SKIN OF
THE WOLF

blue
rider
press

ALSO BY SAM CABOT

Blood of the Lamb

SKIN OF THE WOLF

SAM CABOT

BLUE RIDER PRESS

NEW YORK

blue
rider
press

Published by the Penguin Group
Penguin Group (USA) LLC
375 Hudson Street,
New York, New York 10014

USA • Canada • UK • Ireland • Australia
New Zealand • India • South Africa • China

penguin.com
A Penguin Random House Company

Library of Congress Cataloging-in-Publication Data

Cabot, Sam.
Skin of the wolf / Sam Cabot.
p.   cm.
ISBN 978-0-399-16296-1
1. Indians of North America—Fiction.   2. Murder—Investigation—Fiction.   I. Title.
PS3603.A364S55   2014   2014009560
813'.6—dc23

Printed in the United States of America
1   3   5   7   9   10   8   6   4   2

BOOK DESIGN BY AMANDA DEWEY

A NOTE ON NATIVE LANGUAGES

The Native words and phrases in this book have been rendered phonetically, not orthographically. This is the authors' choice, to help the text read smoothly. Scholars will shudder; we apologize. We thank the experts who gave us their time and attention and we take sole responsibility for any errors.

This book is dedicated to the memory of Pete Seeger,

who loved the river.

1

What he could do, only he could do.

As soon as the thought formed he knew it was un-true. It had arisen from his worst, most prideful self. There had always been others, and would be again. Was that not his purpose and his hope?

Even in his own life, though it pained him, there was one more: his twin, his two-hour elder, named Gata, Prepared, but christened Michael in the white church. He whose birth had been easy and whose life had been calm. He had the Power also, had felt it first, but in keeping with his measured nature used it seldom, and always reluctantly.

He himself, christened Edward, had been called Tahkwehso, Twin, by their father, too dispirited at the loss of their mother to give him a name of his own. Edward's disastrous birth had caused her death, his twisting and flailing, his inability to be comforted even in the womb. The grandmother who received both boys in their blankets as their mother should have passed the peacefully sleeping Michael to their father and held Edward to her, singing softly to him in the ancient language while he squalled and wailed and fought against the world. "He will become a man of consequence. His actions will set great changes in motion," she told their father. But whether for good or for ill, she could not say.

And Michael? Michael, she said, would come to a crossroads. He would have a decision to make, one of great difficulty and great weight. How would he choose? Though she was a seer, that, also, was something she could not say.

Enough. Edward shook himself in the cold New York night, shedding these dark memories. Why was he dwelling on the past? Because his brother was near? Yes, but not near enough to stop him, and unaware of Edward's task, unaware even that Edward was in the city.

The task should have been Michael's. Michael was firstborn, Michael was bigger, stronger: Michael should have led. Edward would have followed, willingly. That would have been the correct beginning. But Michael had made a different choice. He went another way, the white way: university, medical school, research fellowships! Edward found himself snarling at the thought of his brother's choices. What did those things mean? What could they do for their people?

A cold wind raised the hair on the back of his neck. Not even in this slush-soaked February twilight were the city streets empty. His brother was thriving here but Edward hated this place, its never-ending onrush of sounds and smells, its whirling tumult that would not let him rest and silenced the ghosts of his ancestors.

But not forever.

He loped along, staying in the shadows. The thick fur coat that covered him kept the icy air at bay, although his rising excitement as he contemplated the task ahead provided its own warmth. Once he had the mask, preparations would be complete. The ceremony would be held. Others would be freed, first a few, then many. Natural order would be restored, ancient wrongs would be righted. It would take time; but once it began it could not be stopped any more than a raging fire could be hounded back into lightning in the sky.

When all was accomplished the world would be different and the people free. And he would shed the two names he hated, Tahkwehso and Edward, and take his true name.

Ohtahyohnee.

The tracker Wolf.

2

Does it seem to you it's changed much?"

Livia Pietro leaned toward her friend to catch her words, torn away by the wind howling up from the East River. "You mean New York?"

"Since you were last here."

Livia considered. "New York changes overnight, I think. So different from Rome. It's been nearly eight years—yes, I see a lot that looks new to me."

Katherine Cochran laughed. "Oh, so do I. You have to walk down every street in every neighborhood every six months just to keep up. But I meant, the sense of it. With all the building up and tearing down, it always feels like the same place to me. I don't know how it does that. Maybe the Park, and the rivers, the harbor. The fact that it has borders. And maybe the landmark buildings that don't change. I suppose they keep it, I don't know, grounded. Does that make sense?"

"I think so. It's as though this New York is only the latest, just one of many, and the original New York is still here underneath it all." Livia tightened her gloved hand on her collar. They were fighting their way east through the end of a February afternoon. Mounds of frozen slush threw purple shadows and the streetlights had long since come on. "Who decided we should walk?"

"You did."

"Oh. Well, I'd been in those stuffy conference rooms all day, so my judgment was off. I just hope this mask is worth it."

"Now there's gratitude for you. Everyone at the conference would trade their grandmother for a private look at this Ohtah-yohnee. I include my dear friend Dr. Pietro in my exclusive by-invi-tation viewing and she complains about a little subzero windchill?"

"Promise me there'll be hot coffee afterwards."

"If I know Sotheby's"—Katherine reached for the handle of the auction house's heavy glass door—"there'll be hot coffee here."

There was hot coffee. There was also the offer of tea if that was preferred, and a multi-pastel plate of *macarons*, New York's newest pastry fad. All this, of course, the black-clad gallery assistant diffi dently told them, was to be enjoyed only at the end of the confer-ence table that did not have velvet padding set out ready to receive the artwork Dr. Cochran and her guest had come to see.

"Yes, of course." Katherine brushed her fingers through her cap of short silver hair and smiled at the young woman. The assistant had no sooner drifted out with their coats than another woman bus-tled in.

"Katherine! So glad to see you! It's a hideous day, isn't it?" She embraced Katherine and turned her smile to Livia. Her dark hair was gathered into a tight chignon and her black Armani suit and red silk blouse broadcast taste and affluence. "Dr. Pietro! Katherine speaks so highly of you. Estelle Warner. Delighted you could come. My assistant is fetching our Ohtahyohnee. I thought you might want to thaw out first. Coffee?"

They gathered cups, saucers, and *macarons* and sat at the non-velvet end of the polished table. "So," Estelle Warner said, "how's the conference?"

"I'm learning a lot," Livia answered, warming her hands on the delicate cup. "Indigenous art isn't my area, so almost everything I'm hearing is fresh and fascinating."

"Oh, but the Americas aren't exactly uncharted waters to you, either." Katherine turned to Estelle Warner. "Livia's been doing work lately in representations of the New World in the art of Europe. Mostly it's purple mountains' majesty and amber waves of grain, but sometimes our blankets and pots make an appearance."

"The area's not been my main focus for years now, but it's interested me since graduate school," Livia said. "I thought I'd go back to it for a while. Surprisingly little's been written about it." *And a lot of what has is by me, though the learned papers have other names on them; graduate school was a long time ago.* She didn't say that aloud, though, nor did she elaborate on the need, deeper than merely an old interest, that had driven her to this work: the sense that for a while she needed to turn away from medieval art, Renaissance art, the art of Europe, art heavily focused on the Catholic Church and Christian symbology. That art—the paintings, the frescoes, the statuary, and the churches—was her true love, and without question she'd return to it; but what had happened last autumn in Rome needed time to become part of her, to re-shape her understanding of the world. Changing the focus of her work would allow her heart to continue that process at its own pace.

And being Noantri, she could give it all the time it required.

"Livia presented a brilliant paper this morning, tracing the earliest images of maize in Europe," Katherine was saying to Estelle. "Beautiful slides, too. Some frescoes from the Vatican that actually drew gasps. I don't think anyone in the room had seen them before."

She leaned in and stage-whispered, "They're in the private apartments."

"Quite a coup," Estelle Warner said. "Livia—may I call you Livia? Are you the first to study them? How did you know they were even there?"

Livia sipped coffee to keep herself from laughing. Estelle Warner was Sotheby's Specialist in Native Art, so the Vatican was of little use to her; but a historian with access at the Holy See could be a valuable chip in a game of Specialists one-upping each other. "I suppose I am the first, for what that's worth. I've been in Rome a long time. I have friends who can sometimes sneak me into places."

Estelle nodded genially, clearly filing that in some mental database. "Well, I'm very glad Katherine snuck you in here. I think you'll be happy with what you see. Oh, here's Brittany now. Put it down here, darling. Would you like to stay? These are very erudite women. Dr. Livia Pietro from Rome, and of course you know Dr. Cochran from the Met. You'll learn a great deal being a fly on the wall, I'm sure."

A different young assistant, also dressed in protocol black, had entered pushing a cart that held a large wooden box. She retreated to a seat halfway down the table, while the other three women stood. The box, thirty inches in height and width, four feet in length, was simple and beautifully crafted, though of no great age. Native art might not be Livia's area, but she knew enough to be sure that an artifact like the one they were about to view would have originally been wrapped in ceremonial blankets, possibly placed in a deerhide sack. This hard-sided box, no doubt cushioned and fabric-lined, was a collector's way of protecting his possessions.

Estelle put on a pair of white cotton gloves and unlatched the lid of the box. She reached in to remove a large carved wooden mask and laid it on the center of the velvet pad. For a moment no one spoke.

Then, "Oh, my God," Katherine breathed. "I've never seen anything like that."

Nor had Livia. As Arts of the Americas Curator at the Met, Katherine's detailed knowledge was much wider than Livia's, but Livia's studies had given her a glancing familiarity with indigenous American typologies. This mask was something entirely new to her. And not only to her. At the Indigenous Arts conference she and Katherine were attending, this Ohtahyohnee was the talk of the hallways.

Hoping to leverage the gathering of experts and scholars at the biennial conference, many of New York's museums were exhibiting their Native art, presenting speakers and programs, dance and music. Because so many collectors came to New York either for the conference or the satellite events, the major auction houses also chose this week for their Native art sales. Christie's and Bonhams had their own consignments of baskets, blankets, silver and turquoise. The focus, however, was on Sotheby's, and of all the objects on offer, this mask—known so far only from photographs and descriptive text, not to be displayed until immediately before the sale per the owner's instructions—was carrying the day.

Gray-painted, touched with fine lines of black, white, and red, the wooden head shared with the masks of the Iroquois False Face Societies an elongated asymmetry that gave it ferocious vigor. But none of the highly secretive Societies had stepped forward to claim this mask. No one had demanded its return or explained its use. The art historians and the ethnographers were stumped and theories abounded. They all agreed on one point, though. This mask's savage bright teeth, its long, sharp snout, wrinkled as though it had detected a scent, its carved thick fur, its cocked and pointed ears—one forward, one back, so as to miss nothing—and the tremendous muscular power in the jaw and throat left no room for doubt. This was a wolf.

Yet the eyes, Livia thought. Fierce, burning, almost gleeful, the eyes of a predator watching its prey: but in their black-painted depths, in their shape and shading, a shadow of something else. She waited, hoping this sense would become clearer, but felt nothing more.

"It's true, then," Katherine said. "The photographs—it's extraordinary."

Estelle smiled. "I've had time now to get familiar with it, but I have to tell you, it still takes my breath away. You can practically see it sniffing the air, crisscrossing the ground. There's another Mohawk word for 'wolf' but Ohtahyohnee is more active. It means wolf-as-tracker. It's what the owner insists on calling this and it certainly fits. Livia? What about you? What do you think?"

Livia chose her words carefully. "It's astounding. And unique, I think? Wolf masks weren't common in the Northeast?"

"Extremely rare. When this one came to us I was skeptical—I mean, I was knocked over, but still. And I know around the conference there's a lot of doubt. But the mask's provenance is impeccable."

"You can find hints," Katherine said. She hadn't taken her eyes off the mask. "References. Faint, and you have to know what to look for and where. Some of the earliest Jesuit missionaries were apparently allowed to see them, and to attend ceremonies, though they were asked not to speak about them. So even their obsessive note-taking doesn't include much in the way of animal masks. From what I can gather, there were never many, in any case. Even the tribes that used them didn't always have one. Certain kinds of damage would require one to be ceremonially destroyed, and a new one was only created if someone received instructions in a dream."

Livia asked, "What were they used for? What was the ceremony?"

"That's not recorded. The few missionaries who mentioned them never said how they were used."

"Sounds like a major omission, based on the Jesuits I know."

"Oh, it has to be deliberate. And once the Jesuits were gone, animal masks never appear again in accounts of the Eastern nations. Estelle, where did it come from?"

Estelle shook her head. "The seller insists on staying anonymous. The provenance, as I said, is completely convincing and will be provided to the buyer, but even they won't get the seller's name. But Katherine, this will interest you. The provenance starts with a Jesuit missionary. The first mention of the mask, in the household inventory of an Irish family called Hammill from 1790, says it was acquired years earlier from a Father Etienne Ravenelle by the owner's grandfather."

"Really? 1790, someone's grandfather—Ravenelle would have sold it or given it to the grandfather right around the time he was ordered back to France."

"I suppose he didn't want to take it with him."

"Or he was worried he wouldn't make it. In those years the British were hanging Catholic priests wholesale when they found them. How did Ravenelle come to have it?"

"The inventory doesn't say that or anything else about it. Just lists and describes it."

"Specifically enough to be sure it's this same piece?"

"Minutely. A very detailed description, and see this nick next to the stripe at the ear? It's listed, and so is this gouge underneath, here, and a few others. Almost as though the owner didn't want to be blamed for the damage."

"Maybe he was told it was a valuable piece when he inherited it," Livia said.

"Doubtful." Katherine pursed her lips. "In 1790 Indian artifacts only had curiosity value, if that. It's odd someone would have cared enough then to make any kind of detailed record."

"May I pick it up?" Livia suddenly asked.

"Of course. Brittany, please."

The assistant jumped up, opened a drawer in a breakfront, and handed Livia a pair of gloves. Livia pulled them on and lifted the mask, feeling the solidity of it, the weight. She first looked at it straight on, then traced her index finger along the snout, the painted teeth, the curled lip, the tip of one ear. She turned it this way and that, examining the back, the carved fur, the inside. Within, the mask was carved but not painted, and bore what looked like sweat stains where it would have touched the wearer's skin.

"Has there been a lot of interest?" Katherine had also donned gloves, and Livia passed the mask to her.

"Is the Pope Catholic?" Estelle grinned. "Even here, the European Painting Specialists who generally don't give us the time of day are clamoring to sit next to me in the commissary. Our phone hasn't stopped ringing. I haven't been this popular since my junior prom." She added, "I hate to tell you, Katherine, but the estimate's gone up. As of this morning we had it at seven million."

Katherine shrugged. "What can I do?"

Livia asked Katherine, "The Met will be bidding?"

"Yes," Katherine said, turning the mask in her hands. "I have donors who'll underwrite the purchase. They think a major museum is the best place for something this—amazing."

"I happen to agree," Estelle said, "but some other major museums are interested, too. And of course private collectors."

"What about the tribes?" Livia asked. "Didn't I read about a lawsuit? Claiming they're religious artifacts, not art, and shouldn't be sold at all?"

"That involved some of the Hopi artifacts, and they've been withdrawn while it's litigated. But most of what we have here is unattributed or orphaned, or can be supported by bills of sale."

"'Orphaned'?"

Katherine and Estelle exchanged glances. "The tribe that created this Ohtahyohnee is long gone," Katherine explained. "According to the Hammill papers they were one of the Huron tribes, wiped out by European diseases and Europeans. No one's left to lay claim."

Both women had the grace to look sheepish. Livia, a guest here, didn't pursue it. The history of art collecting did not bear close inspection, anywhere in the world, at any time.

Estelle glanced at her watch. "I'm sorry, but I have a meeting and then another showing."

"Of the Ohtahyohnee?" Katherine asked. "And here I thought I was so special."

"Of course you are, darling. It doesn't go on view until tomorrow, after all. You're the only prospective bidder getting a sneak preview. As a thanks for all your help."

"I was Estelle's outside consultant on the items for this auction," Katherine told Livia. "For those very few times she didn't know absolutely everything. But darling, you're lying to my face. You just said you're giving us the bum's rush for your next sneak preview."

"Ah, but this gentleman's not a prospective bidder. He's Native American. Community Relations asks us to give Native people access whenever they request it, if we can. Enrolled tribal members with credentials, of course. Even items like this that are being held back. It can defuse potentially difficult situations."

Livia took one last long look at the wolf mask and then shook Estelle's hand. "Thank you so much. This was fascinating."

"I'm glad you could come. I'm sorry to throw you out so unceremoniously. Perhaps we can get together later in the week? Brittany will show you to the elevator. Don't forget to bundle up!"

Wrapped and buttoned and zipped and bundled, Livia and Katherine headed back toward the Met. "I have a meeting, too, and a few other things to do at the office, but we could get dinner after if you have time," Katherine said as they worked their way uphill in the February darkness. Both walking and talking were easier with the wind behind them.

"Thanks," Livia answered, "but I have dinner plans. A friend who's living here now. Katherine?"

Katherine turned her head. "You sound strange. What's up?"

"The mask." Livia paused. "I think it's a fake."

"What? No, no possible way. Estelle's very careful. If she says it has good provenance then it does. And you saw the carving, the skill—my God, the thing looks alive!"

"It looks alive. But it doesn't . . . feel alive. I think," Livia hurried on, "that the provenance is authentic, but somewhere along the line the mask was switched. The mask in the 1790 inventory may have been the real one, and later than that, too. But this one's not."

Katherine was silent while they crossed the street and said nothing until they were halfway down the block. Then she asked, "Why do you think so?"

This, Livia could not explain. Not to an Unchanged, no matter how close a friend.

"It's just a feeling I have," she said. "The mask does look alive. I think the carver of the original felt that it was, in some way."

"That's often true of a ritual object."

"Yes. But this one, it seems to me to be a copy of a living mask. It's a perfect copy, but I don't get any sense that the artist felt that *this* mask was alive." She paused. "I'm sorry, that sounds absurd. It's not my area and I'm probably wrong. Forget I said anything. I just couldn't let you go ahead and spend your donors' seven million dollars on something that doesn't feel right to me without speaking up."

They'd reached the plaza in front of the Met. The basins, their fountains turned off for the winter, held autumn leaves frozen in ice.

"No," Katherine said. "Something had been bothering me, too. I was just so taken with the beauty of it . . . but something does feel off. Missing. I'm not sure I'd have put it the same way you did, but I'm uncomfortable with something about it."

"What will you do?"

"I'm not sure. If I decide not to bid I'll have to explain it to the donors. But if we're wrong . . . I have to think. But thank you for sharing your misgivings."

"I'm sorry. No one likes to hear that kind of thing, even if it's true."

"Especially if it's true. But better now than after I've spent the money. I have to go. Enjoy your dinner, and see you at the conference tomorrow."

Livia gave Katherine a quick hug and headed to the bus stop. She'd have preferred to walk downtown, but the weather was just too cold.

3

Livia Pietro had been an art historian all her adult life. Forty-two years into that life, in 1915, she put art aside to become a battlefield nurse when her native Italy declared war on Austria-Hungary. A year later, during the Sixth Battle of the Isonzo, she was mortally wounded by a mortar shell.

The night after that, she awoke a Noantri.

A vampire.

The sergeant who'd saved her explained it was the only way; that what he'd done was wrong according to the Laws of his Community, but she'd been so brave, refusing to evacuate, staying to care for the wounded and the terrified, men in pain, boys who were dying. He didn't think it fair that she should pay for her valor with her life. If she was horrified, the sergeant told her, if she didn't want this Change, he'd reverse its effects. She would die, and, he was sure, be welcomed in Heaven. He waited fearfully for her response, while she felt the threads in the roughly laundered linen sheet that covered her, heard the voices of soldiers around the fires on the other side of the ridge—the sergeant had carried her to a copse and woven a roof of branches to protect her—and heard, also, the wind in the trees and the howling of wolves at what she knew, even then, to be a great distance. She looked around, saw the colors in the darkness, deep reds and blues she'd never known before. The scent of loam, and the distant river, and the soldier's coffee, and the sergeant's sweat and worry, she could recognize them all, pick each one out. Her eyes met the sergeant's and though she didn't speak, his face lit with a relieved smile.

Livia had lived as a Noantri now for a hundred years, faithfully following the Laws of the Community into which she had been initiated and of which she felt honored to be part. She remained a nurse until the end of the war—who better, now?—and afterwards she returned to her old work with new abilities and gifts. Blessings, the Noantri called them.

It was these Blessings, indirectly, that had involved her in the events in Rome last autumn; these Blessings that had enabled her to play her role in resolving that crisis; and these Blessings that had spoken to her of the counterfeit nature of the Ohtahyohnee she'd just seen.

The skill of the carver was inarguable. The mask, in its way, was perfect. Livia had no doubt that the tree it was carved from, if tests of such precision were possible, would be shown to have been felled in the fifteenth or sixteenth century and that the pigments and the brushes used to apply them were formulated and made exactly as they would have been then. Katherine had said, *The thing looks alive!* It did. But to Livia's Noantri senses, something was missing.

Contrary to the legends and myths that had always swirled around them, the Noantri had no supernatural dimension. What they had were enormously enhanced human senses and abilities— sight, for example, and strength—and a thirst for human blood. And also, eternal life. In the many, many centuries of Noantri existence before the coming of science, the unearthly explanation was the only one that could account for these attributes, in the minds of both Noantri and Unchanged. The truth, still being unraveled by Noantri scientists, turned out to be both less mystical and more awe-inspiring. The qualities that made the Noantri eternal, and eternally different from the Unchanged, were, the scientists had found, the result of a microbe and the DNA changes it wrought.

When Katherine asked why Livia thought the mask was not authentic she said it was "just a feeling." In truth, it was a lack of feeling. One of the Blessings that had come to Livia with her Change—a Blessing that filled her with deep joy—was the ability, if she contemplated a work long enough and seriously enough, to understand the artist's way through it. She hadn't had nearly enough time with the Ohtahyohnee to fully understand the piece, but the tiny contractions in her hands and arms as she explored it had told her this: the mask had not been made in a state of passion, a fever of inspiration. The artist had worked methodically, carefully, step by step.

Without doubt, stunning, even transcendent art could be produced that way. A muse-driven frenzy was not necessary for beauty, could in fact often be a hindrance. But the original of this Ohtahyohnee, she was convinced, had been made by someone to whom it was alive. More: someone who felt, or hoped, he was bringing it to life by the work he was doing. An artist approaching a work that way starts and stops, fears, rushes in, hesitates, backs out. He may take great care, but he's not methodical. In her brief experience of this wolf mask Livia felt none of that. Her muscles and nerve fibers conveyed to her no emotion at all, save a sharp, steady, single-minded focus.

4

Thomas Kelly had been early to the restaurant, in happy anticipation of seeing Livia Pietro, but became so absorbed in the book he'd brought that he jumped when she spoke.

"Nice to see you're as studious as ever, Father Kelly."

He tried to stand and turn at the same time and nearly knocked his chair over. "I'm sorry, I didn't see you come in! I guess I was distracted—I just always have a book because in case—please, sit down, I'm so happy you could—" He stopped and grinned at her. "This is exactly how we met, isn't it?"

"I ambushed you over a book, yes." Livia smiled also as she moved around the table and sat. "I'm so glad to see you, Thomas. I'm sorry for the short notice and I'm so pleased you weren't too busy. You look well. New York suits you, I think."

"You look wonderful yourself."

"Thank you," she said, her eyes sparkling, and he understood: wonderful, or awful, or anything in between, she looked exactly as she had the last time he saw her.

Before he'd met Livia and others in her Community, Thomas had never noticed how so much of what we look for when we see our friends, especially after an absence, is how they wear time. Thomas himself had a few more lines on his freckled face, a touch more gray in his red hair, than when he and Livia Pietro first encountered each other in the Vatican Library a few months earlier. But Livia, being Noantri, never changed. Her heart, her mind, her spirit, yes; but in appearance, she was and would always be the woman he'd met last fall: a middle-aged *Professoressa*, lively, self-possessed, her eyes still a surprising emerald color, her long black hair streaked with silver.

Tonight she was dressed in a boxy soft black jacket and a black wool skirt, and she wore her hair braided and pinned up. A discreet gold bracelet glowed on her wrist. The scent he faintly caught was not, he thought, the same as she'd worn in Rome; this one was lighter, more citrusy, but maybe women wore different perfumes in different cities and why was he noticing anyway? No, he knew why, and allowed himself a rueful smile. The effect Livia had on him, she'd explained in Rome, was a natural reaction of his Unchanged body to her Noantri one, a result of their different physiologies. But, Thomas thought, not entirely. He accepted that the physical component of his attraction to Livia was attributable to biology. In truth, though, concerning physical desire, wasn't that always so? Did our bodies—Unchanged or Noantri—not have their own laws, their own reasons? Which didn't stop Thomas from bringing his desire, for Livia or any woman, into the confessional, didn't stop it from being something he worked to subdue.

However, he was also sure of another thing. His joyful eagerness for her arrival and his delight in seeing her tonight had an additional component entirely, one as powerful and one that luckily was no sin: a connection begun in mutual antipathy, transformed through painful shared experience, and ultimately grown into a deep and sincere friendship.

"I'd have canceled whatever I had to when you said you were

coming." He settled back into his seat. "My schedule's my own. You're the one who's busy. With the conference and everything. Couldn't you have come for longer? A week before or after?"

Livia shook her head. "I wish I could have. But you know how it is. The university was happy I'd been invited to present a paper so they gave me the week, but even then I'm expected to make it up."

Thomas nodded. A familiarity with the sometimes unreasonable demands of academia was one of the bonds they shared.

That, and the memory of what had happened in Rome last fall.

The waiter appeared and after a brief consultation they ordered a bottle of Frascati, a crisp white from vineyards near Rome. They both took a few moments to contemplate dinner—the restaurant was the Blue Water Grill, Thomas's selection after intensive research following Livia's request for seafood—and then Livia closed her menu and asked, "What are you reading?"

Thomas glanced at the volume beside him. "François Roustang's book on the history of the Jesuits in North America."

She tilted her head to see the cover. "In French?"

"I didn't dare try the translation. He's opaque enough in the original."

Livia's face grew serious. "Thomas, I want to tell you how glad I am . . . When you said . . . When you told me . . . Why am I having trouble phrasing this?"

"I think, because you're not sure how to talk to a priest about his vocation?"

She visibly relaxed. "That's exactly it. I know you left Rome uncertain about your future. It's really none of my business, but I think your decision to remain a priest must be the right one because now that I see you, you seem so happy."

"That may just be because *I'm* seeing *you*. No, I'm joking. I mean, I am happy to see you, but yes, I think abandoning my vocation because of . . . what we learned, would have been a mistake. I still haven't fully assimilated it. I meditate on it daily. But being a priest—it's really who I am, you know?"

She smiled. "Oh, yes, I do know."

The waiter arrived with their wine. He displayed the label for Thomas, but Thomas pointed to Livia; her senses were much more nuanced than his, and he didn't want to accept a bottle that she'd find undrinkable. She tasted it, nodded, and their glasses were filled. He lifted his. "To the future." The meaning of that was different for each of them, but she met his gaze and raised her glass, too.

They ordered dinner, the waiter left, and Livia said, "Now tell me about your research."

"Are you sure? When I get started you know I can go on for hours."

"I'll stop you when you start using words I don't know. Please, I'm interested."

"Well." Thomas sat forward. "I told you I took your advice, right? About changing my focus?"

Livia raised her eyebrows. "I didn't mean that as advice. Just, for me, it seemed like a way to get some distance for a while."

"The more I thought about it, the more it seemed like that to me, too. Fordham asked me to work with two students writing theses in my area, and I told them I would, but that my own research would be heading off in another direction."

"And they're happy with that? Of course they are, they're lucky to have landed that eminent Church historian, Father Thomas Kelly, and they know it." Thomas felt himself blushing. He knew Livia could sense his embarrassment even if she couldn't see his face flush in the dim light, but he'd gotten used to that. "So what is it you're doing?"

"It actually almost touches on why you're in town. The Lily of the Mohawks—is she familiar?"

"The first North American Native saint, am I right? I don't know anything more than that."

He grinned again. "You will when you read my book. Kateri Tekakwitha. Baptized as Catherine. She lived from 1656 to 1680, was beatified in 1980 and canonized in 2012. Church practice when a saint is canonized is to produce a biography. That was done for Tekakwitha but the Pope doesn't like it."

"Francis? He doesn't?"

"Because he's from the Americas and reportedly touchy about it. He thought the biography was minimal, pro forma, not serious scholarship. When I told my department chair—Monsignor Maxwell, Gerald Maxwell—that I wanted to look at early New World issues for a while, he asked what specific areas I was interested in, and when I said I hadn't decided he asked if I'd want to take this project on. Further research into Tekakwitha, to provide something more detailed. It's actually Father Maxwell's own subject, the early Church in North America. He was looking for someone with, well, credentials. To make the Pope happy."

"If you don't mind my saying so, that sounds a little pro forma itself."

"Perhaps. I'm enjoying the work, though."

"She's interesting, your saint?"

"Oh, yes, very. That whole world—the first contact between Europeans and the Native tribes—is fascinating, except of course Europeans didn't acquit themselves very well. Though the early missionaries of my order"—he tapped the book—"seem to have be-haved decently, at times even in ways I'm proud of. Standing for the tribes against the governments—the French, the English, later the Canadians and the U.S."

"Hmm." Livia frowned in mock consternation. "But pride's a sin."

"Not if you're proud of someone else."

"I suppose that's true, as long as you're humble about it. Oh, good, here's the soup. I don't think I'm prepared for a theological debate."

5

Brittany Williams slid the box with the Ohtahyohnee mask into its place on the shelf. The holding room was almost empty; most of the items for the upcoming auctions were already on display. Not quite all: as usual, Native Art had only been given three galleries. Not like Old Masters, which always got a full floor when their big show came up. Or Asian Art, actually three separate departments with three Specialists, eight assistants, and two entire floors for two whole weeks in the spring. No, Native Art didn't even have enough space to exhibit all their pieces and Brittany and Estelle were expected to do everything themselves.

Estelle was a genius, though. The pieces not on display were the ones buyers would be least likely to be familiar with, pieces they might have to be talked through to understand. Making people have to ask to see them was a way to ensure that either Estelle or Brittany would be right there to explain and extoll. Brittany had gotten a French doctor interested in a Spokane doll yesterday and she'd made sure Estelle knew it. If he bought it Brittany wouldn't get a commission—God forbid Sotheby's should work like that, as though any of this were about anything besides money—but Estelle would remember. Even in the backwater that Native art had turned out to be, it was all about people knowing how good you were. And this Ohtahyohnee: according to Estelle the owner insisted it not be shown until the last possible minute, which by Sotheby's policy was the day before the auction. This was the star item for Friday, slated to go on display tomorrow morning. Brittany didn't believe for a minute an owner would hold a piece back that way, especially one causing a big stir. The first Eastern tribe wolf mask to be auctioned in, like, ever? As much as they liked making money, owners liked to show off. There was a lot of *nyaah, nyaah* in the collecting world and this was an absolutely primo opportunity for it. But holding it back was pure Estelle. The only way to create more demand than its existence did was to tell people you had it and then not let anyone near it.

Okay, Estelle might be a genius, but she abused her assistant just like every other Specialist. She was out to dinner kissing some German museum director's ass and Brittany would be here late into the night yet again, getting ready for tomorrow.

She went into the inner office and sat at the computer to key in Estelle's scrawled notes of the people who'd come to see pieces today. After that she'd be last-minuting all the oh-so-fascinating pre-auction details: making sure there were enough black velvet cloths of all the right sizes for the sale pedestals, dusting and polishing each piece one final time. Things no one with an art history degree, and God knows no one with a trust fund, should have to do.

B-o-o-o-oring. She yawned. She'd perk right up with a little coke and a night of clubbing, but no way that would happen. Unless she quit. Which she'd thought about. She didn't want to wake up one morning and find she was like Estelle and her friends from this afternoon. Dried-up old prunes, not even cougars, just three single, sexless, middle-aged women. Well, that Italian one, there was something about her. She could have been hot, but she didn't do anything to help herself and God, what was she, like, fifty?

Brittany didn't want to give Daddy the satisfaction of quitting, though. He hadn't minded that she'd majored in art history, but he'd been incredulous when she'd actually taken a job. It wouldn't last, he sneered to Mom. Some Switzerland ski trip or Caribbean beach would beckon and she'd follow like the airhead she'd always been. She wasn't cut out for working.

So she stayed, because screw him. But maybe she really should reconsider the Native thing. The art was okay, but with Old Masters or Contemporary or even American Outsider, you had a whole gallery scene in addition to the museums and auction houses. You didn't have to be a Slave of Sotheby's, the assistants' name for themselves. Which all the Specialists knew, and didn't care. Sure, there were Native art galleries, but not in New York. They were in the Southwest or in places like Seattle, and no way she was going there. It wasn't like she loved this art particularly, not like Estelle did. And Katherine Cochran, she was even weirder. Brittany suspected they actually bought into it, thought some of the pieces were alive and had powers. Brittany always took care to look thoughtful when they talked like that, but seriously? No, she had to get out of here. No one ever said a Koons had superpowers. Not all that many people even said they were any good. Brittany had only gotten into Native art in the first place because of that Chippewa guy, Stan, from junior year. God, he was hot, and she'd really gotten to Daddy with that one. He'd have been happier if she'd hooked up with a Jew or an Irish potato farmer.

She looked up when she heard the outer door click open. The

Jamaican guard, Harold, this was his night. She'd taken a run at him but he didn't want to lose his job. Maybe she should try harder. He was big, with broad shoulders, and talk about pissing off Daddy! And he was early tonight, so maybe he wasn't as immune to her as he pretended. She swept her golden hair off her forehead—at $300 every few weeks, it better be golden—so it would fall back into place when she looked up. Harold would pass through the storeroom and then, seeing her light on, stick his head in here. She recrossed her legs to reveal a little more thigh.

He didn't show up, though. She didn't hear the outer door shut again, so he must still be in the storeroom. What was taking him so long? He couldn't be, like, afraid of her, that she'd make another pass? She smiled. Or maybe he was trying to figure out a line to use, because he'd decided to do her but he wanted her to understand it was his idea. As if. She stood, tugged the neckline of her sweater a little lower, and went into the storeroom.

Nothing to be seen. "Harold?" A sense, then, that someone had just frozen, that movement had stopped. God, what a coward he was. She stepped up the aisle in her red-soled Louboutins, shoes that turned men to jelly even on women not as beautiful as she. She made a right and halted. Wait. What? She didn't get what she was seeing, couldn't grasp this. The Ohtahyohnee's box was open; the mask grimaced up at her. Standing over it, staring down, quivering in taut-muscled rage, was a huge gray dog. *How the hell did that get in here?* Brittany started to tiptoe backwards. Her stiletto heel caught the rug and she stumbled against a shelf. Just a tiny clunk, but the dog whipped its giant head in her direction. Its eyes glowed and its lips peeled back in a hungry, insane smile. Brittany took two more slow steps back while the dog just stood. Then it crouched to spring.

Brittany spun and dashed for the office, but the Louboutins weren't made for running and she tripped. She tried to scramble up from her knees but the dog crashed into her, knocked her down. Its breath stank, it weighed a ton. She struggled but the mouth slavered and the teeth gleamed and for the first—and last—time in her life, Brittany was prey.

6

While they ate Livia caught Thomas up on people they both knew in Rome. Livia's painter friend, Ellen Bird, was about to have a show of her pastel portraits; Father Franconi at Santa Maria dell'Orto had been delighted with Livia's gift establishing a fund for the care of the church's artworks. "He was embarrassed, though. I told him it was because of how much he helped you when you needed him and he said all he did was hear your confession, that was his job."

"Well, he's right, it is his job."

"Oh, now *you're* embarrassed." Her smile was playful. "Don't worry, he still doesn't know your real name. Or mine. And not everyone does his job so well. I thought that ought to be rewarded."

The waiter removed their soup bowls. Thomas was silent until he'd gone, and then said, "Speaking of confession, I want to say something."

Livia waited.

"As hard as all that was last fall," Thomas said, "there was a part that, even at the time, I loved: working with you. Oh, look, now you're the one who's embarrassed."

"Am I blushing prettily?"

"You are."

"Good for me. Thomas, thank you. That means a lot."

"It's true. This hermit-scholar business, I mean, it's the life I chose, and it's a good one, but . . . well, you know what Keynes said."

"I'm not sure I do."

"'It is astonishing what foolish things one can temporarily believe if one thinks too long alone.'"

Livia laughed. "Well, you're always welcome to call me, if you find yourself thinking foolish things. I agree we work well together, and I'm pretty much of a lone wolf myself."

"I'll take that as a high compliment, then."

"It was meant that way." Their eyes met and held each other. She broke away with a smile and said, "Now. Tell me more about your saint."

"I will, but you know how single-minded I can get."

"Oh, can you?" she asked innocently. The waiter returned, setting down their main course: haddock for Thomas, bluefish for Livia.

"I don't want to talk and talk and then leave here and realize I know nothing about what you've been doing. And you know I could. So first, you tell me about the conference. And 'lone wolf' reminds me: the piece at Sotheby's. The famous wolf mask. You went to see it, didn't you? Was it all it was cracked up to be?"

Livia reached for a piece of bread. "As a matter of fact, no. It's extraordinary and beautiful, but it's not authentic."

"It's fake? But I thought it had unassailable provenance."

"Not exactly fake. With wooden pieces made for ceremonial purposes, there's always a question of what 'real' means. If a piece is damaged or destroyed and one is made to replace it, the new one's as authentic as the original, and as valuable to the users, even if it's less valuable to collectors because it's less ancient. Now I'm giving the lecture, aren't I?"

"I asked for it, in more ways than one. But what you just described, that's not what you mean by 'not authentic'?"

"No. I got the feeling that this piece wasn't made for use."

"Why do you think that?"

"It didn't feel alive to me. I don't mean really alive—it's a piece of wood. I mean, I didn't get the feeling the maker thought it was alive."

If a different art historian were speaking, Thomas would have been skeptical. He was a scholar. He needed evidence, facts, proof. But Livia's Noantri senses brought her close to artworks in ways he credited even while he didn't fully understand them. "What do you think it was made for?"

"To replace the original."

"Isn't that what you just said, though? If one's damaged or destroyed—"

Livia shook her head. "The original was made for use. For a ceremony no one knows anything about anymore. The only Europeans who ever did, by the way, were Jesuit missionaries. But this mask was out of the hands of the tribe who made it and owned by an Irishman as early as the eighteenth century. That's where the provenance starts. I think somewhere after that the original was replaced by this one."

"Why? When?"

"I have no idea."

"Wouldn't the owner have noticed?"

"Maybe he was the one who made the switch."

"Why?" Thomas asked again. Without waiting for her answer,

he went on, "Or is it possible the original wasn't made for use at all? It was made for display, and this actually is it?"

"I don't think so."

As they ate, Livia told him about the tiny contractions in her hands and arms, the tug of the lines of the work; how, since her Change, she understood art not just visually, but viscerally, not just intellectually, but physically. Listening, he marveled that such a thing was possible. That the human body, after a microscopic alteration in the structure of its cells, could be capable of such sensitivity. And how, almost alone among the non-Noantri, Thomas Kelly, SJ, had been accorded the privilege of the knowledge of this.

From the mask, talk drifted to Livia's conference, and then to Thomas's research. His newfound fascination with the Northeast tribes at the moment of first contact animated his conversation; Livia hardly spoke until the coffee came.

"Well," she said, "it certainly sounds like you've found a niche."

"There's so much to learn! Completely absorbing, to a bookworm like me. I hope I haven't been boring you. Lorenzo used to say—" He stopped. His excitement about the work had caught him unawares, driven him into territory he hadn't thought to go.

Livia waited, then gently asked, "What did he say?"

After a pause: "He said, if I were marooned on a desert island with just a phone book, I'd have written three treatises—historical, philological, and philosophical—on the names in it by the time they found me."

She smiled. "I think he was right. Thomas—"

Thomas shook his head. "I'm fine. Really. As I said, I meditate daily on what happened in Rome. So much to understand. So many souls to pray for."

"I'm sure your prayers are well received."

"As yours would be, if . . ."

Now it was Livia who was shaking her head.

"I'm sorry," Thomas said. "I didn't mean to push you. Come on, let's have dessert. The crème brûlée is supposed to be exceptional. There's so much more I want to talk to you about!"

"Me, too. I could sit here with you all night." She checked her watch. "We have time for dessert and coffee. But then we have another appointment. No, Thomas, don't look at me that way. I told you, Spencer wants to see you."

"We weren't the best of friends in Rome."

"On the contrary, it was he who arranged things so that you could go on with this life you're enjoying so much without any pesky interruptions, like getting arrested."

"Yes, that was kind, and I thanked him. By letter. I even sent flowers. Irises. But you know how he feels about priests. He hasn't gotten in touch since he came to New York."

"You haven't called him, either. I told him I was having dinner with you and he insisted I bring you along for a drink. He has a friend he wants us to meet."

"You. Wants you to meet."

"Thomas."

"I don't know."

"I do. This is ridiculous. You got off to a bad start. All right. Now things have changed. A new city, new lives for both of you. And you have so much in common. You're practically mirror-image obsessive scholars. I'm going to go see him. Let's have our dessert, and then, please—come with me."

7

I n a general sort of way," Spencer George announced, burrowing more deeply into his coat, "I do not enjoy this weather. In case you wondered." His eyes watered as yet another blast of cold air hit them.

Bare-headed and gloveless, the larger, younger man beside him laughed. "Why not? It's beautiful! Look at that moon—full tomorrow! Look how bright the stars are! When do you see that in the city? And listen to that wind! Come on, it's a gorgeous night."

"Michael, I am fully prepared to accept that for your people, priding yourselves as you do on your oneness with the natural world, it's conceivable shrieking wind and glowing stars are sufficient to neutralize the discomfort of numb toes and frostbitten ears. I would further stipulate that I myself am a decadent white man who long ago lost touch with Mother Earth." *Longer ago than you can imagine,* he added sourly to himself, *and I can't say I've missed her caress.* "I acceded to this absurd notion of a walk through Central Park purely out of my high regard for you and respect for your wishes. Also my fear that you'd change your mind about joining my friends and myself for a drink if I didn't."

"You weren't afraid of that." Michael grinned.

"That's true. It sounds good, though, doesn't it? It makes me appear unselfish and noble. Willing to suffer for those I cherish."

"Only if I believed it."

Spencer sighed. "Then what am I doing out here? Really, Michael, if this is your idea of a good time, we might be less compatible than I hoped. Talking of 'hoped,' did you see your mask, by the way? Was it as exceptional as you'd anticipated?"

Michael didn't speak immediately. With a small smile, he said, "It's beautiful."

"Hmm. Beautiful. I detect a note of disappointment, however. Are you—" He stopped as Michael grabbed hold of his arm. "What?"

"Shh." Michael stood still. His eyes narrowed and his nostrils flared. He turned his head slowly left, then right, and loosened his grip. "Go," he said.

"What are you—"

"Leave. Go home. I'll come soon."

Spencer didn't move and didn't answer. His own Noantri hearing, acute as it was, detected no sound beyond the howling wind and the hiss of the city's unceasing traffic. Nor did he scent anything unusual riding the rushing air. But he felt something: a current on his skin, a dark voltage new to him but charged, unmistakably, with danger.

A roar blasted the night. A blur of movement: Spencer spun, but not in time. Something smashed into him, knocked him painfully to the ground. Something alive, he knew, because, while he lay on his back, breath knocked out, he saw it bound up and after Michael, who was racing away into the darkness under the trees.

8

Michael Bonnard took off along the darkest route he could find. He sprinted up and over a small hill, loped down the far slope in great long strides. Icy wind whistled around him. He had to lead Edward away from Spencer.

This was Edward, no doubt. It astounded Michael to find him in the city—Edward hated the concrete streets, the crowds, the cars, the steel—but he was here and he was raging. On the bitter air Michael could smell Edward's scent, sense his heat, feel his fury. A fury so great, an anger so overpowering, that Edward had Shifted.

Disaster. For Edward it was always, always anger that triggered the Shift. Michael could use anger, but other states also: panic once, as a child; another time, the exhilaration of first love. It was harder for him, though, no matter what. His flash point was higher. For Michael the Shift had to be intentioned, a matter of determined will.

Plunging into a tangle of shrubs, he tore at his clothes, trying to free himself, trying at the same time to summon that overwhelming, cresting sensation that would be his own trigger. Anger. Fear. Shock. Whatever he could use. Michael didn't know why Edward had come here, what powerful need had driven him so far from home to a place he detested: but right now, Michael knew with certainty, Edward was burning for a kill and he was hunting.

9

Spencer gathered himself, drew a deep breath, used it to mutter an oath, and raced after Michael.

At the time of his Change, Spencer George had been a landed aristocrat with an estate in Sussex. He could ride a horse, wield a sword, shoot accurately with a flintlock pistol, and creditably execute every dance in Ebreo da Pesaro's *De Practica*. Once he'd become Noantri, his grace, strength, and stamina all increased. He was grateful for, and delighted in, that fact in the bedroom; but outside that sanctum, with the exceptions of shooting, swordplay, riding, and dancing, physical exertion had for five hundred years remained on Spencer's list of ways he would rather not spend his time.

Comparable to going to church.

But Michael was in trouble. Spencer ground his teeth as his pounding footfalls up a stone outcropping rattled his bones. He had no idea what had knocked him down—a rabid dog, perhaps?—but two things were unmistakable: Michael was heroically attempting to lead the danger away from Spencer, and Michael had no chance of outrunning whatever this creature was.

Pausing at the top of the huge boulder, Spencer surveyed the undergrowth below. A wild rustle down to the right: Michael, hiding in a tangle of bushes at the center of a copse, his scent exaggerated by effort and fear. Why didn't he stay still? On the other hand, what good would it have done? Spencer could clearly see, even in the shadows, a large shape slinking slowly, patiently, toward the thicket.

Spencer inched down the rock toward the animal, which looked for all the world like a wolf. The trees and the brush cast wind-tossed shadows, though, confusing his sight. More to the point, this was New York City. A more likely explanation made the animal a husky or some other crossbred dog, possibly rabid, and certainly feral or it wouldn't be hunting in the park.

Spencer moved carefully and silently. His intent, once he'd put himself within the dog's striking distance, was to call attention to his presence. He would be an easier target than Michael in the thicket, and the beast would leap. Spencer, whose strength certainly equaled that of a large dog and whose Noantri body could withstand whatever physical insult the dog might inflict, would defeat it. Unfortunately, that would likely mean killing it. It wouldn't do merely to drive it away, back into the streets of the city, now that, rabid or not, it had reached the point of stalking human prey.

Explaining to Michael his victory over the thing might get tricky, but Spencer had had more than five hundred years' practice in such matters. If he was lucky, Michael would remain hidden in the undergrowth and see nothing, in which case no explanation beyond a lucky bash with a large branch might be required. Spencer's gaze scoured the ground for some such branch, and he found one and hefted it. Excellent: a weapon he could wield as he once had his saber. As he crept forward, his mind began to fill with the possible intimate consequences of this episode. Michael had acted courageously, leading the danger away from him, and he was about to play the hero himself, rescuing Michael. Adrenaline-fueled mutual gratitude and relief, in a warm bedroom on a cold night, offered a promising prospect. This ridiculous exertion might be worthwhile, after all.

Near the base of the rock he spied a flat shelf, perhaps three feet above the ground and ten feet from the dog. He leapt lightly down onto it, held his weapon at the ready, and called, "AHOY!" The animal snapped its head up, snarling. Spencer braced for its spring.

But before it could move, Michael burst from the thicket, shouting. Not at him, at the dog. Spencer didn't know what he was saying, wasn't sure it was in a language he spoke, and didn't spend any time on the question: Michael was charging the dog, and Michael was naked.

Spencer found himself momentarily paralyzed, both by the sight—not entirely unfamiliar, but the relationship was new enough that he still found it breathtaking—and by the inability of his own mind to account for it. The animal similarly froze, torn between the two men, but Michael threw himself forward and tackled it and its decision was made.

So was Spencer's. Michael might have suddenly lost his mind but that didn't mean he had to lose his life. Spencer hurled himself off the rock and onto the swirling mass of fur and flesh. The rich scent of earth, Michael's acrid sweat, and the aroma of blood—had the dog already made a kill?—assaulted him. He used the branch as a club, pounding its end on the dog's head, but the dog just snarled and shifted its weight and the three of them rolled, tangled together, into the thicket. Brambles scratched Spencer's face. The combined bulk of the other two thudded onto his chest and he realized three things.

One: the dog was huge. And coarse-furred, and gray. And muscular beyond expectation. This was no dog. This was a wolf.

Two: Michael was holding his own, clamping the wolf's jaws shut with powerful hands, but he had no weapon. What had he expected to do, talk to the beast?

Three: Michael was, in fact, talking to the beast. Half speaking, half chanting, and accomplishing nothing that Spencer could see beyond tiring himself out while the wolf thrashed, kicked, and clawed at him with razor paws.

With Spencer still on the bottom of the pile, the wolf stopped moving. For the briefest second it seemed to stare into Michael's eyes. Then it arched its back and dug its rear legs into the dirt. Snarling, it shook its head left, right, left, until with a roar it broke free. It stood, eyes glowing, jaws slavering. Then it lunged. Michael rolled desperately and lifted his arm in protection. The wolf rolled with him and Spencer was freed. The wolf's pointed teeth, aiming for Michael's throat, instead clamped onto his naked shoulder. Blood began to flow; Spencer could smell it. Without rising, he kicked hard into the wolf's flank. The startled beast yelped, lost its grip on Michael and its footing. It stumbled, scrabbling to right itself.

Man and beast turned shocked eyes to Spencer.

He used the moment to jump to his feet and launch himself at the wolf. He aimed for the ears, vulnerable points on any animal. He'd yank the creature's head up, get its jaws away from Michael. Then he'd break its skull. If he was lucky he'd find a rock to use; but he could do it with his hands. That was his plan. But the wolf was astoundingly fast. By the time he reached it—a second? two?—it had spun to face him. Its huge head angled and Spencer's own momentum drove him into the gaping jaws. They caught his throat. The pain almost blinded him but, choking, he seized the snout and lower jaw, one hand on each, and pulled them apart. Knife-sharp teeth pierced his fingers. He managed to loosen the wolf's grip, kicked at its belly, but his kick was weaker than before. He was dizzy; he was losing blood.

His hand on his own throat confirmed: the wolf had cut his jugular. In the long term—and for Spencer, what was not long-term?—nothing more than a nuisance, but here, now, with Michael in danger, Spencer felt the blood flowing between his fingers as a true loss, a failure, a tragedy. He tried to stand, but couldn't. A strange sound began behind him. He expected the wolf to lunge at him again but its head lifted. It snarled, stood quivering. Spencer, lying on cold rock, turned his head painfully. The hallucinatory vision that met his eyes was Michael, naked, bleeding, bare feet planted on the soil, arms raised to the skies, howling at the moon.

10

Livia exited the taxi, leaving Thomas to pay the driver. That little demand ("A vow of poverty doesn't mean I can't buy you a taxi ride") had been Thomas's final price for acquiescing to this visit. Livia was glad he'd decided to come; he and Spencer were very similar in many things, especially their love for academic study and scholarly details. You just had to get past the fact that one was a young Jesuit priest and the other an eternal Noantri. It was actually Spencer who'd been the more unfriendly when they'd met in Rome. Thomas's reactions had been largely prompted by fear, while Spencer's sniping hostility was the result of centuries of disdain for the Church. They'd each come out of that experience with a deeper appreciation of the other, though, and it was absurd they should be living in the same city and never see one another.

Pulling her coat collar tight, Livia rang the doorbell of the East Side town house just off Central Park that Spencer had recently bought. He'd told her she'd enjoy the brownstone vines carved at the entranceway and the small-paned casement windows. They were indeed beautiful, but she was sure she'd enjoy the warmth of his parlor even more.

That warmth was not prompt in arriving, though. As Thomas

joined her she rang the bell a second time. Ten o'clock was the appointed hour and the first floor was ablaze with light. Where was their host? Livia leaned on the bell, long and hard, in case it was old and unreliable.

"It's ringing," Thomas said. "I hear it."

"Me, too." Livia frowned. Head down, she focused on what her Noantri senses were finding—what she could hear, what she could smell. "Something's wrong," she told Thomas.

"What do you—"

Thomas's words were cut off when the door opened. Livia smiled with expectant relief. She found the doorway filled not by Spencer, however, but by a younger, larger man. He stood shoeless. His short black hair was messy, his face scratched. The jacket thrown over his wide shoulders didn't hide the deeper scratches crosshatching his chest, or the clumsily applied bandages on his left side and shoulder. Mud streaked his slacks.

"You must be Livia." His voice was clear and deep. "I'm Michael Bonnard. I'm sorry we're meeting like this. I know Spencer envisioned something different. But we had trouble tonight—we were mugged coming home. He's all right but he's not feeling well. If you don't mind, I think tonight's not the right time."

Livia looked steadily at him. In his dark eyes a ring of gold surrounded each pupil; they were odd eyes but they seemed kind, his attitude protective, guarding someone he cared for. She liked him right off; still she didn't move. "I'm sorry, but Spencer's an old friend and now you've made me worried. We'll just come in and say hello. If he doesn't want visitors we won't stay, but I'd like to see him."

Spencer was Noantri; almost nothing could truly endanger him, certainly not a common mugging. He'd survive and eventually flourish no matter what had happened tonight. But unpleasant sensations—pain, discomfort—were as heightened by Noantri nature as agreeable ones; and to flourish, depending on the situation, could be a slow path. Livia owed Spencer a great deal and even out here on this landing in this frigid wind she sensed too much pain to allow herself to walk away. "Let us in, please. I'd like to see my friend."

"Michael?" Spencer's voice, weak and rasping, barely carried to the sidewalk. "Is that door open to allow the breeze to soothe my fevered brow? Because I'd prefer a brandy, actually."

"Spencer!" Michael Bonnard snapped his head around. "You're awake."

"Spencer," Livia called, "it's me. I'd like to come in."

"Livia! Michael, you're keeping my friend waiting in the cold? I hope this is some greeting custom of your people, and not simple discourtesy. Tell me, has she got a priest with her?"

"What are you talking about? You can't be thinking you're dying? You don't need a priest."

"I've never needed a priest. I rather like this one, though. Please, let them in."

Thomas tugged at his scarf, revealing his clerical collar, as Bonnard said, "Are you sure you're—"

"Am I to rise and come to the door myself?"

"No! No, don't get up."

"Then I beg you to remember whose home this is."

Bonnard stood for a moment, focusing on Livia and Thomas a dark and steady gaze. Radiating a reluctance so strong Livia felt it as a wall she had to push through, Michael Bonnard stood aside and let Livia and Thomas into Spencer's house.

11

Thomas was happy to be indoors and out of the cold.

He wasn't sure, though, that he was happy to be in this house. His last experience in a house where Spencer George lived had been one he'd never forget, nor want to repeat. The circumstances here tonight did not portend a relaxed evening of cognac and catching up, either.

Michael Bonnard led them through the small foyer and under an archway on the left. Open glass doors revealed a high-ceilinged parlor. The house wasn't among the grandest of Upper East Side residences, but it was comfortable enough, and these days in New York it must have cost a pretty penny.

In Rome last fall Thomas had been granted a look into the lives of the Noantri—lives ordinary enough to those who lived them, but to Thomas, full of amazements large and small. The finances, for example, of eternal life. One Noantri could exuberantly expend all his resources and find himself facing eternity penniless, while another might husband and invest and grow rich. The Noantri leadership—the Conclave, before whom Thomas had stood in awe—were wise, judicious men and women. Prudent investment over centuries had filled coffers ample enough that any Noantri in need had but to ask.

None was refused; what purpose would that serve? This was a policy that Thomas might have wished his own Church, possessed of inestimable secular wealth, would adopt; but Thomas was a Jesuit, devoted to a life of scholarship, forswearing issues of Church governance. Perhaps things were being done as they should be. If not, it wasn't his place to agitate for change. Certainly not based on a comparison between the hierarchy and rules of the Catholic Church and those of a Community of vampires.

Spencer George, in any case, had never needed the Conclave's help. A respected historian of the Noantri people, he had come from wealth, and through the years protected and grown his fortune. The building he'd chosen for his New York home was unremarkable among its neighbors—neither more grand nor more shabby, well kept but, in its context, discreet. In all ways, perfect.

They entered a parlor of dark blue walls hung with prints and paintings. A Persian carpet covered the floor, various coffee tables and side tables stood about, and two upholstered armchairs matched a sofa on which, propped up by pillows, Spencer George was reclining.

He looked terrible.

Spencer George had become Noantri at the age of fifty-two and hadn't changed in the centuries since. Right now, though, he looked twice that age. The brown of his thinning hair only pointed up the pallor of his skin. Nearly healed but still-visible scratches on his long face echoed the raw, angrier ones on Bonnard's. A large bandage circled Spencer's throat and his hands were wrapped like mummies. He didn't lift his head as Thomas and Livia entered, but he smiled.

"Livia, my dear. How good to see you. And Father Kelly. It's been too long."

"Oh, Spencer!"

To Thomas's ears Livia's tone conveyed as much exasperation as concern. Michael Bonnard turned an odd look on her as Spencer said, "Livia, would you mind?" He waved a bandaged hand vaguely. "Downstairs, behind the wine cellar."

Thomas didn't understand what Spencer wanted but Livia clearly did. She turned to Bonnard. "Where's the cellar door?"

Bonnard hesitated, then shrugged. "Under the staircase."

Livia found the door and disappeared through it. Thomas stood uncomfortably under Bonnard's dark scrutiny, but didn't speak. He looked to Spencer for guidance but Spencer's eyes were closed. Best, then, to keep silent and not add to whatever difficulties were under way.

The cellar door creaked. Livia returned. "Gentlemen, please. If we might be alone for a few minutes."

"I don't think so," Bonnard said.

"Michael, it's quite all right." Spencer roused himself to speak. "Livia means me no harm."

"Spencer—"

"Really, Michael, I must insist."

Bonnard stared at Spencer long and hard. Spencer, blue eyes watery in his ashen face, looked back calmly. Shaking his head, Bonnard turned and led Thomas back through the archway and down the hall to the kitchen. Behind them Thomas heard Livia shut the curtained doors.

12

My God, Spencer." Livia opened her bag and took out a brown glass bottle the size of a bottle of beer. "What went on?"

"To tell the truth, I'm not entirely sure."

On the sideboard next to decanters of cognac and brandy Livia found a silver corkscrew. She opened the bottle. "Can you hold this?"

"It would be easier without these annoying bandages. Michael, as it turns out, is an EMT."

"I thought you said he was a microbiologist. Doing a postdoc at Rockefeller."

"That, and an MD, also. With residency rotations in emergency medicine. On the reservation, apparently, one must wear many hats. Of course," he added, brightening, "you yourself were once a nurse, weren't you?"

Livia sighed. "Yes, I was." She picked at the tape and unrolled the bandage from Spencer's right hand. She could see the new pink patches of skin, angry red at their centers, what looked like animal bites. She handed him the bottle. He lifted it to his lips and without stopping downed its entire contents.

"Ah." He sighed in contentment and let his eyes close. His hand dropped back to the blanket.

Livia took the empty bottle from him. "Better?"

In a few moments the color started to return to Spencer's face. He opened his eyes, now their accustomed bright blue. "Much better, thank you. It was one of the fresh ones, though. I should have told you the aged bottles are on the bottom."

"Well, I apologize if it wasn't quite to your taste, but this wasn't really about a gourmet experience. It was about avoiding a couple of months' sleep, which would have been hard to explain to your friend out there. Come on, I'd better rewrap that hand."

"No." Spencer, instead, began unwrapping his other hand. When he was finished he peeled the bandage from his throat. "It's rather too late for dissembling explanations."

Livia nodded. "I'm sorry."

Livia understood what had happened to Spencer; it happened to every Noantri at one time or another. Somehow, one's Noantri nature revealed itself to an Unchanged. One healed from an injury impossibly fast, or emerged alive from what should have been a fatal event, or was forced to use a Blessing no Unchanged should have been allowed to see. Whatever the cause, no recourse remained but for the Noantri to disappear: to leave for foreign parts, or remain nearby but change residence, identity, and sometimes, courtesy of Noantri plastic surgeons, even features. And, of course, to break off contact with the Unchanged who'd been a witness. The process, called Cloaking, was required of every Noantri every few decades in any case. A condition of the fifteenth-century Concordat between the Noantri and the Catholic Church was that the Noantri, though in plain sight, remain hidden, passing unnoticed among their neighbors. Once your neighbors stopped complimenting you on your ageless appearance and began whispering about it, you were no longer upholding that bargain. Since the Concordat also assured each Noantri a supply of blood for sustenance—such as the bottle Livia had just brought up from the hidden room behind Spencer's wine cellar—most Noantri took seriously their Concordat obligations. Those who flouted the agreement faced the displeasure of the Conclave, which every Noantri took very seriously indeed.

Spencer would have had to leave New York sooner or later, but he'd only recently arrived, and he'd come here from a life in Rome he'd been enjoying and was decades away from needing to abandon. He'd left Rome as part of a scheme that, among other things, allowed Livia's own life to continue unhindered. She'd been grateful to him, relieved and pleased to hear that he was enjoying New York, happy that he'd found a new romantic interest. Now she felt dismay that he would have to uproot himself so soon.

All this had been expressed when she said, "I'm sorry." Now she added, to commiserate, "Your friend—Michael—he's already seen?"

Spencer fingered his neck, where shiny pink scars made ragged patterns. "I was positively gushing blood. Like a fountain. I might have thought it quite lovely if it hadn't been mine. We were in Central Park. Michael wanted to take me to a hospital. Of course I refused and demanded to be brought back here. I assured him the damage appeared much worse than it actually was. Since I was conscious and could, with his support, walk, he acquiesced. I was lying; the damage was quite serious. I expended all my strength making our way home, and once here was barely able to move. I was unable to prevent him from applying bandages. When he did, he couldn't help but see. The wounds were already healing."

"Gushing—Spencer, maybe you're exaggerating. Worrying for

no reason. Maybe it never was that bad. Michael's all scratched up, and I didn't see his shirt—I guess he took it off to bandage his shoulder. But I didn't see any blood on his pants. If it was that bad and he helped you walk—"

"I'd stanched the flow by the time he put them on."

Livia stared. Then she started to laugh. "Spencer! In Central Park in February?"

Her old friend snorted. "Hah! Don't I wish. No, nothing that alluring. But Livia?" Spencer sat up, rearranging himself on the sofa. "We were not mugged. What happened is not precisely clear. Before you arrived, as I wandered in and out of consciousness, I thought perhaps I had dreamt certain events. I no longer think so."

Livia opened a drawer in the coffee table, to get the bottle and its crimson-tipped cork out of sight until Spencer was strong enough to return them to the cellar. "Are you sure you should be sitting up? You seem—I don't know, a little agitated."

"I'm perfectly fine. Pour us a brandy, if you don't mind. There's something I wish to discuss."

13

As soon as the kitchen door shut behind them, Michael Bonnard spun on Thomas and demanded, "Who is she?"

"Who? Livia? They're old friends. From Rome. She's a historian, an art historian. They've known each other for . . . years." Was Bonnard also Noantri? Thomas couldn't tell, though he knew Livia could. If he was, Thomas didn't need to equivocate; but if he was, why had Livia been so curt? "She used to be a nurse," Thomas added. "Maybe she just wanted privacy to look at his injuries."

"And that trip to the cellar?"

Thomas, a second late, shook his head, as though he didn't know. He did. He'd seen a bottle's shape outlined in Livia's purse when she returned. The idea of what was in it, even with his knowledge of and respect for the Noantri people, made him a little queasy.

Bonnard's sharp black eyes with their golden rings held Thomas and Thomas knew the man didn't believe him. Bonnard didn't speak. He turned his back and, using his good hand, ran water into a moka pot and set it on the stove. He reached for the coffee canister.

"I'll do that," Thomas said, taking it and twisting off the top. "Sit down. You look like you could use some rest."

"I'm fine." Bonnard, who did not look fine, took the open canister from Thomas and spooned coffee into the pot. Thomas shrugged and sat gingerly in a chair that looked antique but turned out to be surprisingly sturdy. Well, why not? Just one more surprise in a surprising evening. This sort of thing—some inexplicable occurrence that Livia nevertheless seemed to have a handle on—had happened pell-mell in Rome, but now Thomas had resumed his quiet scholarly life and he'd thought all that was behind him.

He did know, though, that it would be a waste of intellectual energy to try to puzzle out what was going on. Sooner or later, the two Noantri would tell him, or they wouldn't. They were of necessity a guarded people, and he had already been allowed access to more of their secrets than most Unchanged would ever know. It would be presumptuous to expect to be brought into every confidence.

Still, his curiosity, at once a useful tool and a hazard of his scholar's mind, was burning.

For something to occupy himself, he examined the room. Botanical prints added color to the white-glazed walls, and pots and pans showing evidence of serious use hung beside the stove. Thomas watched Bonnard, a tall, broad-shouldered man whose graceful movements radiated a tight-coiled strength, like a spring—or an animal ready to spring. Bonnard seemed to know his way around this room. Thomas wondered how long he and Spencer had been together.

Bonnard turned to face him. "Abenaki," he said.

"I'm sorry?"

"Your eyes were drilling holes in my back. Usually that means someone's trying to figure out whether I'm an Indian. Abenaki tribe. Upstate New York. You?"

"I—I'm not—" Thomas caught on and grinned. "Oh. I see. Jesuit. Society of Jesus. From Boston, myself."

Bonnard nodded. "Jesuits were good to us. I was baptized by a Jesuit. You came to convert the savages, like all the missionaries, but a lot of you took on our ways, and you brought us a Jesus we could use. We called you 'Blackrobes.'"

"To the extent that that's true, I'm grateful."

Bonnard took two porcelain mugs from a cabinet. "You take milk?" Thomas admitted he did and Bonnard retrieved a glass bottle from the refrigerator. He poured the coffee and sat.

Thomas said, "Maybe Livia should have a look at your shoulder, too."

"I'm a doctor."

"You can't dress your own wound, even so."

Bonnard didn't answer and retreated into silence, drinking coffee. Something was obviously worrying him. Spencer's condition? The priest in Thomas wanted to offer reassurance—the one thing he did know was that Spencer George, being Noantri, would make a complete recovery—but this was complicated ground.

"I think he'll be all right," he ventured. "He's very strong."

Bonnard snapped his head up. His eyes showed confusion at first. Then he relaxed. "Spencer? Yes."

Something occurred to Thomas. "Did you call the police? About the mugging?"

"No, or an ambulance, either. He wouldn't let me. Just told me to bring him back here."

"But that's a dangerous man, whoever did this. Violent. He needs to be stopped."

Bonnard nodded slowly. "Oh, yes, he's dangerous."

"Then why . . ." Thomas let the question trail off. Of course. Calling attention to himself and especially in the face of injury would be the last thing Spencer George would want. Thomas had once seen Spencer's Noantri body react to a serious wound, had watched it begin to heal itself in seconds. That was something you wouldn't want a doctor to see.

Even a doctor you were close to.

Thomas and Bonnard regarded each other wordlessly. As though reaching a decision, Bonnard put his coffee down. "All right. If she's an old friend and a nurse, he's in good hands. I wanted to talk to him, but I'd better go. I'm sorry we didn't meet under better circumstances, Father." He stood.

That wasn't what Thomas had been expecting. "Wait, you're leaving? He won't—"

"No, he won't, which is why I'm not saying goodbye. Tell him I hope—"

The kitchen door opened. "Gentlemen." Livia stood in the doorway. "I apologize if I seemed rude. It couldn't be helped. Will you please join us?"

Bonnard said to Thomas, "Well. I guess I'll get to say goodbye after all."

Livia threw Thomas a questioning glance. Thomas rose and the three made their way back across the hall.

14

A h." Spencer watched the group enter the room where he now sat comfortably on the sofa, dressed and shod, a snifter at his elbow. "Please, everyone, have a seat. Michael, Father Kelly, would either of you care for a brandy?"

Both the priest and Michael stopped and stared. Really, thought Spencer, Thomas Kelly, who'd been all but initiated as a Noantri—would have been, if he'd requested it—should have known better. Spencer supposed that understanding something was possible and seeing it happen were two different things, but the priest had seen Noantri healing on a smaller scale the day Spencer met him, and he had no business standing in the doorway with his mouth open.

Michael, on the other hand, had a right to his amazement.

Not that anyone who didn't know him as well as Spencer had come to, and didn't have, in addition, Spencer's Noantri ability to sense changes in body temperature, adrenaline level, and heartbeat, would have been able to read Michael's reaction. Michael's people had a reputation for stoicism. To Spencer's mind that was, like any stereotype, rooted in erroneous expectation: in this case, that the outward expression of emotion was identical across cultures. However, it couldn't be argued that Michael was doing an admirable job of keeping his face blank.

Thomas Kelly bestirred himself and sat, as invited. Livia also moved into the room, poured two more brandies, and took a seat on the sofa. Michael, though, stayed standing. He stared and finally shook his head. "Spencer. You look much better. I'm glad. But I have to go."

"If you're in pain, Livia is quite handy with things medical."

"I'm fine."

"I doubt that, but on the other hand, equally implausibly, I am. Michael, please, I'd like you to stay for a bit. I'm sure you'll find the topic of discussion interesting."

"No. I'm sorry, but—"

"It concerns that wolf."

Michael's eyes widened. Spencer was sure that even Thomas Kelly, with his Unchanged senses, could tell Michael's surprise was feigned. "In the park? That was a dog. A husky, or some kind of—"

"It certainly was not. It was a wolf, you spoke to it in some ancient language—no doubt the words of your people—and what's more, it understood you." Michael didn't react, so Spencer added, "Though it didn't seem disposed to agree with your remarks. It snarled and snapped and returned its attention to the task of tearing off my head. At which point, Michael, you uttered some loud imprecation and became a wolf yourself. Now please, sit down."

15

Livia studied Michael Bonnard, waiting for his reaction to Spencer's words. If he chose to turn and walk out the door there would be nothing she or Spencer could do. Or would try to do.

The monumental implications of what Spencer had seen—that the Noantri and the Unchanged were perhaps not the only categories in the human typology—had long been whispered in both Noantri and Unchanged circles. But so had, among the Unchanged, the notions that the Noantri did not appear in mirrors and could fly. The Noantri found these false characterizations useful as diversions and as shields. Revelation of the truth had proved, over and over through the centuries, to be terrifyingly dangerous.

If Michael Bonnard had the power of what could only be called shapeshifting, he also had the right to reveal or conceal that power.

He didn't leave. But he didn't sit, even though from his drawn face and set jaw she suspected he really ought to. Nor did he agree with Spencer's account. "You were delirious," he said. "You'd lost a lot of blood. The dog—"

"Please, stop," Spencer interrupted. "As you say, I had lost a lot of blood, and with it much physical strength. I was not, however, in any way intellectually impaired. I am now well on my way to the complete restoration of my health, which will be fully accomplished, no doubt, by morning." He pulled at the neck of his sweater to show his scars, now almost completely healed. "As has happened to me on other occasions of bodily harm. To one of which Father Kelly was a witness."

Bonnard turned to Thomas. The priest was white as a sheet, brandy notwithstanding, but he managed to nod.

"Michael," Spencer continued. "I saw you wrestle with the wolf. Two wolves, contending together. I also saw this: when the other ran off, you—wolf-you—started after it, but quickly returned, to stare down at me. At that point, to my eyes, you ever so briefly lost definition just as you had in your first transformation. Then you were back, Dr. Michael Bonnard, a man of whom I've grown quite fond, and you ministered to my wounds. Which you could not have failed to notice were already healing. I myself could not help noticing your valor in leading the wolf away from me as soon as it showed itself, nor the effort it cost you to overcome it. Not the least part of that effort was your clear desire to vanquish that wolf without hurting it, although for its part it appeared ready to kill both you and me. That wolf is the cause of some distress for you. I extend my sympathy, but more than that, Livia and I have . . . a number of unusual gifts, shall we say. The Laws of our people dictate that we not reveal ourselves thus, but we both believe this is a situation extraordinary enough that we are willing to contravene those Laws. If we may be allowed to put ourselves at your disposal? Whatever your troubles, you may find us surprisingly helpful."

What surprised Livia was something she was sure only she

caught, though that had more to do with her long friendship with Spencer than with her Noantri senses: a tiny quaver in his voice. He had told her he was touched by Michael's bravery and attentiveness and felt that a debt was owed. But this was something more.

Spencer was in love.

16

Thomas wondered if he himself, not Spencer George, was delusional. Was he really sitting in a New York town house listening to two European vampires accuse an Abenaki Indian of being a werewolf?

To be fair, it wasn't phrased as an accusation, and only Spencer George had said it. Livia, though, didn't look shocked, wasn't suggesting gently to Spencer that he might want to go lie down. Her gaze stayed steady on Michael Bonnard, with a look on her face that Thomas could only read as guarded hope.

In Rome, having finally acknowledged the truth of the Noantri and what they were, Thomas had asked Livia about other peoples whose natures might be beyond what Thomas had understood, up until that day, as "human." Her answer had been that if such others existed, the Noantri had no knowledge of them. Thomas had accepted that; contemplation of the Noantri nature itself was more than enough spiritual labor for a lifetime.

What had not occurred to him until this moment, seeing Livia's face—and Spencer George's, for that matter—was what the Noantri might feel, if such others were found to exist.

The Noantri were alone. For millennia, each individual had

been literally alone, unaware of others, forced into furtive and de-graded lives by hungers they couldn't control. With the signing of the Concordat they'd slowly begun to gather, to create a Com-munity. The ability to live openly—their natures still hidden, but their lives assimilated into the world of those they referred to as "Unchanged"—was, Livia and others had impressed upon Thomas, an enormous relief and a joy to them. No Noantri lived isolated any longer, unless he wanted to.

Still, Thomas suddenly understood, the Community did. In spite of their wide geographical distribution, living in every corner of the earth, at roughly ten thousand, their numbers were small. The over-whelming majority of humans were of one nature; they were of a different one. The discovery, if such it were, of another—what to call it? variety of human?—would fill a void for them that Thomas could only begin to imagine.

It would, if it happened. But this could not be that. Michael Bonnard, standing before them in this room, could no more be a shapeshifter than Thomas himself. Spencer George, weak and delir-ious, had obviously dreamt what he'd seen in the park. Bonnard's brooding dark gaze as he regarded Spencer, then turned to Livia and lastly, now, to Thomas, expressed concern for a man he cared about and a hope that his friends could help. Nothing else.

Secure in that thought, Thomas was stunned by the words Bon-nard finally spoke.

"You should have died," he said to Spencer. He looked around the room. "Now, you should all die."

17

Livia saw Thomas grow pale when Michael Bonnard spoke but she heard no real threat in Bonnard's dark tone, saw none in his stance. She threw Thomas a warning look. He met her eyes and stayed silent.

Spencer smiled. "Why, Michael. I rather thought you'd grown fond of me, too."

Bonnard locked his gaze on Spencer. "You spoke of the laws of your people. In the tradition of my people, one who sees what you say you saw—the Shift—must die. The identities of Shifters, our stories tell us, must be protected at all costs." No one moved, no one spoke. Slow-drifting headlights of a car out on the street swept the room, briefly illuminating dim corners, then vanished.

Bonnard grinned. "Luckily, you were hallucinating. I'm just a guy who chased off a dog. Nobody Shifted and nobody saw it. So everyone's safe."

"Michael," Spencer said gently, "we can go around like this as many times as you like, or we can move on to more important matters. If the Shift is what you call it, then the Shift is what I saw. If on that account your tradition requires my death, however—and by extension, the deaths of my companions, now that they've heard me speak of it—we have a conflict in which I'm afraid your tradition must be the one to step aside. While the death of Father Kelly is possible, it is not something that will be accomplished in this room without a good deal of opposition. The deaths of Livia and myself are flatly outside your capability. Michael, we do not die. I suppose your people have their own name for our kind. We call ourselves 'Noantri.' The English word is 'vampire.'"

Closely, Livia watched Michael Bonnard receive this news. A brief flash in his dark eyes was the only visible evidence of astonishment, but Livia sensed the almost-undetectable tightening of his shoulders, his back. It was a victory of self-discipline that he remained still.

"You're bleeding, Michael," Spencer said. "Your wound was not as bad as mine, yet under that bandage your flesh remains torn. I'm almost completely whole. As a scientist you can't be trying to deny that sort of evidence."

"I grew up on the reservation. I've seen a good deal of healing that science can't explain."

"Not like this. I know it. Unless you had Noantri among you. Which, now I think of it, is of course possible." Spencer leaned forward, tugged open the drawer in the coffee table, and removed the brown bottle. "This is what Livia fetched me from the cellar. It's human blood. Sniff it, you'll see."

Thomas blanched and turned away. Bonnard took the bottle, looked at Spencer, and did as instructed.

"It's blood," Bonnard confirmed. "Whether it's human, I can't tell. All it proves is that *you* believe you're a vampire. Or that you're straight-out kinky."

"In the weeks we've been together, have I done anything to make you think I might be 'straight-out kinky'? Our condition, Livia's and mine, is the result of a micro-organism introduced into the body. The presence of Father Kelly notwithstanding, it has no inherent spiritual or mystical dimension. Come, you're a scientist. Surely you're willing to grant the possibility of phenomena outside your current field of vision?"

Bonnard didn't answer.

"Michael," said Spencer. "This is an historic event." An imploring note crept into his voice. "Maybe not for you. Maybe you've met a dozen different strains of human, maybe your people have a rainbow of abilities the Noantri haven't even dreamt of. But for us. For Livia and myself. Whatever your secrets, we shall keep them. Father Kelly is a priest, he can be counted on to keep secrets, too. Please, Michael. Acknowledge the truth of this stunning moment."

"I might," Bonnard said, "if it were true."

Spencer gripped the arm of the sofa and blew out a frustrated breath. He turned to Livia, but she had no idea what to do, how to help.

Breaking the silence, Thomas Kelly spoke in a strained voice. "But it is true."

All eyes turned to him.

Thomas spoke slowly. "I refused to believe it when I first found out," he went on, his voice wavering but resolute. "I had to have it proved to me, and even then I tried to twist what I'd seen and been told to try to make it mean something else. I don't know what your truth is, Dr. Bonnard. Whether Dr. George is right about what he saw in the park, or whether it means what he thinks it means. But what he's saying about himself and Livia, I know that to be true."

Bonnard kept his gaze on Thomas for a long moment. He shut his eyes and his lips moved, saying words too soft for Livia to hear. Then his eyes opened and looked at Spencer, at Livia, at Thomas.

Slowly, he nodded. He lowered himself into an armchair with the air of an exhausted swimmer finally reaching shore. In that moment Livia understood the effort the past hours had cost him.

"Michael?" Spencer said gently. "Are you all right?"

"I don't know."

Livia rose and brought him the brandy she'd poured earlier. He was ashen; sweat had broken out on his forehead. She said, "I wish you'd let me look at that shoulder. I think that wolf did you some damage."

"Not as much as he wanted to."

Livia slipped the jacket from Bonnard's shoulders and began removing his bandage as Spencer asked, "That wolf—you know it, am I correct? You've encountered that same beast before?"

"I've known him all my life," Bonnard said. "He's my brother."

18

Thomas felt less in a cloud than he had since arriving at Spencer's home. Part of him wondered about that, given that he'd just heard a man identify a wolf as his brother. Maybe it was the brandy, two disorienting forces neutralizing each other. In case it was, he drank a bit more as Spencer said, "I see. A contentious sibling relationship?"

Michael Bonnard laughed. "You really are unflappable, aren't you?"

"No," said Spencer. "But I've seen a good deal. Nothing as momentous as this, in the scheme of things. Yet everyone's life consists largely of personal concerns. History has seen many murderous sibling pairs. Did your brother come here to kill you?"

"I don't know. If he did, I don't know why."

Livia, having cleaned the torn flesh on Bonnard's shoulder, applied a fresh bandage. "That'll do for now, but I think it should be stitched up."

"No. I'll be all right. I heal fast, too. I mean"—he gestured at Spencer—"nothing like that. That, by the way, is why I didn't want to let you in, you and Father Kelly. Even in the park I could see something extraordinary was going on. I didn't know what it was, and until Spencer could tell me, my instinct was to keep everyone away. I'm sorry."

"You were protecting my friend. I appreciate that."

"I do, also," said Spencer, with a smile.

Bonnard leaned forward again and addressed them all. "What you've told me—it doesn't surprise me as much as you might think. Maybe not as much as . . . as what I am surprised you. There's always been room in our world for . . . others. The vampire, the blood-drinker, he's not part of our stories. But when we heard the white people's stories we were ready to believe." He turned to Thomas. "Just as we were ready to believe in Jesus."

Thomas wasn't sure how to respond, but Bonnard didn't seem to expect him to. He went on, "Now that I'd hook up with one, okay, that's unexpected." He smiled at Spencer; then his face and voice grew serious. "I'm sorry. I want to stay and talk. Share our stories. Desperately, I do. But I've got to find my brother. It troubles me that he came here. He doesn't like to leave our land, and he hates this city."

"And you, apparently," said Spencer.

"Yes, but I don't think this was about me. He might not even have been looking for me, until he sensed that I was close. But he'd already Shifted."

"What does that imply?" Spencer asked. Bonnard didn't answer. He started to stand, got halfway, and his legs gave out. He crumpled. Livia caught him and lowered him back into the chair.

"I think not," she said. "You may heal fast, but you're not healed yet."

Bonnard let his eyes close. "Damn city Indian. Getting soft."

Spencer got to his feet, lifted a blanket from the sofa and tucked it around Bonnard. "Please. At least give yourself an hour to recover. All right, perhaps half an hour. You can't go out like that in any case. Give *me* a few more minutes and I'll be strong enough to locate some clothing that will fit your admirable physique. While we wait . . ." He sat and gave a rueful smile. "I must compliment you, Michael. This news has me so nonplussed I don't know what to ask first."

Bonnard opened his eyes and reached a hand from under the blanket for his brandy. "Then let me ask you one. You said, 'micro-organism'?"

Thomas blinked. All the possible questions, all the secrets, all the knowledge, and that was where Bonnard wanted to start?

Spencer, though, laughed. "Spoken like a scientist. Yes, a mi-crobe. It alters our DNA. Our cells repair themselves endlessly. That's one of the effects."

"There are others?"

"Our capabilities improve. Strength, agility. And our senses. It's all part of the same process. There's no breakdown, you see. An-other effect," he added, before Bonnard could respond, "is the need for human blood."

"But that bottle. You get it in bottles?"

"Courtesy of Father Kelly's branch of the family."

"I don't understand." Bonnard looked to Thomas.

"By agreement," Thomas said, "the Church supplies the Noan-tri with blood from Catholic hospitals." He was surprised to find his tone as steady as Spencer's had been. "So they no longer . . . feed . . . on the Unchanged."

"The Church? You're telling me the Church knows? About them? Priests know?"

"Not priests. Only a very few Cardinals in the highest ranks. Some Popes have known, others haven't. The agreement's a closely held secret."

"But you know. Wait, are you . . . what's the word? Noantri? Are you one, too?"

"No. I'm in a—special position."

"Father Kelly did our people a great service," Spencer said. "In return the Conclave—our ruling body—has granted him access to knowledge the Noantri generally take great care to conceal."

"I see." Bonnard nodded slowly, a scientist digesting new facts. Thomas remembered his own panicked reaction the day he'd first heard this same news. "And the hospitals—where do they think the blood goes?"

Spencer said, "They only know they're instructed to sell drawn and donated blood to certain private blood banks. Catholic hospitals are everywhere. The distribution is wide, the supply is steady, and the hospitals can count on a dependable source of income. The system has been working smoothly for six hundred years."

"And before that?"

Thomas felt himself redden.

Spencer answered calmly, "We were hunted. Hounded. Driven out."

Thomas saw a look of mutual understanding pass between the two men. "'Noantri.'" Bonnard tried out the word. "And 'Unchanged'? That's the rest of us?"

"Well, it's Father Kelly," said Spencer, "and those like him. Perhaps, I venture to say, not you."

Bonnard grinned. "No, I guess not. When did you . . . come to be?"

"Me, personally? In 1548."

Bonnard laughed aloud. "It's a good thing I never worried about dating older men. But I meant, the first Noantri."

"Ah. Our scientists say possibly twenty thousand years ago. They're still working on that question."

"You have scientists?"

"Why, did you think all Noantri were effete arts-oriented intellectuals like myself?"

"Until tonight, Spencer, I didn't think there was anyone like you at all."

Spencer spoke in a voice that was quiet, hopeful. "Michael? Will you tell us your story?"

Bonnard sipped his brandy, looking across the room, to the window, to the dark night. "My people say stories have lives of their own. They know when they're being told, and why." A long silence settled. Just when Thomas was beginning to think Bonnard wouldn't go on, he said, "We're twins, Edward and I. Fraternal, not identical. To look at us you might not know we're related. But we both have the Power. Shapeshifting, in English. You'd call us werewolves, maybe, I don't know. We have a word in the Abenaki language but it doesn't matter. We're almost gone."

"The Abenaki?" Spencer asked.

"No. Though Edward and I didn't grow up on Abenaki land. Our father was Mohawk. The reservation we grew up on is a Mohawk one, that's the language we speak. But the Shifters. The Shifters are almost gone."

"There are—few of you?" Thomas heard a sad note in Spencer's voice. Bonnard must have caught it, too; he looked almost apologetic when he nodded.

"I think it's one reason Edward hasn't killed me yet. He hates me. But without me, he'd be alone." Bonnard finished his brandy.

Livia reached across and poured him more. "The Power seems to be genetic. It's not clear why some children inherit it and some don't, but I imagine it has to do with a cluster of genetic requirements."

"And are you saying only the Abenaki have the gene? Among the indigenous people?"

"You can say 'Indians,' Spencer. We do. I told you that."

"And I've told you, it doesn't sound right coming from my mouth. 'Indian.'"

"Sounds fine to me."

The men's eyes met, and Thomas could have sworn he saw Spencer George blush. That, he decided, called for more brandy.

"Anyway, no," Bonnard went on. "My— The research is very new, so a lot of this is still hypothesis, but the gene seems to be widespread throughout the tribes. Not common, but widespread, like other genetic anomalies—somewhere between albinism and left-handedness, say."

"But if that's so, why are—"

"There's another component. You have to be born with the gene, but the Power's not automatic. You need to learn to use it. To bring about the Shift you have to create a specific, precise emotional state in yourself. A resonance, a pitch, like a tuning fork. It's almost impossible to do without being taught. It can happen in flashes by accident, especially when you're young, and it's a spectacular feeling—like a cocaine high times ten. You're invincible, tireless, afraid of nothing. You feel the astounding change to your senses in your animal form. Once you've felt it, you want it again, and again. But without teaching and practice you can't sustain it. Some people, the stories say, can never reliably do it, even so. Edward always found it easy. For me it's much harder." He waved the brandy snifter to indicate himself, exhausted, blanket-wrapped. "And it always wipes me out."

"How is one taught?"

"There's a ceremony. An Awakening, it's called. It's remarkably similar across tribal cultures, and not much else is. That says to me it can't vary much or it's not effective. It involves music, chants, dances, certain objects. Ritual objects. In the past, most tribes had someone who could perform it, or if not, a neighboring tribe did. A medicine elder. Not a Shifter—it's dangerous for a Shifter to even be there."

"Why is that?"

"A lot of the training goes into learning control. It's a knife-edge in any case. Like driving too fast. Like downhill skiing. You almost *want* to lose control. To see how far you can take it. The Ceremony is designed to draw the Power from a Shifter who doesn't know he's got it. To hear the chants, see the dances again once you've learned—the stories say it can drive a Shifter mad."

"I see. And once you've been trained?"

"Once you learn, the Power can be accessed anytime. Edward and I will be able to Shift for the rest of our lives. But traditionally there's a prohibition against Awakening adults. A life lived without the Shift, suddenly interrupted by it—most people's minds can't take it. They never learn to adequately control the Power. Children are different. The world's magical to children anyway, in the sense that pretty much everything is inexplicable. So why wouldn't you turn into a wolf, into an eagle?"

"What is the Awakening process?"

"Traditionally, women brought each child at five or six. The children were told it was an initiation ceremony. If nothing happened, then that's all it was. If the Shift occurred, no matter how brief or incomplete, the child was given as much instruction as he or she needed to be able to access the Power, to control it. The instructions were secret, of course. Everyone in the tribe knew about the possibility, but no one except the medicine man and the Shifter ever knew whether it had happened."

"Not even the child's mother?"

"No. What I said before was true—the identities of Shifters were always protected."

Bonnard stopped and wiped his hand down his face. He looked spent. Now that he'd begun, though, he seemed determined to finish.

"You can see the problem, can't you? It's the Ceremony that's been lost. Few still remember how to perform it, fewer with each generation. It's not clear why they stopped, unless it's just that all our ceremonies and feasts are in shreds. Some of the medicine elders can still do it, in some of the tribes, but even so they might not have the objects. Those are all in museums now. And if they know, and have what they need, no one brings the children anymore. Edward and I were among the last."

"Who did the Awakening Ceremony for you?"

"One of our grandfathers. Technically, a great-uncle, though that's not a term we use. Our Grandma's brother."

"Your parents are Shifters?"

"Our father wasn't, according to Grandfather. Our mother may have been. She died when we were born. Grandma raised us."

"Ah. Are you the younger?"

"I know what you're asking, but no. I was first and my birth was normal. Edward's was complicated. Unexpectedly. There was no doctor on the rez then. By the time the one from town got up there, there was nothing he could do."

Spencer shrugged. "It was too trite a psychological cliché in any case. But can you tell us, why does he hate you so?"

"If you asked him he'd say it's because I've sold out. He thinks

I'm what we call an 'apple Indian'—red on the outside, white on the inside. Boarding school, college, grad school, postdocs. City living. Everything he despises, everything that destroyed our people."

"That's what he'd say was his reason. Would it be true?"

"Not entirely, I think. It may be now, but we've always fought, from my earliest memories. It's as though I'm a part of him that he's been trying to tear out, shake off, leave behind, but what that would mean—killing me—he can't quite bring himself to do."

"He tried to, tonight."

"No. He tried to kill *you*. I was vulnerable before I Shifted. It was his chance, but he didn't take it. He's had that chance before."

Spencer nodded thoughtfully. "Michael, you say Shifters are very few. Have you met others?"

Bonnard shook his head. "I've heard rumors. If others do exist, they must have also, about Edward and myself. But my brother is the only one I know."

19

Maybe the whole damn Job really was a mistake.

Staring at the crimson splashes and smears on the shelves, the carpet, the boxes housing their precious objects, Charlotte Hamilton heard her uncle's voice. "What does it matter that you weren't born up here? You can still come home. This land is where you belong." Uncle James popped into her head with a variant of that sentiment whenever she found herself wondering what the hell she was doing on the NYPD.

In the Academy, when she'd been young and gung ho, the doubts had come only when some no-neck called her "Pocahontas" or let out a war whoop when she walked by. Her response then was to smirk, deck the guy, and dare him to report her to their training officer. After she'd decked half a dozen guys the whoops became scarcer and she questioned the direction of her life less often. But since she'd made detective she'd begun to wonder weekly, and since she'd come into Homicide—and God knows since they'd partnered her with that loony tunes Framingham—it was pretty much daily.

She shouldn't even be here. Seriously, to be pulled out of the rotation and handed this one only because the vic was in the Native

Art department at Sotheby's? What did the captain think, that she'd pick up some tribal vibe, sniff the air and follow the perp to his eff-ing tipi?

"It's not like that, Hamilton," Captain Greg Friedman sighed with weary patience. "Everyone's watching this because Sotheby's is high-profile. It's yours because of the motive."

"You have motive? So there's a suspect?"

"Let me correct that. The possible motive. Come on, the whole thing's politically sensitive and you know what that means around here."

"It means I had to leave a hot date halfway through my first beer. What's the big political issue, if a low-level public servant can be allowed to know?"

The captain ignored her tone in a practiced way. "Sotheby's is about to hold a huge auction of Native American art."

"Go ahead, say 'Indian.' You know you want to."

"Masks, dolls, baskets, stuff like that." He went on as though she hadn't interrupted. "Worth a fortune. Not everyone's happy."

"Meaning, my people want their shit back?"

"Some tribe's filed a lawsuit. Only covers a few of the pieces, though. They've been withdrawn but the rest of the auction's going ahead."

"Oh, don't tell me. You think some Indian offed this girl to stop the auction? Tell me she was scalped. With a tomahawk."

"She wasn't. And I don't know what happened. But if it was some museum up in Harlem I'd send a black cop. That's the way it is in this city."

"Yeah, okay, I know." It was true. Ethnic politics in New York were so fraught and so Byzantine that when she was in a good mood

Charlotte stood back and laughed. All these gate-crashers getting up in each other's grilles. Really, she didn't mind catching this case. Her date hadn't been that hot. He'd actually tried to talk her out of the beer and into a Cosmo. And this killing would be a relief from the domestics and the drug-relateds. Her objection had been pro forma, just making the point. You had to do that in this Department: woman or man, red, white, black, brown, or Chinese. You had to keep everyone on notice that you knew what time it was.

"You'll be the lead," the captain said. "Framingham's with you. You have Ostrander and Sun. For legwork, canvasses, take who you need from the One-Nine, that's the precinct up there. It's high pro-file so you can have detectives, unies, whatever. But Hamilton? Any Native American suspects, witnesses, any connection at all, you han-dle it."

"Oh, Jeez. Even the bullshit ones?"

"When the case is cleared it'll be in your column. But yes, I pulled you in on this because you're Native—"

"Say 'Indian.'"

"Because you're Native, and unless you want to file a racial pro-filing grievance, that's the angle you're going to play."

"All right," she said. "I'm going. But Captain? Tell me this: What if it was Martians? Who'd you send then?"

Friedman smiled wearily. "Framingham, of course."

Here, now, in Sotheby's storeroom, Framingham was drooling over the paranormal possibilities. The savagery of the attack, the si-lence, the stealthy killer no one had seen come or go: all this pointed to only one thing as far as he was concerned. It was a wonder the wingnut ever cleared any cases, since the perps they dealt with were generally not vampires, werewolves, ghosts, leprechauns, or aliens. Unless you counted Mexicans without papers as aliens. Or, as Charlotte had once pointed out to Framingham, "From my point of view, white people."

Snapping on her latex gloves, Charlotte deliberately shut out Framingham's mutterings and silenced Uncle James, too. Uncle James was wrong. Charlotte had been born in New York City. Her people lived in the center of the state, but the land where she belonged—the land she belonged to—was here.

And Framingham, he was a damn good detail man, seeing what was really there even if he was perpetually disappointed he couldn't prove it had been dropped there by black helicopters. His current theory on this one had to do with a botched extraterrestrial dissection. Fine. If that's what allowed him to spot every paper clip, phone call, and pinprick, go with God.

Charlotte herself did it differently. She operated on instinct and always had, on the Job and in her life. Her grandmother had been a seer, a healer, in the tribe, and Uncle James always said the same power was in Charlotte, too. She thought that was probably baloney but she couldn't help admitting she had moments of clarity, of being sure of something she had no way to prove. Her spine and fingertips would tingle, colors would snap to a knife-edge sharpness, and she'd just know.

Sometimes, not always, it happened on a case, though she had no way to know why or when that feeling would kick in. She'd been leery of letting anyone on the Job know until she discovered instinct, going with the gut, was a respected cop technique. She wasn't the only cop to work that way and she didn't have to admit to any Indian woo-woo to explain her high clearance rate—or to be admired for it.

Charlotte knelt beside the body. Methodically, she started to work. Her doubts quieted and backed away. The answer to her question rose up, as always, and always the same: she was on this Job because what had happened here, the fear and blood and death, wasn't caused by ectoplasm, aliens, or New York City. Someone—a person, with a reason, with something inside him that told him he had the right—had done this to this woman. That was an everyday situation. Charlotte's job was to make him pay.

20

Livia hadn't spoken since Michael Bonnard had revealed the meaning of what Spencer saw in the park. She sat enthralled by the possibilities his words conjured.

Earlier, with Michael and Thomas banished to the kitchen, Livia and Spencer had sat in the parlor as Spencer's strength returned. They'd discussed what to do if it turned out Spencer hadn't been delirious and his vision was real. The Noantri had no Law regarding contact with other non-Unchanged humans. That would have been absurd, like Laws regarding behavior during a Martian invasion. It was explicitly written, however, that the Conclave must be informed of anything that could in any way impact the Community as a whole.

"Shapeshifters, Spencer?" Livia had said. "What could fall more squarely into that?"

"You're right, of course," Spencer had replied. "And yet . . . Livia, our Laws require us to remain hidden. Perhaps the laws of Michael's people do the same. He showed himself only in a desperate attempt to save my life. To do so may be punishable. If I'd broken a Law for him, I'd hope not to be—what do they say?—thrown under the bus for my act."

"Spencer, you're suggesting we break a Law right now. He saw you start to heal. Instead of vanishing before he knows you're gone, you want to get him in here and reveal who we are."

"Who I am. I shan't unmask you—there's no need."

"Of course there is. If we do this I'm not going to—as they say—leave you twisting in the wind."

"They still say that? How colorful. I believe I first heard that phrase some three hundred years since. Livia, in addition to my fears for Michael among his own people, my worry is that the excited reaction this news will provoke among ours will somehow cause it to spread beyond the Conclave. Noantri eager to Unveil may try to make common cause with those of Michael's people who hope to do the same, if such exist. Or worse: it's not impossible that certain Noantri would be only too willing to throw Michael's people under the bus to prove to the Unchanged what good, human citizens the Noantri can be."

Livia sighed. "I think, in this case, the expression you want is 'throw them to the wolves.'"

"Possibly, but under the circumstances . . ."

"I agree. All right. Let's talk to him. We can always disappear and Cloak, if we have to. He can say he met vampires, as people have from time to time, and he'll just be thought insane."

That had been their conversation. The story they'd just heard from Michael Bonnard was astonishing, but no more so than their own. What, she wondered, was to be done with this knowledge now?

Michael might be asking himself that, also—how could he not be?—but he slowly began untangling himself from the blanket.

"I'm sorry," he said. "I'll come back, I promise I will, and we'll talk, we'll give all this the attention it deserves. But I've got to find Edward. I'm—"

His words were cut off by the ringing of Livia's cell phone.

"Livia, it's Katherine." The voice was tight, distraught. "I'm sorry about the hour. Something terrible's happened."

21

Thomas listened as Livia relayed Katherine Cochran's news. The story struck him with a horror he saw echoed on Michael Bonnard's face, and even on Spencer George's. In addition, Thomas felt a despair that shamed him even as he recognized it. A young woman had died violently. Livia and Katherine had known her, albeit briefly; Katherine's friend Estelle had been her employer. As a priest it was Thomas's duty to offer solace. He wouldn't shirk that duty; he suggested immediately he go with Livia to Sotheby's, to join Katherine and Estelle. But oh! he was so bad at this. Clumsy, cliché-ridden banalities were all he could seem to muster at times of grief. His own faith ran deep—deeper, he'd discovered in the last few months, than he'd known—but he had no talent for pastoral counseling.

And that was under normal circumstances. This situation, if Michael Bonnard was correct, was far from normal.

"Blood was everywhere," Livia had said. "She didn't scream— the guard says he'd have heard it, that he was on his way there on his regular rounds and she was still alive when he found her, though just barely. They think it must have been an ex-boyfriend, or a stalker, someone so insane . . ."

Bonnard spoke. "She was killed in the holding room? Where they keep the pieces for the auctions?" Thomas saw a darkness in his eyes that seemed to go beyond exhaustion and pain.

"But nothing was taken. At least, Estelle doesn't think so. The room's a mess, boxes all over the floor, but they seem to have been knocked down during the struggle. It's not clear what's damaged, though there's blood on some of the pieces. That's why she asked Katherine to come. Because she was the consultant on these sales so she knows the art. They want to complete an inventory and examine the pieces, get them to conservation as soon as possible if they need that."

"The Ohtahyohnee?" Bonnard asked. "It's still there?"

"Yes. The box was open, and on the floor. She must have been examining it one more time before the sale."

"No," Bonnard said tightly. "Edward was."

"Michael?" Spencer asked. "What are you saying? Your brother did this?"

"I understand now," Bonnard said. "His rage. The reason he'd Shifted. The reason he's in New York at all. And—oh, Jesus!—and the sense I had that he'd already made a kill before he found us in the park."

"The mask?" Livia asked. "He killed her for the mask? But if he came for that, why did he leave it?"

"Because it's fake."

Bonnard seemed to expect this news to come as a surprise, but no eyebrows were raised except Spencer's. "You were disappointed in it," Spencer said. "Is that why?"

"Yes." Bonnard ran his hand over his head. "Those masks. There were never many. Twelve at any one time, throughout the Eastern nations. At war or at peace. The masks were beyond all that. Four eagles, four deer, and four wolves. A new one was only made if one was damaged and couldn't be used."

"Used?" Spencer seemed to get it at the same time Thomas did. "These masks are for the Shifting ceremony?"

Bonnard nodded. "That was centuries ago, though. They were all thought to have been destroyed. The French, the Jesuits, they ignored them or incorporated them into Christian teachings, the way they did a lot of our stories. But the English burned them. Two were said to have been buried when the tribes that held them were on the verge of extermination, but none of the stories can pinpoint a location. Besides, they're wood, so after hundreds of years in the earth, they'd be pulp by now. The idea that one had survived . . . That's why I went to see it. Edward must have come for the same reason."

"Michael, if they were destroyed long ago, what did your great-uncle—forgive me, your grandfather—use for your ceremony?"

"You don't need a mask *per se*. The music, the dancing, the objects—as I said, the point is to create a specific emotional state. Different objects can do it in different combinations, using different songs, different dances. It's not . . . The objects aren't alive. They have power, but it's not as straightforward—as cheap—as people imagine when they say that."

"White people."

"These days, some Indians, too. There's a lot of tin-pot mysticism going around. Those masks"—Bonnard frowned, seemed to be looking for the words—"they were said to work better than other objects. Our stories say masks make the spirit world visible. If for 'spirit world' you read 'any phenomena beyond our current knowledge' and if 'visible' means 'something we can understand,' it makes sense even in terms of hard science. I told you, the Shift is more difficult for me than for Edward? It took me longer to learn, too. Grandfather always said it would have been easier if he'd had one of the masks, though of course he'd never had one, never even seen one. But that's the lore."

"Why do they work better?"

"They're . . . perfect. Within the context of what the artist was trying to accomplish, there were no missteps. If you understood the context, as anyone from any Eastern tribe would have, the mask would have . . . transported you. By the power of its artistic perfection. In a different context, with a different combination of prayers and dances, Beethoven's late quartets or a Ming dynasty peach vase might be able to do the same thing."

"Neuroaesthetics." Livia spoke in a voice of soft wonder. "The brain's response to art. The physical response, the neurological one. It's a new field. The work is fascinating. In that context, what you're saying makes sense. The mask—it's a face. The cerebral cortex devotes more space, more physical space, to reading faces than to anything else. So more of the brain would be activated by a mask than by other objects. That must be part of what's going on."

Thomas thought about what she'd told him, how her own muscles twitched, her nerves fired, as she studied a work of art. It occurred to him that that might always have been true for her, might also be true for others, and that what her Noantri senses had given her was not that response, but the ability to perceive it.

Michael regarded Livia with a look that Thomas understood perfectly. He could tell how much he wanted to hear more, how urgently interested he was—and how an even more critical problem precluded the conversation he desperately wished they could have. Thomas had felt like that himself half the time, in Rome.

"I don't understand," Spencer said. "If this mask is fake, how could it have provoked your brother's Shift? And how do you know it's fake, by the way?"

"Edward doesn't need the mask to Shift. He doesn't need anything external. Neither do I. We've been taught and we've practiced. We can both bring it about. You saw me do it, Spencer."

"So I did. But then—"

"Because it was fake. Any of the ritual objects should provoke a strong reaction in a Shifter. You vibrate with them, in a way."

"And because you and your brother can become wolves—"

"No. Any Shifter will respond to any of the objects. It doesn't have to be your animal-self, your clan, even your tribe. Even if you don't know about yourself, don't know what it is that compels you. A hundred times, I've gone to tribal museums. Hopi, or Navajo. Cree. Just to see who comes and stands in front of certain cases, how long they stay, if they seem to react. Hoping to find someone else like me. I can't tell, though. I can't."

"That was how you knew the Ohtahyohnee wasn't real."

"It was beautiful," Michael said sadly. "But I didn't respond to it. I didn't feel anything."

"And your brother went to see the mask, and when it turned out to be inauthentic, he went mad with rage?"

"I don't think that's exactly what happened. If he'd just wanted to see it he could have walked in the front door, like I did. He keeps his hair long, he wears his medicine bag around his neck—my God, Sotheby's would have fallen all over him. I don't think he wanted to see it. I think he wanted to steal it."

"But why?" Spencer asked. "For the value? I suppose seven million dollars could buy back a lot of Native land."

"No. Edward doesn't think like that. If he had it he'd hide it, keep it in Indian hands. He wouldn't sell it to someone who'd put it on display for the world to gawk at. I think he came down for that reason—to take it back—but if all he wanted was to keep it away from white people he'd have had a big laugh when he found out it wasn't real. He'd think it was just hysterical that people would be making a label for the wall and getting all solemn about a replica. But if I'm right, he came to take it for a much bigger reason. He needed it."

"For?"

"I think he must have found someone who can perform the Ceremony, or could, if he had the objects."

"But you say Edward no longer needs the Ceremony."

"An unawakened Shifter would, though. I think Edward's been doing what I've been doing. Only he's been successful. I think he's identified another Shifter."

22

In the electric silence that filled the parlor, Spencer assessed his own strength. Though a good night's sleep would be optimal, he judged himself capable of activity, and if ever a situation called for uncommon effort, this was the one.

"Very well," he said. "Michael, come with me, we'll find you something to wear. Livia, you'll go to your friend?"

"Yes. Maybe when we find out what really happened it'll turn out to have nothing to do with Edward."

Michael responded with a small smile but said nothing.

"I'll come, if I may," Thomas said. "Maybe there's something I can do. Some comfort I can offer."

Spencer had his own ideas about the nature of the comfort found in the words of a priest, but this was not the time. The good-byes were fast, Livia and Thomas out the door in moments. Up in the dressing room Spencer located a Norwegian ski sweater large enough for Michael. ("From the days before parkas," he said. "One would wear a thermal-knit union suit and two additional wool sweaters under this. It's considerably older than you are.") Socks were simple, and a wool cap, and since Michael's pants, shoes, and coat had been hastily donned in the park and had made it home with them he was garbed and ready to leave within minutes of Livia and Thomas.

"Spencer, what are you doing?" Michael asked as Spencer reached for his raincoat on a hanger in the front closet.

"I can hardly go out in my winter coat. It's drenched in blood."

"You're not going out at all."

"Don't be absurd. I told you, I have certain capabilities that could make me useful to you."

"An hour ago you were unconscious on the couch. Edward's a dangerous man. This isn't your problem."

"You're not focusing, Michael. There is very little your dangerous brother can do to me that cannot be undone."

"He turns into a wolf, Spencer! He's tasted your blood."

"Yes." Spencer smiled, shooing Michael out the front door and locking it behind them. "I wonder if he liked it?"

23

For the second time that night Livia hurried to a door, leaving Thomas to pay the cab. The no-standing zone at the curb held a police van and two dark cars. Estelle Warner stood in Sotheby's lobby, Katherine Cochran beside her.

"Oh, Livia, thank you for coming!" Katherine hugged her as soon as she and Thomas had stepped in from the cold. "This is so horrible."

Livia gave Estelle a brief hug, also. She hardly knew the woman, but Estelle had lost a colleague, maybe a friend. Estelle, so effortlessly elegant just a few hours before, now looked harried and drained. She wore no makeup and strands of gray hair floated about her face from a loosely pinned twist. "I'm so sorry," Livia told her.

"Thank you, my dear. You really didn't have to come, though. Katherine and I will be here quite some time, I'm afraid, evaluating the pieces, as soon as the police"—her voice wavered—"release the crime scene."

"I thought I might be able to offer moral support. And make the coffee. Estelle Warner, Katherine Cochran, this is Father Thomas Kelly, a dear friend of mine. My dinner date, Katherine. He wanted to come, too, to see if he could help."

"Thank you, Father," Katherine said. "That's very kind of you."

"I'm not sure what I can do," Thomas said. "Besides offer a prayer for the poor girl's soul. And help make the coffee."

"A prayer might be in order," Estelle said. "I admit to feeling ghoulish heading upstairs to examine the treasures so soon after what happened to her."

"You have to do that," Katherine said stoutly. "Time will matter. If blood gets a chance to dry on a piece— Oh, my God, that does sound awful. Estelle, could this really have been someone who works here? Someone she knew?"

"It's a horrible thought. But it's hard to imagine how anyone without a key card could have gotten in after hours, and Security performs quite a sweep at the end of the day to make sure no stragglers are trying to stay behind. And the police did another sweep as soon as they got here. They've been in every room, every closet. One of the detectives does think someone could have come in from the café, the rooftop terrace. Maybe snuck in when the door was propped open when the staff was clearing up out there after we closed. The café doesn't use the terrace in the winter but they keep it swept."

"Could that have happened? How could someone have gotten onto the terrace?"

"I don't know. The next closest building is across the street and their roof is much higher. The other detective rolled her eyes when that one insisted—and I quote—'Someone, or some*thing*, could have made that jump.'"

"What did he mean?"

"Spiderman? I have no idea, but she certainly seemed to dismiss it."

"Well, if it was someone with a key card, they'll be able to find out who, won't they? And even if it was an employee who came in during working hours so he didn't have to use his card, it's still a limited pool."

Livia said nothing and carefully avoided looking at Thomas. Katherine seemed to be trying to contain the horror of what had happened, to make it a kind of puzzle, a tragic one to be sure, but one that could be solved. Katherine asked, "Was she seeing anyone at work?"

Estelle pursed her lips. "She's dated in-house, yes. Though I don't really know who. The police asked if anyone stood out, but they don't, to me. I think partly I have trouble imagining that any-one I actually know might have done something like this."

"I— This is all just so awful," Katherine said. "Father, could you lead us in a prayer? It might help." Katherine smiled weakly. "I mean, I know it will help me, and I hope it will help her."

They bowed their heads and Thomas began. "Eternal rest, oh Father, grant your daughter . . ." The guard, seeing them, removed his hat and bowed his head, also. The prayer was a short one. When it was over, the silence echoed.

Then the elevator door opened, an oddly mundane event. A tall woman in jeans, leather jacket, and boots strode into the lobby, fol-lowed by a smaller, wiry man whose bright eyes threw curious glances everywhere. "Dr. Warner?" The woman spoke to Estelle. "Crime Scene's done. They'll be coming down in a minute. The room's yours."

"Thank you, Detective Hamilton. Detectives Hamilton and Framingham, this is Dr. Cochran, Dr. Pietro, and Father Kelly. They're going to help me with the evaluations."

Detective Hamilton, the woman, surveyed the three of them. "Did any of you know the victim?"

Before anyone could speak the other detective said, "Hey!" Without thinking they turned to him. He snapped their photos on his cell phone and grinned.

"Thank you," Detective Hamilton said calmly to the group. "Those will help in the investigation. Now, about the victim?"

Katherine frowned, then answered, "I met her. With Livia—Dr. Pietro. This afternoon. I don't know anything about her, though."

"Dr. Pietro?"

"Just that one time."

"Father? Did you know her?"

"No."

Detective Framingham nodded happily, as though some suspicion had just been confirmed.

Hamilton turned to Estelle. "Dr. Warner, let me ask you this. The mask in the box—it's the most valuable piece up there, am I right?"

"Yes."

"Why?"

"It's the first ever to come to market. Masks like that were rumored to exist but no one's seen one in hundreds of years. Why do you ask?"

"Everything else that's damaged seems to be as a result of the struggle, but it looked to me like that box was opened on purpose and set carefully down. As though someone—either the victim or the killer—was examining it."

"Brittany may have been looking at it, giving it a final cleaning before . . . we're supposed to install it tomorrow." She paused, then said, "Detective, I feel duty-bound to tell you there's been some dispute at the conference about the mask's authenticity."

"Is that a fact? It's a fake?"

"Absolutely not. Its provenance—its history—is inarguable. But because it's so rare . . . I don't know what that could possibly have to do with this but I thought you should know."

Hamilton nodded. "All right. We might be calling you. Any of you. No one was planning to leave town anytime soon, right?" She swept her gaze over each of them in turn. Livia met her sharp dark eyes, and was surprised to see within them an acuity she recognized. Although rare, the heightened sensitivity commonplace to Noantri did appear occasionally among the Unchanged. In reality it was the senses responding to air currents, to odors, to the way light fell; but in the Unchanged it was most often both incomplete and unexplained. Generally they either considered it some mystical gift of intuition, or shook off its messages because nothing it told them made sense. She saw it now in this detective, and wondered, what did she make of it?

"Good," Hamilton said, though none of them had spoken. "Matt, you want to get their contact info?"

Framingham collected phone numbers while Hamilton walked through the high-ceilinged lobby, looking up and around. Without a glance at her partner—but perfectly timed with the completion of his task—Hamilton reached the door. Before the guard could come open it for her she'd pushed out, her long black braid swinging down her back. Framingham followed.

Everyone was silent, watching the pair get into their car and peel away, Hamilton at the wheel.

"I suppose delicacy isn't necessarily a job requirement for a detective," Katherine offered.

"You should have been here earlier. She's Lenape, she announced as soon as she walked in. Given this case to demonstrate the NYPD's cultural sensitivity. She found that funny."

"Well, it's not very color-blind of them."

"The opposite. They're afraid what—what happened here, was politically motivated. An attempt by one or another of the tribes to stop the auctions."

"Oh, my God! Is that possible?"

Estelle paused. "A sale like this always gets a lot of attention. You know the Hopis sued to remove their items, and now they're in court with the individual owners. There weren't any other lawsuits, and as I told you, many of these pieces are orphaned, but all it would take is one unhinged militant, I suppose."

"But you don't sound like you think so."

"There's still the question of how he'd have gotten in. And wouldn't he have taken as much as he could carry, if the point was to return the objects to the tribes? There were no threats, nothing seems gone, and no one's taken responsibility. I think it's doubtful."

"Do the detectives agree?"

"She does. She thinks the idea's laughable. She asked a few questions about the pieces, and I had to give them the owners' names in case any of them have enemies. But she seems to be going with the stalker/spurned lover theory." Estelle paused. "Now, the other detective, he's a little odd. He thinks a political killing's still on the table, and ties in with someone getting in through the terrace. They were both very focused, though, when they got upstairs. And she, Detective Hamilton, she's the one who told me I didn't have to identify Brittany because Harold already had, and they'll have forensics— fingerprints, dental records, that sort of thing. So I'm grateful. They'd . . . moved the body by the time they asked me to come up and see if anything was missing."

"And nothing is?"

"Not that I could see. Detective Hamilton sneered her way

through the holding room. As though any piece we have here is already, I don't know, ruined."

The elevator opened again and three blood-smeared, Tyvek-suited men came out, laughing at something. Carrying boxes and backpacks, they quickly tried to make their faces solemn when they saw the group in the lobby. One of them said, "You can go up now." A blast of cold air blew in through the doors as they wrestled their gear out.

"Well," Estelle said, watching through the glass until they'd loaded their van. "I guess I'd better get started. Katherine?"

"Of course."

"Livia and Father Kelly, you really don't have to come."

"I don't know these pieces, particularly, but I'm an art historian," Livia said. "I may be able to help."

Thomas said, "And I make good coffee."

Together, they walked to the elevator.

24

M ichael? I personally am finding this situation a touch absurd," Spencer said quietly, "but may I ask why you're grinning like a baboon?"

Under his breath, Michael answered, "A vampire and a werewolf walk into a bar? Come on, Spencer, the possibilities are endless." He started to laugh, but took a deep breath and calmed himself. Spencer understood: pain, exhaustion, and worry had brought Michael to the edge. Spencer wanted to put an arm around his shoulders, to squeeze his hand, to do something to let him know he wasn't alone. He did not. Spencer had lived nearly five centuries as a homosexual. In some times and some societies, that identity was accepted, even celebrated. He'd spent some marvelous years in Shogun-era Japan, for example, and a few lovely decades in Constantinople around the time this new America was shrugging off British rule. Ah, the perfumed flowers, ah, the water flowing in the secluded gardens! In other places at other times, though—most of them, if truth be told—his desires had been as necessarily hidden as his Noantri identity, each revealed only when he sensed he was among his own.

In the cab on the way uptown, Spencer had asked Michael, "I felt this too delicate a question to bring up in the presence of the others—as much for Father Kelly's sake as yours—but I shall ask it now: Is your choice of romantic partners among your brother's complaints against you?"

"It never has been, but he hasn't met you yet. Seriously, no. Edward's straight himself, but he's radically old-school. Pre-contact good, post-contact bad, no discussion. Pre-contact, a man like me would've had a place in the tribe. Two, actually—among the warriors, and among the women. Though when they found out I can't cook they'd have chased me back to the battlefield."

"I'd have taught you."

"Thanks. No, my being gay has never been a problem for Edward, but my being with white men has. It's just more proof that I'm throwing away my heritage. Accepting the identity the white world forced on us."

"Have you ever felt that you are? Accepting that false identity?"

Michael gave Spencer a searching look. "Boy, is that a question for a long evening by the fire."

He fell silent, and Spencer did the same, watching the city streets roll by, people wrapped in scarves and hunched into coats hurrying through the dark.

"Spencer." A new tone rang in Michael's voice.

"Yes?"

Michael threw a glance at the cabdriver, who was absorbed in the upbeat music from the radio. "You said you'd have taught me to cook. You could have, couldn't you? Pre-contact. You could have been there. You could've come with Champlain, with the Jesuits. When our nations and our cultures were whole. You'd have seen us, known us. Spencer, my God, were you—?"

Spencer shook his head. "I'm sorry. No. First: my affection for Father Kelly notwithstanding, I'd have gone nowhere with the Jesuits.

Second, though it's true I've traveled extensively, the appeal of a continent as rife with physical privation as this one was reported to have been was lost on me. It's said there were Noantri among the earliest Europeans to arrive, but I was not one. I'd never touched toe to American soil until last October, a few weeks before you and I met."

The taxi slowed and rolled tentatively to the curb at a desolate Washington Heights corner. The driver turned to announce, "GPS says we're here. You sure this is where you want to be?" Spencer, peering out at the closed auto body shops, the shuttered check-cashing storefront, and the one open bodega, thought the question entirely reasonable and the answer "No." Michael, however, paid the fare without a word and got out. Spencer sighed and followed. A few steps along the side street brought them to a steel door beside a window lit with Budweiser neon. Without hesitation Michael pulled the door open and stepped inside.

Now that door swung shut behind them, cutting off the icy air and replacing it with warmth and the aroma of beer, whiskey, and something that smelled distressingly like the lavatory in the rear, where a good many drunks probably missed their target. And sweat, as many discrete strands as there were people in the room—eighteen, perhaps twenty—plus, Spencer thought, two or three who'd recently left. How much of this was Michael also picking up? How lupine were his senses, and how different in his human and Shifted states? Michael used reading glasses, which had struck Spencer as odd for a man in his thirties; but wouldn't vision be a wolf's weakest sense, far outweighed by hearing and smell? Michael was a lover of nature, as well, a passion not shared by Spencer, and up until tonight ascribed by Spencer to Michael's reservation childhood and the culture of his people. Which might still be true, but an entirely new dimension of that affinity had now been revealed. And

Michael loved music: classical, which Spencer also enjoyed (sometimes remembering his own first reactions to pieces now revered but startlingly avant-garde when he'd heard them premiered in some palace or drawing room); and jazz, to which Spencer was allowing himself to be introduced. At the clubs Michael favored, he preferred the quiet styles to the brass-heavy larger ensembles. Spencer didn't love loud brass or powerful percussion himself, a distaste shared by many Noantri because of the acuteness of their hearing. Were Michael's reasons the same? And though it was true Michael couldn't cook, he did have a discerning appreciation, possibly based in his olfactory sense, of fine cuisine—and a trencherman's appetite.

A few heads turned when the door opened. A jukebox was playing a sad ballad, of the style Spencer had come to learn was "country." Some nods and lifted beer bottles of recognition came Michael's way, some skeptically raised eyebrows were directed at Spencer. Many of the faces, both men and women, shared Michael's sharp nose, his high cheekbones. Others Spencer might have passed on the street and thought black or white; at the table in the back was a man he'd have sworn was Asian. But this place—inexplicably called "Stonehenge"—was, Michael had assured him, an Indian bar.

Michael greeted the bartender with a casual offhandedness that impressed Spencer, suiting as it did neither the pain he must be in nor the gravity of his brother's presumed crime.

"Must I drink this?" Spencer asked *sotto voce*, taking the bottle of Budweiser Michael handed him. "Or is it merely a prop?"

Michael grinned without answering and headed toward the back table, where he nodded Spencer to a chair. They both sat. Michael took a long pull on his beer.

"Hey, Doc," said the oldest of the men there. Lines webbed his dark face and he wore his gray hair loose and long.

"Pete." Michael responded to the greeting, then pointed his beer bottle at the other two men in turn. "Harry. Lou. This is Spencer. So far he only knows me. I thought it was time I brought him here to meet some real Indians."

Spencer settled back in his vinyl-covered chair and said, "Pleased to meet you, gentlemen."

At his words, the man called Harry snickered, while Lou, the Asian-featured one, rolled his eyes.

"Shit, listen to you," Pete said, pulling on his beer. "You come to invade us again?"

Spencer shook his head. "That didn't work out very well the first time."

"For us. You made out like bandits. Hell, you *were* bandits."

All three men laughed, though without rancor; even Michael smiled. Michael drank some beer and said, "I'm looking for my brother."

Pete nodded, and Lou said, "He was here, yeah."

"Tonight?"

"No. Three days ago. Maybe four."

"Do you know where he's staying?"

"Didn't say."

Pete said, "Last time he was down he went to Donna's."

"She keeps that place open through the winter?" Michael asked. "I didn't know that."

"There are Indians stupid enough to stay on, even in February." Pete indicated the group of them. "Englishmen, too, I guess."

Spencer raised his bottle in acknowledgment and took a drink.

"Hey, Englishman, you like that?" Pete asked. "Bud?"

"In fact, no."

"Doc, why are you making your friend drink that shit? Frankie,"

he called to the bartender. "Get this guy a Labatt's. Doc's a city Indian, forgot how to drink beer."

"That's why I come in here, Pete. To be reminded of the traditional ways."

Spencer thought it an odd joke, but the other men laughed.

"You want one too, Doc?" the bartender called.

"No, I'm good."

"No one's good drinking that shit," Pete said, a sentiment Spencer would not have expressed in that fashion but with which he
couldn't help but agree.

The bartender opened a bottle and set it on the bar. Michael
started to get up for it but a woman with curly hair slipped down off
a barstool and brought it to the table.

"Hey, Doc," she said. She put the beer in front of Spencer,
turned around a chair from the next table and sat. Harry scraped his
chair along the floor to make room for her.

"Ivy. Spencer, this is Ivy Nell."

Spencer and the woman acknowledged each other. She looked
at Michael critically and said, "What the hell happened to your face?
And what's wrong with your arm?"

"I fell on the ice, got banged up."

"Want me to look at it?"

"No, thanks. A friend took care of it already."

Spencer wasn't sure whether Ivy Nell, or any of the men, believed Michael's story, but the subject was not pursued. Ivy Nell said,
"I heard you say you're looking for Eddie."

"Have you seen him?"

"Didn't know he was down."

"I didn't either. Heard from someone else."

Ivy shook her head. "Such crap," she said. "Your only family, and you treat each other like this. I saw you at Midwinter. Nine days, you didn't speak a word."

"It's Edward whose back is turned," Michael said quietly.

"So what? He's your brother! Find a way."

Michael didn't respond. None of the other men at the table said anything. The music on the jukebox changed, another mournful ballad following the first.

Ivy picked at the label on her beer bottle. Without looking up, she said, "He's in trouble, Doc. I don't think he knows it, but he is."

Spencer wondered whether she referred to the killing at Sotheby's. If so, how did she know? He didn't react, though, remaining as impassive as the others.

Michael asked, "What kind of trouble?"

"He's been hanging around with a white man. Braids, cowboy hat, turquoise. Feathers and shit. You saw him, Lou. Harry, you too."

"Don't know him, though," Harry said. "Those guys from the Wannabe tribe, they all look alike." He and Pete laughed.

But Lou nodded. "Yeah. Eddie was in here with him, September, October."

"You know his name?" Michael asked.

Lou shook his head.

"No," Ivy said, adding, "he calls himself 'Abornazine.'"

Michael's eyebrows rose.

Harry said, "What's that mean?"

"The baby-naming websites will say 'Keeper of the Flame,'" Michael said. "In Eastern Abenaki. But that confuses a couple of things. The real meaning is 'random archer.'"

"That fits. If I saw that guy with a bow and arrow, I'd run."

The men all laughed and Lou said, "Wonder what *he* thinks it means?"

"This guy . . ." Ivy, unsmiling, looked at Michael. "He's bad news. He's trouble."

"What kind?" Michael asked.

"I don't know. Big. Bigger than just Eddie. Lots of people . . . He needs to be stopped. Eddie's not trying to stop him, though. He's trying to help him."

"Help him do what?"

Ivy paused. "I don't know, Doc. I had a dream."

It seemed to Spencer that all four men sharpened their attention, focused on Ivy Nell more closely.

"People running," she said, gazing at the scarred tabletop. "Screaming. Through the trees, then in a city. Then eagles, wolves, deer, but crazy, like something was wrong with them. And then fire."

The men all waited, but she didn't go on.

Michael asked, "Edward was there?"

"He was . . . somewhere. You were, too. You and Eddie . . . it's about you, but not about you. I don't know. I don't know what it means."

Michael drank, looking across the room, to old black-and-white photos and a small drum that hung on the wall.

"You find that white wannabe," Ivy said. "You find that Abornazine, you'll find Eddie." She looked up and held Michael's gaze. "It's important. Not just Eddie. And Doc? Soon. You need to find him soon. Whatever it is, if you don't . . . You've got to stop them. Soon."

"All right." Michael pushed back his chair and stood. Spencer also rose. "Anyone sees him, will you call me?"

Pete said, "Sure thing, Doc." The others nodded, and Spencer followed Michael to the door.

25

L ivia leaned back, sipping the coffee Thomas had just brewed. The group had been in the holding room for two hours, examining and sorting: what was unharmed, what could be cleaned with mild soap and water—a task Livia took on, with assistance from Thomas—and what required serious conservation. They'd all stopped, daunted, when they'd opened the door, overwhelmed by the fallen boxes, scattered precious objects, and the fingerprint dust that covered everything like snow. They were relieved, in the end, to find little actual damage. Sotheby's didn't have its own conservation staff but it did have a Disaster and Damage Protocol, which Estelle had followed with precision and efficiency. Owners had been contacted, permission requested and received. Conservators in wood, paper, textile, stone, and pottery had been awakened and were standing by, ready to rush to their labs and receive whatever Sotheby's sent.

"All right, I suppose I'd better report in." Estelle removed her cotton gloves and smoothed her hair. "Reporting in" involved going up to the executive floor, where the managing director and the head of public relations fidgeted and fretted along with a crisis-management consultant. They'd been fending off reporters since police scanners had first squawked the discovery of Brittany Williams's body. New York loved nothing better than a juicy crime involving people with lots of money. If sex and passion were part of it, so much the better. And, Livia reminded herself, that's what this still might be: a lover's fury, not a shapeshifter's rage. For Michael Bonnard's sake she hoped it was.

But she didn't think so.

Estelle stood. She'd spoken to the managing director on the phone twice already and had gently escorted him back to his office when he'd come to inspect the situation firsthand. As she gathered her notes, Katherine asked her, "Are they still planning to go ahead with the sale?"

"Not today's." Estelle checked her watch; it was just past two. "They've put out a press release that all auctions are canceled today out of respect for the deceased. Whose name they had to ask me, by the way. They're folding today's pieces into tomorrow's sales. We'll be open for viewing, though. They still want me to install the Ohtahyohnee and everything else that hasn't been shown yet, so they can open at ten."

"My God, Estelle, by yourself? That's impossible!"

"They're lending me an assistant and an intern," Estelle said wryly. "From Impressionism."

"Will the police allow it?" Livia asked.

"Unless they impound the whole building they can't stop it, and apparently the mayor would rather they didn't do that. Anyway, Detective Framingham thinks the killer might come back, to be here during the sales."

"Why?"

"To see where the objects are going. He thinks maybe the point was to get blood on them, so now they're cursed, and the people who buy them will be cursed."

"That's not any native thinking that I ever heard," Katherine said. "And most of the blood ended up on the boxes, not the objects."

"The Lenape detective wasn't impressed, either. But she's interested to know if any of our employees don't show up for work or are acting strange. I'll try not to be upstairs long. Katherine, can you get that rug boxed and ready to send to Brown's, and the map packaged for Reba Fishman at the Morgan?"

"And the kachinas? You want them to go to Ted Morse?"

"Of course." Estelle and Katherine both smiled wearily. Katherine turned to Livia and Thomas. "Inside joke. Ted Morse is the best wood restorer in the country for Native art. He's part Iroquois, which he claims gives him an instinct for these pieces. His business cards say, 'Morse, of course.'"

Estelle said, "Thanks so much, all of you," and pushed out the door.

"Well"—Katherine looked around—"it's not as awful as it could have been."

By unspoken agreement, they'd been conducting operations in the end of the holding room farthest from the bloodstains. They'd moved all the affected pieces to the long worktable, examining them minutely. Now, while Katherine packed up rug, map, and wooden figures, Livia excused herself to make a phone call.

"Livia, my dear," Spencer said. "How are things progressing? How is your friend?"

"It's dismal here, but Katherine and Estelle are both holding up and most of the art is undamaged. Including the Ohtahyohnee. Spencer, did you find Michael's brother?"

"No. We met an interesting lady and some gentlemen, friends of Michael's, and drank an unspeakable beer. Michael was eager to continue the search, proposing to visit a person named Donna who runs an informal boardinghouse, but he's falling off his feet. I persuaded him that this Donna would be more disposed to welcome him at a decent hour, particularly so if he didn't look as though he were likely to expire in her foyer. He was reluctant to pause in his efforts but he does think his brother will probably need to rest soon, also. Moreover, though Michael didn't say it, I suspect that he wishes to regain as much strength as possible prior to another encounter with brother Edward. We've just reached home and I've sent him off to sleep."

"That's probably wise. He might be interested to know, by the way, that the New York police sent a Native American detective."

"Did they really? Is that politically correct, or just the opposite?"

"It's hard to know. The thinking is, it might have been a political killing. To stop the sale."

"Interesting. It could be a useful red herring, though. I suppose it might even be true."

"Do you really think so?"

"No. I'll update Michael when he wakes. Livia, I've just had a worrisome thought. If brother Edward came for the mask and became enraged when he discovered it wasn't real, might he attempt to find the consignor? Sending a forgery into the marketplace while retaining ownership of the authentic work isn't unheard of. If Edward suspects that's happened here—"

"I follow you. Estelle says the owner insisted on staying anonymous. Let me see what I can find out, though."

"I think that would be wise."

"Take care, Spencer. Talk to you later."

Returning to the staging area, Livia found Katherine and Thomas drinking coffee together. ". . . way back in my childhood," Katherine was saying. "I grew up in Florida, near the Seminole people. They're great craftspeople, the Seminoles, beaders, quilters, basket weavers. I loved the colors and the patterns I saw everywhere. I used to sneak away and spy on them. You know how it is when you're a child. Everyone else's life is far more exciting than yours and anything you find out in secret is twice as thrilling as it would be if someone just told you."

"I sometimes still feel that way. When I'm researching."

Katherine smiled. "And my mother always said her mother was part Cree. I don't even know if that was true, but I believed it. It meant I was part Indian and that made it tremendously unfair for me to have to live my boring subdivision life when my real people were just down the road having secret ceremonies and feasts that I could only hide behind trees and watch." She laughed and turned to the door. "Oh, hi, Livia, there's fresh coffee if you want some. I was just telling Thomas how I got into this field. He tells me he's researching Kateri Tekakwitha, under your influence."

"I take no credit for the eminent Father Kelly's academic choices." Livia sat. "Katherine, there's something I need to ask you. The Ohtahyohnee. Did you tell Estelle how we felt about it?" Seeing Katherine glance doubtfully at Thomas, Livia said, "I already told Thomas what I thought."

After a moment and a sip of coffee, Katherine answered, "No. What could I really say? That you and I had the same bad feeling? She's nearly as much of an expert as I am—in this field, more than you, Livia—and she's examined it minutely. The provenance is unbroken. If it's a forgery it's one of the best I've ever seen and I have no idea who could do that kind of work. Or really, why? And based on what?"

"What if the original were destroyed or damaged and the owner, knowing how much it was worth, had a fake made so he could sell it?"

"No one would own a piece like this without insuring it. That would've covered any loss and believe me, the insurance company would notice if an identical item came up for auction." After a moment, Katherine added, "Livia, we may be wrong. In any case, my donors may still want me to bid."

"Have you told them?"

"Not yet. But I'll have to. It may be just a feeling but it's their seven million dollars."

"I don't think we're wrong." Livia looked directly at her friend. Katherine met her eyes and after a moment nodded in agreement.

Livia asked, "Do you know who the owner is?"

At first Katherine didn't reply. Then she shook her head.

"You don't know," Livia said quietly. "But you have an idea?"

A long pause. "There's a gentleman in Riverdale. Do you know where that is?"

"In the Bronx, along the Hudson?"

"That's right. There's a man there who's a major collector, but he's kind of an old-fashioned recluse. Keeps his distance from the art world, thinks of his fellow collectors as Johnny-come-latelies, and fools. He's studied Native cultures all his life. He often buys privately, not just through dealers or at auction. He's good enough to know when he's found gold in someone's trash heap. And he sells exclusively through Sotheby's. I got the idea from some things Estelle said that he might be the owner of the Ohtahyohnee."

"Will you give me his name?"

"I— Why?"

"I want to talk to him."

"Livia, *why?*"

"I want to trace the mask back. To see if I can find when the fake appeared. Art forgery's a long-standing interest of mine." Livia felt a pang of guilt; while that wasn't untrue, it also wasn't relevant. From the look on Katherine's face, she wasn't convinced, either, so Livia added, "And I can't shake the feeling that these things aren't coincidence—the appearance on the market of an Ohtahyohnee mask, the fact that it's fake, and what happened here tonight."

Katherine bit her lip, and said, "I can't either."

"Then tell me who the owner is."

"But Livia, if you think the mask is involved in"—she spread her hands—"this, shouldn't you tell the police?"

"They already have all the owners' names and they'll be following up. They've been told there's talk the mask's a fake, but Estelle insists it's not and there's no definitive way to settle the question. And it wasn't stolen. As you said: What could I really say?"

"Then why do you want to know?"

"Because what the police *won't* do is trace the mask back through its provenance. I want to do that. If the fact that it's fake matters, then finding the real one may be important."

Katherine looked at her, and then away, sipping her coffee. Was she buying it? Livia hoped so, because what could she say next? "A friend of mine, he's a shapeshifter and so is his brother and we think the brother killed Brittany Williams and wants the real mask and we need to find the owner before he tears his throat out, too?"

Unexpectedly, Thomas spoke up. "Katherine, if I may?"

"Of course, Father."

"If you're worried you'd be breaking Estelle's trust, you won't be. She never told you who the owner was. You're guessing."

"No, that's true." Katherine gave Thomas an odd look. "Why are you interested?"

Thomas reddened. "This isn't my area. But what happened here—it's hard not to want to know."

Could anyone be better than a priest at sounding sincere while saying nothing? Livia wondered. Another long pause. Then, "All right," Katherine said suddenly. "I don't know why I'm being so secretive. As you say, the police already know. I think the owner's a gentleman named Bradford Lane. I can get you his address. It's one of the big mansions by the river. Just please don't let either Mr. Lane or Estelle know where you got the information. If it got out I was revealing the secrets of eccentric collectors"—a smile—"the Met would have a cow."

26

Charlotte Hamilton pulled in and cut her engine. This was a no-parking zone, but though she lived forty blocks south, every traffic cop in this neighborhood knew her car and none of them wanted to piss her off. A couple of times, one or another of them had. Once, having pissed her off, one said something about her being on the warpath. None of them said that anymore, either.

God, what a night. Out of her shift rotation, a gruesome crime scene, no forensics—what the hell did this guy do, wear gloves and lick his shoes clean?—hours of overtime, a string of dead ends, and no damn progress worth the name. Framingham was still in the squad room pushing papers, nursing God knew what whackjob theory, but Charlotte recognized the moment when her brain stopped doing useful work. She needed sleep, but before that, she seriously needed a drink. Any number of places on her own block could have helped her out with that, but New York only had a handful of Indian bars and this was the one she liked best. On nights like this, when Charlotte didn't have the energy for barstool cowboys, stockbrokers smitten with her cheekbones, or, so help her, some moron who'd lift his hand and solemnly say, "How," she did what a lot of city Indians did: she came up here, and thanked God the Stonehenge never closed.

Though it did pretend to, between 4:00 a.m. and 8:00 a.m., as the law required. They clicked off the neon, pulled the curtain, and you actually had to knock in code on the steel door.

Charlotte's knock was answered by Leonard Moore, who owned this place with his brother Frankie, trading shifts irregularly as the spirit moved them. "Hey, Len. Frankie go home?"

"He got tired of looking at a bunch of drunken Indians. What can I get you?"

"A beer, thanks. What, he took the drunks with him? Jesus, there's no one here." Even the back table was empty. Two guys she knew and wasn't crazy about sat in a booth; one she didn't know surrounded a beer at the bar. She dropped herself onto a stool and took a long pull on the Labatt's that Len slid in front of her.

"Hard night?" he asked.

"You better believe it. I need another line of work."

"I need another beer." The guy down the bar spoke to Len. Len opened a bottle and put it down on a coaster. The guy looked over at Charlotte with a sharp grin. "If it'll help, I'll buy you one, too."

Well. This was something she hadn't considered. Maybe a drink and some sleep weren't the only things she could use right now, not the only ways to drain the adrenaline raging through her blood and calm her nerves, jangled by frustration, weariness, and too many hours spent with Framingham.

She lifted her bottle. "I'm not ready."

"I can wait."

His black hair hung down his back in a braid bound in leather. That was good; Charlotte liked leather. Her own hair, until recently in a similar braid for work, fell loose about her shoulders. Curious gold circles surrounded the pupils of his dark eyes and under his sweater she could see the bulge of a medicine bag. With the older

Indians that was one thing, but with a young guy it was usually a tip-off that he was a pretentious jackass. When that was true, though, the jackass was making a statement so he wore the bag where the world could see it. Maybe this fellow really was newly down from the rez; maybe wearing a medicine bag was just his way. He was big and good-looking and radiated an energy as charged as her own—with, she thought, a weariness as great underlying it.

"Okay." She put out her hand. "Charlotte," she said, and then, in case he really was a traditional kind of guy, "Lenape."

He leaned over from his barstool but made no move to come sit closer. That was classy, she thought. His hand was big, rough, and warm as they shook. "Good to meet you, Charlotte. Tahkwehso. Abenaki."

27

Bone-tired, Katherine Cochran hailed a cab to head for home. It almost wasn't worth it. It was past four, and she had an 8:00 a.m. breakfast with a curator from Chicago. After which she'd have to face the decision she'd been putting off since late in the afternoon: whether to let the donors know the mask wasn't real.

When Livia brought up her doubts, Katherine had been surprised. For even the most erudite scholar to feel so definite about a piece outside her own area was unusual. But one of the qualities that had always impressed Katherine was Livia's sensitivity to the tiniest nuances of a work. Katherine would have taken Livia's misgivings seriously under any circumstances, but this afternoon she hadn't needed them, except to confirm her own. From the moment Katherine held the mask, she knew.

No, the honorable thing would be to tell the three donors their money would be wasted on the Ohtahyohnee. Those would not be easy conversations. Talking to Livia she'd used the phrase "eccentric collectors" but what collectors weren't? These three had been chasing stories of the lost masks for years. When this Ohtahyohnee had surfaced she'd done some delicate dancing to persuade them to pool their resources to buy it for the Met. They only agreed once they realized the price would go too high for any one of them alone. That they were willing to share it with each other and the public so it wouldn't disappear again marked the keenness of their desire. To learn it wasn't real would break their hearts. They'd want to know how she knew, how she absolutely *knew*. They'd want her to be wrong, and what could she say? *I don't feel a current. I don't hear it sing. It's a piece of wood, gentlemen. Beautifully wrought. As a work of art it deserves a place in any museum. But art is all it is.*

At least Peter van Vliet wasn't one of them. In him you had a genuine eccentric, though a serious scholar, as serious as Bradford Lane. Van Vliet had traveled most of the native lands, spent time with elders of various nations, and, he said, been taught some of the vanishing ceremonies. She believed him; he was odd but he wasn't a blowhard. He had a bit of P. T. Barnum in him, true, but in a way that corroborated his stories: all the medicine people Katherine had met were charismatic charmers. That van Vliet shared that temperament made it more likely that he'd be allowed into the inner tribal circles he claimed to have penetrated. She and he had been trading pieces for years, van Vliet donating works he'd bought in return for ones she deemed less valuable for the Met's collection but which he, for whatever reason, wanted. To her knowledge he hadn't seen this Ohtahyohnee, but he'd declined to join the bidding consortium. Nor was he planning to bid against her. She wondered, belatedly, if van Vliet's lack of interest should have raised a red flag.

She sighed. Letting her mind drift to a collector she wouldn't have to call in the morning was one giant avoidance technique and she knew it.

When she did call, would they believe her? Would they insist she ignore her "feelings" and bid because other authorities disagreed, other experts had authenticated the mask? If they did, would that be so bad? The Met stood to acquire what was widely accepted as one of the greatest Native treasures to come on the market in decades. No one else except Livia, who had no credentials in the area, believed it was a fake. The real one might never come to light.

Even if it was found.

She leaned back against the seat, her mind racing, as on edge as her body was exhausted. She thought about Brittany Williams, whose blood they'd spent the night carefully, clinically cleaning from precious objects. What had the girl's final moments been like? What terror, what confusion? Katherine hoped she hadn't suffered but from what she'd learned about the crime she thought she must have. For someone to be so full of desire and rage that they were willing to kill, how horrible; to do it with such savagery, was beyond words.

That was most of what Katherine was feeling now, as the cab rolled through near-empty streets: sorrow, helplessness, a kind of resigned horror. But another, brighter note had crept into her thinking, one she felt ashamed for caring about in the face of this tragedy but one she could not, if she were being honest, deny. For reasons of their own—and the ones they'd given sounded thin, but what would have been the point of questioning them closely?—Livia and Father Kelly seemed determined to trace the Ohtahyohnee. Katherine herself could not be part of that hunt; her position at the Met required a high level of discretion. Particularly from the curator of a secondary department. Oh, no one would call it that aloud, especially in this era of political correctness. No one could say the work Arts of the Americas handled wasn't in every way—design, workmanship, materials—the equal of pieces from Renaissance Italy or Expressionist New York. But Katherine had learned in her student years that in the art world "artist" trumped "artisan," "attributable" trumped "anonymous," and European trumped everybody.

To have suggested Bradford Lane's name to Livia was a serious breach of protocol. But though Katherine had to keep her distance from the hunt for the true Ohtahyohnee, it brought her an electric thrill of excitement to think that Livia and Father Kelly might find it.

Still, she hadn't been entirely truthful with Livia. As the cab neared her block she took out her cell phone. On the second ring her call was answered. "Morse, of course."

"Hi, Ted. It's Katherine."

"The kachinas are here." In his usual breathless flurry, the wood restorer went on, "I just started. I just got off the phone with Estelle. Unless one of you gorgeous women is going to bring me coffee, leave me alone and let me work."

"I would if you weren't in Brooklyn."

"You would not. Katherine? That young woman—it's terrible what happened to her. I'm so sorry."

"It is terrible. It's hard to believe. You only read about these things, you know? They happen in other people's lives."

"I guess, not always." An uncharacteristic pause; then, "So, is this it? For the damaged wood pieces, I mean?"

"Of course, Morse. If there were other pieces, you think Estelle would have sent them to anyone but you?"

"That's lucky, I guess."

"Ah. You're wondering about the Ohtahyohnee."

"Well, no one's talking about anything else."

"It's just fine. Have you seen it?"

"No. I was going to come up when it's on display. Now, if these kachinas have any chance of being ready for the auction I really do need to get to work."

"If you think you'll have them tomorrow midday, I'll come pick them up."

"They'll be done by then, but I can have them delivered. You must be up to your ears this week."

"No, I'll come. Estelle would feel better, I think. And there's something else I want to talk to you about."

28

Detective Matthew Framingham threw his pen down and rubbed his face. Nearly 5:00 a.m. He'd stayed in the squad room hoping for forensics on the Sotheby's vic but so far, nothing. The ME was digging bullets out of a gangbanger when Brittany Williams was delivered, and though the rich-and-powerful thing bumped her to the head of the line, they weren't about to push aside an open corpse. She'd be next, instead of next week, but it would still be hours.

Framingham's partner, Charlotte Hamilton, had gone home to sleep. "Jesus, Matt. A shift and a half already, not even our rotation, I'm dying here. We hit the heights, it's enough for now." Hitting the heights had involved rousting three of Brittany's ex-boyfriends out of bed. All three turned out to have alibis, though, two of whom they'd also rousted out of the suspects' beds. Whether the alibis were solid would require checking, but that was slow work. "Let Ostrander and Sun chase their tails for a while," Hamilton said. "I'll meet you back here at eight."

In retrospect, it had been a good idea. Hamilton, nine years his senior on the Job and three in Homicide, had a lot of good ideas. She was sharp-eyed, quick, and relentless as a headache. Framingham didn't mind admitting she'd taught him a lot in the two months since his transfer. Any cop paying attention could learn from her, but the attitude in the squad room about being her partner was pretty much *better you than me*. That was because she had a short fuse and when it was lit she got up in your face. Framingham understood, though. All the Pocahontas shit. Long black hair, long legs, high cheekbones—she was one headband short of a corny image of an Indian princess. Which she'd told him Indians didn't even really have. Growing up in New York, she'd learned to fight that battle in schoolyards. Framingham, a skinny, studious kid with, until he'd trained himself out of it, his expat parents' Brit accent, frankly admired her for it.

Her refusal to be put into that Indian box, though, explained what he considered her major flaw: her absolute denial, her positive mockery, of the idea that powers beyond the obvious might be at work sometimes, in some places. Indian stuff, shamans and medicine men and the Great Spirit, she wouldn't even talk about. Okay, fine; that was her business and all that conjured up was Johnny Depp with that thing on his head. But Roswell, the grassy knoll, spy satellites? Different category entirely. Last year the NSA admitted to collecting citizens' phone data, something Framingham had been warning people about for years. Hamilton gave him that one, but it didn't do anything to bring her around. She wouldn't concede the slightest possibility of any theory you couldn't outright prove, wouldn't consider ETs, a sixth sense, any paranormal phenomena whatsoever. Or conspiracies, even, and really, who had suffered more from lying, treacherous governments than her people?

Hamilton's disdain for the paranormal wasn't affected by her own flashes of intuition. Framingham could tell when they happened, and they were another reason other detectives avoided partnering with her. On some cases, not all but some, she'd get bitten by an idea and want to head off in a direction the evidence couldn't justify. It made the captain grit his teeth and it had gotten her into hot water more than once, but it also cleared cases that had the whole squad room sitting around with their thumbs up their butts. Framingham had tried to get her to explain why she made the leaps she did, but she just snapped at him to get back to work.

She played down her intuition, he figured, because she was an Indian and a woman: she had to be Spock, steer clear of anything that smacked of what she called "woo-woo" so she'd be taken seriously. Okay. But Framingham didn't. Most of the cases they caught were straight-up homicides. A woman popped her husband's hottie, a dealer caught it from a turf-war rival, why would Framingham try to make those out to be anything they weren't? But a corporate whistle-blower found with a suicide note, a pistol in his hand, and *two* gunshots in his head? Sixteen people in a Brooklyn neighborhood passing out after a "fiery streak" in the sky, and one of them dying of a "heart attack" while unconscious? Hamilton wouldn't admit the slimmest chance that all might not be as it seemed in those kinds of situations.

This Sotheby's case, it was another one. Stalker? Enraged lover? Yeah, maybe. But even the ME was unsettled by the size and shape of the wounds, their obvious ferocity and their ragged edges. He'd suggested they might have been made by an artifact the killer grabbed in the holding room, a serrated bone knife or something. They hadn't come up with anything, though, and the Sotheby's Specialist said nothing was missing and nothing like that was in this auction, anyway. Of course, you couldn't discount the possibility that she might have been involved herself, and taken away whatever it was.

The other thing they hadn't found, which Framingham thought

was interesting but Hamilton shrugged off, was any record of any-one carding himself in at the door after working hours, any reports from Security of unusual sounds or unexpected lights anywhere in the building. The one thing they *had* found was what Framingham could swear were skid marks on the slate of the roof terrace, the kinds of streaks you'd make if you landed there after a leap. A long leap, across Seventy-first Street. He'd gone up to the roof of the medical building opposite to take a look; that roof was asphalt, not easy to read by flashlight, but damned if he hadn't seen what looked to him like a matching set of marks, the kind of digging-in ones you'd make when you were pushing off. Hamilton laughed. She might have bought a zip line if they'd found signs of grappling hooks to catch the cable—stranger things had happened in New York—but Framingham wasn't thinking that was it.

He was thinking, someone had made that leap, for the purpose of killing Brittany Williams. He had no idea what the motive was, but he suspected it had little to do with love. And he did have this idea: the someone wasn't human.

29

Thomas Kelly's footsteps made no sound as he walked through the dark, gigantic room. A library of some kind, but not the one he'd meant to come to. There was information he desperately needed. Could he find it here, though he didn't know how this place worked, what the system was? He looked for a member of the staff but saw only indistinct figures moving through the stacks or hunched in carrels. When he tried to speak he found he had no voice. He tried again, to no effect. His panic mounted; then a bell rang and someone spoke to him.

"Hello? Thomas? It's Livia. Hello? Are you there or is this voice mail?"

"What? Hello. Hello. No, it's me. Where am I?"

"Don't you mean, 'Where are *you*?' Meaning me? I don't know where you are. You said you were going home to bed."

Thomas, slowly waking, looked around. The murky library faded, replaced by his small, plain room in the Jesuit residence in Chelsea. A winter dawn leaked in around the window shade and the clock read 7:30. His hand held his cell phone. "Yes, you're right, it's me and I'm here. Where are you?"

"In the Bronx, in a tree."

"What?"

"I went back to my hotel, changed, and came up here to keep an eye on Mr. Lane."

"From a tree?"

"I told you, I was what you'd call a tomboy. He lives in a large house with grounds. I wanted to be able to see if anyone came near."

"Did anyone?"

"No. Michael was probably right about his brother needing to rest before he goes out again."

It occurred to Thomas that anyone eavesdropping on this conversation would assume it was in code.

"Did you sleep?" Livia asked. "Can you come up here?"

"Into the tree?"

"Don't be silly. I want to talk to Mr. Lane as early as possible and if I were with a priest I think I'd have a better shot at not getting thrown out."

"Ah. You want my calm, clerical presence."

"Correct." She gave him the address. "We'll call him when you get here. The hour should be decent by then. But Thomas? Not too calm. Before you come up, have some coffee."

30

Spencer was rested, showered, dressed, and scrambling eggs when Michael came into the kitchen. "Well." Spencer turned. "You look much better, I must say."

"Better than what? I feel like hell." Michael dropped into a chair and looked Spencer over. "You, on the other hand, are completely healed, aren't you?"

Spencer shrugged modestly. "I'm pleased to say I'm suffering few ill effects, it's true." As he met Michael's eyes Spencer found himself hesitating. By nature both men were reserved, even in private; still, Michael had been through a lot last night, and a show of affection—a kiss, a brief embrace—would not be out of place. Spencer's situation, though, was new to him. Spencer believed the Noantri Law forbidding the revelation of one's true nature, although enacted for the protection of the Community, was a wise safeguard to one's personal relations, also. Few indeed were the Unchanged who could accept the truth. What Michael had learned last night could not help but alter his view of Spencer. Perhaps Spencer's touch was no longer welcome. He berated himself for his cowardice as he turned back to the stove, not yet ready to find out.

"I assume you're hungry?" He poured Michael coffee and carried it to the table.

"Starving." Michael tried to lift the mug with his left hand, tentatively, testing his arm. He got it an inch off the table, drew a sharp breath, and changed hands.

"How is it?" Spencer asked.

"The coffee? Delicious."

"The arm."

"Not even capable of handling a cup of coffee."

"I'm sorry. Is there something I can do?"

"You can answer this: last night. I wasn't hallucinating, right? Drunk? Delirious? Edward, your friends, what you told me—I didn't dream that?"

Spencer placed a platter of eggs and bacon on the table and pulled out a chair. "I might ask you the same thing. Now, we could be coy all through breakfast, neither saying what he thought the other told him, but each trying to maneuver the other into revealing what he thought he was told. It seems a lot of bother, though. Let me just say that you and I had an extraordinary encounter in the park, Livia Pietro and Father Thomas Kelly were indeed here, a young woman was reported killed at Sotheby's auction house, and I accompanied you to an intriguing tavern in Washington Heights. Also, I'm fairly certain you told me you and your brother are shapeshifters, and I know I told you I'm Noantri, which in your language— or at least, in English—makes me a vampire."

"Ah." Michael nodded slowly, as though considering a scientific theorem advanced by a colleague. "Yes, that's pretty much what I remember. And the fact that we're sitting here in sunlight? That I can swear from experience you can be seen in a mirror?"

Spencer smiled, remembering the evening with the mirror.

"Myths. The more outlandish, the more useful to us. We don't make any attempt to correct misapprehensions about our nature."

"I see." Michael raised his coffee and Spencer did the same. They clinked mugs and drank. Michael put his coffee down and loaded his plate with bacon and eggs.

Spencer let Michael eat in peace. He even had a strip of bacon and a portion of scrambled eggs himself. In Rome, of course, he wouldn't have taken any breakfast beyond a cappuccino and a *cornetto* or some other small, sweet pastry, but that had only been the fashion for a hundred years or so. In China he'd breakfasted on the rice porridge called *congee*, a tasty dish if one added pickled vegetables or salt fish. He'd had morning meals of flatbread with white cheese in Syria, herring in Scandinavia, and on his estate in Sussex he'd been partial to smoked pheasant.

"Michael? What do your people eat for breakfast?"

"Berries. Pancakes. Cornmeal pudding with maple syrup. It's good. If I could cook I'd make you some."

"Give me a recipe and I'll make you some."

Michael laughed. "That's one of the reasons I can't cook. We don't use recipes. Kids stand and watch and chop. I went to boarding school when I was eleven, so after that I wasn't around to watch."

"You went, but your brother did not. Why?"

"Edward hated school. He felt confined, choked."

"You didn't share that feeling?"

"I was a science whiz. Give me a rock and a microscope, or a beaker of something that stank and turned blue, and I was happy. It got so the reservation schools couldn't keep up with me."

"Was it difficult, leaving home?"

Looking into his coffee, Michael said, "We don't like to leave the land we're raised on. My father didn't want to send me off the rez but Grandmother said it was important that I go and that I wouldn't be any less of an Indian for going."

"Do you feel that was true?"

Michael looked up. "Do I feel like an Indian? Yes."

"But your brother faults you."

"He quit school as soon as he could, and when he did go he spent as little time and paid as little attention as possible. Since we were small he followed the traditional ways, learned from the traditional people. To him, every step I took into the white world twisted me, turned me away from our people. Because of . . . what we are, he feels doubly betrayed."

"It must be hard for you."

Michael didn't answer.

Spencer said, "When we find him, what will happen then?"

A long pause. "I don't know. I need to know why he's here. Whether I'm right about the mask, and why he wants it. But if he really killed that woman—God, I think he did."

"Is it his first?"

Michael stared. "His first what? *Human kill?* What are you talking about? He's not a murderer, Spencer. What the hell—you think he's on a crusade to single-handedly wipe out the white race?"

Evenly, Spencer said, "I didn't mean that."

"But it occurred to you. And now you're wondering about me, too. Whether I've ever killed anyone."

"I wasn't."

"You would have."

Spencer nodded. "As you will eventually begin to wonder about me." From the reluctant doubt behind the anger in Michael's eyes, Spencer could tell that he already had. "Michael, we have a lot to learn about each other. I suggest we accept that fact, look forward to our mutual education, try not to lose sight of our mutual affection, and concentrate on the matter at hand. To relieve your mind: I have never, to my knowledge, killed a fellow human. Though in my Unchanged state I did have the opportunity twice, in duels." He added, "Both opponents walked away, wounded but not mortally so. Under the right circumstances I'm quite the swordsman."

Michael stared, then laughed.

Spencer gave an answering smile. Michael's anger drained away, a process Spencer could discern in his falling adrenaline level and slowing heartbeat.

Michael finished his coffee and said, "I'm sorry. This is . . . Oh, shit, Spencer. You asked what happens next. I don't know. I don't *know*. This is my responsibility. It's down to me. Grandmother, my grandfathers, the elders, they're all gone."

"Surely," Spencer said, "there are elders among the traditional people? Not your relatives, perhaps, but some to whom you might appeal?"

"Elders, yes, but not Shifters. On our rez, no one who can do the ceremony, even. No one who knows about Edward and me. Or knows for sure that it's even possible. That knowledge—the identity of a Shifter—that's a tremendous weight for someone to carry. I can't ask any of the elders to take this on." He paused. "Or maybe, I'm supposed to. Spencer, Jesus, I don't know what I'm supposed to do."

Spencer regarded him. "I'm afraid I have nothing to offer but sympathy. And whatever help I'm capable of providing, once your direction is clear."

"And coffee."

Spencer did have that, so he poured Michael another cup. Michael drank in brooding silence. He'd almost finished when he set the mug abruptly down and asked, "What would your people do?"

"I'm sorry?"

"If a—Noantri—were dangerous. To others. Outsiders. What would you do?"

"Ah, I see. I'm afraid we're in a rather different position, though. There are, for one thing, a good many of us. We have laws and a ruling body. The laws are not many, but infractions are not well tolerated."

"How are they dealt with?"

Spencer took a moment to ponder. The working of the Noantri Community was not something he'd ever considered explaining to an Unchanged. For one thing, it was against the Law. But the most critical Noantri Law—not betraying their existence—Spencer had already broken. And Michael had broken the same law about himself.

He poured Michael more coffee and filled his own cup also. "It's the case with us," he began, "that the physical proximity of other Noantri is, it turns out, of immense importance. Emotionally, psychologically." He smiled. "I say this as one who has spent decades on end as a recluse. But hear me out. Until, in historical terms, relatively recently, few individual Noantri knew of the existence of another. If one's interactions with a mortal brought about that person's Change, possibly the two might be aware of each other. But perhaps not. A Noantri's life in those times was furtive and frightening. After satisfying what must have been an inexplicable, tormenting, but uncontrollable craving for human blood . . ." Spencer paused and regarded Michael, his calm exterior belying a pounding heart and a hope that felt to him absurd: that Michael would not blanch, shift his position to gain distance, or smile to hide disgust on hearing those words aloud. Last night they'd been said while Michael was in a whirlwind of exhaustion, shock, and physical pain; but now that they'd sunk in and here in the light of day, would his reaction alter?

For a moment Michael appeared to have no reaction at all. Then he reached across the table and touched Spencer's hand. Just briefly, just lightly; but Spencer wondered when the sun had learned to come bursting through his north-facing kitchen window. *You'll be hearing bluebirds next, you silly man!* he told himself, and listened for them.

Michael sat back and waited. Spencer exhaled. "After—there is no other way to say this—feeding, a Noantri in those times would have moved on. Staying in one place would have been sure to bring suspicion. Also, it's possible to feed without causing the Change. Thus for most Noantri, either another of their nature was not created, or one was, but they never knew." He paused, collecting his thoughts. "These times I'm describing were not years I lived through. By the time of my Change the agreement Father Kelly told you about had been in effect for a century. Noantri had begun to gather, to live in communities; in a larger sense, in Community.

"Imagine, Michael, if you came upon a community of Shifters. People who shared your knowledge, your fears, your outlook on the world. The odd quirks, the amusing moments, the difficulties that come about not because you're Michael Bonnard, but because Michael Bonnard is a Shifter. Would you not feel immediately . . . at home?"

"God. I can't even think what that might be like."

"For us, it's that, and much more. The alteration in our DNA causes our bodies to respond to the bodies of other Noantri in a way that's similar—few Noantri like it when I say this, but it's true—similar to the reactions of pack animals to each other. Dogs will gather into packs. As, I imagine, will wolves."

Michael nodded.

"Camels will form herds, and sheep, flocks. These animals are miserable if kept isolated. Cats, on the other hand, try to avoid groups of other cats. Throughout the animal kingdom you find examples of both kinds of behavior. Noantri, it turns out, need one another."

"But you said you were a recluse."

"Yes—but in Rome. The center of Noantri life. My home was in Trastevere, where perhaps three percent of the population is Noantri. For years I interacted with very few people, but I was comfortably surrounded by my own."

"Three percent of the population of Trastevere? Spencer, seriously?"

"Indeed. We can discuss that, and many other facts which will interest you, I'm sure, at a later date. Let me answer your original question, though, to which all this is relevant. You asked how infractions are punished and how dangerous Noantri are dealt with. From what I've said, you can understand, perhaps, what exile would mean to us."

"Exile."

"In a practice similar to the Amish 'shunning,' violators of the Law are sent away. Those whose infractions are relatively minor but who are thought to require discipline nevertheless, are ordered from their homelands to some distant place. They may dwell among other Noantri but may not return home until their sentences are lifted. Serious lawbreakers are required to dwell at a distance from other Noantri. They are supplied with the blood they

require for nourishment but forbidden other interaction for a pre-
scribed period."

"What if someone violates his exile?"

"At first, it is reimposed to a farther place and a longer time. If
that fails, there are two further steps. Our leadership operates a
prison. Small, but effective. And I imagine, quite boring. You can
understand how tedious being locked in a cell might be, when your
life is eternal. Very few exiled Noantri commit the additional trans-
gression of violating that sentence for fear of what comes next."

"And after that?"

"There is only one step possible, after that."

Again, Michael didn't speak.

"Some Noantri are deemed so dangerous to the Community
that they cannot be allowed to continue. When one's life is eternal,
even a prison must be seen as temporary. An earthquake, the failing
of a bolt: nothing built lasts as long as we do. Rarely—very, very
rarely—a death sentence is imposed."

"But you don't die."

"There are two causes from which we do."

"I'd guess one would be lack of a blood supply."

"In fact, no. A long-term deprivation would cause what you
might call suspended animation. Such a state might last for centuries, but Noantri in this state can be revived."

"Then what? Silver bullets? Stakes through the heart?"

Spencer rolled his eyes. "Certainly not. Those are fictions useful
for misdirection, but they have nothing to do with us. The facts are
these: once a Noantri has made another, the two become recipro-
cally lethal. It has to do with an autoimmune response of the blood.
Should either attempt to feed on the other it will be a fatal mistake
for the one fed upon. An execution is rarely carried out in this fash-

ion, however, as it forces another Noantri, who may be innocent of the crime, to become the executioner. The other cause is fire."

"Fire? That seems so mundane."

"Perhaps not mundane as much as elemental. Another of the effects of the microbe is an increased vulnerability to fire. We're, shall we say, more flammable than you. Our longevity depends upon cellular regeneration. Fire destroys soft tissue. There's nothing left to regenerate."

"And this is a sentence your leadership would impose?"

"You look horrified, and quite rightly. Yes, they would, and yes, it's horrifying. Our lives are precious to us. Our enhanced senses and literally all the time in the world to explore their uses—ending a fellow Noantri's experience of that is a decision never taken without long and somber deliberation. But it has been done, and the knowledge that it has is usually enough to cause even the most apostate among us to reconsider his or her path."

Michael rubbed his eyes and looked away, out the kitchen window. Spencer didn't know what Michael was seeing, but he thought it was not the brick wall of the building behind Spencer's home.

"All right," Michael said. "I don't know how to think about this, Spencer. I want to know more. I want to know everything. At the same time I wish I'd never heard any of it. My own secret, Edward's . . . Now this . . . It's enough, it's too much. But I can't deal with it now, no matter what. Right now, I've got to find my brother." He stood.

Spencer remained seated. "I do understand," he said. "I've had centuries to get used to my own Changed existence. I shan't impose myself. Last night I insisted on accompanying you out of concern for your weakened physical state. You do seem to have recovered admirably. Perhaps at a later date we can discuss the particularities of your . . . situation. I continue to believe I have gifts I might be able to put at your service, but if you'd prefer to carry on alone at this point, I can appreciate why."

Michael regarded Spencer with an unwavering gaze, which Spencer met. "No," Michael said. "No, if you're willing, I think I'd rather you came."

31

A starched, unsmiling woman led Livia and Thomas through a series of oddly bare rooms and down four stairs into the blossom-scented air of a greenhouse. "Please sit." The "please" notwithstanding, this was less an invitation than an order. "Leave that chair free for Mr. Lane. He'll be along soon." She turned and trotted briskly up the stairs with the air of the stepmother abandoning Hansel and Gretel in the forest.

Livia and Thomas found places to sit that did not include the chair for Mr. Lane. The damp jungle aroma and lush shades of green contrasted sharply with the gray, icy morning visible through the foggy glass.

Livia lay her coat beside her on the love seat and smoothed her hair. She no longer wore yesterday evening's black cashmere skirt and heeled boots; now it was heavy wool tweed and sensible shoes, and a down parka. She had, after all, spent the night in a tree.

"You're sure no one—um, nothing—came near?" Thomas had asked when he arrived, handing her a paper cup of steaming coffee.

"I'm not sure, no." She'd sipped, unimpressed with the thin and bitter coffee but grateful for the warmth. Cold, like every other natural phenomenon with the exception of fire, was harmless to a Noantri. Some of Livia's people—those from, say, Scandinavia, or the high plateaus of Peru—enjoyed icy winds and blade-sharp air. Livia, however, was Italian. She skied in the Alps, she skated on frozen lakes, but those were lively events of short duration. Cold as a long-term encompassing environment was not to her liking, at all. "But," she said, "I didn't sense anything out of the ordinary. No sounds or smells I wouldn't have expected in a wooded residential area like this."

"Can you detect a wolf?"

"I'm not sure I could. I don't have experience with their scent, the sound of their breathing, anything like that. But the birds and animals would have noticed, for sure, and I'd have felt that. And I can tell you no one, and nothing, entered the house."

"You'd have sensed that?"

Livia grinned. "They have an alarm." She finished the coffee. "I didn't detect anything worrisome when I got here, no panic, no blood. He hadn't come before I arrived and he didn't come during the night. We're ahead of him, if he's coming here at all."

Now soft footfalls alerted Livia to the approach of their host. She stood, and Thomas, following her lead, did the same. A white-haired man, slightly stooped, wearing a suit, a tie, and very thick dark glasses, stopped momentarily in the doorway, then grasped the handrail and slowly took the stairs down into the sunroom. "Bradford Lane." He extended a hand in their general direction, shook sharply once with each of them, and said, "Please sit down," employing the same "please" they'd heard earlier. He strode creakily but with determination to the empty chair.

"Thank you for seeing us this early, Mr. Lane," Livia began.

"I'm an old man, Dr. Pietro. The old don't sleep well. Calcification of the pineal gland. You'll find out. So I don't care how early it is. That explains why I'm seeing you but not why you want to see me. You say you're here for the Indigenous Arts conference, yet you were ten minutes from my house at eight in the morning. You can't be staying near here because there's nowhere to stay, so you must have come up to see me without knowing whether I'd even let you in. So whatever your business, you think it's important. You mentioned my Ohtahyohnee but not your interest in it nor how you know it's mine. Very cagey. Calculated to make me curious. Congratulations, it worked. Though I hope it doesn't mean Estelle's breaking my trust after so many years. I'd hate to have to start doing business with Christie's. Enlighten me, please."

Well, all right then, thought Livia. "Sotheby's hasn't called you?"

"My pieces aren't going to auction until tomorrow. Why would they call me?"

"They will, later in the day. They're just being polite. I'm afraid the police may be calling, too. A woman was killed in Sotheby's last night, Mr. Lane. Estelle Warner's assistant. There's some indication the killer was interested in some of the Native items, including your Ohtahyohnee." Quickly, to be reassuring, she added, "Nothing was taken and nothing was damaged."

Lane stiffened. "I— Killed? What do you mean, killed? Interested in the items, what does that mean? What happened?"

Astonishing, Livia thought, how it's always the same. None of us, Unchanged or Noantri, can absorb the idea of unexpected death on first hearing. "What do you mean?" What could she mean? His mind was just playing for time. Such a human reaction.

"It's not clear what happened. She was killed violently, in the storeroom where they keep items not on display yet. The police think it was a jilted lover, a stalker, something like that. Some of the boxes were open, including your Ohtahyohnee's. They think that was accidental, that it happened in the struggle. I don't agree, though."

Bradford Lane sat silent a long time. "Don't you?" he finally said. "And who are you to agree or disagree? Why are you delivering this news, and not Estelle? Dr. Pietro, you'd better tell me what's really going on."

"I'm an art historian and a friend of Estelle's. I think that what happened at Sotheby's has to do with your Ohtahyohnee. What the connection is," she forestalled the question, "I don't know. But I have to tell you, there's been some talk around the conference about the mask's authenticity."

"Of course there has. No one's ever seen anything like it."

"That doesn't make it real."

"Its provenance does, though. I'm sure Estelle will show you that if she hasn't already, which she may have done since she was willing to give you my name."

"No, she wasn't. That was something else I picked up at the con-ference. Deductive reasoning with some of my colleagues. It's been quite a guessing game."

"That's ridiculous and I don't believe you. It would be interest-ing to know why you're lying, though."

Livia said nothing.

"You got my name from someone, not from a guessing game." Lane tapped the arm of his chair. "But as long as it wasn't Estelle—and I'll ask her later—I really don't care."

"It wasn't."

"Fine. The mask is real."

"I have colleagues who don't think so."

"Then they won't bid. But if rumors start in an effort to drive the price down, I can promise you I have lawyers who know their way around a slander suit."

"You mistake me, Mr. Lane. I'd like the mask to be real and in fact I think it is." Thomas had started to stir uneasily as Livia strayed progressively further from the truth. "So would Father Kelly," she said. "He's also a historian, of the Church."

"Are you?" Bradford Lane turned in Thomas's direction. "And what's your interest?"

"My interest," Thomas echoed. He swallowed, and said, "Well, sir, I haven't seen the provenance, either, but I understand it begins with a Jesuit."

Oh, not bad, thought Livia.

Lane barked a laugh. "And so you want to grab the Ohtah-yohnee for the Church? That's a damn odd idea of repatriating. You priests, what an audacious crowd."

"No, no," said Thomas. "I mean, if it's repatriated anywhere, shouldn't it be to one of the Iroquois nations?" He radiated such an air of sincerity that Livia had to suppress a smile. "I'm only interested in Father Ravenelle."

"Ravenelle? I don't know anything about him. Too bad, dead end. All I know is that he gave the mask to a friend named Liam Hammill, whose family listed it in their household inventory forty years later and kept it, generation to generation, for the next two hundred and fifty years. Until I bought it in 1965. That's three hundred unbroken years, which is usually provenance enough in this field. If the Iroquois want it, let them sue me."

"Mr. Lane," said Livia, "how can you be sure the mask you bought was authentic? Hadn't been substituted?"

"In 1965? Are you really asking? I thought you were an expert. Here for the conference."

"From Italy. My field's tangentially related but there's a lot I don't know."

"Ha!" Lane slapped the arm of his chair. "I knew it! I never heard of you and I've read pretty much everyone. What's your real field?"

"Early representations of the Americas in European art."

"Oh, God, such crap. It's mostly awful, you have to admit."

"Interesting to study, though. But the mask . . . ?"

"You don't agree. You like those silly here-be-monsters paintings. Well, it's your funeral. Indians weren't a hot commodity in '65, especially the Eastern tribes. Navajo silver, Seminole beadwork, maybe a little, but woodlands baskets, carvings, forget it. No one was collecting, just a few cranks like me. Before that—in the two hundred and fifty *years* before that—there was even less interest. I bought that Ohtahyohnee from a Hammill who was clearing old family junk out of the attic. That was my collecting secret, in case anyone wants to know. Yard sales, fire sales, pawnshops, Goodwill. Why the hell the Hammills had even kept the mask, no one seems to know, except that the Irish never bury their dead and great-great-great-great-whatever-grandfather Liam had made it a point in his will that the thing was important. But the depreciated third-rate Hammill I came across no longer gave a damn. I hope Liam's haunting him. Dr. Pietro, a lot of what I acquired over the years—and curated and preserved and saved from the landfill—were the kinds of things burned as primitive garbage by Europeans so they could substitute their own primitive garbage. Which is the long way of saying, for what I paid for that mask, it wouldn't have been worth a forger's time."

"It is now. I've been told it's estimated at seven million dollars."

"Talk to Vincent van Gogh's brother. There was no serious market for Indian art until about twenty years ago. I promise you, for the last twenty years I've known where that mask has been every minute of every day. Now suddenly the market's booming and I'm selling. Aren't I a lucky man? And if you're suggesting I could have had it forged myself, which of course I could have, I'll throw you out."

"I wasn't," said Livia. "There would be only two reasons to do that. One, to sell it twice. But though the Native art market has grown, it's still a small world. You wouldn't get away with a double sale of an item this unique and you certainly know that. The other reason would be to rake in your seven million dollars but still be able to enjoy the work yourself. I can't help noticing, though, that your walls and shelves are pretty empty. For a man who's supposed to be a major collector, there's not much collection here."

Livia caught Thomas's eye as she said that. He nodded; he'd noticed, too, then. She glanced at Bradford Lane. He didn't catch her eye. Or Thomas's. Or, she realized, anyone's, anymore.

"No," Lane said, his voice dispirited. "Very little is left. As I'm sure you've discerned by now, I'm nearly blind. Another of the disasters of age." He paused. "Whatever you say about the value of the Ohtahyohnee, I bought it for its beauty and I made time to admire it, and my other pieces, every day of my life. Until I was unable to see them any longer. After that, what was the point? I began selling things off. The Ohtahyohnee is among the last to go."

"I'm sorry. It must be hard."

"Oh, spare me the pity. I had a good run. I was whole until I was eighty-eight. How many people can say that? Frankly, the power of that Ohtahyohnee's so tremendous I might still be holding on to it if we hadn't had a fire in the house last year. Nothing was damaged, but it was a wake-up call. Fire's every collector's worst nightmare. You balance the risk of calamity against the joy of living with beauty. Then a lamp cord shorts and your house is burning and you realize all that beauty could have been destroyed, and you? You haven't seen any of it for years anyway. I called Estelle the next morning."

"I'm so sorry," Livia said again. "Not pity, just a statement of fact."

"Yes, well, in that case, thank you. Now you'd better leave. Hilda will be here any minute to tell you I'm tired. I'm not. But I told her half an hour with you would be enough. I think it has been. Based on what you said, I'm likely to be dealing with Estelle and probably the police starting any minute now and after that I will be tired."

"Mr. Lane, there's one more thing."

"Does there have to be?"

"I'm afraid so. As I said, I think whoever killed Estelle's assistant was interested in your Ohtahyohnee. It's possible he decided it's not the authentic one, which would be why he left it behind. If so, he might come looking for the real one."

"He might come here, you mean?"

"Yes."

"And kill me, too, when he doesn't find it?"

"That's what I'm worried about, yes."

Bradford Lane laughed. "He's welcome to it! First, I find your reasoning faulty, but let's say I accept it so we don't prolong this conversation. In that case: second, I'm a rich old blind man living alone with a housekeeper. It's possible someone might get onto the grounds but this house is protected like Fort Knox."

"We got in."

"If Hilda hadn't liked your looks through the security camera you wouldn't have. She's an excellent judge of character. With, by the way, a pistol permit. And a pistol. And third, I'm an old blind man who finds being rich less and less of a comfort. I'm arthritic, I have gout, I take nine pills a day. If I had the stones I'd kill myself but I'm a coward and Hilda won't tell me where she keeps the gun. She's very devout, you see. Makes a novena every day, or whatever the hell it is she does, and she thinks suicide is a sin. Ask me, mine would be a gift not just to myself, but to the world."

"Sir—"

"Oh, put a sock in it, Father. I've heard the arguments and they're all bunk. If this killer does get in, if he won't believe there's no other mask and if he gets angry enough about it to kill me, then bravo. And Hilda will shoot him, and bravo to her, too. Now, please leave. I'd like to sit here for a while and remember what it was like when the Ohtahyohnee hung on that wall. The moisture in here was good for the wood. Right there, it was. Now I can't even see the wall anymore. Dammit. It's a beautiful piece."

"Yes," Livia said. "It is. Thank you for speaking with us."

Unexpectedly, Lane smiled. "I can't say it was a pleasure, but it was interesting. I was never much for small talk, but this house can get to feeling like a desert island. I hope they find whoever killed that girl."

Livia looked at Thomas, then said, "Mr. Lane, will you do something for me?"

"Why would I?"

"I'm not sure. But if someone whose looks Hilda doesn't like tries to come see you, will you let me know?"

"Oh, I suppose so. If you think it will help catch this fellow."

"That's exactly what I think. Thank you."

"You're welcome. Leave your number with Hilda. Goodbye. Oh, and Father Kelly?"

"Yes, sir?"

"If you're really interested in Ravenelle, there was a priest who came to talk to me about him and the Ohtahyohnee maybe four years ago. That's why I called you an audacious crowd. Because I didn't invite him, and he didn't call, he just showed up one day. I let him in because he was a man of the cloth and Hilda said she'd shoot me if I was rude to him. I regret now that I didn't take her up on it but four years ago I wasn't prepared to die. Since he seemed to know so much about the whole business already I swore him to secrecy— which I assumed would be all I'd need, based on his collar—and we sat in this room and admired the Ohtahyohnee."

"If I may, sir, why the secrecy?" Thomas asked.

"Because by the time he came the Indian market had heated up. I knew two things: one, the Ohtahyohnee would create a sensation at auction; and two, given the progress of my eye disease—progress, how's that for an oxymoron?—I didn't have much more time with it. I wanted to be left alone as long as possible. It turned out I had almost four more years, which surprised even me. This priest and I discussed the Ohtahyohnee's history, which he knew as well as I, and I allowed him to photograph it. All of which I'd bet Dr. Pietro already knows, since now that I think of it, if Estelle didn't give her my name, he must have. Proving you can't trust anyone, not even a priest who's been sworn to secrecy."

"You'd lose that bet," said Livia. "It wasn't Estelle and it wasn't a priest."

"Yes, that's right, it was a guessing game. Which I don't have the patience to play with you. So: he saw the Ohtahyohnee and took his photos, but he really came here to talk about Ravenelle. I couldn't help him—he already knew more about Ravenelle than I did. You might ask him."

"I'll do that," Thomas said. "Do you know where I can find him? Do you remember his name?"

"My memory's the one thing that hasn't faded. I'm pretty certain I'd be happier if it did, but you don't get to pick and choose. He's at Fordham, at least he was then. A Father Maxwell. Gerald Maxwell."

32

S hit, you look perky," Framingham said as Charlotte dumped her backpack on her squad room desk.

"Only you would use those words together and mean something good," Charlotte said. "Didn't you go home?"

"Do I look that bad? I slept here, a couple of hours."

"Then you need more peaceful dreams."

"Like you had?" He snuck a grin across the room to Ostrander and Sun. "One of those nights, huh?"

Charlotte felt her cheeks flare. "Oh, screw you, Matt. You guys, too. Do we have forensics?"

"We have doughnuts," Ostrander said.

"And coffee," Framingham said. "Bet you could use some."

"Keep on like that and I'll make you try to say my real name."

"Why, would that turn me into a bat?"

"Why not?" said Ostrander. "She's already a fox."

"And you, Matt, are already an ass. Enough, you guys."

Charlotte's tone must have gotten through to them. It usually did. Ostrander shut up and Framingham went hastily on, "Actually, we do have the ME's preliminary report. They're still saying a serrated bone weapon. They're hoping we find some jaw thing, that the killer could've snapped shut on her throat."

"The jawbone of an ass. I'm looking at one right now." Charlotte blew the dust out of a coffee mug. "Matt, the only Indian jaw things I've ever seen are masks from the Northwest tribes and they're made of wood."

"Meaning no disrespect, oh wise one"—Framingham put his hands together and bowed—"but is it possible you don't know everything about every Indian thing? Maybe there's some secret ritual object you haven't heard of."

"'Secret ritual object,' right. I know, it's a land shark. And it flew across Seventy-first Street. Can land sharks fly?"

"Give me a hard time, I won't tell you what we do have."

"You'd better tell me, I outrank you. We have something?"

Framingham lifted a sheet of paper. "Sotheby's visitors' log from yesterday. Late in the day, after Pietro and Cochran left—we met them last night—"

"I remember."

"Of course you do. After them, someone else came to see Dr. Warner."

Charlotte inspected the paper. "Michael Bonnard? What about him? He left twenty minutes later. Did he know the vic?"

"Nothing says he did, no."

"So?"

"Dr. Warner had meetings all day, you can see that, but with collectors and art people."

"How do you know who they were?"

"I got bored sitting around waiting for you, so I called her and we ran down the list. Had to be done sooner or later."

"She was there this early?"

"Are you kidding? She was there all night. Show must go on and all that. So this is the part you won't like, but it's where the captain pats himself on the back for putting you on the case."

"Oh, Christ, Matt, seriously? Bonnard's an Indian?"

"Correcto."

"Did he bring a secret ritual bone thing with him?"

"If he did Warner didn't tell me about it."

"Maybe she's in on it. With the FBI and the CIA."

"And the land shark. The only thing Bonnard wanted to see was that big wolf mask. He saw it, said it was beautiful, and went away."

A tingle Charlotte recognized came and went at the mention of the mask. "So?"

"So you know we have to talk to him."

"We have to talk to all of them." Charlotte tapped the visitors' log.

"No, Ostrander and Sun have to talk to most of them. You, and therefore I, have to talk to the Indian."

Charlotte sighed and picked up a doughnut.

"But luckily for us, there was something interesting about him."

"Says who?"

"Dr. Warner. Bonnard's not an art guy, which would be one reason to go see the mask, but as far as she knows he's not a muckety-muck in the tribe, either."

"You know that's an Indian word?"

"Tribe?"

"Muckety-muck. Comes from Chinook, hayo makamak. Means 'plenty to eat.'"

"Loosely translated as 'Ostrander brought doughnuts.' Bonnard's a microbiologist. She doesn't know what his interest is. He didn't seem to have a chip on his shoulder like you, he didn't say anything about wanting the thing back—in fact she said he seemed disappointed."

"In a seven-million-dollar mask?"

"Seems like it."

"And so what, he came back later, flew across the street, and killed Brittany Williams because he didn't like the art?"

"Who knows? But he's not answering his home phone."

"Oh. Slightly more interesting. Where does he work?"

"He's a researcher at Rockefeller U." Ostrander, a gray-haired man with a gray mustache, got up with his empty mug and crossed to the coffee machine. "Kind of a rising star, from what I hear. Labs are open twenty-four hours, but the office opens at eight. I just got off the phone with them. Receptionist says he called in sick."

"That a fact? He have a cell phone?"

"Sure does," Framingham said. "You don't want to call him, you want to ping the phone and find him, right?"

"Right. Indian or whatever, guy doesn't answer his phone, doesn't go to work, that's enough for me. Wonder how fast we can get a subpoena for the cell."

Framingham slapped his desk. "Oh, I am good like that!" He waved a sheet of paper in the air. "I got the wheels in motion after I couldn't get him at home. Came through just before you walked in the door."

"That was fast."

"Upstairs wants this cleared up fast," said Ostrander, perching on the edge of Charlotte's desk. "In case you were wondering, they also want it to be a personal crime and not a political one."

"And yet they're sending an Indian after an Indian. Dangerous, opening that can of worms," said Charlotte. "Might end up having to give the whole island back. But this time I think they're in luck. Ask me, we'll do a lot better chasing the cowboys than the Indians. Unless this Bonnard happens to be both. Steve, you got anything yet?"

From across the room Steve Sun said, "Not a thing. I dumped her phone and went through her work computer and her iPad. Lots of texts, mostly bitching with her girlfriends about guys or sexting with those same guys. This Bonnard doesn't turn up, not his number, not his e-mail."

"The name Michael? Mike?" Charlotte thought for a moment. "Chief?"

Framingham laughed. Charlotte threw him a scowl.

"I tried those. Including 'Chief.'" Sun smirked at Framingham. "And other things, like 'Crazy Horse.' Nada. If she knew him, she wasn't talking about him. Or to him."

"Anyone you think we should look at?"

"Not really. She dumped a guy a month ago but he went to Gstaad to cure his broken heart. I called. He's still there. Pissed that the local cops kept him off the slopes for an hour checking him out."

"How too bad. Okay, those other guys, get on them. And the girlfriends she was bitching to." Charlotte turned to Ostrander. "Parents here yet?"

"In a couple of hours. Steve and I'll get them at JFK."

"Good. Ask them about Bonnard. See if they can narrow down the boyfriend list to guys she might have had a problem with."

"What else? Don't give me the stink-eye, I can see something's bothering you."

"The mask," Charlotte admitted. "I don't know what it has to do with anything, but . . . Vinnie, you and Steve go talk to the owner.

See who his enemies are. See if he has anything to say about the rumors the thing's a fake. And put a surveillance team on him. From a distance. He lives in one of those mansions in Riverdale. Don't let them park a unit in front of the place, for God's sake."

"Why?"

"Because I don't want anyone to see them!"

"Not why that. Why are they there?"

"If the mask's a fake, and the killer knows it, he may go looking for the real one."

"So you do think this is about the mask."

"No. I think it's about sex. And maybe drugs and rock 'n' roll. But that mask . . . just do it, Vinnie, okay?"

Framingham, behind his desk, waved two papers in the air: the subpoena and the visitors' log.

"Well, Matt, goddammit," Charlotte said. "What are you waiting for? Get the ping going."

"I needed orders. You outrank me."

While they waited, Charlotte Googled Michael Bonnard. She didn't learn much. The only hits were on the Rockefeller website, where he had an impressive but impersonal résumé. He was good-looking, in a serious-scientist way. His research had to do with smallpox. Jesus, an Indian working on smallpox. What was he thinking, he'd cure it retroactively and bring everybody back? Apparently he was from "upstate New York." Where? she wondered. Lots of reservations upstate. Assuming he was from a rez at all, which maybe he wasn't.

Now, Tahkwehso last night—even before he told her he was from Akwesasne, she knew he was a reservation Indian. Tahkwehso, that was a Mohawk name, and if he had white ones, first or last, she didn't know them. That was Charlotte's way when she picked a guy up, Indian or not. The less you knew that first time, the better. The mystery made everything more exciting, and if the night turned out to be a mistake you could wipe it away more easily. If it was good and you wanted more, there'd be plenty of time to learn lots of things.

Her own Indian name was the same. Charlotte's Lenape name was Keewayhakeequayoo, Returns to Her Homeland. Uncle James chose it for her. *Every time you say your name, you'll be reminded,* he told her when she was small. Maybe; but she didn't say it very much. She didn't give it to many people, not even many Indians—God knows she'd never told Framingham—but something about Tah-kwehso, some electrical charge, made her want him to have it and she'd told him before he asked. He'd whispered it, over and over, and his hands traveled her body, seeming to know at every moment what she wanted, and then moving beyond that, offering what she'd never known before. And that electricity, that feeling of a circuit completed: even after, when he was asleep and she was lying beside him, it didn't end. Here in the squad room, she still felt it.

She wondered if he was going to call her. Sometimes, when it was magical, those were the guys who didn't call, like they were worried it would never be that good again. And the kind of magical it was last night—

"Got it!" Framingham clicked his keyboard. "He's in the Bronx. Near West Farms Square. Let's go before we lose him."

"Son of a bitch," Charlotte said, reading the ping on her computer. "Would you look at that? Forget 'near,' Matt. I know just where he is."

"You do?"

"Sure," she said. "He's at Donna's."

33

The cab left Spencer and Michael in front of a small brick house in the Bronx and sped away. Michael watched with a grin. "I guess we're going back by subway."

"Every minute with you is an adventure."

Michael mounted the steps and rang the bell. Spencer, he noted, was looking with interest up the shabby street, considering its cracked sidewalks, sagging overhead wires, and vacant lots. A man might be five hundred years old, yet apparently the world still held new things to see.

In front of Michael the door opened. A chubby, long-haired woman smiled and said, "Doc."

"Donna."

She stepped aside for them to enter. "You okay? How'd you get scratched up like that?"

"Fell on the ice." Michael reached into his pocket and handed Donna a pouch of Prince Albert tobacco. She led them into a front room on the left. A military-neat metal-framed bed, two upholstered chairs, and a TV made up the furniture population. Michael took one of the chairs and gestured Spencer to the other. Donna sat against bolsters on the bed as though it were a sofa. She tamped tobacco into a pipe, lit it, puffed, and finally nodded; Michael waited until then to speak.

"Full house?"

"Bah. In winter? No construction, no work. No work, no Indians." She waited, smoking, then said, "Your brother's staying."

"I heard. I'm looking for him."

"Not here now, though."

"You know where he is?"

"Didn't come in last night."

"Could he have gone back?"

She shook her head. "He owes me rent. Wouldn't stiff me. He does this sometimes, Eddie. Takes a room, then comes and goes. Maybe he got lucky." She gazed steadily at Spencer as she said that.

Michael smiled. "Spencer, this is Donna McKay. Donna, Spencer George, a friend of mine."

Donna nodded and puffed smoke. "Good to meet you."

"The pleasure is mine," Spencer said, and though Donna raised her eyebrows at Michael when she heard Spencer's accent, she didn't say anything else.

"Donna," Michael said, "I need to find Edward. He may be in trouble."

"What kind?"

"I'm not sure. Ivy Nell had a dream."

A long pause. "That why you're looking? Because of the dream?"

"No. That's why Ivy told me the dream. Because I was looking."

Donna's pipe had gone out. She set it down. "Don't know about the dream, but you may be right. He's keeping bad company."

"A white man, calls himself Abornazine?"

"That one. You know him?"

"No. Ivy, Pete Travis, a couple of other guys, they know him. Couldn't tell me where to find him, though."

"He's been here with Eddie, a couple of times. Silver, turquoise, deerskin boots. Long hair. Has maybe three words of Mohawk, says them wrong. Waiting for him to show up in one of those Comanche war bonnets. I'll throw him into the snow."

"Have you seen him lately? Did Edward bring him this time?"

"No." With a silver reamer she cleaned the bowl of her pipe. "Don't know what the hell Eddie's doing with him. You can tell he's wrong, he's off." Tamping in a new pinch of tobacco, she said, "Lives up the Hudson. Near Esopus."

"Where is that?" Spencer asked.

Michael said, "About an hour north of here."

"Yeah," Donna said, "he's got some big estate on the bluff. Where the rich people are."

"He's rich?"

"Yeah." She flicked a lighter and pulled on the pipe until it caught. "Eddie never told me his white name. Like they're both pretending he doesn't have one."

"You think Edward might have gone up there? Maybe that's why he didn't come back here last night?"

"No idea. But you go up there, ask around, somebody's gotta know him. Even in a crowd of rich crazy white people, guy like that stands out."

They said thanks and goodbye and stepped out again into the gray day. Michael started down the steps but stopped and looked up the street. "Spencer," he said low, "I brought you here to meet

Donna. She's an old friend. We talked, we smoked. That's all. If you can manage not to mention Edward, I'd appreciate it."

"I don't think I'm following. Mention him to whom?"

Michael nodded to a blue Impala, where a man was getting out from the passenger's side and a woman from the driver's. "Them."

34

ichael Bonnard?" Charlotte asked, although she'd seen
enough photos of Bonnard to know that if the guy
coming down Donna's stoop wasn't him he had a twin.
The difference was, the guy in the photos wasn't as battered as this
one. This one was scratched, tired-looking, and holding his left arm
gingerly. Like, say, he'd been in a fight. "NYPD. We need to ask you
some questions." She and Framingham showed their badges.

"I'm Michael Bonnard." After a brief, searching look at her he
added, "Abenaki."

Abenaki? Lot of that going around. Tahkwehso, he was Abenaki,
too. Thinking about him gave her spine a tingle. She wondered if he
knew Bonnard. Not likely. There were maybe ten thousand Abenaki
all told, in five or six states and a couple of Canadian provinces.
Tahkwehso lived at Akwesasne; Bonnard, she could see already, was
as city as she was. But she wouldn't be much of an investigator,
would she, unless she followed up? Tahkwehso had no cell phone,
but she could find him. To help with the case. And maybe he'd tell
her when he was coming back.

Charlotte put Tahkwehso out of her mind and said to Bonnard, "Detective Charlotte Hamilton. Lenape." She turned to the man with Bonnard and waited.

"Spencer George," he said. "Tribeless."

"Sorry to hear it. Dr. Bonnard, shall we talk out here, or would you like to come downtown?"

"I don't understand. Have I done something wrong?"

"You tell us."

"As far as I know, no. What's this about?"

"What happened to your face?"

"We were mugged. Spencer and I."

"When?"

"Last night."

"Where?"

"Central Park."

"Did you report it?"

"No. They didn't get anything and neither of us got a good look at them, so what's the point?"

"The mugging," and Charlotte let a little skepticism leak into her voice, "was that before or after you were at Sotheby's yesterday?"

"After."

"Why did you go?"

"To Sotheby's? To see an item they're listing for auction."

"Which item?"

"A wolf mask."

Framingham's cell phone beeped and he stepped away to read something on his screen.

"You're not a collector or a historian," Charlotte said. "Why did you want to see the mask?"

"My grandfather was a medicine man. He used to tell me about masks like this but he'd never seen one. They're extremely rare."

"So you just thought you'd check it out?"

"Yes."

"Do you know a young woman named Brittany Williams?"

"No."

My ass, thought Charlotte. People who really didn't know someone almost always asked to hear the name again.

"Hey!" said Framingham, beside her again. "Smile!" He snapped a cell phone photo of Spencer George.

George scowled. "I object! Is he permitted to do that without my consent?"

"No expectation of privacy on a public street," said Charlotte.

"Really? How disagreeable."

The front door to the small brick house opened. Charlotte looked up and nodded. "Donna."

"Charlotte. Everything okay?"

"Fine."

"Doc?"

"Thanks, Donna, no problem."

"Whatever you're doing, want to do it in here? Cold out there."

"Whatever we're doing"—Bonnard turned to Charlotte—"I'd like to know what it is."

"It's okay, thanks, Donna," Charlotte said. "This won't take long."

"I, for one, am relieved to hear that," said Spencer George.

Donna nodded and closed her door. A moment later her round face appeared at the window.

Charlotte turned back to Bonnard. "When you went to Sotheby's, who did you see?"

"Detective, what's going on?"

"Answer the question, please."

"I saw Estelle Warner, the Specialist in the Native Art section, but really, it's cold out here and I'm getting annoyed."

"I'm annoyed, too. Brittany Williams was killed at Sotheby's a few hours after you left. Homicide irritates the hell out of me."

"My God." That wasn't much of a reaction, but hell, he was an Indian. Spencer George said nothing.

"What happened to her?" Bonnard asked. He didn't, Charlotte noticed, ask again who Williams was.

"Someone tore her throat out."

"Jesus."

"Was it you?"

"Was it *me*? Why would I— Are you crazy? No, of course not."

"But you knew her."

"No, I— Was she the assistant? Blond young woman who brought the mask? Then I met her, yes. But I didn't know her."

Charlotte turned to Spencer George. "What about you?"

"About me? What would you like to know?"

"Who are you in all this?"

"In all this criminal activity? I don't believe I'm anybody. In the larger world, I'm a friend of Michael's."

"Did you know Brittany Williams?"

"No, I did not. Nor have I ever been to Sotheby's."

"But you are a collector," Framingham interjected. Charlotte raised her eyebrows but let him run with it.

"Of art, yes, I am, and how clever of you to know that. But the artifacts of Michael's—and, I assume, Detective Hamilton's—people are not within my area of expertise."

"No, yours is more European art. Items from the Vatican, say."

Spencer George eyed Framingham. "My collection includes some pieces the Vatican has deaccessioned, yes," he said evenly.

"And how do you two know each other?"

"Michael and I? We met at a gallery opening, as a matter of fact. The works of Jeffrey Gibson. Do you know him? Quite a talented young man. One of your people," he said to Charlotte. "Though not of your—what is it you say? Your nation."

Framingham smiled but seemed to have no more to say, so Charlotte turned back to Bonnard. "Why didn't you go to work today?"

"I was pretty wiped out. I decided to sleep in and take the day off."

"To come to the Bronx."

"I've been wanting Spencer to meet Donna."

"Tell me this," Charlotte said. "What was your reaction to the mask when you saw it?"

"The mask? I thought it was beautiful."

"But you were disappointed."

"Who told you that?"

"Is it true?"

"Is that what Dr. Warner said? She's very perceptive."

"Disappointed, why?"

"As I said, the elders used to talk about masks like these when I was a kid. Maybe you heard the stories, too?" When Charlotte didn't answer he went on, "I guess I just expected something more spectacular."

"Where were you last night around nine?"

"Walking in Central Park. Waiting to get mugged."

Charlotte looked at Spencer George, who smiled and nodded.

"After that? Did you go to a hospital, get medical attention?"

"We went back to Spencer's. He wasn't hurt and I took care of myself."

"Michael is a doctor," Spencer George added helpfully.

"So no one can confirm your story?"

"No," said Bonnard. "Do I need that? Are you seriously thinking I killed this woman?"

"Should I be?"

"Not unless you want to waste your time. Detectives, I wish we could help you, but it's really cold out here and I have things to do. If we're at the point where you're accusing me of murder, I think—"

"If someone, some Indian, killed Brittany Williams to stop the auction, who would that have been?"

"Are you— No one would do that."

"You're sure? I've seen Indians kill for a bottle of beer."

"And you see that as a political statement?"

"I see it as desperation. The same as this would be. You know anyone that desperate?"

Bonnard just shook his head.

"All right," Charlotte said. "Stay available. I want to be able to find you if we need you."

"How did you find me this time?"

Charlotte grinned. "Lenape tracking secret. Matt, you have contact info for Mr. George?"

"Doctor," said Spencer George. He handed Framingham a business card. "Though I'm sure you could find me just as you took my photo: whether I want you to or not."

Charlotte said, "Okay, you can go. Come on, Matt, as long as we're here, maybe you should meet Donna, too."

She trotted up Donna's front steps, Framingham following behind. As Donna opened the door Charlotte saw Bonnard and his friend turn and stride away.

35

You lied to the authorities," Spencer said, walking beside Michael on the way to the subway.

"Technically, no. She asked if anyone could confirm my story. It's not true, so how could anyone confirm it?"

"That," said Spencer, "is the sort of sophistry I'd expect from a Jesuit."

"I just couldn't see an easy way to explain that the people with us last night were the people she met at Sotheby's later. If I were a cop I'd see that as one coincidence too far."

"And yet, that's the innocent part of the story."

"I know. I just don't want to spend the day in a police station convincing them. In my defense, she wasn't straightforward with me, either. She asked why I went to Sotheby's but she knew I'd gone to see the mask. She already knew I was disappointed in it."

"She asked that to see if you'd lie. I believe that's her job."

"And on that I told the truth. That must have bought me some credibility."

"If you don't mind my saying so, you didn't appear to have a great deal of credibility in her eyes."

"Her partner doesn't seem to think much of you, either. What was he talking about, 'items from the Vatican'?"

"That's a long story, best told beside a warm stove. About our lonely night last night, I assume you'd like Livia and Father Kelly to tell a similar tale?" Spencer took out his cell phone.

"Yes, though we won't be able to keep it going. They'll put it together eventually. But I'd like to find Edward before that."

Those words hung in the air between them, begging the question of what would happen then; but Spencer had asked that once, and would not again. Before he entered Livia's number, he said, "I must warn you, I'm not sure I can convince Father Kelly to tell a lie. In that he's rather different to most other men of the cloth."

"Takes his vows seriously, does he?"

"According to Livia, all of them. Michael, am I to be surprised that this Lenape detective knows your friend Donna? Or is she known to every Native person in New York?"

"Not everyone. But her place is on the Indian grapevine. You're new in town, looking for work or whatever it is, you need a place to stay, ask around and someone will tell you about Donna. Mind you, she runs a tight ship. No drugs, no alcohol. Still, if I were an Indian cop, I'd make it my business to stay on Donna's good side because she always knows who's coming and going."

"And you're not worried that Donna will reveal to these detectives our true reason for coming to see her?"

"No. Edward . . . It's hard to explain, but people care about him in a special way."

"Including yourself."

"Well, he's my brother. But Donna, Ivy, Pete—people look out for him, protect him. You heard Ivy, her dream, how worried she was. Donna won't volunteer anything. Though I guarantee, if any-one besides Edward had shown up in her place with a wannabe like this Abornazine she'd have kicked them both out."

"May I ask you about Ivy, and her dream? I had a sense that you and the others put special credence in it."

"Ivy's a seer. I don't know if your people have anyone like that?" Spencer shook his head, and Michael went on, "Ivy's dreams have always meant something. Since we were children. She's from Akwe-sasne, too. We grew up together. No one discounts Ivy's dreams, even guys like Pete and Lou, from the West. But Ivy can't always explain them."

"I see. Thank you." They were nearing the subway entrance, so Spencer thumbed Livia's number.

"When you're done," Michael said, "do me a favor and turn the phone off." Michael had his own phone out and was powering it down.

"Why would I do that?"

"That's how they found us. 'Lenape tracking secret.' They must've traced my cell phone."

Livia answered on the second ring. "Spencer. How are you feel-ing? And how's Michael?"

"I'm quite well, thank you. Michael's much improved. Were you able to locate the owner of the mask?"

"We spoke with him. A man in Riverdale by the name of Brad-ford Lane."

"Riverdale, in the north Bronx? Has Mr. Lane been approached by anyone other than yourselves? Does his situation seem secure?"

"I'm a little worried about him, actually. No, no one's been there, and I don't know how Edward would learn his name, but it's not impossible. I suggested he might take extra precautions until we know for sure whether the mask had anything to do with the murder but he refuses."

"I see. And on the subject of the mask itself?"

"He's convinced it's real. Or at least, that the one he sent to Sotheby's is the one he bought fifty years ago, that had been in the Hammill family since the French priest brought it to them in the seventeen hundreds. But that's an interesting point."

"What is?"

"The French priest, Père Ravenelle. Mr. Lane said someone came to see him a few years ago asking about Père Ravenelle and about the mask. Research into the early Church in North America. He turns out to have been Gerald Maxwell. Thomas's department chair at Fordham."

"My," Spencer said. "That's an odd coincidence."

"Not necessarily. The early Church is his area. It may turn out to be convenient, though. We've just gotten to Fordham, on the other side of the Bronx. Thomas is going to go see him."

"How marvelous that we all find ourselves in the Bronx. Perhaps we can reconvene at my home in, say, an hour? We can compare notes. But before that, please know this: we've just had an encounter with two police detectives. When asked whether anyone had been at my home with us late last night, after the mugging in the park that accounts for Michael's injuries, Michael replied that we were alone. He thought the coincidence of your having been with us and then at Sotheby's was too much to bear."

"Spencer, that's perfectly innocent and explainable. Why would it matter unless—"

"—unless they were suspicious of us? I believe they may have formed that opinion, which would be why they wanted to know where we'd been."

"Formed that opinion, based on what?"

"I'm not certain. Viewed from a certain angle, Michael's responses may have appeared a bit evasive. Perhaps I did my part, also. In any case, I'm not asking you, and certainly not Father Kelly, to join in our deception. I'm just making you aware of what's been said. No one, of course, has so far mentioned brother Edward."

"I understand. It's possible the police won't be interested in us anyway. Was it the same detectives I told you about last night?"

"A young woman of Michael's people, though apparently a different tribe—"

"And a smiling, weird man? They were suspicious of us, too, just for being at Sotheby's. It might not mean anything."

"The smiling man, who I believe is called Framingham, did mention the Vatican to me."

"Oh, Spencer, really? I thought all that had been wiped clean. Do you suppose it will be a problem?"

"I have no idea. I'm rather annoyed, I must say. However, at the moment there are more pressing issues. It's important to Michael that he be allowed to continue his search for his brother unhindered. And that no one else begin a similar search."

"All right, Spencer. I'll tell Thomas. And we'll see you at your place in an hour."

"Everything all right?" Michael asked as Spencer slipped the phone back into his pocket.

"Yes. Though Livia is uneasy about Mr. Lane."

"She's worried Edward will find him."

"I don't like to put it that way, but I'm afraid so."

"She may be right. And it may be a way to find Edward." Michael turned his phone back on, scrolled through for a number. He thumbed it, waited, then, "Lou? It's Doc. Give me a call. I need a favor."

When he lowered the phone Spencer said, "Lou—he's one of the gentlemen I met last night?"

"I'm going to ask him to keep an eye on Lane's place. He'll love it. He's a hunter, grew up in the woods. The L'Anse rez in Michigan. Did two tours in Afghanistan as an Army Ranger. His father was Army, too. You must've noticed he looks Asian?"

"I wouldn't have inquired about it, but indeed I did."

"God, Spencer." Michael grinned. "For a historian, you're amazingly not nosy."

"On the contrary. I'm attempting a certain discretion, as I understand it to be an attribute valued by your people. In the normal way of things I'd be clamoring to have my questions answered."

"I can't see you ever clamoring, but I'm flattered anyway. Lou's dad is Potawatomi. He met his mom in Vietnam and brought her back to the rez. It hasn't been easy for Lou, especially since the Army. He's been in and out of trouble, kind of lost his way. But he's a good guy." Michael's phone rang and he lifted it to his ear. "Lou? Thanks for calling. No, not yet. Listen, maybe you can help me out. I wouldn't ask, but you heard Ivy— Yeah, okay, I know I don't, sorry. It's like this. There's a guy in Riverdale, I think Edward might be headed his way. Any chance you could go up there, keep an eye on the place, call me if he shows up? Come to think of it, anyone. Whoever shows up there, let me know, okay? But not this number. I'll call you with the number in a few minutes. Yeah, good." Michael gave the particulars of Lane's home. "Thanks, Lou." He powered his phone down again and pocketed it. "Come on, Spencer. I need to pick up a pre-paid phone, and if we're meeting Livia and Thomas in an hour, we just have time to stop by my place on the way. I appreciate the loan of your antique ski sweater, but it's making me itch."

36

E dward Bonnard walked with long strides through the fluorescent-lit expanse of Penn Station. The odors of burnt coffee, frying doughnuts, and disinfectant crowded the air, which itself had to be pummeled through metal ducts and fiberglass filters to force it down here. All around him, people looking miserable rushed to destinations he couldn't imagine would make them any happier. What was wrong with white people that caused them to make places like this?

Some of the elders went back to the stories. When the Creator baked the earth to make the people, they said, he'd kept each one—black, red, yellow, and white—in the oven for different lengths of time. Black, red, and yellow men, though they'd come out looking different, had all cooked thoroughly and were complete. The white man, though, was unfinished. White people were like children, unable to look ahead, not seeing the consequences of their actions. Children weren't by nature malicious, but their heedlessness could cause great damage, great pain to themselves and others. They needed to be guided, instructed, reined in.

Edward, though he didn't contradict the elders, did not agree. Even children learned from their mistakes. They couldn't see ahead, but they looked behind. Try too far a leap, sprain your ankle, next time you'd find a rope to swing from. If white people were like children, they might have built this sort of building once, maybe three times or ten times, but eventually they'd realize how horrible it was and stop. Edward spent as little time as he could manage in the white world, but "little" didn't mean "none." From what he could see, white people must like this sort of space and the life it gave them because it was these spaces and that life with which they covered Mother Earth.

Even Abornazine, a white man who loved Edward's people, wasn't immune. His home, though beautifully made, was so huge that half the population of Akwesasne could live there and never bump into each other. No, of course that was an exaggeration. And Abornazine hadn't built the house. His ancestors had, and he'd inherited it—a concept that only made sense if you believed that land could be owned like a pair of pants and that buildings were meant to last as long as the grass grew. Abornazine didn't believe those things, but for now, he said, the house was necessary: for the number of people it could safeguard, for the land around it and the river you could see from its porch. The people were Edward's people; the land was where they would Awaken, and the river was Cahohatatea, called the Hudson by whites as though before they'd sailed up it no one had seen these waters and they had no name. Cahohatatea, the river that would carry the people back down to the island that had once been theirs.

Edward searched the confusion of lights, signs, and advertising, looking for track numbers. He felt much better now than he had last night. Waking this morning to a strange dawn in an unfamiliar room had given him, not the disoriented jolt he might have expected, but a pause, a long blank moment that separated night from day. The smooth skin of the woman beside him had been warm and comforting, talking to him of what was to come, not what had been. As he gazed on her she woke. She touched her finger to his lips and slipped her leg over him. He was as ready and hungry as she, though their lovemaking last night had been long, powerful, and so complete that once they were both, finally, satisfied, Edward had fallen into a deep sleep without dreams he could remember. This morning had been like that also, in tune but syncopated, each action and reaction both surprising and inevitable.

After, he lay in bed while Charlotte showered, then watched her emerge from the bathroom, a white towel tucked around her brown body, her hair a glistening dark tangle down her back. Wordless, she smiled and disappeared into the kitchen. He headed to the bathroom himself; when he came out she handed him coffee. By then she was dressed, already wearing the gun and holster that had thrown him last night when she took off her leather jacket. "I'm a cop," she'd said, seeing his face, the words sounding half challenge and half invitation; and then she locked up the gun and her daily life with it. Edward had trouble understanding why an Indian would opt to live in the white world at all, and to choose, beyond that, to enforce that world's laws, was beyond him. But Charlotte made it clear she didn't want to talk about work, didn't want his white name, didn't want to speak much at all, and that suited him. Here in the frantic city he missed the quiet of the woods, of Indian companionship. White people seemed afraid of silence. They filled the air with talk, with music, with blare and buzz. Edward thought he knew why: in silence the ancestors' voices could be heard. No matter how white people screamed and shouted, raced their cars and threw their towers up to the sky, their hearts must know how wrong the direction of their lives had become. They didn't want to hear their ancestors, the anger and the disappointment. But the voices were not gone, not even stilled. They were speaking, and they wouldn't tolerate this heedlessness for much longer. Nor would they need to. White people were part of the Creator's plan, and they would be included in the world as it started to change, very soon.

All this went through Edward's mind when he was with Charlotte, but he said none of it, last night or this morning, asking only, as they walked to the subway, where her people lived.

"I was born here in the city," she said. "I was brought up Indian, we go home for Midwinter, stuff like that, but I've never lived on a rez."

"You said Lenape?"

"Right. My dad's people, they're Mohawk, Tuscarora, and there's my exotic Italian great-granddaddy but we don't talk about him. What about you? Abenaki, you said?"

"Yes. My father's people are Mohawk. I live up there at Akwesasne."

"Come down to New York much?"

"Not if I can help it. I'm leaving today." For some reason he didn't fully understand, he added, "I'll be back soon, though."

"Call me," she said.

They'd parted with a nod and a smile, no kiss, no touch. She'd descended into the subway to go to work. He'd wanted to be out in the day, even as degraded as the day was in the city, and so had walked downtown to Penn Station, feeling energetic, feeling peaceful, feeling grateful to Charlotte.

Because until he met her, last night had been a calamity, a series of disasters.

He'd come to the city fully intending to return with the Ohtah-yohnee mask, but they weren't unrealistic, he and Abornazine.

They'd planned for the possibility that he wouldn't be able to obtain it. They had next steps prepared. But it had never crossed their minds, either of them, that the mask might not be real.

Edward was sorry about the young woman he'd killed. She'd feared him, been repulsed, been outraged that he should have invaded a place she thought of as hers, but even in his rage and disappointment he wouldn't have taken her life if there had been another way. There was not. If she'd lived she would have told what she'd seen. She might not have been believed; but the goal they were working toward was of such profound consequence that any risk was too great. Edward had killed her and offered prayers to the Creator, as hunters did when they shot a deer or farmers when they slaughtered chickens. He'd expressed his gratitude for the life she gave and his hope that this death would nourish the people equally with those.

Encountering Michael after that had seemed at first just a colossal stroke of bad luck. Edward had left his clothes hidden in the park, to be recovered after he'd completed his task and returned to human form. That Michael should have chosen that same hour to walk through the park with his friend—that could never have been predicted. But as he thought about it later, Edward was forced to admit that he'd stayed in the park, racing, bounding, slinking, stalking, much longer than he'd needed to. That his fury over the mask, combined with the metallic tang of the young woman's blood—a heady, disorienting taste he'd never known before—had caused his heart to speed, his nerves to buzz; that in this city he hated so much he felt powerful, safe, in his Shifted state and he'd been unwilling to return to his man-self prison.

And he had to admit, also, that when, bounding through the icy night, he'd picked up Michael's scent, he could have avoided the encounter. Instead, he'd sought it out.

Michael, though, had done what he'd done many times since they were boys: kept Edward from an act he'd have regretted. He didn't mean killing Michael's friend. Unlike the young woman's death, that one wouldn't have been necessary, but Edward's frustrated fury and the man's obvious importance to Michael—and the man's ridiculous bravado—goaded Edward on. For a man in his fifties he'd been staggeringly strong and the taste of his blood a searing, unpleasant sensation. It was something to smoke on, Edward thought, to consider, that in the space of a few hours he'd tasted his first human blood, and then tasted it again with such a different result. He wondered how much more of it he'd have to spill before their goal was reached.

But no, the death of Michael's friend wasn't the act he was glad Michael had thwarted. Not for the first time, it was his failure to kill Michael himself that Edward was grateful for.

Edward's heart ached for Michael. It always had. The beat of Michael's pulse was the sound he knew best, the first rhythm of his world. They were one-as-two, they completed each other: the dark and the light, the storm and the sun, the burn and the balm. But from the moment they'd come into the world Michael had drawn away. Edward saw their destiny clearly, even as a child, and embraced it though the path was difficult. Michael refused. Refused, Edward thought, the Creator's will, though no one could be sure what the Creator intended and Edward thought those who spoke as though they knew sounded painfully like the priests of Christian churches. But in his heart he wondered, could it be otherwise? Twin Shifters, a birth as rare as that of the white buffalo—how could it not have a meaning as sacred? They'd been born to a vital task, a duty for the people. Edward welcomed it, thankful to have been chosen.

Michael slipped away, away, into the white world.

Edward didn't long for Michael's death. Not truly. He longed for Michael to awaken to their joint destiny as they'd both Awakened to their natures in their early years. But at times the pain and sadness of knowing that wouldn't happen were overpowering. Then Edward's rage and hurt consumed him and he wanted Michael gone. If Michael wouldn't walk with him, Edward wanted to destroy his brother and then grieve for him, and walk in the world alone.

That desire, though, like the ocean waters, ebbed and flowed. Last night he'd have killed Michael and exulted; this morning, he was relieved he hadn't. It was possible, still, that once this task was complete, once the people were free, Michael would understand and take his true place.

Edward would go back up north now, not all the way home, but to Abornazine's grand house on the cliff overlooking Cahohatatea. They'd burn tobacco, and pray, and plan. The worthlessness of the mask was a setback but not, in the end, a disaster. He was sure of it.

In the glare of the lights he found the gate to the train he was taking. He disliked travel by rail, but a train was preferable by far to the air-debasing, earth-destroying, soul-devouring automobile. He showed his ticket, went down the stairs, and took a seat on the river side, where he could watch the water and the cliffs as the train hurtled north.

No, what had happened last night wouldn't force them off the path they were walking.

Tonight was the full moon, but they'd have to let it pass. Still, in a month there'd be another.

They would be ready.

37

Thomas! Come in, come in." The history department chair gestured from behind his desk. "Is there something you need?"

"A few moments of your time, Father, if that's possible."

"Of course." The chubby and balding Monsignor Gerald Maxwell, wearing a clerical collar and a tweed jacket—badges of his dual professions, Thomas reflected—closed the manila folder he'd been reading and gave Thomas his attention as the younger man sat. "Is everything all right, Father Kelly? Are you enjoying your work here? I met with Andy Burns the other day and he couldn't stop singing your praises. He said you found the organizing principle for the entire first section of his thesis."

"I didn't have to look very hard. He's a gifted scholar."

"Well, I wouldn't be surprised if he dedicates the book to you. Or names his firstborn 'Thomas.' How's your own work coming?"

"It's completely fascinating. I suppose you knew it would be, but besides the facts themselves, to me it's so entirely different—like a whole new cuisine, I suppose. Or a new language. Different emphases, different rhythms. I'm enjoying learning so much."

"I'm delighted. So, tell me what I can do for you."

"I've come across a man I'd like to know more about, and I've been told you researched him once yourself. I thought perhaps you could point me in the right direction."

"Who would that be?"

"Père Etienne Ravenelle."

Maxwell twirled a heavy silver ring on his left hand, a habit when he was thinking. It bore a crest Thomas didn't recognize, a cross on a full moon. Some society within their own order. More than once, Thomas had meditated on that curious inevitability of human endeavor, that nations break into states, cities into boroughs, faiths into orders and sects and societies. As though the totality of human experience were too much to encompass.

"Ravenelle?" said Maxwell. "He's far afield for your work, isn't he? He was here a full century after Kateri Tekakwitha. What brought you to him?"

"Just following my nose, I suppose. Kateri's relationships with the Jesuits and with her own people were tangled, and Ravenelle seems to be the end of one of the threads." *When did I learn to do that?* Thomas wondered. *Give an answer that tells nothing, even borders on actually lying?*

"He is that," Maxwell agreed. "The end of a thread, I mean. Ravenelle came to New France in 1742. He'd read the biography Claude Chauchetière had written of Tekakwitha—I imagine you got that far?"

"I've read it, yes." Not exactly the answer, but apparently the Monsignor, knowing the answer he expected, assumed he'd gotten it and went on.

"Ravenelle arrived certain of what it had taken Chauchetière years to come to believe—that there was value in the Native way of life, and that saving Native souls involved nothing more than in-troducing them to—revealing to them, really—the mystery of the

Savior. They would, he thought, find their own way to Him." Father Maxwell smiled. "A touch apostate, even now. You can imagine what his superiors thought two hundred and fifty years ago. But you understand, New France in the mid-eighteenth century was what we'd call today a difficult posting. Not every priest was willing to go."

"Yes, I can see that. By then the thrill of first contact would have been long gone and both the Iroquois and the Huron had turned on the Jesuits."

"Because of the behavior of Europeans—including some Jesuits—toward them, and because of the European diseases that were decimating them." Father Maxwell focused a stern eye on Thomas, to make sure his point had been taken. Thomas nodded. The Monsignor continued, "In any case, Ravenelle was decades too late for the romantic missionary work he'd imagined himself doing. All the missions in Native territory had been abandoned and the priests withdrawn to Quebec, Montreal, or Ottawa. Ravenelle reportedly did venture out among the Iroquois against the orders of the Superior General. He seems to have gone more than once, with the tacit approval of his Father Provincial, so it's likely he was well received. But there are no records of his meetings with the tribes."

"I wonder why?"

"Why there are no records?"

"Well, yes, but also why he went, and why, at that point, he'd have been well received."

"It's a good question. I couldn't say. In any case Ravenelle seems to have made the mistake of staying on after the British dissolved the Jesuit order in New France. He must not have kept his head down because he became a hunted man. He headed south, perhaps to find a ship to take him home to Europe. I never found any evidence that he'd made it back, though. He did get as far as New York.

I suspect he died here. As you know—or maybe not, since you've been concentrating on Italy until now, but as you'll find, missionary records from that period are quite sketchy, the more so the farther south you go, into British-held territory. Especially Jesuits. Anyone still here was hiding, running, desperate to escape the British. They were hanging priests, you know."

"Yes, sir, I do know."

Maxwell took a brief moment of silence, perhaps to consider the dangers once inherent in being a Jesuit priest in the New World. Thomas offered a prayer for the souls of those who had not escaped.

"Well, Thomas," said the Monsignor, "there you have all the news I could find of Father Ravenelle. He's really a little outside my area, too, and quite outside yours. I understand the lure of new knowledge, those secrets that glow just beyond the horizon. But I'm not sure you have time to, as you say, follow your nose every place it tries to lead you. I'm told Pope Francis is very much looking forward to the results of your original charge. All's coming along well with that work, is it?"

"Yes, thank you. And I'm sure you're right. I should be narrowing my beam instead of widening it."

"Exactly. Tell me, Thomas, how did you come to know I'd looked into Père Ravenelle in the first place?"

"My Italian historian friend, Dr. Pietro? She's in town for the Indigenous Arts conference. We were talking about this Ohtahyohnee mask that's such a sensation, and someone said you'd once been interested in it and in Père Ravenelle."

"Really? That was years ago. Who remembers that, I wonder?"

"A man called Bradford Lane. He's a collector."

"He was at the conference?"

"We spoke with him." *All right,* Thomas thought, *that's not an outright lie, but close enough that I should probably jump up and run to the nearest confessional. Or maybe Father Maxwell will hear my confession. Forgive me, Father, for I've shaded the truth, because if I didn't you'd know two of my friends are vampires and the gay one has a shapeshifter boyfriend. . . .*

"Thomas? Are you all right?"

"Oh! I'm sorry, Father. I just—remembered something I'd forgotten." *Which is that I'm different from my brothers and sisters in the Church now, and I always will be from here on, since I've been granted access to some of those secrets glowing beyond the horizon—knowledge I never asked for, can't share, and seem to continue to accumulate at an alarming rate.* "Did you ask me something?"

"I wondered how Mr. Lane is doing."

"Sadly, he's lost almost all of his sight."

"Yes, that deterioration was under way by the time I saw him four years ago. I'm sorry to hear it. Is he otherwise well?"

"Creaky. But mentally he certainly seems sharp."

"I'm glad of that, anyway. Well, I'm sorry I can't be more help to you, Thomas. Ravenelle was—how did you put it?—the end of a thread for me, too. And the Ohtahyohnee, I never saw it."

Thomas smiled. "You don't have to keep that secret any longer, Father. Mr. Lane said you and he sat admiring it, and then he swore you to secrecy."

The Monsignor paused. "He told you that?"

"He said you even photographed it."

"Oh." Father Maxwell shrugged. "I suppose now that he's selling it he doesn't mind people knowing about it. Yes, I saw it and I took photographs. I thought they might be useful if I ever found any mention of it or Father Ravenelle in any other records. I never did, though."

"Thank you, Father," Thomas said. "I can't say my curiosity's been satisfied, but as you point out, my own work calls. Let me ask you one more thing, if I might. I understand you were looking at Ravenelle, but what did you think of the Ohtahyohnee? There's been some talk at the conference that it's not authentic."

"Really? Well, art's not my area, but I thought it was beautiful. Powerful. People think it's a fake?"

"People are unsure."

"Because it's the only one anyone's ever seen, maybe. Because no one was even certain they ever existed, much less still exist. Or"— he raised his eyebrows—"I suppose, because it's a fake. Myself, I really don't know."

"It's going on display this morning, for tomorrow's auction. Will you go over to see it?"

"I think I will. Something like that, the last of its kind—yes, I think I'll have to take one more look."

38

As Charlotte and Framingham trotted back down Donna's front steps, Framingham said, "Do I get the feeling your friend Donna was hiding something, or is she just being an Indian?"

Charlotte shook her head. "I hate to admit it but I agree with you. Michael Bonnard felt so lousy after he was mugged that he didn't go to work, but instead of staying home in bed he decided to come up to the effing Bronx on a crappy cold morning like this— and all he wanted to do was to introduce his friend to Donna? And all they did was sit around and chat? Bullshit."

"Why aren't we taking her downtown?"

"Donna? Based on what? That we think she's lying about what she talked about with a guy we have no reason to suspect of anything? I mean, no reason besides his cultural curiosity and our racial profiling. And have you ever tried to lean on an Indian? We close up tighter than a duck's ass. I need to get some angle on what she's hiding and then I can take it to her. She won't respond to a fishing expedition, and God knows, not to intimidation. But if I ask her straight on she might talk to me. Anyway, I want to ask *you* something."

"Me?"

"Yeah. How did you do that?"

"Do what?" Framingham asked innocently.

"'Do what.' You knew Spencer George was an art collector and what he collects. You couldn't have found that out between when he told us his name and when you came back and sprang it on him."

"You don't think I'm just good like that?"

"You may be, but the department system isn't. It might have told you if he was known to us, but not anything else about him. Did you Google him?"

They stepped over a pile of last week's snow. Framingham grinned. "Yes, and no, and that's what's interesting. I Googled him before and got nothing. That e-mail I just got? That was Interpol."

"Before what? Interpol? What are you talking about?"

"After Dr. Warner told me about Michael Bonnard, I thought I'd check him out." Framingham slid into the car. "I found two photos of him at events with this Spencer George. So I thought I'd check *him* out."

"I didn't find anything like that. All I saw was the Rockefeller U. links."

"You probably didn't look for misspellings of his name."

They reached the car and got in. Charlotte started it and steered out onto the Bronx street. "Not too shabby," she admitted.

Framingham snapped his fingers. "See, I *am* all that. Spelled with one *n*, with a *t*, all kinds of things. Told you I was bored. I found him twice with this Spencer George guy and that was enough to get me interested. You have to admit, they don't look like they belong together."

"Love is blind."

"You got that feeling, too?"

"I did, and by the way, it makes Bonnard less of a suspect in our killing."

"If you're still thinking crime of passion, sure. But that wasn't what interested me."

"What was?"

"At first, I was just bored. Like you said, I was fishing. But I didn't catch anything. I couldn't find a thing on Spencer George anywhere. No Wikipedia entry, no Google hits, no nothin'. He has no online presence. The photos with Bonnard were it and both of them get his name wrong, too. One spells 'Spenser' with an *s* and the other gets it backwards. George Spencer. He probably doesn't know they exist or he'd make them go away, too."

"He's scrubbed out?"

"Thoroughly. He must pay a service to do it, untag photos and so on, though I'll bet there wasn't much to begin with. That kind of thing's expensive. Now I ask myself, why would someone do that?"

"To protect their privacy?"

"That's a lot of trouble to go to so no one knows you went to an art opening. So on a hunch I ran him through Interpol."

"And?"

"He's almost invisible there, too."

"Almost?"

"Now, you can't laugh at me."

"Matt, laughing at you makes my life worth living."

"When will you learn?" Framingham paused dramatically. "He's been scrubbed from Interpol, too."

"That's impossible."

"I don't think so. My guy there—a Brit, by the way, a fifteenth cousin on the Framingham side—"

"A cousin? Really?"

"Who knows? But it's like Indians, like your clan system. We upper-class Brits are all related and since we're under attack from all sides—"

"Jesus, Matt!"

"We stick together, I'm trying to say. Please don't crash this department vehicle. He just e-mailed me, my cousin whose name isn't Framingham. He found a short obscure line in a long obscure bulletin alerting departments worldwide to an endless list of persons of interest, including one Spencer George, a collector on the run from Rome after the bust-up of a scheme to rob the Vatican."

"Rob the *Vatican*? Matt, you're insane!"

"I'm just reporting. Come on, Charlotte, think about it. Even if there was no such plot, if some agency ever thought there was, shouldn't there be more paperwork? A cybertrail, I mean. One little bulletin, that's it? Interpol's just a fancy cop shop. Cops are all alike. Everything in triplicate, nothing thrown away. If the guy was referred to once, he was referred to a dozen times. If there's a bulletin, there are lists the bulletin's on. There'd be surveillance shots, photo arrays, progress reports, false sightings. Something. And"—he thrust a triumphant finger in the air—"there'd be a record of his arrival here."

"Here? The U.S.? There isn't?"

"No, there isn't. But he seems to be here, doesn't he? This guy who got himself erased from the Interpol system. Here, and hanging around with a man who was disappointed in a seven-million-dollar mask a few hours before a woman was killed in a violent and unexplained way in a room with same. Admit it. Something strange is going on."

"All right," said Charlotte slowly. "You might have a point. We should look into it. As long as you don't put the flying leap across Seventy-first Street back on the table."

"You know"—Framingham put on the innocent face again—"there are some animals that could make that leap. Not regular normal animals, of course."

"Oh, no. No, no, I know you don't mean—"

"Just sayin'. Special ones. A special kind of wolf, or deer. An eagle could have flown."

"Special ones. Matt. Please tell me you're not saying what I know you are. My God, you are. You think she was killed by a were-wolf. Shit. You are out of control."

"Your people say shapeshifter, don't you? Now, Dr. Bonnard, he looks like a normal human specimen, but Spencer George strikes me as a guy with sharp pointy teeth. I should've told him a knock-knock joke, so he'd have smiled and we could've seen them."

"The jokes you tell, that would never work." Charlotte looked over at him. "Oh, crap. You're pulling my chain, aren't you?"

"Well, hell." Framingham grinned broadly. "You make it so easy." He settled back with a satisfied air. "Really, I'm just asking you to keep an open mind."

"The fact that I haven't chucked your skinny white-boy upper-class Brit ass into the East River proves how open my mind is."

"Of course it does. But Charlotte? About that leap being back on the table? As far as I'm concerned, it was never off."

39

His long gray braids drawn back by the wind, Abornazine stood on the bluff looking over the river. The Hudson, he'd learned as a child to call these magnificent waters, this river that flowed two ways. He'd called it that before he'd understood the mortifying arrogance of naming things that had names already.

He'd been born Peter van Vliet, to the descendants of colonizers, a child of power and privilege. And wealth: oh yes, a good deal of wealth. The injustice of his position had disquieted him from the time he understood it. As he grew so did his shame in what he had and his guilt in the ways his ancestors had acquired it. His family lived the empty life of the idle rich: travel and parties and fretting about the delicate parsing of their ranking among other equally meaningless people. No one paid any regard to the young boy, cringing at every gift of gem-encrusted jewelry and each invitation to a benefit gala in aid of some group trampled by those dancing and dining on its behalf.

Sent away to school with others of his caste, he was repelled by the easy certitude of his fellows that they did, indeed, own and rule, and that it was right and just that they should. He was drawn to solitude, to the forests. Spreading tracts of woodlands surrounded his home, others encircled the school, and what time he could steal he spent among the trees and the creatures who lived there, learning their ways. Often he'd sleep in the woods; the school did not approve, but his mother, who in the general way showed no particular interest in her son, coolly informed the institution that she would prefer if they left him to pass his time however he pleased, including the time he spent sleeping, providing he fulfilled his academic obligations. He therefore made a point of succeeding in his course work on a high level, and his athletic skills also grew, if only in the solitary sports: running, swimming, riding, shooting.

He spoke little, but became a magnet for the few others like himself who understood the catastrophically wrong course on which the entire world had been set when Europeans conquered this beautiful land. His small group would sit in clearings in the forest, telling tales of the people who used to walk these woods, live easily on this earth; and tales of what the world should be like, what it would be like if the afternoons they were spending could stretch to encompass their entire lives.

In classes, he learned that the conquerors write history, though that wasn't the intended lesson. And then on the day he turned sixteen, as he sat in a course labeled "Diversity"—an earnest, condescending survey of ethnic traditions around the world, "ethnic" meaning any civilization not their own—he was hit by a figurative bolt of lightning. He understood he had been shown his meaning and his purpose. He understood who he was.

He'd been born among the colonizers, yes, but he wasn't of them. He was of the people. The Native people, who had lived on these hills and by these rivers for millennia in ways so inextricably woven into the life of the earth that their souls and the souls of the other living creatures were able to touch. The Native people, who had been so downtrodden, so dominated, exploited, and abused, that it was only right that one such as he should devote his life—and his power, and his wealth—to raising them up again. The Creator had sent him, born Peter van Vliet, to learn and to serve.

To become Abornazine. Keeper of the Flame.

40

As Livia steered the car around a wide curve Michael watched the great house rise into view in the distance. He'd fought the idea that he couldn't drive up here alone, objecting to both the company and the helplessness. But the three of them—Spencer, Thomas, and Livia—had ganged up on him and they'd been right. He couldn't have managed the car. Even now, just sitting for an hour as they rode beside the ice-pocked river, his shoulder was stiffening, pain stabbing down to his fingers and up his neck with every jolt in the road.

Livia Pietro had been appointed chauffeur. She'd rented a car and she'd been good company on the drive up. By which Michael meant, good Indian company: she hardly spoke. She left him to his own thoughts, which were few. He cleared his mind and concentrated on seeing. The silver river, the changing grays of the sky, the black lace branches on bare trees.

Livia had been chosen because Spencer, as it turned out, didn't drive. Michael had been both amused and relieved by that. He wouldn't have let Spencer come; this way there was no anger and no arguing. Well, little arguing. Spencer had protested, but turnabout is fair play and a gang-up can work in more than one direction. Grudgingly, Spencer had accepted the plan, especially once Thomas suggested a useful line of research that he and Spencer, as historians, could follow.

Michael's argument, that his first choice would've been to go alone, and since that wasn't possible he'd accept a driver but not an entourage, was true but incomplete. It angered Michael when Spencer asked if Edward had ever killed anyone besides Brittany Williams but the truth was, he didn't know. He did know this: in his own Shifted state he'd hunted, many times. The compulsion to finish a kill, to chase down and devour escaped quarry whose blood he'd already tasted, was formidable. In this, his needs and Edward's were the same. While he understood that there was no harm Edward could do to Spencer that couldn't eventually be undone, "eventually," from what he'd learned over the past twelve hours, could be a long, long time.

They'd only been together a few months, he and Spencer. If each had been a normal man, their differences of background, of age, of culture, might have doomed the relationship in any case. Under the circumstances, that they'd found each other was almost laughable; but then, that either of them existed at all was beyond most people's ability to take seriously. Whether they had a future together, especially since their definitions of "future" were so different, was unknowable. If they did, though, Michael—the one of them whose time was limited—would rather not spend years of it waiting for Spencer to regenerate himself. Or whatever the process was called.

Watching the sliding clouds, he wondered what the process *was* called. The Noantri had their own vocabulary. Their Community had organization, it had laws and traditions. Had Shifters once been the same? Had they been a separate, hidden band within the tribe and clan structures of the continent's First Peoples, known only to one another, recognizing and welcoming each other when they met?

He wanted to know. He wanted, badly, had always wanted, not to be alone. To know there were others like him beyond his twin, people who understood and shared his singular way of being in the world. That was where his work was; that was what his research had always been about. Though even if he succeeded, his achievement would be now and its outcome would stretch forward from the present. He'd never understand what it had been like before. But knowing that the future would be different—maybe that would be enough.

Michael roused himself, sharpening his focus as something moved through the woods beside the road. Something pale and quick, running toward them. It broke from the trees and onto the roadway. Livia slammed on the brakes and pain shot through Michael's shoulder as the car jolted, fishtailed, and stopped. The figure froze, then turned and sped away back into the woods.

"I'm sorry," said Livia. "I didn't see it in time. But . . . What *was* that?"

"It must have been a deer."

"It looked . . . upright. And pale."

Livia eased the car forward again, driving slowly until they emerged from the canopy of trees. Before them, winter-frosted grass sloped up to a tall portico. White columns fronted a lodge whose roof levels kept changing. The house looked accrued, amassed, the way wealth would be. Piled up, collected because it was possible, not because it was needed.

The lawn, that broad sweep, though, was surprising. Even now, in winter, sheep dotted it, foraging for what they could find. In spring their dung no doubt would turn this slope into a glorious expanse of green; but as Michael took in the sheep pen, the rail fence surrounding stubbled corn rows and tripod beanpoles waving last year's leaves, as he heard a cock crowing from inside what had clearly been built as a three-car garage, he wondered if the van Vliet ancestors were happy with the rustic turn their stately home had taken.

It hadn't been hard to locate Abornazine. Donna had been right: even in this enclave of Gilded Age mansions—most in new-money hands now, though a few original families still clung to moldering brick and flaking plaster—all he'd had to say was "long hair" and "turquoise" and the affable kid behind the butcher shop counter was pointing to a road leading east off the town's main street.

"You mean Mr. van Vliet. His place is up that way. It's called, I don't know, Air House or something. What's going on up there?"

"What do you mean?"

"Well—" He flushed, as though he suddenly realized he might have gotten it wrong. "You're an Indian, right?"

"That's right."

"That's what I thought." The kid grinned again. "Lots of Indians up there. Maybe a hundred since fall, living in tents and stuff, and now a bunch more in the last couple of weeks. It's like a powwow or something?"

Michael wanted to say, *In winter?* but the kid's ignorance wasn't his fault. "When I find out, I'll let you know. Thanks for the help."

Now, at the wrought iron gate that stood just beyond a bend in the drive, they stopped and Michael spoke to a short, round man who came out of a stone booth.

"Michael Bonnard. Abenaki."

"Lee Stearns. Choctaw." Stearns glanced briefly into the car. Michael made no move to introduce Livia, but said, "I want to speak to Abornazine."

"He's expecting you?"

"No."

Stearns went back inside the booth and made a call. Through the window, he waved them in. The gate slid open.

"What would we have done if that hadn't worked?" Livia asked, driving on.

"It was bound to work. The butcher's kid said Indians are still arriving."

"Those might be people van Vliet's invited. People he knows."

"Then his curiosity would be killing him. You haven't met these wannabes. Any Indian who shows interest in them, they'll follow him like a baby duck."

Livia pulled up to the portico and stopped the car. Michael got out and leaned in the window. "Thanks," he said.

"Are you sure—"

"Yes. I'll call you when I'm done."

"You really think you can just walk in and out? He tried to kill you."

"He'd Shifted."

"How do you know he hasn't Shifted now?"

Michael didn't answer her. He straightened, turned, and headed for the wide green door.

41

Beyond the house the long drive curved to head back to the road. Three pickup trucks and a half dozen cars, none of them new, stood in a frozen field down the slope. Livia pulled the rented Malibu in beside them and left it, stretching her legs in strides through the bracing air. She took out her cell phone and called Spencer.

"Livia. I trust you arrived safely?"

"No problem. This man Abornazine, he's Peter van Vliet and he's from one of the old families up here. In fact I've heard his name before. Katherine's mentioned him to me. A big collector. He comes down to see her at the Met sometimes. She says he's full of good stories."

"And have you talked with him? Is Michael's brother there?"

"Michael just went into the house but he asked me not to come. If his brother's here he wants to see him alone."

"But you haven't wandered afield?"

Livia smiled at Spencer's tone. "I'm nearby, Spencer, don't worry. If he needs help, I'll be there. How are you and Thomas doing?"

"Thank you for your reassurance. As for myself and Father

Kelly, our research has just begun but I'm afraid neither of us is upbeat."

"The material's not there? Father Maxwell was right?"

"On the contrary. I fear the good Father was less than forthcoming. Just when I had begun to re-examine my long-standing position on the untrustworthiness of the clergy, too."

"A re-examination based entirely on knowing Thomas, I'm sure."

"Indeed. Which proves the absurdity of using a sample of one."

"What do you mean, though? About Maxwell not being forthcoming?"

"Despite his claim that he'd been able to discover only very little by, or about, Père Ravenelle, it's become clear that rather more documentary evidence exists than he acknowledged—and that he's seen it. Father Kelly, I must say, appears to have a gift for research, and I, of course, have many years' experience of filling in gaps. Ravenelle might, or might not, be relevant to the story of this Ohtahyohnee mask in the present day. But the fact that Father Maxwell, the most recent researcher to investigate Ravenelle, won't admit to his findings, gives one pause."

"It certainly does. What is it that you've found, that he denies?"

"Ah. There's the rub. Though we can see there is more to be had, it seems to be under lock and key at the Jesuit mother church."

"I'm sorry?"

"La Chiesa del Gesù. Back home in Rome."

"Oh." Livia stopped at a rail fence and looked out over the frost-rimed garden rows at rest for the winter. "Can you tell anything about it?"

"No. Father Kelly, as one of his order's bright lights, is allowed access at a fairly high level to the Jesuits' private archives. Still, no matter the angle from which we approach, we are able to discover

SAM CABOT

no more than that contemporaneous documentation both by and about Ravenelle does exist, and that the last researcher to access it was Father Gerald Maxwell. Father Kelly informs me that the abstruse abbreviations in the various online catalogs are indications that such a one as he, were he at Il Gesù itself, would be permitted at least to review the description of the material, and possibly the material itself, though he can't be certain of that from here."

"Spencer, that sounds beyond 'private.'"

"I agree, and the question that brings up is, what are they hiding? It seems the only way to find out, however, would be to dispatch Father Kelly to Rome."

A breeze rattled the dry husks of cornstalks. "That might be a fool's errand, though," Livia said. "He might not get access even there. And if he does, we still don't know that what's there will matter to what we're doing."

"Now you mention it, I hate to say this, but I, for one, don't actually have a firm grasp on what it is we are doing. If Michael's found his brother, or at least has learned how to accomplish that task, perhaps our continued search for the mask—or indeed, our continued involvement in the situation at all—is no longer helpful."

"I don't know, Spencer. There's something odd going on up here." Livia described the scene to Spencer: the gardens and barns, the livestock. "We've been told there are dozens, maybe hundreds, of Indians here, living in tents, in RVs, in tipis. And more still coming. It's as if they're getting ready for something."

"Have you any idea what?"

"No. I'm hoping Michael will be able to shed light on it after he talks to his brother. Though what happens then . . . Do you have any idea what he's planning to do?"

"None. If indeed his brother is responsible for the death of this

202

young woman, Michael is in a difficult position. I suggest we take our lead from him."

Slipping the phone into her bag, Livia headed back toward the house. She wanted to stay close to Michael, in case she was needed, though since he'd gone inside she hadn't sensed any disturbances. No voices raised in anger, not the sudden smell of fear or the heat of fury. All these were physical responses to emotion. They were detectable by the Unchanged at various levels depending upon an individual's sensitivity to others, an attribute that, when brought to the fore, was referred to as empathy. One of the alterations in Noantri bodies produced by the microbe was an amplification of the senses, no different in kind from the enhancement of Noantri muscles, the strengthening of Noantri bone. A body with no need to shore itself up, to compensate for deterioration, or to spend effort counteracting natural decline, could focus on optimizing the potential of each cell. That, at least, was the current thinking among Noantri scientists studying the microbe itself. Add to that the years, the decades and centuries of learning from experience of the world, and the Noantri ability to read people's emotional states lost all its mystery

It was this ability that made Livia pause on her way up the slope. She was passing a field where horses stood, grazing as they could on the frozen grass, though from their glistening coats and solid flanks she could see that they had the benefit of a plentiful winter diet. Livia had grown up with horses, still rode at a friend's farm outside Rome as often as she could arrange it, and the sight of them always both calmed and charmed her. As she stopped to watch these, though, she became aware that something was not right. Not here, among the horses, but in an outbuilding beyond the horses' enclosure. Animals had no structure of rational thinking as a barrier

between the world and their senses. They were therefore more re-
sponsive to the emotions of others than most Unchanged, more
than some Noantri. The rapid heartbeat of anger, fear's acrid smell,
and the bone-shaking tension of frustration radiated palpably from
the outbuilding and accounted, she was sure, for the way the horses
avoided that end of the field, leaving a semicircle of unmunched
grass as though a line had been drawn.

Livia followed the fence around the field. It was probable that
this was nothing important, and certainly it was none of her business. A sick animal, most likely, one needing to be isolated for its
own sake or that of the others. Though she was unsure—an animal?
If so, what kind? The sweat in the air smelled like a man's, but
the heartbeat was so rapid that a man surely couldn't sustain it for
long. Yet it didn't slow.

No one was near when she approached the building, a new-
looking metal shed. A heavy lock secured the door and the windows
had been soaped up inside. Through the film Livia could see thick
black bars. One whole side of the sloping roof consisted of a large
skylight in a metal frame. Livia studied the steel sheets of the roof's
other slope. They looked capable of bearing her weight.

The agitation of whatever was inside the shed increased as Livia
drew near. It heard her coming, maybe smelled her as she smelled it.
From close up she re-examined the roof, but it offered no surprises,
as the ground around it offered no stepping-stones or springboards.
If she wanted to be up there she'd have to jump.

So she jumped. Even her Noantri strength couldn't get her up
onto the slope from a standing start but it got her to where she could
clutch two of those raised square seams in her leather-gloved hands.
Some contracting of the biceps and triceps, a swing of a leg and the
thump of a boot, and Livia was on the roof.

Whatever was inside the building went completely silent when she landed. She could still sense the quick breathing and the heartbeat, but it stopped all movement and sound.

Staying low to keep her balance in the wind, Livia crab-walked to the roof ridge and lay flat. She pulled herself up until she could peer over the ridge and down through the skylight.

Looking back up at her, unblinking, was a man.

He was naked. His upturned face was not far from hers because he sat, not on the floor of the shed but on a beam six feet above it. Not sat; he perched. Feet and butt on the beam, knees up, arms at his sides balancing lightly.

For a moment their eyes locked, he and she both frozen. There was a strangeness to his eyes: rounder than most, irises yellow and completely surrounded with white. His hair was white, also, and appeared both shaggy and fine. His scent, now that she was closer, was peculiarly layered, something in it she couldn't define. Livia stared, fascinated.

Then he opened his mouth and screeched. He lifted his arms and, still balancing on the beam, raised and lowered them. As if he were flapping wings. As if he were trying to fly.

The screeching continued. Livia could feel fury and fear pushing against the skylight glass; she could feel a murderous bloodthirst starting to rise. She eased away from the ridge, slid down the slope, and jumped to the ground.

42

A long-haired young woman in boots, jeans, and a flannel shirt—Indian winter regalia, Michael thought—smiled as she admitted him to a wide central hall. Polished wood and gleaming white walls surrounded them, a patterned marble floor lay under their feet, and a leaded glass window lit the curving staircase. Open doors on left and right revealed high-windowed rooms with carpets on parquet floors. A third doorway, farther back, offered a glimpse of a dining table among walls of paneled oak.

These European spaces were built to hold European objects: Revolutionary-era oil paintings, thin-legged wooden chairs, delicate blue-and-white china. Art and furniture to evoke centuries of tradition, to comfortably connect the frightening, raw New World to the tamed fields and pacified forests of the Old.

What Michael saw, though, was Native pieces everywhere. The carpets on the parquet were Navajo rugs; Hopi masks hung from the moldings. On a rough chest stood a pair of Mohawk wedding baskets, the kind his parents had exchanged in the Longhouse. Ojibwe dream catchers swayed overhead, and a beaded, fringed shawl lay over the railing. The dining table was made of thick, uneven timbers and surrounded by hand-built chairs. The air jangled with the mismatched confusion of it all.

With a shyness that surprised him, the young woman asked, "You're Michael Bonnard?" and when he said he was she smiled again and ushered him to a fourth, closed door. She knocked, opened it, and said, "Abornazine, he's here." Giving Michael another quick look—an almost awed one, he thought, as though he were a person of note—she stood aside for him to enter, then withdrew.

Across the room a white man sat smiling behind a desk in front of the windows. His weary, weathered face was framed by long gray braids. Turquoise-studded silver bracelets circled his wrists and a medicine bag lay against his chest.

"Gata," he said. "You are welcome here."

Michael strode forward, tamping down a flash of anger at hearing his Indian name used by someone he hadn't given it to. "Peter van Vliet?"

"Abornazine."

Ignoring the correction, Michael said, "I'm looking for my brother. Edward Bonnard."

"Tahkwehso." Van Vliet nodded. "I've sent for him."

A new voice spoke. "And I am here."

Michael spun around.

Edward stood in the open doorway, black hair loose around his shoulders. "Welcome, brother." The fringes on his buckskin jacket swayed as he walked into the room. He held his right hand out. Michael hesitated, was immediately ashamed, and stepped forward. He gripped Edward's forearm as Edward gripped his.

"Thank you," Edward said. "I thought you might not greet me."

"You're my brother."

"But we fought."

"We've fought before."

Edward gestured to Michael's shoulder. "I'm sorry. Have you—"

"I'm fine." Michael cut him off.

"And your friend—I didn't mean to—"

"Spencer's fine, too."

Edward's dark eyes held Michael's. "That's very good. Brother, I'm surprised to see you here. I don't know how you found this place but I hope I can hear you say you've come to join us."

"I've come to talk."

"You're angry."

"Yes."

Into their silence, van Vliet spoke. "I think when you understand our work here, your heart will change."

Michael looked wordlessly at van Vliet, then turned back to Edward. He spoke in the Mohawk language. "Will you walk with me?" He nodded to the field beyond the windows.

"Happily." Edward answered in Mohawk, also. "Since we began here I've wanted to tell you, to show you our lives and our work. It's been my dream that you'll join with us. Even, that you'll lead us. That would be your right and nothing would please me more." Edward moved around the desk to stand beside van Vliet. Switching back to English, he said, "But we'll talk here."

Van Vliet's gaze stayed steady on Michael. "You'd honor me, Gata," van Vliet said, "if you sit while we talk. I can see you're tired and in pain. Shall I call a healer?"

Michael didn't move. "I'm a doctor. Peroxide, antibiotic ointment, gauze, adhesive tape. I said I'm fine." None of that, he knew, was as good at its job as the teas and poultices his grandmother used to brew. If there really was an Indian healer here his shoulder and side would benefit from a visit. But what was an Indian healer doing here? What were any of these people doing here? "What is this place?"

"My home," said van Vliet. "And therefore the home of my friends." He spread his hands. "My ancestors named this place 'Eervollehuis.' Honorable house. No honor is to be found in the lives they lived. But sheltering the work Tahkwehso and I are doing here, the house will earn its name."

"Your work?"

"In this place," Edward said, "our lives will start to change. *All* our people's lives will start to change. That's our purpose here—to begin that change."

"Double-talk," Michael said. "Another off-rez Indian settlement, another taking-back-the-land? Old news. And whatever your so-called purpose is, a young woman died last night so you could accomplish it. Or am I wrong?"

"No," said Edward, without heat. "You're not wrong."

Michael didn't let his face change, but he felt as though he'd been stabbed. Until that moment he hadn't realized how much he'd wanted to be mistaken about what had happened at Sotheby's. Nor how sure he'd been, at the same time, that he was right.

"She gave her life," Edward said. "The cause was just. Once our goal is accomplished, we'll honor her gift."

"I don't think she'll care."

"The dead hear our words."

"Edward." Michael looked at his brother. "Edward. Why?"

"She might have said what she'd seen."

"Who'd have believed her?"

Edward nodded. "Brother, you may be right. I wasn't thinking clearly. I'd Shifted."

Michael's eyes flew wide. He looked to van Vliet, smiling behind his desk.

"No, it's all right," Edward said. "He knows. Some of the others also know."

"The identity of a Shifter?" Michael spoke in disbelief. "You've revealed yourself?"

"And though I've said nothing to them, the ones who know about me also wonder about you."

Michael looked over his shoulder at the door. "That young woman—the way she looked at me—"

"Yes. Kuwanyauma. She's Hopi but she was educated in white schools." He smiled. "Your own scientist ways, she understands them. Her learning in genetics tells her that my twin may well have the same Power I have."

Michael continued to stare at his brother. "I don't understand. The Law, our grandfathers—why did you do that? Why did you reveal yourself?"

"It was necessary. Some of the ones who come, come believing, but some are skeptical. They come in hope but they have strong doubts. Abornazine says doubt can obstruct the Awakening and the Shift."

"Of course it can. You don't need him to tell you that. Anything that interferes with the intense emotional state. That's Grandfather's teaching."

"Gata, the wisdom you possess is precious," van Vliet said. "Please stay and share it with us. With the people."

"I have no wisdom. What I have is knowledge. From the traditional people, and also the good that can be taken from the white world."

"There is none," Edward said shortly.

"Really? Yet you stand beside a white man in a white man's house and ask me to stay. Tell me: the people who come here—what is it they come believing? Hoping?"

"They believe in the Awakening Ceremony. They hope it will succeed."

"The Ceremony?" Michael stared. "You've revealed the Ceremony? Edward, what are you doing? Are you throwing away everything we were taught?"

"Of all men, you can ask me that?"

"I've never broken my oath."

"Your life is a broken oath."

"My life has been about us! My research, my work—"

"White man's science. It destroyed us."

"No. White man's greed did that. Science is neutral. Edward, you've always refused to hear, but listen now. Come walk with me."

Edward shook his head. "Speak, but speak here."

"No."

"Then"—van Vliet stood, silver bracelets jingling—"then, Gata, listen. You and Tahkwehso, you've been taught, you've trained, you've practiced. You're the only ones. When the Shifters Awaken they'll need someone to teach them. Someone to help them. Tahkwehso is just one man. Please stay with us and help your brother. Help your people."

"What are you talking about? Are you saying there's someone here who can perform the Ceremony?"

"I can," said van Vliet.

Michael looked at him hard. "No," he said. "Ceremonies are passed through generations. The Awakening is no different. Families have rights to their objects, to their dances. A medicine elder will pass the Ceremony to a son or daughter, a niece, nephew, cousin.

Not a stranger. Not a white man." He turned to Edward. "I've found six. Hopi, Cree. Two women among the Coeur d'Alene. A Seminole in Oklahoma and a Saulteaux Ojibwe, in Saskatchewan. Edward, this is my work. This is what I've been doing, all our lives. You've refused to hear my story but I can tell you. I can—"

"There was a Navajo," van Vliet interrupted. "Atsa. He taught me."

Michael frowned. "Atsa died ten years ago. Before I began searching. I was never able to speak to him." Reluctantly, he added, "I'd heard rumors."

"They were true. He was a hundred and three when he died. I had lived with him for nearly a year. I was his student. I learned many things. One was the Awakening Ceremony."

"He taught a white man?"

Van Vliet shrugged. "None of his children, no one around him, wanted to learn. They scoffed. He knew my heart was sincere."

In the silence Michael became aware of the ache in his shoulder, the burning in his side. "The children here," he said, "have you done the Ceremony for any of them?"

Van Vliet and Edward exchanged a look Michael didn't understand. "I've done it seven times," van Vliet said.

"With what result?" If, at that moment, Michael had been asked whether the scientist or the Shifter in him wanted the answer more, he couldn't have said.

Van Vliet shook his head. "Not successful."

Michael felt an odd sensation: relief, gratification, and disappointment in equal measure. "That's what I thought. You were taught nothing." He could see the scene: a Navajo grandfather, his children scattered, no one to take notice of him. Van Vliet was company, he was someone to tell stories to in the chill of the desert night, someone to teach dances and songs to in the blazing heat of the day. But the Awakening Ceremony, its correct way, its chants and its secrets? Not that.

"You're wrong," said van Vliet. "Four times when I did it, the Shift was provoked. But each time something . . . went wrong."

Michael's stomach tightened. Before he could speak, Edward said, "It's why we need the mask, brother."

"I worked so hard," van Vliet went on. "I tried to learn the intricacies, to master everything Atsa wanted to teach me. I fasted, I sweated, I danced for hours under the hot sun. Everything he asked. But I was only able to do the Ceremony once under his direction, and that child didn't react. And then Atsa died. His family didn't want me to stay, wouldn't let me take his drums or dolls. So I came back here. I've spent the last ten years collecting the objects I thought I needed. When I met Tahkwehso I knew the time for the work had come."

"And I knew the same," Edward said. "We were brought together for this. For the people."

"I've done the Ceremony seven times," van Vliet went on, "four with results that prove I'm doing it correctly. But it's not enough. The objects I have aren't powerful enough to make up for my lack of nuance, of skill. I need the mask."

"Four results from seven Ceremonies?" Michael shook his head. "You're doing nothing. You're just seeing what you want to see. It's much too high a percentage for the genetic reality."

"Brother, your genetics—"

"Edward! Truth is truth. Four out of any seven children won't have the Power, no matter how well the Ceremony's done."

Again, Edward and van Vliet looked at each other.

"You say something went wrong," Michael said warily. "What was that? The children—what happened to the children?"

"Not children, brother. The farmers, the ranchers. Auto mechanics, housewives, teachers, and steelworkers. From the reservations, and from the cities. Men and women. Not individually, and not children. There's no time for that. In groups, for adults. That's why these people have come. Abornazine has been doing the Ceremony for them."

43

Edward watched his brother stride in fury from the room. The last quarter hour had been spent in fruitless argument. Edward and Abornazine had struggled to explain their work, their methods and their goals. Michael wouldn't hear them. His words when he'd learned what they were doing were bitter and harsh, aimed particularly at the numbers of people at each Ceremony—fifty, sometimes sixty—and the fact they were adults. His predictions were dire and his heart would not soften. Finally, enraged, he'd turned on his heel. Now he was leaving.

Edward was torn: his heart went with Michael but his duty lay here. Damn Michael! Damn him for this anguish, this cleaving of himself that Edward had known since childhood. Edward was inseparable from Michael in the deepest of ways, but he was also inseparable from their people. These two opposite, unbreakable connections pulled him agonizingly apart now, as they had from the day Michael chose the white world over their own.

"Go to him," Abornazine said.

Edward shook his head. "The way he spoke, the things he said about our intentions—you heard. His heart is flint. He won't be persuaded."

"Go in any case. If you talk to him alone it might be different. Right now he can't see past me. Regardless, it will ease your own heart to try. Go, Tahkwehso."

Edward hesitated; then he hurried from the house.

Michael was on the roadway when Edward caught up with him. "Brother," Edward said, speaking in Mohawk, "I thought you wanted to walk together."

Michael stared wordlessly, but he left the gravel and set off uphill across the ragged grass. Edward fell into step with him, into the icy wind.

"You're wrong," Edward said into Michael's angry silence. "Please hear me. Your words just now, the fears you expressed: some of that may come to pass. The Power might overwhelm some new Shifters, people without the traditional ways. But they'll learn. They'll study and practice. As we did. As you and I did, when we were young."

"We were young! These are grown men and women. Their ways of being in the world are set. Do you think you and Abornazine know better than our grandfathers? The Ceremony's always been done only for children. Don't you think there's a reason for that?"

"The world was slower then. Now, to find the children, one by one, to Awaken them and train them and wait for them—brother, there isn't time! The seas are rising. The land is poisoned, the birds are dying. If the Shifters aren't Awakened soon, Mother Earth will die before the children come of age."

"And who will train them, Tahkwehso? You? All these men and women blinded by new ways to see, deafened by sounds they've never heard? Thrilled beyond words by the sensation of the Shift itself, as we were at first, wanting nothing but to feel it again? Who'll teach them? Abornazine? Look at him! He's old and feeble. The man's a joke. The worst kind of white man."

"He's not a joke, brother, and he's a white man but he loves the people. Our people, our nations. And he's dying."

Michael stopped walking. Edward turned to face him squarely. "That's the other reason it has to be soon. And why we need the mask. He's weaker than he has been. His powers are fading. He can do the Ceremony, but he won't live much longer."

Quietly, Michael said, "That's why the healers are here?"

"The healers are here because they come to us, with the same hope as the others. Living here now, there are nine. None have been able to cure him, not even to slow the disease. He's been to white men's doctors, too. They told him to go home and prepare himself to die."

"I'm sorry."

"If you are, it's weakness. A man you despise is dying. A warrior would rejoice."

"You love him. My sorrow is for you."

"What I'm asking of you is not your sorrow."

"Edward," Michael said. "Edward, other people can also do the Ceremony. Our people. I told you, I've found six. There must be more. We can bring them the children—"

"What children? How will you find the children? How will you coax the parents to do something they haven't done for generations? And what if the people you've found are mistaken? Are lying, are wrong, have forgotten? What if they don't have the dolls and the drums and the masks they need? Abornazine can do it now, brother. But not for much longer."

Michael stared across the field. "My research, Edward. Please listen. Please let me tell you."

"No! Your science is a deception. Science can't explain the Gift the Creator gave us."

"You're wrong."

"No. *You're* deluded. You're blinded by the white world as you always have been. Gata, come back to us. Stay here and help me teach. Help us free the people. Your science—all right, then use your science. Use it for us, for the people. Use it to find the children. And the adults, the Shifters who don't know their Power."

"I can't—"

"You can! Help us show the world our strength. Once it's known people have Shifted, more will come. Some won't be Shifters but they'll be medicine men and women, able to learn the Ceremony, able to go home and perform it on their own lands. Think of it! Think of how you feel in your wolf-self. Think of hundreds, thousands of our people, feeling that way! We'll be strong once again. Mighty and unstoppable."

"Unstoppable."

"Yes! And united. The nations together. The dream of so many grandfathers, we can create it. This land that was stolen can be ours again. The Shifters will lead. The people will follow. Brother, stay. Help us take back what was ours, so that something more than ashes and dust can be passed to the children."

"Take it back? You think you can turn back history? You think you can drive the white man back over the ocean?"

"With Shifters leading, so many from all the nations, with our Power not hidden any longer but shining in the sun—yes. We can. We will."

Michael stared long over the field, and Edward, hope warming his heart, stood silent beside him. Finally Michael spoke. "People will die. Edward, Ivy Nell had a dream." Edward attended as his brother recounted Ivy's vision: deer, eagles, but something wrong with them; and fire.

Worry subsiding when the story was over, Edward said, "That's already been. Abornazine told you. Four times at the Ceremony, responses but not complete Shifts. I'll hide nothing. Two died, brother. Two survive but cannot complete their Shifts and cannot recover their first selves. These were tragedies, but with the mask this won't happen anymore."

"And the fire?"

"The Ceremony is done at a fire. Our fires have been large."

Michael shook his head. "People will die," he said again, harder this time. "Three already have. Edward, you've trained, you've learned, but last night you killed in anger. You say you weren't thinking clearly. How can you expect the newly Awakened, wrenched from the lives they've known and drowning in new scents and sights and sounds—how can they think more clearly than you did? People will die and people will go mad. What you're doing will end in disaster for the nations, the people you love."

"It will end in victory. In honor."

"Honor? No. Your heart knows this: your wolf-self killed that woman, but it was your man-self who wanted her death. Thousands of men and women with the powers of their animal forms, intoxicated with the Shift, and with the violent hearts of their man- and woman-selves—don't you see the calamity of it?"

"The Creator made us—you and me, brother—made us men with the powers of wolves. We must use those powers—the Power—to free our people."

"Our people can't be free until the white man is free, too."

"The white man is the jailer!"

"And the jailer is also in the jail. Do you know why we were given the Power? What I think?"

"What, brother? What do you think?"

"The wolf, the eagle, the deer—the animals, they're better than men. They kill for food, but not for sport, or in anger. They don't poison the water or ruin the land. Shifters know both lives, both ways of being. We can lead, as you say, but not by force. Our task is to bring an understanding of the way of animals to men. Not to give men new ways to kill and ruin."

"And so what would you do? Find the children one by one? Train this one, teach that one, over the years while Mother Earth sickens and dies?"

"Mother Earth will live. We can cause great damage, but in the end if we can't live in peace with the earth, the earth will survive and we'll be gone. Yes, I want to find and teach the children. They can learn. They can bring peace. What you're doing will cause catastrophe. Tahkwehso, please. Stop this."

Edward stood in the wind, feeling nothing at first; then icy disappointment began in a place deep within him, replaced almost immediately by a fiery rage. "Don't call me that. Call me by the name I'll take. Call me Ohtahyohnee."

"'Ohtahyohnee.' Is this your dream?"

"The name should have been yours. But I'll wear it proudly." Edward felt his shoulders tighten and his thighs tense to spring. The sight and scent of his brother enraged him. "You've deserted us, Michael. Gata—that's the joke! You were never prepared. You fled from your duty, from your people, as soon as you could run. I can't look at you. Leave this place."

"I'll stay until I persuade you."

"Then you'll die here."

Michael stood, facing Edward, feet apart, head high.

Edward's vision started to fade, his hearing and sense of smell to sharpen. His skin stung, his blood raced. *Choose now,* he told himself: *stop this Shift, or let it happen.* He smiled, baring his teeth. Always, they had a choice. But since the end of their childhood days, when Grandfather had demanded they stop the Shift, over and over, learning to control it, since the time when the exhilaration of inhabiting his wolf-self, his ancient, fierce, unconquerable self, had been denied him, over and over, and he was made to sit and learn prayers and incantations while the sounds and scents faded and the dreary, limited world accessible to human senses grew to choke him once again—since those days Edward had never, ever, made the choice to stop.

He'd Shift, soon, here in the wind and the cold. But he had another choice. His injured brother stood before him, obstructing his path as he intended to obstruct his work. Truly they were estranged now, all hope lost. With one spring, Edward could make his own words come true. Or he could turn his back before the fury inside him grew too powerful to control.

Michael spoke. "Don't, Edward. Stop the Shift. Talk to me."

Edward saw nothing but crimson fury, heard nothing but his own thunderous howl. He leapt and slammed into Michael with all the power roaring through him. For a moment he stood over his fallen brother, whose face was full of pain but who made no move to rise. Their eyes met and locked. Another howl tearing from his throat, Edward turned and raced toward the trees.

44

Livia Pietro was walking up the slope, trying to comprehend what she'd seen in the shed, when the wind brought new sounds: an argument inside the house. Even her Noantri hearing couldn't make out the words from this distance but the timbre of anger was unmistakable. Three voices, and she thought one was Michael's. Of the others, one sounded similar to his, a man of his own age; the third had the pitch of an older, weaker man. The voices rose, warring. Then they stopped. The door opened and Michael stalked out. She could see his rage in the length and speed of his stride. She veered to go to him but checked herself when another man burst out the door. The wind streamed his long hair out as he loped up the hill. Michael slowed and the other fell in with him. They walked together, stopping at the top of the bluff, both looking toward the river. They were arguing. She saw that in their tense stances, heard it in the angry snatches of conversation the wind brought her, now that she was nearer: *We were young. There isn't time. Please, listen.* And then: *Don't call me that.*

Their fury grew, and something else, a change in the other man.

Nothing Livia could see or scent but it was surely there. She started toward them and wasn't fifty yards away when the long-haired man, howling, threw Michael to the ground and stood over him, quivering in rage. Livia sprinted with Noantri speed. She was almost there, ready to grab him before he could reach down and do Michael more harm but he didn't reach down at all. He howled once more and took off running toward the trees.

Livia bent over Michael. "Are you all right? Is that Edward?"

"Yes." But as Livia stood Michael said, "Don't go after him. He's Shifting."

"He can't hurt me."

"He can." Michael leveraged himself to a sitting position. "Maybe he can't kill you, but he'll hurt you badly. Like he did Spencer."

"Spencer wasn't prepared. I can protect myself and subdue him."

"He won't let you. If he can't kill you, he'll fight until you kill him. Please."

"Michael," Livia said gently, "if he killed that girl, if he's willing to kill me, he's dangerous. I'm sorry but we can't just let him go."

"I know that. But please—let me find the way." Michael stood slowly, gripping his left shoulder. For a long time he stared into the woods where his brother had vanished. Then he turned and walked forward on the bluff, to a place on the edge. Livia followed. The silver ribbon of the Hudson flowed below.

Looking down, Livia asked, "What do your people call it?"

"Cahohatatea." Michael stared silently for a time; then he slipped his hand into his jacket and brought out a small brown pouch. He spilled some of the contents into his palm: tobacco, she saw. He replaced the pouch and held his hand out, open, letting the wind take the tobacco. Eyes closed, he started to chant low, under his breath. Livia stood transfixed. She found no meaning in the words and she wasn't sure there was any, as such. Michael's deep voice seemed to sing the notes of the wind in the trees, the rhythm of the river curving through the valley. The sound and the pulse hypnotized her with wonder.

She wasn't sure how long Michael's song lasted. When it was over he opened his eyes, lowered his hand, and slowly sat. From the edge of the bluff he looked out across the trees and the river. Livia sat beside him. For a long time in the cold wind, Michael didn't move.

Finally, with effort, he rose. "Will you come?"

"Of course."

She walked with him back to the house. He tried the door. It was unlocked and she followed him through a wide entry hall to a study in the back. Like the hall and the other rooms she saw through open doors, the study was furnished with Native artifacts, some of them very old, all of them very fine. Peter van Vliet clearly had not just money, but discerning taste.

The study, though full of beautiful pieces, was empty of people. Michael stopped at the door, then walked past the desk to the French windows, looking out at the bluff they'd been sitting on. He and Livia both turned when a voice came from behind them. A young woman in a flannel shirt asked, "Dr. Bonnard? Are you looking for Abornazine?"

"Where is he?" Michael said.

"I don't know. He left."

"To go where?"

"He didn't say. Or when he'd be back, either." The young woman smiled. "I'm sure you'd be welcome to stay."

Michael gave a small, cold smile. "Yes," he said. "I'm sure I would." He strode past her and Livia once again followed him, out the door and down the hill, to the car.

45

I want to look at that shoulder again," Livia said as they neared the car. "And don't tell me you're fine."

"I'm not fine. The damn thing is killing me. I wish I'd gone looking for a healer."

"Where? You mean, here? There are healers here?"

"According to my brother, yes."

"You want to go back and find one?"

He shook his head and didn't say anything more. She briefly kept her silence, for which he was grateful; but what was he expecting? That she'd be content to be his driver and leave him to—to what? What was he hoping for, what was he going to do?

He looked back up the hill, at the house, then turned again to the bleak woods where Edward had disappeared. Wearily, he got into the car. And of course Livia wasn't content. Even an Indian, consumed with the questions she no doubt had, would have had trouble staying quiet. As the car crunched down the long drive, she asked, "Did you find out what it's about? Why all those people are here?"

Michael thought he saw a gray shadow moving among the

trunks and branches, keeping pace with them. Near the main road he lost sight of it. "Yes," he said.

Livia waited again, then asked, "Can you tell me?"

He changed position, which did nothing for the pain. "It's so . . . Telling you goes against everything I was taught."

"I understand that. Believe me, I know how hard that is. But whatever's going on, I think you need us, Michael."

He wished it weren't true. All his training rebelled against sharing this work—whatever that turned out to mean—with anyone. And with white people? But it was what he'd heard on the bluff, in the voice of the wind and the words of the river, when he'd asked for counsel: *Accept the hand that's offered. This is not a task for one man alone.* And if two of the people offering hands weren't quite—or were more than—human, and the third was a wide-eyed Jesuit priest, did that make a difference? Surprising himself, Michael laughed.

Livia threw him a glance. "Something's funny?"

"Among my people, pretty much everything. It's how we survived. The stories say the Creator likes to hear us laugh and we honor him when we do it." The car turned onto the main road, the growl of gravel replaced by the soft whirr of asphalt. "I said I thought Edward wanted the mask because he'd identified another Shifter. A child who'd need to Awaken. I was almost right, but in grad school we used to say 'almost' blows the lab up. He hasn't identified anyone. He needs the mask to do the Ceremony wholesale. They've been doing it that way already. Fifty, sixty people at a time. To Awaken any Shifters among the people here. That's why these people have come."

"I'm not sure I understand. These people are all Shifters?"

"No. Some of them may be. They all apparently hope they are."

"And Edward can do the Ceremony? I thought Shifters weren't the ones who did it."

"We're not. He can't. Peter van Vliet claims he can. He's the one who's been doing it."

"And? What's happened?"

"Van Vliet and Edward both say they've had four 'partial successes.' Two people died, Edward says, and two had incomplete Shifts. I don't believe it, though. The Ceremony—it's mesmerizing. Most likely what happened is, someone, some people, got carried away. Thought they felt something they didn't feel. Tried to fly, who knows what? And Edward and van Vliet thought they saw something they didn't see, because they wanted to see it."

"Maybe," Livia said slowly. "But I'm not sure."

"What do you mean?" Michael asked, but his heart knew. He felt no surprise, just a growing, icy dread, as Livia described what she'd seen in an outbuilding on the edge of the horses' field. When she was through he sat silent for some time; then he said, "As we were driving up. In the trees—I said it was a deer. I was lying to myself. That's what I wanted it to be. It was a woman, wasn't it?"

Livia nodded. "I think so. Naked, lithe, and frightened. She moved like a deer."

Michael let out a long breath. "Damn it. Oh, goddammit. They're right, then. Edward and van Vliet. They've had Shifts. But they're incomplete. The Shifters can't control it and they can't go back."

"Shifters." Livia's voice was quick with excitement. "Then there *are* more. More than just you and Edward. And they've found them."

Her words echoed in his head: *there are more.* Others like him.

He felt it, too, that excitement. Up that hill behind him, Indians, from the West, from the South, Mohawk and Sioux, Navajo and Seminole, native people of this land, the small tattered remnants of great nations. So many now with nothing left, no land, no language, no clan, no culture. But they had this: they had this gene.

He'd been right. This was his proof. The results Edward and van Vliet had achieved were disastrous, but they weren't failures. This was the empirical evidence his research needed. These were the experiments he'd never have done. The deer-woman in the woods, the eagle-man in the shed: they were his corroboration. He'd been right.

Almost, in his exhilaration, Michael wanted Livia to stop. *Let me out here,* he nearly said. *Let me go back. These are my people. Doubly so. I've been asked to stay: I'll stay.*

But they'd reached the edge of town, were rolling down the main street, past the butcher shop where the kid had asked, "What's going on up there?" *If he had known,* Michael thought. The heat of his excitement dissipated, revealing the ice in his spine that had not left him since Livia's story of the shed. No. They had to be stopped. Their results weren't failures. But they were disastrous.

Livia pulled the car into a parking spot. "Wait here." She got out, and he sat and watched the people on the shopping street of a pretty town, a pretty white town, where Indians were sports teams' mascots, or war-paint-wearing primitives battling cowboys in some mythical long-ago.

"Here." Livia got back in the car, handed him a large coffee and a bottle of aspirin.

Again, he laughed. "It's that obvious?"

"You're dead on your feet." She peeled back the top on her own coffee. "And I'm freezing." She started the car, steered through the town back to the highway. "Michael, talk to me. Other Shifters: this is what you hoped for. You told us that. And in case it wasn't obvious, it's what Spencer and I hoped for, too."

"That was clear."

"All right. Your brother's found them. What do we do now?"

The coffee was old and bitter but she'd sweetened it with honey, thickened it with cream. "I wish," Michael said, "I wish we could celebrate. But even disregarding the three deaths they've already caused: if they succeed it'll be catastrophic. In a lot of ways."

"How? If they can identify Shifters—"

"They can't. Like the elders who've always done the Ceremony for the children, they don't know who can Shift until it happens. But the elders knew what to do. How to help, how to control it once they saw it starting. Edward and van Vliet have no idea."

"Is that what went wrong, then? The eagle-man I saw. He can't . . . He'll be like that forever?"

"I don't know. I've never seen that. The stories say it can happen that way, though." He threw back three aspirin. "But that's just part of it. The other part is, these are adults." A hawk wheeled against the gray sky. Michael framed his thoughts. "To children, the world is magical. I don't mean unicorns and rainbows. I don't even mean benign. I mean, causation isn't obvious. Or a possibility. My people tell children to walk slowly in the dark because that's when the ghosts come out. If you run you might bump one and anger him, and he'll hurt you. So if a child runs at night and falls and breaks his leg, he's perfectly willing to believe he offended a ghost and the ghost threw him down. An adult would believe he couldn't see and he tripped. The child will move slowly at night from now on. The adult will buy a flashlight and if he's in a hurry, he'll run." Michael looked over at Livia. "But what if there really are ghosts? The child's learned a different way of being in the world now, and it'll matter. He won't offend any more ghosts and he'll be fine. The running adult, even with his flashlight, will break his leg again when he bumps another ghost."

"I'm not sure I understand."

"I don't really believe in ghosts. But I try not to run in the dark. And I know I can become a wolf. I learned that when I was too young to understand that it was impossible, or even strange. I could, my friends couldn't. One of my friends on the rez, he had blue eyes. None of the rest of us did. In my mind, those phenomena were equal. Do you see? I was told I'd been given a gift, that it was to benefit our people, that I'd have to learn to control it, that I couldn't talk about it except with Grandfather and Edward. None of this seemed odd to me. I learned how to live in the world in both skins, before I was old enough to have established any other way to live."

"You don't think adults can learn what you did as a child?"

"I don't know. I want to think they can, but there you have the curse of science—I can't believe things just because I want to." He drank more coffee. It wasn't melting the ice inside him but it was warming his arms, his legs. "Livia, your people. You Change as adults. Is it always easy?"

She met his eyes, then looked back to the road. "It's never easy. For new Noantri, there's an initiation, a period of learning. Sometimes it doesn't help at all. Some people are overwhelmed from the beginning by their new, heightened senses. They never learn to filter or ignore. Others seem to adjust without difficulty, but slowly it grows on them: eternity is a very long time."

"What happens to them?"

"Some go mad. They have to be protected and cared for. Others . . . Spencer told you there are ways we can die. Suicide is a problem among us."

They rode in silence for a time. Finally, Livia asked, "Will the mask help? Or do they only think it will?"

"It will. The real one, if they can find it. If they've done the Ceremony seven times, conservatively figuring fifty people each time, and had four responses, that's just over one percent. It's not high enough. It should be closer to one and a half or even two. Van Vliet's obviously good but he's not good enough. He needs more powerful tools. Why are you smiling?"

"The way you rattled those numbers off. In case I didn't know you were a scientist. But Michael, the one percent, the one and a half. How do you know those numbers are right?"

"It's my work. It's always been my work."

46

Michael had fallen silent again. Part of Livia wanted to let him be, to let him digest what they'd learned and choose a course of action. But she felt a growing sense of urgency. "You say this is your work," she said. "But you study smallpox, Spencer told me."

"That's how I get grants. I wouldn't get far if I told the NIH I'm looking for the werewolf gene." He finished his coffee. "And on one level it's true. Smallpox took a disproportionate toll on Shifters. It's a hard trail to follow. Whites weren't keeping records of who died where, just shoveling them into mass graves as fast as they fell, but some of the tribes did, in the wampum, in the buffalo robes, in the stories. I've spent years piecing it together. The same way blacks are more likely to develop sickle-cell anemia, or Ashkenazi Jews, Tay-Sachs, people who carry the Shifter gene seem to have even less ability than the native population as a whole to fight off smallpox. I've found if I follow the virus, I can follow the gene."

"So your work is the gene? What you told us back at Spencer's about the research—"

"It's my research. No one else is doing it and no one knows. My whole life's been about this. But Edward won't hear me." His voice wavered; then he went on. "My thought was to be able to identify the children. If I could find them, if I knew . . . At the same time I've been searching out people who can do the Ceremony. I've found some. They're all old, so in a way I'm racing the clock. But in a way, not."

"How, not?"

"When I first told you about the Ceremony, about the specific emotional state, you brought up neuroaesthetics. The brain's and the body's response to art—to anything—it's all physical. The cause isn't the point. It's like . . . You can put a potato on the fire and cook it from the outside in, or you can put it in the microwave and cook it from the inside out. It's cooked either way."

"But cooked differently."

"In a way that matters? I'm not sure. If I can identify the bio-chemistry, what goes on in me as I Shift, maybe I can give a child that same experience without the Ceremony."

"Or an adult."

"No. Just because it would be controlled still doesn't mean an adult could handle it."

"But a child . . ." She trailed off, unsure how to put into words what was bothering her.

Michael looked over at her. "You're worried it's unethical. Inter-esting, isn't it? When it's demystified, when it's just a physical state and not the magical result of some romantic ancient ritual, it's different. If I chant and dance and a girl turns into a deer, she's ful-filling her fate. What the Buddhists call her dharma. If it happens because I gave her a shot, it's a bizarre kind of human experi-mentation. Well, don't worry. I'm not nearly there yet." He rubbed his eyes. "And I'll never get there if Edward and van Vliet aren't stopped."

"Why not? Why is your work and their . . . whatever they're doing, even connected?"

"You don't see it?" He gave another laugh, but a humorless one. "That's because you're not American. Do you know much about our history—my people's history, Indian history, I mean?"

"I'm sorry, no. The art that comes into my area is from early in the discovery of the continent."

"Right there, that's a loaded word, 'discovery.' We 'discovered' this continent fifteen thousand years ago when we crossed the land bridge from Siberia. When Europeans first came we were curious but not impressed. They had oceangoing ships but they couldn't paddle a canoe. They didn't know how to hunt or farm this land. We helped them out the way we helped each other, and you can see where that got us. We were destroyed. By the nineteenth century we were hunted for fun."

Livia made no response. What could she say?

"Now," Michael said, "now there's a museum in Washington and everyone claims to have a Cherokee grandma. We're romantic figures. Mother Earth, medicine men, the Seven Generations—no one has any idea what the hell they're talking about but boy oh boy, do they admire us. But in the 1970s when Indians started demanding rights, like women and blacks, that didn't go over well. At Wounded Knee, on my own rez at Akwesasne, there were gun battles, armed standoffs. It's what Spencer said. It's what happened to your people until your Concordat was signed. Once it's known that this is an Indian gene, once it's clear that all Shifters, even if they look white or black, must carry Indian blood or it wouldn't be happening, once the Shifters all go mad or die—or kill—Jesus Christ, it'll be open season on us again."

Livia went cold. She flashed back to last fall, to being told by the

Conclave that she must not fail at the task she'd been given. She heard Counsellor Rosa Cartelli saying that if she did, *the fires will come again*. She hadn't wasted a moment imagining that Cartelli might be wrong.

"And you want to talk about human experimentation?" Michael said. "A gene that gives this Power? Just wait. The NSA, the CIA, whoever the hell, they'll be all over it."

Quietly, she said, "I can't argue. It's an ugly picture but I'm afraid it's true. Michael? Just now, when we went back to see van Vliet, and he wasn't there. What were you going to do if we found him?"

For a long time, Michael didn't speak. Then: "You were right, wanting to go after Edward. I shouldn't have let him go."

"What do you mean?"

"I was thinking with my heart. Hoping to find a way . . . But now I understand: they're not deluded, ineffectual dreamers. They're dangerous and they have to be stopped."

"Stopped, how?" Livia asked, but she knew. "Michael, he's your *brother*."

Miles passed in silence. She asked, "If you can't find them? If they move their operation, do the Ceremony somewhere else?"

"They want the mask. If they get it they'll do a Ceremony as soon as they can. If it succeeds, they'll go underground, traveling rez to rez. As van Vliet has more Shifts, as his confidence grows, his power will grow. Soon he won't need the mask. He'll pass it to someone else and he'll teach others. He's dying, Livia. Edward told me. But if he teaches, if they can see it happen while they learn from him . . . Ivy Nell's fire. In her dream. I don't know if it was real or metaphorical. Or both. This could be it. It could be coming."

"If they don't find the mask, would it stop them?"

"It might, because they think it would. They think their failures are related to van Vliet's weakness. The same way confidence will make his power grow, self-doubt will diminish it. It's not magic. When you're uncertain, you stutter, you stumble, you sweat. He won't perform the Ceremony perfectly and he won't get as many Shifts, even partial ones, if he's not sure of his power." Michael paused. "And then he'll die."

"And then? What about Edward?"

"He'll need to find someone else who can perform the Ceremony. I'll need to find him before he does."

Livia didn't ask again what would happen then. "Then we need to find the mask. Or at least be sure they don't."

"Yes." Michael blew out a weary breath. "But I have no idea how."

"I don't either. But there's someone who might be able to help."

47

Rosa Cartelli sat on the Via Veneto in the sidewalk café of Harry's Bar. Even in the wan light and cool air of a February afternoon she enjoyed this place, had come here frequently to take a late-day hot chocolate—or in the heat of summer, a Campari—since the first confectioner's, the Golden Gate, had opened on this corner in 1918.

Rosa Cartelli was among the Eldest of her people. Vividly, she remembered the first time she'd seen Rome. She'd arrived in what present usage referred to as the third century, in the year Diocletian became emperor. Much travel was behind her and much ahead at that point, and like most of her kind she kept, by and large, to sparsely settled areas. She avoided her fellow humans until a hunger she could neither understand nor control drove her to feed; afterwards she'd retreat again to regret, self-loathing, and solitude. It was a life of heartache, wary loneliness, and physical discomfort, a life she did not understand to be endless until she could no longer count the years since she herself had been attacked by a man none of the members of her household, or any of the citizens of Uruk, had ever seen before. She was not young then, and her children and grandchildren feared for her life, but her recovery was rapid and complete.

More than complete. She grew stronger, more able, more adept at every task; but as she became powerless to avoid her dark desire for the blood of others, as she watched her family age around her, she was forced to admit the gods had treated her with a different hand. Eventually her grandchildren began to have children of their own and they in turn neared the age of marriage, while she did not, any longer, change at all. As people in the town began to whisper and to turn from her, she understood she could not remain in the Mesopotamian valley that had until then been her entire world.

One night, without goodbyes, she left her loved ones and walked into the hills. The world, she found in the centuries that followed, was much, much larger than she had ever imagined. She saw great swaths of it, from the early dynastic towns of what would become the towering Chinese empire to the cold, rough fishing villages along the North Sea. Then one day she came by ship to the center of the Roman Empire, for no reason other than that she had not been there before. The hot and dusty hills, with their umbrella pines and vineyards, captured her heart. She stayed; eventually, as she had to, she left; but throughout the centuries she continued to return. It was here, outside the walls of the city proper in the dock quarter now called Trastevere, among peoples of all the Old World's races coming and going, that she first became aware of others of her kind.

Eleven centuries after her first sight of these hills, ten after her first meeting with others like herself, the Council of Constance and the signing of the Concordat made it possible for her people—known to themselves, by then, as the Noantri—to settle permanently and together, if they chose. She did, taking the name Rosa Cartelli, leaving Rome after that only for the periodic Cloaking Noantri life required. As her formerly scattered, furtive people began to create the Laws and structures that would define their lives henceforth,

Rosa Cartelli engaged wholeheartedly in the debates and deliberations that helped build these systems and their uses. Her eloquence, passion, and clear thinking had brought forth from their acknowledged leader, the Pontifex, an invitation to take a seat on the newly formed Conclave. Though many Counsellors chose to serve for a time and then return to private life after some decades or centuries, Rosa Cartelli had remained in service to her people. She sat now on the right hand of the Pontifex, acknowledged as second only to him in wisdom and fineness of perception.

She was, however, with all that, still a fairly private person who would rather not be interrupted over her chocolate and biscotti. Thus when her cell phone rang on this afternoon in Harry's Bar and the screen informed her the call was from the Conclave offices, she considered not answering. Duty won out, however; the Noantri administration rarely contacted a Counsellor except in a situation of importance.

"*Salve. Sum Rosa Cartelli,*" she said, speaking in Latin as was the custom when discussing affairs of the Community.

"*Salve, Consiliaria,*" replied the familiar voice of Filippo Croce, the Pontifex's private secretary. Continuing in Latin, he told her, "Livia Pietro has called from New York. She wishes to speak to you."

"Livia Pietro? What on earth could she want?" Five months ago the task Pietro had been set was the most urgent business in the Noantri world. Any communication from her then was given the utmost priority. But that situation had been resolved satisfactorily, and Pietro had gone back to her uneventful life in the study of art history.

"I don't know, Counsellor. She said her concerns were private, to be shared only with you. I have her on the line and can send the call through, or I can tell her you're unavailable if you prefer."

"No, it's all right, I'd better speak with her. I can't imagine what it's about—you say she's in New York?"

"Yes."

"Thank you, Filippo. Please put her through."

A pause, an electronic hum, and then, "Professor Pietro, here is Counsellor Cartelli. I'll absent myself now, and the line is secure. *Salve.*"

In the early days of this technology, until not long ago, one would at this point have heard a click. Now nothing but a subtle silence announced Filippo's departure.

"Signora Cartelli?" came Livia Pietro's voice, speaking Italian. "Thank you for taking my call."

Rosa switched to Italian, also. "I must admit to a certain concern, Professor Pietro. If you wish to discuss an issue of importance to the Community, a protocol exists that you, of all people, know very well. Thus I wonder why you insisted upon contacting me individually. If you have something else in mind, my perplexity is all the more. Tell me, how can I be of service?"

"I'm afraid your concern is justified, Signora. The issue I'm calling to discuss is of enormous importance to the Noantri, but I don't feel I can talk about it at this point with anyone except yourself."

"I don't recall us being the closest of confidantes." Rosa signaled the waiter for another chocolate. "Please explain yourself."

"Yes. I assume Signor Croce told you I'm in New York. Spencer George and Father Thomas Kelly are here, also."

"An embarrassment of riches for New York."

Pietro didn't respond to the mild barb. "We've met two men here. Not Noantri, but also not Unchanged."

"Don't speak in riddles, Professor. It's tiresome."

"I apologize. But when I tell you—" Pietro took an audible

breath and began again. "Signora Cartelli, these men are what the legends call shapeshifters."

During the long pause that followed, a *motorino* buzzed up the street and a truck rumbled the other way. Rosa stared at the ancient bricks of the Porta Pinciana, recalling the hot summer when it had been built. "Livia Pietro, be very careful what you say. These are not concepts to be trifled with. Down the ages many people have claimed many abilities. Some have known themselves to be liars, while others have believed their own words. All, though, have turned out to be charlatans. America is no different from the Old World in this, except that the impostors may be both more persuasive, and unfamiliar to you. Whatever these men are claiming—"

"No." Pietro interrupted her. "They've claimed nothing, in fact they've tried to hide it. Spencer saw it happen."

"Spencer George? He saw? What did he see?"

The waiter placed Rosa's chocolate in front of her and backed discreetly away. The cup sat untouched as Rosa listened to Pietro's narrative of a cold night in a park in the heart of the giant metropolis, where, according to Spencer George, a man had turned into a wolf.

When Pietro was finished Rosa said nothing, but lifted her cup to her lips and sipped. The sweet warmth of the drink broke the spell. It was a seductive tale; but it was nonsense. "Spencer George was injured. He was hallucinating."

"I don't think that's true."

"You may not. There it is nonetheless."

"The young woman who was killed—"

"Was killed by a madman of one kind or another. A tragic story, but an old one."

"I disagree."

"Professor Pietro, have you seen this Shift, as you call it?"

"No."

"Until you do, please don't spread unsubstantiated rumors. Especially from an academic, it's bad form. Furthermore, if this is a phenomenon you're requesting that the Conclave investigate, as is your right, I still don't understand why you felt compelled to contact me directly."

"I'm most emphatically not asking the Conclave to investigate. That's part of the point. I'm calling you because when I was Summoned before the Conclave you were the Counsellor most forcefully opposed to Unveiling. You insisted vehemently and categorically that revealing ourselves would result in disaster for our people."

"That encounter was not so long ago that I've either forgotten it, or changed my opinion. What of it?"

"Assuming for the sake of argument that what Spencer saw was real and these men do have this Power, it's both contrary to their Law and a genuine danger to them to reveal their existence. As it would be for us. In fact I'm directly contravening their Law by calling you, although I do it with the approval of one of them."

"I do not accept your assumption, but since you apparently do, let me ask, then, why you're calling at all?"

"Because a greater danger is imminent and I need your help."

"What danger?"

Again, Rosa listened as Pietro described a scenario that, if it were to come to pass, would admittedly be horrible. Men and women with no experience of powers simultaneously vast and subtle suddenly invested with them, with the changes in perception they brought and the alterations in consciousness that went along with them. Rosa was taken back to her own beginnings, when her new Blessings and dark needs appeared simultaneously, with no warning, no guidance, no way to understand.

"Many will not survive, I'm told," Pietro said. "Some will, but be unable to choose rationally how and when to apply their Powers—a terrible form of insanity. Many lives will be forever changed, irrevocably destroyed. But that's not the worst."

"And what is the worst?"

"It will be the same as it would be with us. Once it's known this can happen, once people become aware that it's the natives of this country who carry the gene that makes it possible, and especially in view of the chaos this ill-considered Awakening will unleash, there will be disaster on a grand scale. You spoke about the fires coming for us once again. They'll come here, too. The killing mobs, people who've been wronged screaming for blood, and people full of fear, and soon after, people whom the destruction hasn't touched but who are all too willing to seize a chance to brutalize and kill. Unlike with us, the Power to Shift doesn't convey immortality or anything near it. The stories say Shifters are difficult to kill, but the truth of that depends on their skills and abilities in their animal forms. Most of these people will have none. In our case, only the fires can harm us, and to escape them is to survive. But a Shifter can be captured, hurt, and destroyed in any of the ways an Unchanged can. And of course, as it was when the Noantri were the target of violent persecutions, many people who aren't Shifters will be hunted and killed, caught up in the panic and the frenzy.

"And something more. Like ours, the Shifters' difference is based in their physical natures, in their genes. To fear government-decreed mass arrests and imprisonment, and human experimentation—

especially considering the history of this country regarding its First Peoples—is not to go too far."

Rosa sighed and sipped her chocolate. "You're an eloquent speaker, Livia Pietro. All those years of trying to motivate undergraduates, I would suppose. The picture you paint is quite dark but you haven't yet explained my place in it."

"The men who plan to perform this Ceremony have hidden themselves. I'm not sure we can find them to stop them. But they need a specific artifact, an ancient mask. Or at least, they believe they need it, which amounts to the same thing. The murder of the young woman came about when they tried to obtain the mask, but the one at the auction house is a fake. They're looking for the real one. Signora Cartelli, they *must* be stopped."

"I assume you've come to the point where I learn why I'm involved."

"Yes. Spencer and Father Kelly have followed the trail of the real mask to Il Gesù, in Rome."

"The mask is here?"

"It may be. Certainly, information on the last man known to have possessed it is there. He was a Jesuit priest who lived in the early eighteenth century in what was then called New France. A certain Père Ravenelle, on a mission to the Iroquois. The information that could lead to the authentic mask is in the secret archives at Il Gesù. Even Father Kelly can't get at it."

"A circumstance which has fueled your suspicions, no doubt."

"Yes."

"But your nemeses, they can?"

"I don't know. They may be able to, or they may find the mask another way. For us, this is the only path we see."

Rosa finished her chocolate, watching dusk settle over her beloved Rome. Four millennia, and the problems of people living in this world never got any easier. People Changed or Unchanged—or, barely possibly, Other. She wrapped her cashmere scarf more tightly as a breeze came up.

"What you want me to do, then, is send someone to burrow into Il Gesù to unearth this material."

"That's it exactly. But without informing the Conclave. I realize this puts you in a difficult position. But as I said—"

"Yes, yes. Whatever I choose to do will be my own responsibility." Rosa took another long pause. "Very well. Although I seriously doubt the veracity of this claim to shapeshifting powers, the consequences you describe are too dire to be ignored. On the possibility that there is truth in this story, I will help you. After the danger has passed we will discuss the necessity of Conclave involvement. In the unlikely event that what you say is true, this is not a secret you have the right to keep."

"I understand that. As does my Shifter friend. But many delicate issues will have to be involved in that deliberation."

"As you say. So we will proceed with an attempt to resolve the current situation. But Livia Pietro, sending someone to Il Gesù is unlikely to serve your purpose."

"Why is that?"

"It's true there are Jesuits among the Noantri, and two, I believe, with access at a level high enough to penetrate the secret archives. Neither of them is at the moment in Rome. I can call them here, and will. But the urgency of your situation indicates you haven't time to wait. However, there is another way."

"What way?"

"In 1497 a ship sailed for the New World from Bristol, in England. Her captain was a man whose name has come down through history as John Cabot, but who was by birth an Italian called Giovanni Caboto. He had been some time in England then because he was Cloaking."

"He was one of us?"

"Yes. And he took with him on his voyage another Noantri, an Augustinian friar calling himself Giovanni Antonio de Carbonariis. Carbonariis's Change came about in the second century, when he was a monastic in a Christian hermetic order near Jerusalem. By the time he sailed with Cabot he had begun to feel oppressed by both the collective nature of the religious society in which he lived, and the growing communal aspects of Noantri life. John Cabot returned to England within a year, later feigning death in a shipwreck. He has since taken other identities in succession. But Carbonariis remained. He is still there."

48

S tanding on the shoulder of the highway, Livia drew a breath, digesting what Rosa Cartelli had just told her. Michael stood some distance away, outlined against the sky. "Signora Cartelli," Livia said, "this man, Father Carbonariis—he was here when the Indian nations were thriving? He was here when this Ceremony was regularly performed?"

"If there ever was such a Ceremony, yes. If there is a mask such as the one you describe, and if it was last seen in the hands of a Jesuit missionary to the Iroquois, chances are good that Carbonariis can shed light on its travels."

"Can you put us in touch?"

"Why would I have mentioned him otherwise? But Livia Pietro, take care. Carbonariis's dedication to his Church and his loyalty to the Noantri are both intense, but they are matched—overshadowed, possibly—by his devotion to the peoples he first encountered in the New World. In today's parlance one might say he had 'gone native.' I'll contact him and order him to speak with you and he will obey, but he will not thank me. Carbonariis is a recluse, living in the dwindling but still untamed forest of what is now Canada. He has never embraced the joys of Community."

"Never embraced—he's an Old Way Noantri?" Livia said in wonder. "They do exist, then? I've only heard stories."

"As always in this world, some stories are fabrications and others are true. There are indeed Old Way Noantri. As to the story you've just told me, I've no idea into which category it falls. I'll have Carbonariis speak with you. But know this: Carbonariis will help only to the extent that he believes what you want will benefit the native peoples. If he sees a threat to them, he'll disappear. That would be a cause of great dismay for the Conclave. Old Way Noantri are not required to come into Community but they are forbidden to feed as they did before the Concordat. If Carbonariis feels it's in the best interests of the native peoples for him to vanish, he may break off contact with the Conclave and return to his original ways. Under various circumstances other Old Way Noantri have done the same. This exposes us all to an unacceptable danger of discovery. If he chooses that path, Carbonariis will be dealt with in whatever way the Conclave deems necessary. That danger to the Noantri, and the consequences to Carbonariis, are things for which you, Livia Pietro, would be answerable. Do you understand?"

"Yes." Livia shivered in the cold wind; then, in a voice that she hoped sounded stronger than she felt, she said, "I do understand, and I'll be very careful how I approach Father Carbonariis. Signora, how soon can you reach him?"

"He has no modern conveniences, of course. I'll call the intermediary who delivers his provisions. She'll have to go to him, but once in the woods she can travel as fast as she might. It should not take long."

"Signora Cartelli, thank you. For your help, and for believing me. As I say, I know asking you to keep a secret like this—"

"As you say, you've said that. I shall be in touch. *Salve.*"

Driving down the highway, Livia turned the heat up in the car and told Michael about Cartelli, the Conclave, and what little she knew of Father Giovanni Antonio de Carbonariis. "You heard from Spencer how we feel most comfortable when we live in physical proximity to each other. But as with anything, there are exceptions. Certain Noantri—no more than a few dozen, I think—who were made hundreds, in some cases thousands, of years before the Concordat allowed for the possibility of Community, have never given up their solitary lives. They live as recluses, as hermits. They're required to abide by the provisions of the Concordat and so they're supplied with . . ." She faltered, wondering if Michael's reaction to her reality, to Spencer's, was anything like Thomas Kelly's had been when he'd first learned.

"Blood." Surprising her, Michael grinned. "I'm a biologist, I'm a doctor, I'm an Indian, and I'm a shapeshifter. You think a little blood is going to bother me?"

She smiled back. "They're given supplies of blood and they're forbidden from feeding as they used to or making new Noantri without Conclave permission. Beyond that they're left alone and their identities and locations are closely guarded. I've never met one of them and I don't know anyone who has."

"When was this Father Carbonariis—the word is 'made'?"

"In the second century. He was a hermit even then. By the time he came here he was an Augustinian friar, and apparently he'd made it clear he had no interest in Community."

"And he's been here since? Your process of going somewhere else, changing identities—he hasn't done that?"

"I suppose if you live deep in the forests of Canada you don't have to."

Michael said nothing in answer to that, just sat and watched charcoal clouds slip through the iron sky. Livia, used to his silences by now, stayed quiet as she drove, feeling the soft shifting tugs as the road curved and curved again against the rocky hillside. As they started the descent to the river Michael said, "Carbonariis would have been here at first contact. Before the diseases, before the slaughter. He'd have heard the lost languages. Heard the songs, and seen the dances."

"Yes."

"Maybe, when this is over . . . Do you think he'll sit with me? Tell me what he remembers?"

"I don't know. All we can do is ask him."

Michael nodded. Livia watched the river come closer, saw Manhattan rising in steel cliffs to answer the stone ones of the Palisades. As they reached the George Washington Bridge Livia's phone rang. She slipped the earpiece in and answered it.

"Professor Pietro," came Rosa Cartelli's dry voice. "It seems there may be some truth to your story after all."

"Carbonariis says that?"

"Carbonariis says nothing. I reached his contact in Halifax. Carbonariis has gone to New York."

"To New York? A recluse from the woods of Canada?"

"It seems so. His contact was quite surprised and asked him why. He told her there was a mask he wanted to see."

49

Charlotte threw her pen down on the scratched steel desk. She'd rather have punched out the computer but the Department didn't like it when you broke the technology. She and Framingham had spent a frustrating morning running down the list Brittany Williams's furious father and tearful mother had supplied of their daughter's ex-boyfriends. Ostrander and Sun had been in the same business; among the four of them they'd been out on half a dozen interviews covering all five boroughs (Brooklyn twice) and made dozens of phone calls. The first set of calls was to ascertain that some of these exes lived far away and the second set, more roundabout, was to make sure they actually were far away right now.

"Before goddamn cell phones," Charlotte said to no one in particular, "when a cop called a guy in Buffalo and he answered the phone that was all you needed to know."

"Scuse me, child, but how do you know that?" Ostrander asked mildly, not looking up from his computer screen. "You and Matt were born with cell phones in your hands."

"She was," said Sun. "Matt was born with the tricorder to call the mother ship."

Framingham hurled his pencil across the room and Sun, with a practiced move, ducked.

Charlotte got up and poured herself the burnt dregs of the coffee. She dropped behind her desk again and scrolled through the preliminary forensics report, hoping something would jump out at her. Nothing she saw was any more useful than it had been the first four times. All the blood was Brittany's, and though the room was plastered with fingerprints, the ones they'd checked so far all belonged to Sotheby's personnel or consultants. Which didn't mean someone with a right to be there hadn't killed her, but it did mean if that's what had happened you couldn't prove it by fingerprints. One of the ME's people thought he had some anomalous DNA in the rip in her throat, but he couldn't even tell if it was human, and Charlotte was ready to strangle him when he admitted that a musk perfume, or sloppy kisses from her poufy little dog, would have left those kinds of traces.

"Well," Sun said, looking up, "I might have something. Charlotte, don't take this wrong."

"Screw you."

Sun nodded as though she'd agreed to be reasonable. "I was going back through these guys. Her exes. Her father can't tell them apart but he says one of them obviously did it and since they're all goddamn leeches they should all be shot."

"It's good to be the king," Framingham said.

"Her mother, though, seems to have memorized each one. If it were my mother that would be because she was already naming the grandchildren. She gave me a complete roster."

"Isn't that what we've been working from?"

"Yes, but get this. In college Brittany dated a guy named Stan Miller."

"I called him," Ostrander interrupted. "He's in Omaha."

"That's not the point. He's Chippewa."

Charlotte narrowed her eyes but said nothing.

"According to her mother, that's where her interest in Native art started. And here's the thing: two of the other exes are Indians, too. Enrolled tribal members. A third, he's not enrolled, but I Facebooked him. He's got long hair and that round face, like Nanook of the North."

"Hey!" Framingham complained. "How come he can say shit like that and you're not breaking his balls?"

"He's Chinese," Charlotte said. "Steve, you're telling me she had powwow fever?"

"That's what you call it? With us we say she liked rice."

Charlotte swung her legs off her desk. "That's what we call it. You know what it means?"

"I do! I do!" Framingham raised his hand. "It means we get to take another run at one of the last people, who also happens to be an Indian, to see her alive. Michael Bonnard. I should ping again?"

"You bet."

A few minutes and the rest of the coffee dregs later, Framingham looked up to announce, "We are pingless. His phone must be off."

"How about that? Who turns their phone off?"

Ostrander and Sun said together, "Bad guys."

"Okay. Come on, Matt."

"Where?" To her glare Framingham said, "Though of course I'd follow you anywhere so I don't need to know, do I, I'll just trail along puppy-dog like and worship at your—"

"Oh, shut the hell up. This is right up your upper-class Brit alley. We're going to see his Brit pal, Spencer George."

50

I was not expecting so many."

Livia, Spencer, and Thomas stood in Spencer's parlor, facing the glowering man who'd stopped short in the arched entryway. Thomas found himself fighting not to flinch as the dark eyes swept over them.

At Spencer's suggestion it was Michael who'd gone to greet Giovanni Antonio de Carbonariis at the door. "If the good father's identities as priest and Noantri are secondary to his love for Michael's people, it might put his mind at ease to be met by—listen to this, Michael, I'm learning to say it—an Indian "

Michael had smiled and they'd all settled in to wait.

Thomas himself had a hard time staying still. The man on his way to them had passed through Thomas's research on Kateri Tekakwitha, though like Père Ravenelle he was what Father Maxwell referred to as "far afield." In the other direction, though. At the dawn of the sixteenth century Antonio de Carbonariis had been involved in the establishment of a Christian settlement in Newfoundland, the first in North America. After a few years the settlement had foundered and the monks, it was reported, had returned to Europe. Thomas had searched for more information but hit a puzzling wall: the Scottish scholar whose life's work had been that expedition and Carbonariis had ordered all her research destroyed when she died. At the time he'd wondered why anyone would do that, spend a painstaking lifetime adding a piece to the puzzle that was human knowledge and then remove it and throw it away.

If her research had led her to Carbonariis's true nature, though, he understood.

Even Livia and Spencer, it seemed to Thomas, engaged in an uncharacteristic level of banter and bustling: making coffee, straightening pillows. Only Michael didn't speak, barely moved. He drank the coffee Spencer brought him, and after that leaned back in his chair. Thomas wondered if he'd fallen asleep; yet he sat up, alert, and stood to walk to the door a few seconds before the bell sounded. Spencer and Livia also lifted their heads; it was only Thomas who needed the doorbell to know their guest had arrived.

Michael and Carbonariis had exchanged words at the door, words Thomas heard but couldn't understand. A Native language, most likely. Now Carbonariis stood in the parlor entrance, a tall, thin figure in the loose black wool habit and shoulder cape of an Augustinian friar. His gray hair was cut in a tonsure, a style long abandoned among most orders—including, Thomas was sure, the Augustinians. Around his neck hung a silver crucifix and a small leather bag.

Carbonariis spoke to Michael, again words Thomas didn't understand. At Michael's response Carbonariis snorted, said something more, and in waves of cloth strode into the room. The upholstered furniture earned a scowl of disdain; he chose a wooden side chair. He turned to Livia and said, "You are Professor Pietro?" His English carried a slight accent, an odd guttural roll. Not of the native Italian speaker, for of course Carbonariis wasn't that. The tongue of his youth, Thomas realized, would have been Aramaic.

"Yes, I'm Livia Pietro."

"I've been ordered to speak with you. Who are they?"

"Dr. Michael Bonnard—" Livia began.

"Gata. We have just met. These two."

"I am Spencer George. This is my home. I—"

"Your home is grand. I wish you great joy of it. And you, Jesuit?"

Taken aback, Thomas answered, "Thomas Kelly," in a voice less forceful than he might have liked. "I'm very glad to meet you, Father."

The Augustinian's response was a sardonic gaze. "Gata tells me you are all to be trusted. Fine. Let us proceed. Why have I been called?"

"Will you have coffee?" Spencer asked. "Or a brandy, perhaps?"

"I prefer to keep this encounter as brief as possible." Carbonariis had not taken his gaze from Thomas, who was doing his best to meet the glinting eyes.

"As you wish," said Spencer. He looked from one priest to the other. "Father Kelly is a friend," he said, and added, "of the Noantri."

Now Carbonariis glanced at Spencer. "Is he? This is new. And disquieting. We are Unveiling to priests, now? And," he added, looking at Michael, "to the Haudenosaunee?"

"No. Father Kelly's position is unique. As is Michael's. As is yours, Father Carbonariis."

"Unique, because I am both priest and Noantri? You delude yourself. There are many."

"No, Blackrobe," said Michael. "Because of your memory of my people. And though my language is Mohawk and my home is at Akwesasne, the Haudenosaunee are my father's people. I'm Abenaki. Wolf Clan."

Carbonariis nodded to acknowledge the correction. In the silence that followed, Thomas realized he alone was still standing. He took to the armchair again, but perched on the edge, eyes on Carbonariis. *There are many.*

The friar turned to Livia. "All these men have spoken, yet you are the one to whom I was sent. Why?"

"Why have they spoken?" Livia smiled. "It's their nature. Why are you here? About the mask."

"The Ohtahyohnee."

"You don't seem surprised."

"Little surprises me."

"But some things impress you. You traveled a long way to see the mask."

Carbonariis made no answer.

"And have you, Father? Have you seen it?"

"Yes."

"What did you think of it?"

"Why does it matter?"

"Because it's a fake."

A pause. "You've brought me here to tell me that? Nothing like this Ohtahyohnee has been seen for centuries. I'll make my own judgment. I doubt you would know."

"I've seen it," Michael said. "I know."

Carbonariis regarded Michael for a long, silent time. He said slowly, "You were able to tell?"

"Unmistakably." Michael switched to Mohawk. Thomas watched the exchange, saw the Augustinian's eyes widen as Michael spoke. Carbonariis asked sharp questions. Michael responded calmly. Finally Carbonariis settled back and gave a cold smile.

"New, indeed," he said. "The Noantri Unveil to a Jesuit, and a Shifter reveals his identity—and to white people. The world is changing."

Thomas saw Livia and Spencer glance at one another. "You know?" Livia asked. "About the Shifters?"

Carbonariis didn't answer.

"You know?" she repeated. "You knew the Noantri weren't alone?"

"You pronounce that as an accusation."

"No, no. Just—that knowledge, it means so much. If we'd known . . . The Noantri—"

"Are Europeans!" Thomas recoiled as Carbonariis's roar struck the room with physical force. Lowering his tone, the friar went on, "Not all, of course. Even when I came to this land there must have been Noantri in Asia and in Africa. But the Concordat was signed by Europeans. The Noantri are governed"—he smiled thinly "like the Holy Mother Church, from Rome. But there were no Noantri here. None that I met. None that were rumored. None, among the native people."

"I told you that," Michael said to the others, his eyes still on Carbonariis. "There are no blood-drinkers in our stories."

"Each of us," Carbonariis said, "when he becomes Noantri, remains the man he was. What reason did I have to expect that my eternal brethren would love the people of this land any more than my mortal brothers did? As for the Church, her love for the native peoples was such that she held learned debates to determine whether they even had souls. I had been here forty years before *Sublimus Dei*, and I saw that papal bull and its radical idea that the natives were human given lip service and immediately ignored. For centuries I watched priests and Noantri land on these shores and, side by side with the unchurched and the Unchanged, wantonly destroy all that was beautiful and sacred. In the hands of such people, knowledge is a weapon. Why would I give them such a powerful one?"

"A weapon," Livia said, "but also a tool. Knowing this could have changed our people."

"Our people? The twin hierarchies in Rome, you mean? No. Those who welcomed me half a millennium ago to lands they inhabit but do not conquer, forests they use but do not destroy, seas they fish but do not poison—they are my people." He stood. "If I've been sent here by the Conclave to be berated—"

"No," said Michael, standing also. "You've been sent to help your people. Please, Blackrobe. Sit with us."

The air sparked with tension. Thomas searched for pacifying words. Before he could find them, Livia said, "I'm sorry, Father. I didn't mean to offend you."

"No. You meant to criticize and expected me not to be offended." Abruptly, Carbonariis sat again. "Shifter," he said to Michael, "why are you here?"

"To help my people."

"By living in the white world? Your Power was given to you for a purpose."

"Everything I am, and have, was given to me for that same purpose," Michael said. "I'm a scientist. I study the Power."

"Study?" Carbonariis's words dripped with acid. "White science teaches nothing but how to destroy."

"Science teaches nothing at all. As Livia said, knowledge is a tool. Its use is what you make of it."

"And what use do you, Shifter, make of your studies?"

"The Power is genetic," Michael said evenly. "If I can trace the gene I might be able to identify the Shifters."

"That's not for a Shifter to do. It's the work of a medicine man."

"It's not being done."

"Perhaps there are reasons." Carbonariis narrowed his eyes. "How will you do it?"

"I study smallpox. The virus killed Shifters out of proportion to their numbers among the people. If I can find—" He stopped; Carbonariis was shaking his head.

"Smallpox did not kill Shifters."

"The Shifters fade from the stories in the same pattern as the disease swept through the nations. My work—"

"Is white man's work!" The friar gave a sneer of triumph. "Smallpox was a potent weapon. It helped destroy the nations. But not Shifters. Not the way you think. Shifters survived the disease. Almost always. But the Power was gone."

"I . . ." Michael trailed off. He began again, "The historical record . . . I can see the virus—"

"You look through white eyes! You can see the virus? Can you see the people dying, warriors, women, children? Can you see the helpless medicine men as they weep? Can you see Shifters, desperate to summon the Power—as though the Power would turn the battle against white man's filth!—but trying because their oaths demanded it, and achieving nothing more than a pitiful, partial Shift, an interrupted Shift they could not reverse? You say you can see Shifters vanishing as smallpox spread. Yes, they vanished. The medicine elders stopped performing the Ceremony! It was too dangerous. Infected children could not complete their Shifts and the elders had no way of telling whose blood was poisoned. And Shifters also vanished because many walked into the forests and killed themselves, rather than let their identities be revealed by their failures to return to man-self or woman-self. In that last act they honored their oaths, as they could not in any other way. As you, Gata, do not." He glared around the room. "If I have knowledge that will be of use to what is left of the people I love, let me employ it. If not, I will be grateful to be gone."

51

Livia waited for Michael. These were his people, his brother, his story to tell. His face remained stone, but when he finally found words, his voice was bleak. "My work," he said. "My people."

"Your work will not help your people."

In silence, Michael's gaze met the friar's. Livia saw desolation in one, bitter triumph in the other. Spencer leaned over and pressed Michael's hand.

Carbonariis gathered his habit around him, stood, and strode to the door.

"Father," Livia called out.

The Augustinian spun to glare at her.

"The partial Shift. The destruction of the nations. These are the things we've asked you here to prevent."

"The nations are already destroyed."

Slowly, Michael turned to face him. "The people still live."

Carbonariis pursed his lips and nodded. "For which I say a grateful prayer every day."

Livia heard more acid than gratitude in that, but said nothing.

Michael answered, "I do, also."

Carbonariis took another step toward the door. He stopped; with a hissed breath he turned. He looked angrily to Livia. "Speak."

"The mask," she said. "The Ohtahyohnee. It's a forgery. We think, though, that the real Ohtahyohnee still exists. Someone had this one made to replace it."

"It was not I."

"Of course not. But the real one—others are searching for it."

"For reasons of white man's greed?"

Before Livia could answer, Michael spoke. "No. To use in the Awakening Ceremony. To Awaken not children, but adults."

Carbonariis stared, then shook his head. "No medicine man would do that."

"This is a white man. With him, a Shifter. My brother."

Michael's voice gained strength as he told the story: Edward ("Tahkwehso," Michael said), van Vliet (whose Abenaki name Michael didn't use), the gathering at Eervollehuis. The Ceremony being performed over and over for people unprepared for the Power and unable to control it. Livia watched color drain from Carbonariis's face as the enormity of the peril dawned.

"The Shifters who Awaken—most will die or go mad," Michael said. "All of my people—your people—will be in danger. Even those without the Power, even those who don't believe it exists—"

"No." Carbonariis held up a hand. "Don't speak it. I saw it once. I don't doubt it will happen again." He crossed himself and walked to the window, where he stood, silent, for a long time. No one moved. The very air in the room was still, waiting for the friar.

Finally, he turned back to them. A slow, mordant smile stretched his thin lips. "They will all die. Death is the fate of all things living. The people will vanish as the nations have. You, and you"—nodding at Michael, at Thomas—"will be gone in the blink of an eye. We three will be here when the civilizations that destroyed the nations dissolve into dust, we will live for aeons under the wheeling stars, but the end of days relentlessly approaches, and when it comes it will be our time, also. Our Savior will greet us—the nations, the people, even we—in the afterlife.

"Only a fool, then, would allow his heart to ache at the story you tell, Shifter. Only a fool would try to prevent what you say is coming." He strode back through the room to the wooden chair and sat. "And so, I am a fool. Tell me: How can these men be stopped?"

Michael stared; then, as he had earlier, he surprised Livia by laughing. Spencer smiled with him. Thomas looked confused. Michael's face grew serious again as he said, "We can stop them if we find them."

"And a hermit monk from the forests of Newfoundland can help you to do that?"

"They're searching for the Ohtahyohnee. If we find it we may find them. The trail of the mask leads back to the middle of the eighteenth century, to a French Jesuit named Etienne Ravenelle. Ravenelle left papers but they're locked up at Il Gesù in Rome, and even Father Kelly can't get at them."

The friar threw a scornful glance at Thomas. "The Jesuits protect their precious knowledge. So this is why the Conclave sent me to you—on Ravenelle's account. I remember him. What of him?"

"Did you—did you really know him? I'm sorry, Blackrobe. I don't doubt what you say. It's just, it's not twenty-four hours since I learned such a thing was possible."

Carbonariis gave the thin smile again. "And hundreds of years since I was called by that name. Ravenelle was a missionary to the Iroquois. Not a fool. A man with more questions than answers. Unusual among Jesuits. But if Ravenelle possessed one of the twelve masks, I never knew it. If that was what you were hoping for from me, I can't help you."

In the silence that followed, Livia heard children laugh on the street outside. Their joy only underscored the despair around her.

"Father," Thomas spoke suddenly, "maybe you can." All eyes turned to him but he kept his on Carbonariis. "Forgive me. I'm thinking aloud."

"A common affliction of Jesuits."

"Yes, perhaps. Let me ask you this. The incomplete Shift. My recent studies have been on the life of Saint Kateri Tekakwitha."

"'The Lily of the Mohawks,'" Carbonariis said with curled lip. "She was Algonquin, you know. Wolf Clan. Her hagiography says Mohawk and Turtle Clan, but those were her father's people. Not that the Church has any reason to care."

"But we do. Follow me. Tekakwitha founded a community, a sacred society of Native women. They lived for their commitment to each other and devotion to the Savior. Tekakwitha wore a hooded robe. We're told it was to hide smallpox scars. But we're also told that from a young age she refused to marry, that she was meek and practiced mortification of the flesh. Why would a woman like that care if people saw her scars?"

The friar's eyes glittered. Livia got it just before he spoke. "Jesuit! You think she was a Shifter."

"I do. And she contracted smallpox. From what you've said, I think her Shift was incomplete and that's what she was hiding. You say she was from the Wolf Clan. Would that have been her—what do I say, her animal self?"

Michael nodded. "It would have, yes."

"Her mother's said to have died of smallpox. Maybe that's true, maybe not. Maybe she was one of the Shifters who killed themselves, may God have mercy on their souls. But Tekakwitha was devout and suicide's a sin. I wonder, now, if they were all Shifters, all the women she gathered to her. Christians, and Shifters, women who rejected suicide but wanted to keep their Shifter oaths of secrecy."

"It is possible," Carbonariis said. "The members of her society did not associate with many, as I understand. A cloistered order, if they'd taken vows. I did not know her. But the stories say she celebrated both the Mohawk ceremonies of her childhood and the sacraments of her Christian faith."

"Which means," Thomas said, "they'd have had a priest with them. At least one who visited regularly to celebrate Mass."

"But clearly not Ravenelle. He came a century later."

"Not him. But a Jesuit."

"Yes, one of your missionary brethren. What of it?"

"If we knew who he was, that priest, we could follow his trail. Ravenelle had the Ohtahyohnee. Where did he get it? When Ravenelle's life was in danger he gave the mask to a friend and extracted a promise to keep it safe. Why? Did Ravenelle know what it was, how it was used?" Thomas looked around at the others with a quiet excitement Livia recognized from their days in Rome. "Do you see? The Jesuit who ministered to Tekakwitha's community may have known the women were Shifters. If the Ceremony wasn't being done and the masks were being hidden one by one, if the medicine men were dying, too, then maybe a mask—this one— came into Tekakwitha's care. And she gave it to her priest. Maybe that knowledge is what's under seal at Il Gesù."

"Knowledge of the Shifters," Livia said softly. "Like knowledge of the Noantri, hidden by the Church for its own reasons." It would have meant so much to the Noantri to know this, she thought sadly. But been so dangerous to Michael's people, if it had been known.

Michael spoke. "All of this could be true. But what good does it do us? Ravenelle gave the mask to Hammill. Following Ravenelle might teach us something, but going back a hundred years before him—where will it get us?"

"And how will it be done, except at Il Gesù?" Carbonariis said. "I know nothing that can help."

Thomas's shoulders slumped. "No, you're right. I was just hoping . . . I suppose it was a long shot. Tekakwitha's society left no records, and it doesn't seem to have survived her death."

Carbonariis said, "It didn't. It dissolved, as though it had never been." He shook his head. "Gitgoo ungehsege wahgwenyu. *Omnia vanitas.* They honored only briefly, and they did not live on."

"Then we're wasting time," Michael said, standing. "I'm heading back to van Vliet's estate. I shouldn't have let Edward go. It was weakness. Someone there will tell me where he is. I—"

"Wait." Thomas lifted his hand. "Father Carbonariis, what did you say? They honored only briefly and they didn't live on?"

Carbonariis fixed his eyes on Thomas. "Gitgoo ungehsege wahgwenyu. In what is—now—an ancient dialect of Mohawk, 'to live on to honor it.' Tekakwitha had that as her society's name. Her symbol was the cross on the full moon."

"Grandmother Moon," said Michael. "She protected the twins who made the world. We honor her still."

"The full moon," Thomas said. "And the cross. And the motto *Praevalere et veneror.* 'Live on and honor.' I've seen it."

"Where?"

Thomas looked around at them all. "On a ring that Father Maxwell wears."

52

axwell?" Spencer saw Michael's brow furrow as he said to Thomas, "At Fordham? Your department chair?"

Thomas nodded. "He said he—"

Spencer held up a hand to silence them. A car door had shut in the street outside. He listened to the approaching footsteps and his Noantri sense of smell brought him additional information. "Michael. We're being visited by those charming detectives. I imagine their interest is rather more in you than me. Perhaps you'd care to wait in the kitchen until I send them away?"

By the time the bell actually rang, the kitchen door was clicking closed.

Spencer opened the front door and smiled. "Good afternoon, Detectives. How can I help you?"

"We're looking for Michael Bonnard," Charlotte Hamilton said. She appeared no more beguiled by Spencer than she had earlier in the day.

"I can't help you," Spencer said, still smiling.

"Can't or won't?"

"Does it matter?"

Before she could answer, the other detective, Framingham,

leaned past Spencer into the vestibule. "Hey!" He grinned and waved. Spencer turned and saw Thomas in the armchair in the parlor, just within Framingham's line of sight. "How ya doin', Father Kelly?" the detective called cheerily. "Hey, Hamilton, did you know these guys knew each other?"

"No, I didn't. Dr. George, what the hell is going on?"

"Many people, seeing a priest in my parlor, would ask the same."

"Now, Dr. George," Thomas said, rising. He came to stand beside Spencer at the door. "I've told you, it's nothing to be ashamed of." He smiled serenely at the detectives. "I'm Dr. George's spiritual adviser. He requested a scholar, someone who would understand him. A historian, as he is. I was sent."

"Really? What a coincidence. You being at Sotheby's last night, and now here."

"I was there for the same reason. To offer spiritual counseling to scholars."

"It's something of a specialty of Father Kelly's," Spencer said drily. "Comingling the immanent with the transcendent."

"And of mine." Another voice rang out, and the spectral form of Carbonariis loomed on Spencer's left.

"And you are?"

"Giovanni Antonio de Carbonariis. I was also sent to Dr. George, to offer a more rigorous interpretation of Scripture than my Jesuit colleague. A mind as fine as Dr. George's deserves no less."

"Surely, Father," Thomas protested, "the narrow pathway you propound—"

"Father, your own slippery, world-based formulations—"

"Gentlemen, please." Spencer looked to the detectives imploringly. "Do you see what I have to contend with? No wonder Michael refused to stay."

"He was here?"

"Until these two pious sages squared off. I rather enjoy such Catholic contentiousness, but Michael will have none of it."

"Where did he go?"

"I really couldn't say. Back to his laboratory, I would imagine, where nothing speaks in nonsensical ambiguities."

"We called. They say he's not there. And his cell phone goes to voice mail. Yours does, too, by the way."

"I've turned mine off so as not to be disturbed while I contemplate the spiritual gifts these holy men are offering. Michael often has his off when he's working, for much the same reason, though he's contemplating bacteria." Spencer looked both priests up and down, and shrugged.

"We need to talk to him. I'd like to come in."

"Entering my home will bring you no closer to your goal. And it might keep me from my spiritual one."

"What do you know about Bonnard's relationship with Brittany Williams?"

"I'm not aware he had one."

"Has he ever mentioned her to you?"

"He has not. Detectives, I really can't expect to keep these fine gentlemen here all day. If I'm to avail myself of their wisdom—"

"We'll come back with a warrant if we have to."

"At that point, I will let you in, as I will have to. Until then, I have the labor of the devout ahead of me and I'm anxious to get to it."

Spencer closed the door on the detectives. He turned to find Thomas grinning behind him. Even Carbonariis couldn't hide a dour smile.

"'Spiritual adviser'?" Spencer said. "Father Kelly, I commend you on your creativity, if not your devotion to objective possibility."

"Thanks. And I commend Father Carbonariis on his ability to usefully confuse the situation. A forte of Augustinians, that kind of obfuscation, if I'm not wrong."

Carbonariis glowered. "If you really are this man's spiritual adviser, Jesuit, I fear for his soul."

"On that score, you have no reason to worry," said Spencer. "And now I propose we leave this house at once, before another encounter with the forces of the law demands some even more outlandish response."

"I can't think what that could possibly be." Livia joined them from the parlor, where she had managed to remain hidden. "But don't you think they'll be watching the house?"

"I'm quite sure they will. Fortunately, this door is not the only exit. Another, in the rear, leads to a cramped but serviceable passageway to the next block."

Livia smiled. Spencer knew what she was thinking and if pressed he'd be inclined to agree. Livia's Change had come about in the twentieth century, when the fires were long past. The chary prudence of Noantri like Spencer was considered understandable but unnecessary by those younger; still, Spencer would not have been comfortable in a home without a second, and preferably hidden, exit. Adding that feature to his list of real estate requirements limited the housing inventory he was invited to examine—but not as much as he'd assumed it would. As it turned out, Prohibition, nearly a century before, had provided any number of exclusive dwellings with concealed escape routes.

Livia crossed the hall to open the kitchen door. "Michael, Thomas scared them away, you can . . ." Her words faded. She turned to the others. "He's gone."

53

The Protector had thought the mask was safe, at least for now. The Ohtahyohnee was a great deal on his mind lately, the inevitable result, he thought, of the upcoming Sotheby's sale and all the excited talk. But he'd thought its hiding place secure.

Now he was worried, though. Probably he was overreacting. Probably the sanctuary he'd given the Ohtahyohnee was as perfect as it had been when he'd selected it. But too much was going on. Questions now swirled, and people were taking notice of him, he who should have been invisible in the life of the Ohtahyohnee.

He himself, not the role he played, was the problem. He understood that. Another man might have done better. Another man might have been more equipped for the keeping of such a powerful secret. A man braver, or wiser, or more ruthless. Or were those the same? But there was no other man: the time and thus the duty had been his.

He hadn't sought out the obligation but he'd not turned from it, either. He'd searched for the Ohtahyohnee, as he must, as his predecessors had done; it was his honor and the mask's bad luck that he was the one of them who'd found it. He'd done what he could. And now again, he must do what he thought best. He must move the mask out of here, change the hidden shelter. The Ohtahyohnee had to be lodged in a place with no connection to him.

He wished he could consult with his brethren but the oath they'd taken forbade that. Through the centuries the members of the society had sworn to uphold two sacred trusts. The first, the identity of a Shifter, was a secret he himself had never been called upon to protect. Though how he wished he had been, how he wished he'd just once seen the Shift, seen the Creator's generous gift made visible before him. In that same way, the location of a mask was never to be shared until the mask was transferred to a new Protector. He and his brethren were to act as stewards, their sole duty to hold the masks in their care until the rightful owners could return for them. Centuries ago when their society was established it had seemed the wise path: each mask with its own guardian, no information shared. It wasn't his place to question the wisdom of those who had gone before, but he was disquieted at the knowledge that nothing now stood between the Ohtahyohnee and the world except himself.

But that was the circumstance, and he had to act upon it.

He pulled open the heavy door, entering the darkened space with great care. Earlier in the day when he'd gone out he'd had the odd feeling he was being watched, though he'd seen no one, nothing. He'd shaken that sense off, telling himself it was because he was fearful that he felt he had something real to fear. But his unease had underscored the rightness of his decision. He'd already determined to move the mask and had gone to its new home to assure himself everything was in order. He was grimly amused by his choice: a safe-deposit box very difficult to trace to him that he'd established years earlier, in case it was needed. The mask would rest in the vault of a bank whose fortune was rooted in the long-ago devastation of the animals and forests from which, in the beginning, this Ohtah-yohnee had come.

The door shut behind him and silence settled. He was alone here as he'd known he would be at this hour. The outer door, as always, was unlocked, but in the middle of the day no one came here—a shame, as the place, like others of its kind, had been built as a help to people hoping to rise above their lesser selves.

As he moved into the echoing room it gave him back no sound but his footsteps. A wan winter light struck odd colors from the high windows, barely enabling him to make out his own faint shadow on the stone floor. A shadow like his heart, he thought as he strode to the front: not strong, but nevertheless continuing forward.

A sound behind him, the faintest rustling. He turned sharply. No one, nothing. In the stillness he decided it had been no sound at all, just his dread taking external form. He continued on, turning left at the aisle. In the wall at the end nestled a small door, an unassuming element in the grand space. It gave access to a spiral staircase no longer used. Behind the staircase, between its enclosure and the next room, was an empty space, a stone cavern, of a kind that in this age of obsession with the value of every square foot would never be built. When this building was erected, though, pleasing dimensions and proportions of rooms were judged paramount. If empty space was required to achieve them, so be it. For his purposes, empty did not mean useless, and the philosophy of waste behind this aesthetic was a valuable if ironic aid.

Inside the tiny staircase-room, the walls faceted into a series of curved panels, three rows circling the room, seven panels making up each row. Their grainy oak surfaces appeared identical and undisturbed, but there the falsehood lay. In the center row, a light push on the smooth wood caused a delicately crafted panel to swivel, revealing the dark space within. He'd had this hidden niche built many years ago, not with any thought of ever truly needing it but for the same reason he'd acquired the safe-deposit box: his oath required him to be prepared. He wondered sometimes what sanctuaries his fellows had established, if any were like his. His curiosity was all the greater because he could not ask.

He lifted out the box from the shadowed shelf inside, feeling the heft. When he'd first held the copy he'd commissioned, now making such a stir at Sotheby's, it had proved heavier than expected. He'd expressed his misgivings to the maker and was assured the wood was identical, the depth of the carving the same. He had no option but to take the man's word for it. The maker—who'd never held the real one, never even seen it, but had done his remarkable work from photographs and descriptions—had proved correct. The Protector recognized from the moment he finally held the real Ohtahyohnee that it was as unyielding and substantial as the promises of the Creator.

The panel swung back into place with a click. Box under his arm, the Protector opened the stairwell door. He saw only dim stillness and left the small room, shutting the door behind him. He should take the mask and go, now while he knew he was alone; but he found himself unable. He had to see it again, to look once more upon its power. He couldn't leave this room without the chance to feel the glorious sensation—at once wildly electric and deeply tranquil—the sight of the Ohtahyohnee created in him.

He sat, placing the box on his lap. He opened the padded lid, untied the cord on the deerskin sack, slid out and unwrapped the blanket within, and the Ohtahyohnee was revealed. Even in the dim light, what force, what majesty! As always when he gazed on it he had a sense of a flame springing up deep within him. He regarded the Ohtahyohnee, felt himself smile, and silently told it, as he had before: *Your time will come again.*

He had just returned the mask to the darkness of the deerskin when he heard a sound, a rustling, nearby this time. He snapped his head around. In shock and fear, he choked: right behind and looming over him, a face, close, fearfully distorted. No sound came from it, but he could hardly look into the eyes, so full were they of fury and yearning. Arms reached for the Ohtahyohnee. He batted them away. Bent over the mask, cradling it, he started to stand. A blinding swipe, and fiery pain tore the side of his face. Hot blood obscured his vision. He staggered forward, clutching the mask all the tighter. He felt it being tugged, wrenched, but he wouldn't release it. Another blow knocked him forward. Screams echoed around the high stone room; he realized with a shock they were his own. Repeated blows fell on his head and shoulders. He tried to pull away, managed two steps, but slipped and fell. His head struck the cold stone floor. He saw a sickening swirl of colors; through it he kept as tight a grip as he was able, but his strength failed and he felt the Ohtahyohnee pulled from his grasp. As the colors faded and darkness took him, he offered a prayer, apologizing to the mask and the Creator for not being the man he should have been.

54

Matt Framingham climbed in the passenger door as Hamilton, dropping into the driver's seat, yanked out her cell phone. "Afternoon, Captain," he heard her say after a moment. "Charlotte Hamilton, Homicide. Can you send me a couple of unies for a surveillance on the Sotheby's case? Good, thanks." She gave Spencer George's address. "I'll stay until they come." Clicking off, she turned to Framingham, who spoke before she could.

"Captain Patino at the One-Nine. You don't think we have enough for a warrant but you want these guys watched because either Bonnard's really there, which is why they won't let us in, or he might show up. Or they know where he is and they'll be heading there. But you want unies to do it because you have something more exciting in mind for us."

"For extra credit," she said, "what is it?"

"Rockefeller? Maybe he's really in his lab?"

Charlotte jabbed the air as if hitting a button. "*Baaaap!* You fail. Rockefeller gets public funds, tax breaks, that shit. They know better than to lie to the NYPD even if a star scientist tells them to." She grinned. "Luckily, there's more than one way to track an Indian.

Soon as we turn this over, I'm hauling your white ass to an Indian bar."

The uniformed officers from the One-Nine came and settled in, armed with photos of Spencer George, Father Kelly, and the spooky-looking Carbonariis. "I didn't think you got him," Charlotte said when he showed her that shot. "You didn't make him look at you like you usually do."

"I snuck it in. I'm telling you, that is not a normal man. I didn't want to piss him off so he'd go back inside, and they'd slam the door and you wouldn't get your subtly intimidating interrogation done. Or he'd vanish in a puff of smoke. Or attack me and bite my head off."

"Literally?"

"Of course literally. Until I checked the screen I wasn't even sure he'd appear in the photo."

Framingham e-mailed the photos back to the squad room. On the drive to upper Manhattan Charlotte called Ostrander to tell him to dig deeper on Thomas Kelly and Spencer George, to find if there was any way to tie either of them to Brittany Williams, to Sotheby's, to Indian art, to anything Native at all. "Besides that, George seems to be dating an Abenaki guy we think might swing both ways," she said. "What? Abenaki, for God's sake, look it up. And see what you and Sun can come up with on this Carbonariis. He's some kind of priest, too. I just think something's going on here that's weirder than shit."

She laughed and clicked off.

"Ostrander was funny?" Framingham asked.

"Yeah. He said 'weirder than shit' makes it for sure your kind of case."

The Washington Heights block Charlotte pulled up on was like a thousand other run-down streets in New York and the bar beyond the pitted steel door was like a hundred other dives Framingham had seen. Except maybe for the drum on the wall and the old photos of long-haired guys in buckskin cradling rifles across their arms.

"Charlotte," said the bartender, and then with a noncommittal glance at Framingham, "this a social call or an official one?"

"Frankie," Charlotte acknowledged. "Detective Matt Framingham, this is Frankie Moore. He and his brother Len own this dump."

"Welcome to the Stonehenge, Detective," the bartender said. His manner didn't change, but Framingham guessed he was on notice now: Charlotte had announced this was business. "You guys on duty or you want a drink? Or you want a drink even though you're on duty?"

"Beers," said Charlotte, settling on a stool. "And whatever you're having, Frankie, if you want one."

Framingham understood and he sat, also. Alcohol on duty was against NYPD official policy, but some guys wouldn't trust you if you didn't drink with them and the brass had always appreciated that. The bartender uncapped two Labatt's and poured himself a Johnnie Walker Black. Ah, the high price of information.

"Looking for an Abenaki," Charlotte said, sipping her beer. "Name of Michael Bonnard. Know him?"

Frankie nodded. "Doc. He was here last night, a couple hours before you were. I was gone by then, and I forgot to tell Len about Doc or he'd have told you to call him."

Framingham thought he'd missed something but if he had, so had Charlotte. She said, "What?"

"You're looking for Doc to tell him you found Eddie, right?"

"Who's Eddie?"

"His brother." Frankie looked puzzled. "He was here last night looking for him. Doc was, I mean, for Eddie."

"Bonnard was here last night?"

"Sure. With some English guy. He said it was important that they find Eddie, but by the time Eddie got here they were long gone and so was I."

"Son of a bitch. They didn't tell us they were here."

Frankie hesitated. "They, who? Doc and the English guy? You found them already?"

"Lost them again, though."

Charlotte's voice had barely changed but Framingham could see anger in her tight jaw, in the straightening of her spine.

The bartender seemed to sense it, too. "Oh. Anyway, I don't know where Doc is but I can give you his number."

"I have it. He doesn't answer."

"Oh," he said again. "Maybe, you can ask Eddie. Maybe they even found each other already."

"Where do I find Eddie?"

"I don't know. I thought you would."

"Frankie, why the hell would I? I never heard of the guy until just now."

The bartender's face slipped from puzzled to uncomfortable. He cast a glance at Framingham, who smiled back brightly. "Um," Frankie said. "Eddie Bonnard. Tahkwehso. According to Len, you left with him last night."

55

S on of a bitch!" Charlotte, her face burning, slammed the car
door and grabbed for her phone. Framingham had barely gotten his side shut when she threw the car into gear and peeled
out. She drove with one hand and speed-dialed with the other.

"Ostrander."

"Get me warrants on Michael Bonnard and Spencer George.
And Father Thomas Kelly, while you're at it."

"You have something new?"

"They lied about their whereabouts last night."

"All of them?"

"At least two of them. Yeah, probably the priest, too."

"Good enough. I'll get on it."

"You know what? Carbonariis, too."

"Okay," Ostrander said. "I was about to call you anyway. You
sound pissed off."

"Goddamn right I am."

"Should I ask why?"

"No. Call me about what?"

"There's a body in the Bronx you might want to look at."

"Why would I?"

"One, it's an unexplained violent death where no one saw the perp come or go."

"A dime a dozen. And I'm kind of busy."

"Two, there's a box on the scene that's similar to the one the Sotheby's wolf mask is in, except it has more Indian stuff on it."

That stopped her. "There's another mask?"

"There's another box. Empty when the responding officers got there."

"What the hell do you mean by 'Indian stuff'?"

"Ah, there's the Hamilton I know and love."

"Screw you. What do you mean?"

"Trees, animals, I don't know. I can send a photo."

"Send it to Framingham, I'm driving. Who's the vic?"

"Framingham, if you're driving. I know, screw me. A priest named Gerald Maxwell."

"Who's he to me?"

"Maybe no one. But he's the head of the department at Fordham where your pal Father Kelly teaches."

Charlotte thumbed the phone off. She screeched into a U-turn on Broadway and was rewarded with blasting horns. Framingham, braced on the dashboard, said mildly, "I'm not sure you can arrest a guy and his friends because you slept with his brother."

"Shut the hell up!"

She drove like a rainstorm, siren blaring, lights flashing. She swerved and honked and used the adrenaline flood to let her muscles and her fingertips take the lead. It was a kind of meditation, driving like this, a space where her body could come forward and her mind retreat. It was like running or skydiving and it was working fine until Framingham yelped, "Jesus Christ, Charlotte! He won't be any more dead if we get there five minutes later!"

That smashed the mood, switched the autopilot off. She snarled, said nothing, but was forced to slow; and when she did, the question she'd been trying to outrun jumped out in front of her: *What the hell is she so upset about, really?* Spencer George and Co.? People lied about their whereabouts all the time. No, obviously it wasn't that. Yes, she seemed to have slept with her prime suspect's brother, but she'd been put on the damn case because she was an Indian, and when you factor in the Indian bar, her going home with Tahkwehso—Eddie goddamn Bonnard!—could be written off as just one big sick coincidence. Embarrassing, but when had she ever given a crap about being embarrassed? But she was mad. She was furious. Why?

Tahkwehso. Eddie Bonnard. Whatever the hell his name was. Reluctantly she forced her mind to stay with him until she got it.

She didn't want him to be a suspect's brother.

She didn't want him to be any part of this case. Of any case. Of anything dirty. Earthbound. Bad. She wanted him to be—*what, Charlotte, for God's sake? The Noble Savage? The Indian at the End of the World?* What the hell was she thinking? He was a great lay, a nice enough guy, but . . . She tried to shake it off, this odd feeling of both connection and protection. How many one-night stands had she had? And how many had been Indians? It was a minor specialty of hers, and now, suddenly, she found herself spoiling for a fight because this one guy, some damn long-hair just down off the rez, was turning out to be what he shouldn't have been: human.

She was grateful when, in what might have been record time from Washington Heights, they roared through the gate into the Fordham parking lot. The security guard pointed them across campus before Charlotte asked. Crime Scene and the ME's crew were already there, vehicles and cops and techs scattered around the stone chapel. A three-deep crowd of gawkers stood shooting pictures with their phones. Charlotte parted them like an icebreaker, Framingham in her wake. At the yellow tape she barked, "Who's in charge?"

"That would be me," a chubby, mustached man said. "John Ciara, Bronx Homicide, out of the Four-One."

Charlotte showed her badge, said, "Charlotte Hamilton," and had the irrational urge to add, "Lenape." She was saved by Framingham, who gave his name and, with an odd look at her, wagged his thumb back and forth between them and said, "Midtown South Homicide."

"They told me you were coming." Ciara led the way into the chapel. In the high stone room Crime Scene's brilliant lights gleamed off polished pews and banished the winter dusk to the corners. "What's your interest?"

"The Sotheby's vic from last night," Charlotte said. "You heard about that? This could be related."

"No shit." They reached the eye of the cop-tech hurricane and stopped. "Well," Ciara said, "this guy went down fighting."

Tape perimeter, fingerprint powder, lights and noise and white-suited techs: all the bustle faded as Charlotte knelt over the body. Open eyes, blood pooled under the head, deep scratches on the face. Without touching him, she leaned closer, to examine the hands. Hallelujah, blood and gunk under the fingernails and on the priest's gold ring. Unless he'd scratched up his own face, it was the killer's and there'd be DNA. She let her gaze travel the body, its position, the eyes and the angle of the head. As Ciara said, he'd put up a fight, this priest, and he'd died terrified. But bending over him, Charlotte found her spine and fingertips tingling, saw colors get sharper, and her instinct, that whatever-it-was that kicked in sometimes, was telling her those facts weren't related quite the way Ciara seemed to think. This man hadn't fought because he was afraid to die. He was in danger of losing something and he was fighting to keep it. To save it from someone else. His killer had taken—had come for, she was rock-solid sure—whatever was in the box, and Father Maxwell had died trying to protect it.

"Do you want it?"

"What?" Squinting against the lights, Charlotte looked up at Ciara. "Do I want what? What was in the box?"

He frowned. "The case. Yours if you want it, otherwise we'll keep it in the Bronx."

"No," said Charlotte. "I want it. This box—it was like this when you got here?"

"Yes. Open and empty."

"Do you know what was in it?" She stood and slipped between the pews to where the wooden box sat.

"No. Or where it is now. Or whether it had anything to do with what went on here, even. We printed it and we're working on the pews and everything else around here, but the place is never locked, so good luck. I have a preliminary list of his coworkers and friends, and people out canvassing for witnesses. The president of the university's been calling every ten minutes."

"Keep him away from me. Give the info you have to Framingham. Keep the canvass going." Charlotte spoke vaguely, not looking at Ciara. "The box. It's been swabbed, printed, everything? I can examine it?"

"Knock yourself out."

She sat on the smooth cool pew, taking the box onto her lap, closing the lid. She hadn't realized she was cold, but she must have been because the box warmed her. Probably because it had been under the lights for a while, that was why. She peeled off her latex gloves. The carved wood felt good, oddly familiar under her fingers, though she'd never seen this box before. It was roughly the same size and shape as the one at Sotheby's that held the Ohtahyohnee mask, but where that box was beautifully crafted, padded inside, but unadorned—something commissioned by a collector for the protection of his investment—this one seemed considerably older, with evidence of wear. It was beautiful but more crudely put together, as though made by a skilled craftsman with less refined tools. Its hinged lid bore lines of stylized river water and pointed pine trees, and images of eagle, bear, and wolf. She let her fingertips wander along the river and then slowly opened the lid. The box was unlined; whatever had been in it, then, must have been well wrapped. On the underside of the lid she saw a carved cross superimposed on Grandmother Moon, and the words *Praevalere et veneror*. Latin? She traced the words with a finger.

"Charlotte? Hey, Hamilton. Anyone home?"

Framingham's voice reached Charlotte from a long distance away. She looked up at the bright lights and chapel walls and blinked. Grandmother Moon? When had she ever thought like that? She gazed once more at the cross, at the words. Without answering Framingham she put the box aside, worked her way back to Maxwell's body, and lifted his hand. On the bloodied gold ring on the priest's fourth finger she saw the same image, and the same words.

Straightening, she spoke to the ME's men, who were drinking coffee in a nearby pew. "You can take him away now. Bag the hands," she said to make sure, and was rewarded with an eye roll. She turned to her partner. "What, Matt?"

Framingham's brow creased. "You okay?"

"Yeah, just great. What is it?"

"Uh-huh, you look great. Okay, don't slug me. One of Ciara's canvassers found a witness you might want to talk to."

"About what?" Charlotte followed Framingham out of the pew and down the aisle.

"She was almost knocked down by a guy tearing out of here like he'd seen a ghost. Maybe the same ghost you just saw." He gave her a sideways look and she scowled at him.

"Did she give a description of this guy? Aside from if he's seeing ghosts, he's crazy like you?"

"Big. Moderately dark-skinned—she thought maybe Hispanic. And he's favoring his left side, as though his shoulder hurt."

"Son of a bitch. Michael Bonnard?"

"That was my first thought."

"Was he alone?"

"You mean was his brother with him?"

"I mean, was he alone!" But she meant, *Was his brother with him?* Framingham was smart enough not to pursue it.

Charlotte met the witness, a backpack-toting student, and tried for more details. She showed the girl Bonnard's picture and got a shrug, maybe yes, maybe no. Would she recognize the man again? Maybe yes, maybe no. Which direction did he go? Like, sort of that way. Was anyone with him? Didn't see anyone, but like, I wasn't looking, you know? While Charlotte's blood pressure rose, Framingham answered his ringing cell phone. She heard, "Great," then, "No shit," then, "Okay, I will." He held his phone out to her. "Ostrander. He called me in case you were still driving."

"Get her contact details." Charlotte pointed at the witness as she took Framingham's phone. "What, Vinnie?"

"Got your warrants. Michael Bonnard, Spencer George, Thomas Kelly, Father Whatshisname Carbonariis. Material witnesses, all of them."

"Good enough for now. That it?"

"Hardly. The unies up in Riverdale called. Three people showed up at that house. Two men—long hair in braids, the older one with silver jewelry—"

"Just say, 'They look like Indians.'"

"I don't have the balls. And a woman a little later."

"Do they know who? Do they have photos?"

"No. They're at a distance and they have binocs but not long-lens cameras. Budget issue."

"Screw it. We're on the way."

"You need backup?"

"We'll use the unies, and the precinct up there, if we do."

"There's one more thing, but ask Framingham, because it's bullshit."

"Okay. Thanks." She clicked off and tossed the phone back to Framingham. She started across the campus at a fast clip.

He trotted after her. "Where are we going?"

"Riverdale. I'm supposed to ask you about something."

"Carbonariis."

"I don't know."

"That's what Ostrander said."

"To me he said it was bullshit."

"He did? I'm supposed to Wikipedia him."

"Carbonariis? He's got an entry?"

"Maybe he's famous."

They climbed in the car. While she slammed it into gear and

drove, Framingham bent over his phone, his thumbs tapping. "Oh. Oh, holy crap. Charlotte, you have to see this. No, dammit, wait till you stop!"

She leaned over anyway. On the screen of his phone she saw a black line illustration, like an old woodcut. "Son of a bitch!" She turned her attention back to the street and the honking traffic. "That's him. He is famous."

"Yeah, well," said Framingham, "he's also really, really old. What he's famous for is founding the first Christian settlement in North America. In 1497."

"Oh. I guess we met a descendant. Do priests have descendants?"

Framingham didn't answer. He'd enlarged the picture on his screen and was staring at it.

"Matt?"

"Not a descendant." Framingham spoke in an odd mixture of trepidation and excitement. "I told you, there was something seriously weird about that guy. This"—he waved his phone—"is the guy we met."

"Please tell me you're just trying to lighten the mood."

"Charlotte. It's this guy. You felt it, too, I know you did. His totally weird vibe. *Totally* weird. And how many of these guys could there be?"

"At least two."

"No. It's him. The simplest explanation is always the best. The simplest explanation: he's not human."

"Sure," Charlotte sighed, "I get it. A weird pale guy centuries old—he's a vampire. Jesus Christ, Matt, if I didn't know you were crazy, I'd think you were crazy."

56

Abornazine drove steadily south on the last leg of their journey. Next to him, Tahkwehso sat, back straight, staring ahead. The lack of connection to the road and the unnatural speed with which distance could be covered made Tahkwehso uncomfortable traveling by car. Abornazine, knowing this, always hesitated to ask him to make a trip, but this time it was Tahkwehso himself who'd insisted.

"He won't stop," he'd said, returning to Abornazine's study after Michael Bonnard had driven away from Eervollehuis earlier in the day. When the brothers left the house, Abornazine let himself be seen leaving also, and then hid in the woods, understanding that Michael would come back for him if Tahkwehso couldn't turn his brother's heart to their cause. If twin would not respond to twin, no words from Abornazine would convince, and his own physical powers were waning. There was no shame in retreat, no glory in howling defiance into your enemy's teeth to spark a battle you knew you wouldn't win.

When Michael drove away Abornazine came back to the house, and when Tahkwehso also returned Abornazine could tell he'd Shifted, had inhabited his wolf-self for a time. The deep weariness that always accompanied his return to his man-form was with him, the weariness but also the electricity that came: the charge Abornazine could all but see throwing blue sparks around him. "My brother doesn't stop," he said. "From the time we were young. He moves untiringly along narrow paths. If he can't find us he'll find the Ohtahyohnee. If it's in his power to stop us, he won't let us continue. I had him. I should not have let him go."

"He'd have fought you," Abornazine said, hoping to comfort. "Only one of you would have come out of that battle."

Tahkwehso had turned away, to the windows and the winter field beyond. "I would have been the one."

"Still. There must be some other way. He's your *brother*."

Tahkwehso had not answered.

Nor had he spoken since they'd left, just sat watching the road and the winter cliffs. Now, as the purple dusk gathered and they turned off the parkway to roll slowly down the curving Riverdale street, Abornazine said to him, "I may be wrong."

At first, silence. Then, "If you're wrong, we'll continue searching. We can't stop now. It's too important, and our goal is too near, to stop. Or to let my brother stop us."

They drove past large homes fading in the twilight. The irony was not lost on Abornazine: to the great estate they were headed for, from another—his own. What was wrong with his people, he asked himself as he had so many times, that they made "good" synonymous with "large"? For himself, he was thankful to have been permitted to put his house and his wealth in the service of the People.

He gave his name—his white name—at the gate and was rewarded with a long silence and then a wordless buzz. Their arrival must have created the stir he'd anticipated, because the door opened before the car was parked and, alongside the redoubtable Hilda, Bradford Lane stood waiting in the doorway.

"Christ!" Lane cackled as they approached. "It really is you, Peter van Vliet, you old fraud! I didn't believe it when Hilda told me, and I can't see worth a damn anymore but I'd know you anywhere— you still wear enough silver to sound like Santa's sleigh." He paused and frowned. "Who's with you?"

"Tahkwehso." He introduced himself, reaching for Lane's hand with both his own. "Abenaki. We're grateful to be received in your home."

"Oh, Jesus. Van Vliet, you never change, do you? Fine, Tah-kwehso, welcome. Hilda, they're in, so you might as well bring coffee. Getting to be a regular Grand Central Station around here." He turned and, with stiff but even steps—he was counting, Abornazine realized—he walked back through the entryway. They followed him across a living room bare-walled and empty-shelved to the warmth of the sunroom, where Lane settled into an armchair and waved his guests to seats. "So, Peter"—he grinned as though an argument were over and he'd won it—"what the hell are you doing here? If you were hoping to get your hands on the goodies before everyone else, you're out of luck." He spread his arms joyfully. "It's all gone. You'll have to go to Sotheby's tomorrow and bid with the rest of the vultures."

"I can see everything's gone," Abornazine said. "I'm sorry. I know how you loved the things you had."

"For God's sake, if it's my funeral you've come for, you're early. Write a eulogy if you want but don't try it out on me. Tahkwehso, who the hell are you?"

"A friend."

"Not of mine, so you must be a friend of this charlatan's. You understand there's nothing real about him except his money?"

"I've found the truth to be different, but I'll consider your words."

"You do that. Peter, I don't think I've seen you in fifteen years. Last I heard you were out West living with some old Navajo."

"Atsa. He taught me many things."

"'He taught me many things.' You even talk like a B movie. Or maybe I don't get out much. Tahkwehso, do real Indians talk like that now?"

Tahkwehso smiled. "People speak in many different ways."

"What are you, an Abenaki politician? Now: I don't know any-thing about the murder at Sotheby's. I never met the girl. I under-stand all my pieces are intact. The sales are going ahead. If any of those things are what you came about, there you are and you can leave before the coffee comes."

"We're not here for those reasons," Abornazine said.

"Then I can't imagine why you *are* here, and I can't wait to find out. Where the hell is Hilda?"

"I'm right here, Mr. Lane." The unsmiling woman came down the steps and set a tray on the wicker side table at Lane's elbow. "It's getting toward evening. Your guests need light."

"Then turn it on, for God's sake."

Abornazine bit his tongue. Soft winter twilight filled the room, the dusk within identical to that beyond the glass walls. No electric light could be as welcoming or as profound; nevertheless Hilda flicked a switch. Abornazine narrowed his eyes against the sudden, mundane brightness. Hilda cast an ominous look at the visitors as she turned and left.

"Help yourselves," Lane said. "Someone pour me one. Black with two sugars."

Abornazine did that, and poured a cup for himself. Tahkwehso rarely took caffeine, but a guest didn't refuse a host, so he prepared a cup with a lot of milk.

"All right," Lane said. "You're not here for the gory murder details—you knew about that, though?"

"Yes."

"Did you bring *me* any gory details?"

"No."

"Oh, hell. And you didn't come sniffing around for anything I own?"

"No."

"Then please enlighten me. To what do I owe this dubious honor?"

Abornazine exchanged a glance with Tahkwehso. "We want to talk about the Ohtahyohnee."

"Hah! I should've known. I've had people here all day talking about the damn Ohtahyohnee. Detectives, and a priest, and some woman who's as phony as you are, Peter. Claimed to be here for the conference but about Native art, she doesn't know her ass from a hole in the ground."

"What about an Abenaki?" Tahkwehso asked suddenly. "Has another Abenaki come to ask about it?"

"Not unless one of those detectives was one. I suppose that's possible, now that I think about it. If either one was, though, they didn't say."

"The Ohtahyohnee," Abornazine said, watching Lane closely. "I was right, then? It is yours?"

"So what? That cat's out of the bag. I don't care."

SAM CABOT

"Bradford, it's not real."

"Oh, no!" Lane gulped coffee and clinked his cup into his saucer. "Don't *you* start! That woman tried the same thing on me. Peter, if you're trying to drive the price down, I swear I'll have your head on a platter. Though I'd heard you weren't bidding."

"No, I hadn't planned to." Quite the contrary: Abornazine had taken pains to conceal his desire for the Ohtahyohnee, avoiding the auction house, the talk and the fuss, the consortium of his fellow collectors hoping to buy it for the Met. He and Tahkwehso had no doubt of Tahkwehso's ability to acquire it as they needed to, and the ease of his rooftop leap and entry into Sotheby's through the open terrace had proved them right. The only catastrophic hitch in their plans had been the mask's false nature.

"Then what do you care whether it's real or not?" Lane demanded. "And how would you even know? The Met says it is, the Quai Branly says it is, Sotheby's experts say it is. What do you know that they don't?"

"He knows nothing," Tahkwehso said quietly. "I know."

Lane frowned. "You've seen it?"

"Yes."

"And you're an expert? A scholar? You have some secret knowledge no one else has?"

"I have no knowledge. But I have a way of knowing. About these masks, there is a way to know."

Lane sat silent. "No," he said finally. "Really. You cannot be trying to feed me that line. Gentlemen, I may be old and blind but my mother raised no stupid children. If you think you—"

"There is a way," Abornazine said with gentle firmness, "and Bradford, you clearly know what that way is. The mask's not real."

296

"The only way I know"—Lane spoke carefully, as though enunciating for people having trouble following him—"is what's written in the oldest stories. If that's what you're trying to say, that amounts to you, Tahkwehso, telling me to my face that you're a shapeshifter. Since, for one thing, no real shapeshifter would ever do that, and since, for another thing, *there are no goddamn real shapeshifters*"—he leaned back in his chair—"I have to ask myself what is the point of all this. And whether it might be time to call Hilda to throw you two lunatics out."

Abornazine looked in the direction of the unseen river beyond the windows. Their own reflections met his gaze, and nothing was visible in the blackness outside. He turned back to Lane. "The point," he said, "is that we need the real mask. I believe you had that, once. I believe the one now at Sotheby's was substituted at some time and you never knew. We're asking you to help us. Please. To try to find out when the switch was made, and by whom, and why. And where the real Ohtahyohnee is now."

"You're insane. Get out of my house."

"We need the mask," Abornazine went on as though Lane hadn't spoken, "to perform the Awakening Ceremony. Yes, Tahkwehso is a Shifter. He breaks his oath to say it, and that should give you a sense of how urgent our need is. There are others like him, and once we've performed the Ceremony with the power of the Ohtahyohnee, there will be many more. Think whatever pleases you, but what harm could come from giving us your help?"

"You do need help, but not the kind I can give. Tahkwehso, are you as crazy as he is?"

"I know the same truths he knows."

"So the answer's yes. If I could see, I'd say prove it. Turn into an

SAM CABOT

eagle or a wolf or whatever it is, right now. But you know I can't do that, don't you? You know you could put on a fur coat and tell me anything you wanted to. Get out, both of you."

"Bradford—"

"Goddammit, Peter! Even a blind man can see through this! I stand to make several million dollars tomorrow on that Sotheby's sale. Provided no one suddenly says, 'Lane isn't sure anymore. He thinks that madman van Vliet might be right when he says the masks were switched at birth.' One word of doubt from me on the Ohtahyohnee and the authenticity of *everything* in the collection is suddenly in question. What are you trying to do to me?"

"Whatever you tell us, no one would know."

"Really? How do I know you're not wired for sound? You could be transmitting every word we say back to that consortium you say you're not part of. You might—"

Abornazine's cell phone started to ring.

"Hah!" Lane chortled. "That's them, telling you to give up now that you're busted. Hello, you thieves! Go to hell!"

Abornazine looked at Tahkwehso as he took his phone from his pocket. Little was more important than what they were doing now, but this could be someone from Eervollehuis to tell him Michael had returned. The number wasn't familiar, but once he answered, he knew the voice and the name. He was about to say he couldn't speak now, when he heard words that froze him.

"I have the mask."

"What?"

"The Ohtahyohnee. The true one. I have it now."

Abornazine was at a loss.

"You know the one at Sotheby's isn't real, don't you? I have the real one. I want to give it to you. But there's something I want, too."

298

57

ivia focused on her driving, trying not to get caught up in the riptides of emotion around her. Her Noantri senses picked up heart rates, stress hormones, and sweat as easily as strained voices and tense postures; in a car with Spencer angry and worried, Thomas Kelly confused and anxious, and the extraordinary Giovanni Antonio de Carbonariis glittering with doom, it was all she could do to stay steady on the road.

They were in her rented Malibu heading for Fordham's Bronx campus. "Where else would he have gone?" Spencer snapped once they'd discovered Michael had slipped away while they were busy with the detectives. "He'd just learned from Father Kelly that Father Maxwell had a connection to Tekakwitha and possibly to the mask. He has to assume his brother might have somehow learned the same, and in any case it's the only new idea we have. Oh, *why* won't he answer his cell phone?"

"Because it's off, Spencer. He told you he was keeping it off. And in case the police are tracking yours, you should turn that off, too."

"Damn the police. Then please give me yours."

She had, and Spencer, sitting beside her, was using it to try to reach Michael every ninety seconds.

He'd just lifted it to his ear again when it rang. Scowling, he handed it to Livia. "Whoever it is, explain that you're busy."

She took the phone and said, "Livia Pietro."

"Livia, it's Michael."

"Michael! Where are you?"

Livia got no further; Spencer snatched the phone from her. "Michael? What are you doing? Of course you couldn't, you insisted that I turn it off. Where are— What? I'm sorry, what?" He listened, and when he spoke again his voice was more subdued. "Oh. Oh, I see. Yes. No. As it happens we're already headed there, and if you'd waited— Of course we are. Well, I'm sorry if that's what you want, but I categorically refuse to stay away if you— No, I'll— What? He is? Now? No, Michael, don't hang up! Put me on hold, I'll wait— Michael, do *not* hang up! Michael! Michael?" Spencer lowered the phone, his lips pressed tight together. "Extraordinary. Father Carbonariis, are all Indians like that?"

"It's not an easy question to answer," said the spectral form in the backseat, "since I have no point of reference. What do you mean by 'that'?"

"Livia, that man Bradford Lane, in Riverdale. Do you know how to get to his home?"

"I can figure it out."

"Please do so, and change our course appropriately. Father Carbonariis, in answer to your question, I was inquiring whether in your experience Michael's people tend to be headstrong, stubborn, and obdurate to the point of absurdity."

"Some do. Like priests, I think. Or Noantri."

"That is neither an explanation nor a recommendation."

"You didn't request either of those."

"Spencer, why are we going to Bradford Lane's?" Livia interrupted. "Is that where Michael is? He didn't go to Fordham?"

"He did, and he's leaving there now. Clandestinely, I might add. Bradford Lane's home is his destination, if I'm correct."

"If you're correct? He didn't tell you that?"

"He hung up because his friend Lou was on the line. Lou is the gentleman Michael sent to keep an eye on the home of Bradford Lane. He was to inform Michael if his brother Edward, or indeed anyone of interest, appeared. If Lou has called, a strong possibility exists that Edward has gone to see Mr. Lane, in which case, we ourselves might want to do the same. In the meantime"—he turned in his seat to face Thomas—"Father Kelly, I'm afraid I have rather bad news for you."

58

The old blind man, Bradford Lane, was having trouble waiting. Edward could tell that Abornazine was, also. Neither spoke, but they drummed their fingers, rubbed their foreheads, crossed and recrossed their legs as they sat in the warm, plant-filled room. Some of the elders said it was a fault in white people's blood that caused this lack of patience. Edward thought not. He blamed a weakening of the spirit that came from long experience, both personal and cultural, of getting one's way. Of defining one's way as apart from and in opposition to the way of the rest of Creation. But when he saw Abornazine stand, take three steps to nowhere, and sit again—Abornazine, who'd done his best to walk the path of the People since boyhood—Edward considered if it might be true. A genetic failure, his brother would call it. Michael's work, his wasted life, was his own failure: studying the genetics of the People, the makeup of their blood, instead of learning and being transformed by the simple truths he'd been born to understand.

Edward himself sat unmoving, smelling the damp soil in the clay pots around him, feeling the moist warmth on his skin. He was as anxious as they to see this Ohtahyohnee, to know if the mask being brought to them was the true one, but nothing he could do would make it arrive sooner.

Bradford Lane, at first, had not wanted it to arrive at all. Abornazine, after listening to his caller with obviously growing excitement, agreed to some arrangement and said into the phone, "Bring it here." He gave Lane's address.

"What the hell are you doing?" Lane had barked at him. "Whoever that is, I don't want them here and I don't want you here, either, Peter. Leave now, unless you're prepared to tangle with Hilda."

"It's the Ohtahyohnee," Abornazine had said, lowering his phone. "She's bringing it."

"Who is? Estelle? She's bringing it back? What are you talking about?"

"Not Estelle. Though why don't you call her? Ask her if it's at Sotheby's. The one you sent."

"Why should I?"

"Because, Bradford, I'm fairly certain that the one that's coming is the real one."

Lane had made that call, and, thumbing his phone off, said, "It's there. It's fine and it's going nowhere and the whole place is under armed guard. What the hell is coming here and who the hell is bringing it?"

"The real mask is coming. Katherine Cochran is bringing it."

Lane frowned. "What makes you think it's any more real than the one at Sotheby's? Where did she get one? And why is she bringing it here?"

"She knows what I can do."

"What the hell are you— Oh, my lord. Not seriously. The Ceremony, you're talking about? She wants to see you do an Awakening Ceremony? Am I the last sane person left on earth?"

"Maybe, Bradford, you're a cynic whose faith is about to be restored. Now, we'll wait."

For twenty minutes the three of them had sat, Abornazine vibrating with excitement, Lane irritated, though curious and growing more and more impatient, and Edward quiet. If this was the real Ohtahyohnee about to arrive, he would need his strength.

59

Even sitting a few feet from the bundle as she drove, Katherine could feel the power of the Ohtahyohnee through the blanket, through the deerskin. She regretted leaving the box. It had its own history, it might have had things to teach. But it would have slowed her too much. The weight and heft of the mask alone had been almost more than she could handle.

Remorse for the death of the Protector came and went. Perhaps she could have found another way. She'd gone hoping—expecting—only to talk to him. To thank him for his untiring attention to the mask and to relieve him of the burden she knew it must be. The Protectors, the stories said, were stewards, keeping the masks safe until their true owners came again to claim them. They were priests, the Protectors, a line of Jesuit religious men from a society founded at the time of the wars and diseases, when the nations were just starting to understand that the new pale tribe from over the sea had not come to share the bounty of the land, but to seize it to use and destroy. The society and its oath remained a secret so deep that its existence was hidden even from others of its order.

Katherine was not a medicine woman. She couldn't perform the Ceremony and it would be wrong for her to try. But nothing happened by accident. Almost exactly a year ago Peter van Vliet had told her, as though sharing a confidence he couldn't keep to himself any longer, that he'd been taught the Awakening Ceremony. And now, the Ohtahyohnee had appeared. A false one, to throw others off the trail; and the true one, a path to which had been opened to her. She'd first understood the possibilities when Livia confirmed Katherine's own doubts. What followed had been a great deal of thought and a tense conversation with Ted Morse, filled with gentle, veiled threats from Katherine and stammers and sweat from the restorer, and then, finally, her answer.

So she'd hurried to talk to the Protector. A helpful student had seen him go in the direction of the chapel. Katherine had no idea when she followed him into the vast, dim room that the mask was near. If he hadn't unwound the blanket, if the resplendent face of the Ohtahyohnee hadn't leapt at her out of the gloom, her response might have been more measured. But the unexpected sight had called forth that ferocity from deep within that she'd first felt on a summer evening so many years ago, as a young girl on the edge of the swamp spying on the secret ceremonies of the Seminole. The naked young boy kneeling in front of the singer seemed to have no reaction at all, but Katherine, hidden in the cypresses, had been staggered by a wild, skyrocketing exaltation. When it passed, hours later, she found herself in a different part of the cypress grove, exhausted and hopelessly bereft. From that night on she'd devoted her life to the understanding of what had happened, in the faint hope that she might find it again. Van Vliet's boast had triggered a hunger in her that she'd barely dared to admit, and when Morse led her to the true Ohtahyohnee, that hope blazed like the light of angels.

But Father Maxwell had tried to keep the Ohtahyohnee from her. She was sorry he'd died. Yet the purpose of his life was to serve this mask, and the mask no longer needed him. His place in the afterlife was assured, and she had no doubt the Creator would greet him with thanks and praise.

Katherine had reached her destination. She announced herself at the gate and was buzzed in. Leaving her car, she cradled the bundle and ran toward the house. A wild north wind whipped bare tree branches overhead, changing, second by second, the pattern of the stars. Oh, glorious! Just before she stepped onto the porch she turned to look at the moon, starkly white and full. A promise, an abounding hope, like her own, and inexorable. Nothing men could do could stop the phases of the moon. Nothing any man could do, now, could stop her from reaching her true self.

She rang; she was admitted. In the jungle warmth of a plant-filled solarium she found Bradford Lane, and Peter van Vliet, and a long-haired man she didn't know. Van Vliet and the other man stood as she came down the steps; it was keenness, not courtesy, she could see that in their eyes. Lane remained seated but he leaned forward, as tight with anxious desire as the other two.

"Peter." She nodded. "Bradford." She was mildly astonished to hear her own voice, speaking normal words in normal tones as though nothing had changed.

"Are you all right?" van Vliet asked. "Your face—"

"What?" She touched her cheek where it stung and was surprised to see blood on her fingertips. "Nothing, it's nothing." She turned to the third man. "Who are you?"

"Tahkwehso." Smiling, he reached for the bundle in her arms.

She took a step back. "Not you. Peter. If you can do what you say. Otherwise I'm gone again."

"I can," said van Vliet with quiet confidence. "If the mask is real. Give it to Tahkwehso. He'll know."

She frowned, but after a moment lay the bundle in the man's arms like a mother handing her newborn to a stranger. Tahkwehso sat and she watched his long fingers untie the deerskin cord. The folds of the blanket slipped to drape over his knees as he lifted the mask free of the sack. Little about him changed. His impassive face, his quiet body, appeared as they might have if he'd been inspecting a cooking pot someone was offering for sale. But the light Katherine saw in his eyes was identical, she understood, to the dazzling hope inside herself. Only in him, it wasn't hope: it was knowledge.

"The mask is real," he said.

"Give it to me!" Bradford Lane burst out. "What the hell do you people know? If it's the real one—if it's *mine*—I'll be able to tell."

Tahkwehso rose to walk across the room. As he did the angle at which he held the Ohtahyohnee changed. The black, bottomless eyes stared straight into Katherine's. Her breath caught, her pulse hammered. She'd seen the mask only in the chapel's dimness and she'd wrapped it as soon as she held it. Now, in the bright room, the Ohtahyohnee's gaze seared her, scorching the lifelong layers of her own mask to find and ignite her true heart. Icily terrified, burning with need, she couldn't turn away.

It turned away from her, allowing her to breathe again, as Tahkwehso laid it across Lane's lap. The old man ran his fingers along its carved surfaces, inside and out. He wrapped his palm around its muzzle, traced the savage teeth. No one made a sound. Van Vliet smiled softly, his gaze riveted on the mask. Beside Katherine, Tahkwehso stood, taut, without movement or expression.

Hoarsely, Lane spoke. "This is my wolf mask."

Katherine answered, "The Ohtahyohnee."

"What is at Sotheby's?"

"One made to replace it."

"Where did you get it?"

"From the man who stole it."

"Who was that man?"

"Monsignor Maxwell."

"He was a thief?"

"He was a Protector."

Lane shook his head. "The oldest stories . . ."

Katherine said, "The stories know."

"Tell me how *you* knew."

"From the man who made the other."

"That man?"

"Ted Morse."

"He can't have."

"He had photographs."

"Photographs are nothing."

Katherine walked slowly forward to stand beside him, beside the mask. "The photographs, and the details. From the Hammill papers. And Maxwell's knowledge. And," she added, "you had no sight."

Lane drew a sharp breath. "But when I held it, why didn't I know?" He stopped. His face changed. "It was the fire. It was the fire, wasn't it?"

"It took years to make the mask. Years, from the time Gerald Maxwell came here. Maxwell knew your sight was failing. By the time of the fire it was gone. No one else had seen the Ohtahyohnee."

"Maxwell set the fire?"

"Making sure it wouldn't come near this room. In the chaos he slipped inside and switched the masks. Morse said that's what Maxwell planned, and he understood everything had gone well. After the fire you never took the mask down until Estelle came for it, did you?"

"No. No, I didn't. I couldn't bear to. Why did he do it?"

"Morse? Because Father Maxwell paid him well and promised never to sell it or show it. Father Maxwell didn't say more, but Morse understood."

"Understood what?"

"That Father Maxwell was this mask's Protector. Each mask has one."

"The masks are all gone."

"Or they're not. This one is still here. Every Protector has sworn an oath to continue to seek his mask and safeguard it if he finds it."

Lane sat silent; then he smiled. "The copy—tell me. How good is it?"

"It's very, very good."

Lane nodded, still smiling, his hands on the Ohtahyohnee. Katherine turned to van Vliet. "Peter. Your promise."

"Yes," he said. "Although . . ."

"Oh, here it comes!" Lane roused himself from his reverie. "You told her to bring you my mask and you'd do the Ceremony. You promised to turn her into a deer or some damn thing, didn't you?" Katherine could see a laughing anger kindling in him, driving out the clouds of uncertainty, of confusion. "But now you're going to tell us why you can't. The night's too dark or the wind's too strong or the Great Spirit isn't talking to you right now, is that it, Peter? So you'll just take it with you, and maybe another time? In your dreams, bully boy."

"To do it here"—van Vliet spoke uncertainly to Tahkwehso—

"where we haven't prepared, where there are two without the Power who'll merely observe . . ."

"You've performed the Ceremony for hundreds and most have turned out to be nothing more than observers. And"—Tahkwehso grinned—"how can you know neither of these two will respond? The blood of the People flows through many veins."

"Oh, my God!" Bradford Lane bellowed. "You think Hilda and I are Indians, too? Holy smokes, I haven't had this much fun in years."

"The moon is full," Tahkwehso went on, "the wind is high, and the sky is clear. It is a good time."

"The moon will be full again next month." Van Vliet turned to Katherine. "Come to Eervollehuis. You'll meet others, you'll share our life. I can prepare."

"Not there! Not next month!" Katherine felt a jolt of fear, a blaze of rage. "Now! Here! Or I'll take it away with me. I'll find someone else." Before she could reach for the Ohtahyohnee a powerful arm wrapped her shoulders and held her in place. It was Tahkwehso; immediately she calmed, feeling his heartbeat. He spoke to van Vliet.

"A month is a long time, and for you as well, my friend. The power in this mask will buttress your own declining strength. A successful Shift will increase it yet more. I wouldn't want to see you wait another month." Van Vliet still looked uncertain, and Tahkwehso said, "She is ready. Tonight is good, I think. You will succeed."

"The other crazy man speaks!" yelped Lane. "You'll do it tonight, Peter, and by God, you'll do it here, or I'll get Hilda to shoot you all."

Van Vliet looked from one to the other and nodded. "Tonight, then. And here. But I'll need a drum."

"Hah! Another goddamn excuse! You think the best I can offer is a stewpot with a wooden spoon, and then you can tell us that's why it didn't work. Unfortunately for you, Peter, I have a drum. Too new for Sotheby's to care about, they wouldn't take it. A Chippewa drum, deer hide, with a rising sun and bear tracks. Wait, I know. Bear tracks are the one thing that screws the Ceremony all up, right?"

"No." Van Vliet smiled. "Bear tracks will be fine."

60

With great care, Edward stacked the wood to build the fire. Once they'd chosen the location for the Ceremony—a level stretch of lawn between the house and the trees—he and Abornazine ferried firewood from a storage room.

"Stack it up high as you want, boys," Lane said. "I have no use for it. Haven't had a fire since I had the fire, you know what I mean?"

Hilda's disapproval of the undertaking was obvious but Lane squelched her objections. "Come on, Hilda, where's your sense of adventure? How can you resist this? This quack's offering to turn a woman into a deer right under our noses!"

"Not a deer, necessarily," Abornazine corrected him. "I can't know until she shows herself."

Edward wondered why Abornazine wasted his breath in discussion. If Katherine Cochran Shifted, Lane would have to believe. If not, he'd assume Abornazine was a fraud and no words would convince him otherwise.

"But," Lane went on to the scowling Hilda, "what's really going to happen is, Peter will dance and drum and make a fool of himself and fall flat on his ass! With my mask and his jingle-bell silver and his lunatic friends here. Won't that be tasty? I can't wait! The real question is, what the hell do I do with the Ohtahyohnee once this farce is over? I have half a mind to hold on to it and see how high the bidding goes on Ted Morse's little masterpiece. Let those morons spend their millions on a fake. I'll say this one is a replica and I'll sit with it every day until I die, and when I do, I'll leave it to the Met because Katherine's the one who found it. Of course, she'll have to explain why the Met already has a phony one in the collection, but that'll be her problem, won't it? Where the hell did she go, anyway? Come on, people, what's taking so long?"

Edward, striding past Lane with an armload of logs, recognized this chatter for what it was: a white man's inability to bear an uncomfortable silence. Though he himself had never been sure which came first: perhaps that desperate need for talk was what made silences uncomfortable for them. The idea that moments not filled with talk were therefore silent was also an error. When the flow of words paused Edward heard footsteps, his own and Hilda's. From the bare-walled living room he could make out the measured in and out of Katherine Cochran's breathing as she prepared herself according to Abornazine's instructions. Soft thumping came from another part of the house as Abornazine adjusted the heads on the drum, tried them, pulled their deerskin cords tighter. And on a night like this, the wind! The trees circling the mound of logs leaned and reached, now this way, now that, like people at a dance. The wind gave them voice, and they sang and howled, keened and whispered. Broken branches cracked, torn twigs whipped along the brown grass and scratched the sunroom windows. Lane's blindness, his helplessness to be part of the preparations, Edward thought, contributed to his impatience. But a blind man filling silences with meaningless words, when so much more was available to his ears than to most people's—*the white world,* Edward thought, pulling open the door and stepping once again into the wind and the dark, *the white world, I could never live there.*

He arranged his logs and stood back, felt the wind push on him as though it were a friend inviting him to leave his chores and wrestle. The pile was complete. The low outer barrier around the fire site was laid, also. The fire would kindle and burn hot, just long enough for the Ceremony to be held. If Abornazine sang well and Katherine Cochran truly had the Power, she would Shift before the flames died down. About Abornazine, Edward had no doubts. The mask and the presence of a woman who claimed not just hope but experience, no matter how incomplete, had ignited his spirit as never before. Edward saw it in his eyes, heard it in his voice. Abornazine would do the Ceremony as well as he ever had. If the fire faded and no Shift had occurred, the thing Katherine Cochran so desperately hungered for—the thing he and Abornazine wanted so badly, also— would not happen.

If that was the outcome, so be it. They'd take the Ohtahyohnee with them and continue their work.

Once the Ceremony started he himself would keep a distance from it, not looking directly at the fire or the dance, far enough that the howling of the wind would interfere with the drumming and the chant. And the mask, especially the mask. He'd had to struggle to control the sensations roiling within him at his first sight of the Ohtahyohnee, and that was within walls, among unbelievers, lit by electric lights. Under the moon, at a fire, with the chanting, to see the mask as it was intended to be used—no, the prohibition on the presence of an awakened Shifter at a Ceremony was ancient and wise. If the need arose for him to Shift he would do it, but he would control the time and place.

A rectangle of light sliced onto the lawn as the back door opened. Bradford Lane, swathed in a thick down coat and a giant scarf, lifted his feet over frozen tufts of grass. Beside him, holding his arm in a vise grip, Hilda radiated disapproval into the night. Her disgusted scowl made Edward wonder if she should be barred from the circle. It, plus Lane's cackling cynicism, created a sizzle of ill will like a second, maleficent fire. But no. The strength he felt in Abornazine tonight, the power of the Ohtahyohnee—what was mistrust born of ignorance against them?

Hilda went back in and returned with two folding chairs, for herself and Lane. They sat; then the door opened again and Katherine Cochran emerged. Her feet were bare, her face hard and set. She hugged a thick blanket around her; under that, Edward knew, she was naked, but if the cold reached her she didn't show it. Abornazine came out last, carrying drum and mask. At the sight of the Ohtahyohnee a flash of fear, of excitement, of yearning, raced up Edward's spine. Katherine Cochran stepped into the circle and knelt in the place Abornazine showed her. The wind picked up in sharp gusts, as though impatient, now, with any delay.

Edward stepped into the circle, also. He looked from his friend to the kneeling woman. Then he turned his back to them. He raised his arms and sang a prayer to the wind, to the moon, and last, to the fire that was to come. Finished, he knelt and put match to tinder. A gust made the flame shiver but he'd laid the wood so that the wind wouldn't blow out the spark, but make it roar to life. He waited, not long; soon the center began to glow and fingers of fire cast conflicting shadows across the frozen earth. Edward stepped back, hearing the crackle, watching the dancing light. He met Abornazine's eyes one more time, and the light was in them, too. Edward walked past

Abornazine, past Katherine Cochran, over the barrier, out of the circle and away from the growing fire. He didn't stop to watch Abornazine don the mask. Behind him the voice of the drum started to rise, and soon, over it, came Abornazine's steady, insistent chanting, echoing through the Ohtahyohnee. The Ceremony had begun.

61

Michael hunched into his coat, staying in shadow on the curving Riverdale street. Blocks away he'd paid off the cab that had brought him here from Fordham. Better to approach on foot, taking stock.

Riding across the Bronx, many things had weighed on his mind. He had no doubt the priest he'd found lifeless in the chapel was Father Maxwell; the cross and moon on the priest's gold ring told him that. He had no doubt, as he knelt beside the body, that the man had only been dead a short time; if Michael had moved faster he might have saved him. And he had no doubt the open box on the pew nearby had once contained a mask. The true Ohtahyohnee? How, and why? And where was it now?

And was the inert form of Father Maxwell, with its staring, frightened eyes, another disaster to lay at the feet of his brother?

He wished he hadn't called Spencer. It was weakness, his need for connection masquerading as a desire to keep Spencer from trouble. The same flaw had stopped him from leaving last night as he should have, as soon as he'd gotten Spencer home from the park and been sure he wasn't going to die. It was a failing compounded of many parts: a man's affection and a scientist's curiosity, plus a researcher's hope to be able to continue his work and, he knew, a Shifter's arrogance. It seemed complex but it amounted to a simple thing: greed. A white man's disease. Michael had wanted to have everything, to give up nothing. All his life Michael had denied his brother's charge, but it was true: living in the white world had changed him.

But now he'd do what he should have done already: he was going to disappear. If, first, he could confront Edward here, he would; if not, he'd go back north. He'd follow his brother and van Vliet until he found them and stopped them. After that, whatever path presented itself was the one he'd take.

He wondered suddenly if the real reason he'd called Spencer was to say goodbye.

A whisper in the dark: his name. Michael snapped his head up, sprang back ready. A shadow stepped from under a linden tree.

"Relax. It's me." Lou moved into the light.

"Jesus. Lou, I told you to leave."

"Fat chance. The hell good's a recon man doesn't pass his intel on?"

"You already did that when you called."

"I have more. Tried to call again but you didn't answer."

"I threw the phone away. I can take it from here, Lou."

"Maybe, maybe not. There are five of them in the house."

"Five?"

"Didn't know that, did you? The old man, his housekeeper—or maybe she's his bodyguard, she looks it—your brother, that white wannabe he hangs out with, and a lady who just came."

"A lady?"

"Short white hair, scratched-up face. In a hurry. Carrying something heavy in a deerskin sack."

"How big?"

"Big. Like this." Lou spread his hands.

"Hell." A shift in the wind brought the pulse of drumming. Michael listened: a chant began. Ice raced up his spine. "Oh, my God."

Lou cocked his head; he'd heard it, too. "What?"

"Nothing. Lou, I'm asking you, leave. It's my problem."

"You have more problems. Two cops in an unmarked car, over there. Eyes on the same house."

Michael followed the direction of Lou's nod. "Dammit."

Lou held up night vision binoculars. "I've been watching them. They must've seen Eddie go in but they haven't reacted."

"I don't think they're looking for him."

"Then who?"

"Me."

"You? Doc Bonnard, on the wrong side of the law? Give me a minute, let me call Pete. He'll laugh his head off."

"It's a misunderstanding."

"I think I heard that inside."

"But it would take time to unravel it and I don't have time."

"Guys on the inside had nothing but time, never got theirs unraveled. Seriously, Doc, you in some kind of trouble?"

"Go home, Lou." Michael started forward.

Lou grabbed his arm. "Not that way, for God's sake. At least make them work for it. Come on, I can get us down to the house and they'll never know we were here. Can city Indians climb a fence or you gonna need a boost?"

Michael stopped but didn't answer.

"Doc, what's it about? What's going on?"

"I can't tell you."

"I think I know, though. Ivy's dream."

"What?"

"I think this is what she meant and I think you need help, whatever it is you're supposed to do."

"Lou—" Then the words of the river came back: *Accept the hand that's offered.*

What if he sees?

Then he was meant to see.

Michael looked at Lou's angled eyes, evidence of the blood of two continents carried in him, and his cocky grin, evidence of who he was in himself. "All right," he said. "You hear the drumming? What they're doing—it needs to be stopped. Disrupted. If they have a wooden mask, take it away from them if you can, but don't damage it. Leave Edward to me. Do not go up against him."

"Eddie? Why would I? Ivy said to help him."

"Don't go near him. You get me?"

Lou raised his eyebrows, but just said, "Yessir." He turned. Michael grabbed his arm.

"Lou? Whatever you see, it's real, you're not losing your mind. But you can't, ever, talk about it."

Lou grinned again and took off, leading the way.

62

J ust those three," the uniform in the unmarked sedan told Charlotte, as she leaned in his window. She read his nameplate: Petersen. "The two men, then the woman."

"Describe them."

"The men, they had some Indian thing going on. Both of them with long hair in braids. The young guy was big, wearing a leather jacket. The older guy was smaller. He had on some fringed thing that looked like what I had when I was a kid. I wanted to be a cowboy." He laughed and nudged his partner but Charlotte's look stopped him and he swallowed and went on, "The woman, short hair, white or blond, in a helluva hurry."

"And the thing the woman was carrying?"

"Looked heavy," said the driver, a chubby guy named Klein. "Wrapped in something. About this big." He spread his arms wide.

"Okay. Your captain says you're our backup. Come on."

"On foot?" Petersen made that sound like an idea he'd never heard before.

"I don't want them to see us."

"They've got a locked gate. How're you planning on getting in?"

She scorched him with a look. "How're you? Floor it and crash through?"

"That's not what I—" He stopped when Framingham shook his head. Grumbling, the two uniforms climbed out of the car.

"And shut up," Charlotte said.

Half a block closer, she could hear drumming. The wind brought chanting, too, and the smell of burning wood. Big houses like the ones around here, a lot of them would have fireplaces; but that's not what it was and she knew it. Another half block and she could look straight through an iron picket fence to a plant-filled glass extension on the side of the house. Beyond its foggy windows, on the lawn in the back, a fire blazed. A few yards from the fence she stopped. If the gate had a security camera she didn't want it to find them. She edged around the fence to where she could see the fire. Two people sat in chairs; a blanket-wrapped figure knelt; and someone in a wolf mask sang and beat on a drum. Tahkwehso?

"Holy crap," said Framingham.

"You shut up, too. Can you climb this?"

"I—"

"You," Charlotte said to Petersen. "Come boost him over. You two, can you climb it? Oh, shit, forget it. Matt, Petersen, come with me. When we get inside, Matt, you come back around here and open the gate." She took off at a run to the north side of the house, where they'd be hidden from the glass room and the fire.

63

Thomas sat stunned by the news Spencer had delivered. Father Maxwell, dead; and dead because he had, it appeared, been in possession of the real Ohtahyohnee. For how long? Why? *Praevalere et veneror.* Father Maxwell and Kateri Tekakwitha, with the same motto. Chance? Not possibly. A society, then, within the Jesuit order, stretching back to the time of Tekakwitha, for the preservation of the masks. Secret, unknown. Could such a thing be? Oh yes. From its founding, many circles had existed within the Society of Jesus, some deep in the shadows of the order and the Church. This could mean nothing else. The early Jesuits in the New World, the Blackrobes the nations had loved—they must have understood the power of these masks. Had they seen or just been told? Did it matter? They knew about the Shifters, the way the Church had known about the Noantri for so long. The members of Father Maxwell's society knew. Father Maxwell had known.

Who killed the priest, and why? Was this yet another death for which Edward Bonnard would have to answer?

Where was the mask now?

And how many other secrets, world-altering secrets, existed? And how many were known to, and shielded by, Thomas's Church?

Thomas chided himself for dwelling on questions when a man's soul was in need of prayer. For the second time in twenty-four hours he began, "Eternal rest, oh Father . . ." This time he offered the words silently, but no less sincerely. He'd just finished when Livia spoke.

"There's an iron fence around the property." They were driving down the curving street toward the Riverdale estate. "There's a gate with a security camera, but I didn't see any other cameras. Spencer, I assume you want to get as close as we can without being seen?"

"Indeed, that's what I was hoping."

Livia made a left and parked the car a block from Lane's home. Everyone climbed out, including Father Carbonariis, who hadn't spoken since Spencer's news. "This way," Livia said. "There's a place we can get to the fence and not be seen from the street. It's where I went over last night to get to my tree. It's not a hard fence to climb, but someone might have to boost Thomas."

64

Following Lou, Michael slipped through the trees at the edge of the frozen lawn. They'd come over the fence on the north side, away from the fire. The iron rods were high and smooth and Michael's injury had made climbing them tricky. In the end he'd needed Lou's help, which had come with a wiseass smirk.

As they neared the fire Michael struggled to retain control. Even with the house blocking his view of the flames he could see their glow and the weaving shadows of the trees. And he could hear the chant. *The Ceremony,* he'd told Spencer and the others. *Similar across tribal cultures, that's why it's effective.* Van Vliet claimed he'd been taught by a Navajo. If so, he'd learned well. The drum called and the chant demanded. The howling wind whipped the sounds around Michael and drove them deep inside him. Chant and drum reverberated past Dr. Michael Bonnard, who lived in the white world, past Gata, who was born on ancient land, scorning both to reach the wolf-self within.

No. No. Whoever was at the center of this Ceremony—the woman who'd brought the mask?—could not be allowed to Shift. She'd be destroyed. And van Vliet's power would grow. Michael felt the ice and the heat start together within him. He fought them. As though on the side of the chant and the drum, a gust of wind staggered him, knocked his breath out as powerfully as a blow. Lou reached out to offer help, but his gaze snapped immediately to something else. Michael followed Lou's eyes. A figure stepped from the shadows of the house.

Edward stood, arms raised, lit by the half-hidden glow of the fire. Michael's eyes locked with his brother's. A moment of stillness, of silence; then Edward spoke, in the voice of the thunder: *"No."*

65

Charlotte left Framingham climbing onto Petersen's shoulders, which didn't make either of them happy but why would she care? She crept around the house toward the fire, moving fast but keeping to the shadows. This bastard Michael Bonnard, was he here? Petersen and Klein hadn't reported anyone who looked like him but those two weren't the brightest bulbs. God knows how many people could've slipped past them.

It bothered her that the woman had arrived carrying a bundle, but there was no reason Michael Bonnard couldn't be working with a partner. In her mind it ran like this: Bradford Lane found out a second mask existed. What else could that box be for? He wanted it and sent his to auction, maybe so he could afford to buy it. But it wasn't for sale. He saw his chance when Michael Bonnard killed Brittany Williams, probably in some lovers' spat. How did Lane know about that? A detail; later. Lane blackmailed Bonnard into stealing the second mask for him. The priest at Fordham didn't want to let it go, a fatal mistake. Bonnard passed it to his partner and let himself be seen leaving the church as cover for her.

And what the hell was going on here, now? Charlotte had a guess. Lane was a wannabe, one of those collectors who amassed

Indian stuff because it was as close as he could get. Stealing this mask—especially if Lane knew the priest had died—had soaked it in bad juju and it had to be cleansed. Some bogus chanting and drumming around a fire under a full moon and it would be good to go.

So she had her theory and it was sound, she was inside, and her partner was about to let her back up in the front gate. She was a few steps away from a dynamite collar. Why was she so pissed off?

Because when you want a cleansing chant by a fire, who better to sing it than a long-haired Abenaki just down from the rez? Petersen and Klein hadn't described anyone like Michael Bonnard, but a big guy in braids and a leather jacket sounded like Tahkwehso all over. Which meant whatever his brother had done, Edward Bonnard was probably up to his medicine-bag-wearing neck in it, too.

66

Following Livia, Spencer swung himself down over the fence. If he hadn't been sure of his feelings for Michael before this, he'd have found undeniable evidence in his willingness to engage in absurd derring-do on two successive bone-chilling February nights.

Spencer watched Giovanni Antonio de Carbonariis, with a hard smile, jump up onto the stone base of the fence and extend a hand to Thomas Kelly. Thomas took it and Carbonariis yanked him up with such force that Thomas yelped; but the momentum hefted Thomas high enough to grab the pickets at their tops. With a scowl at Carbonariis he propelled himself over. Carbonariis did the same, and they were all inside.

The howling wind brought the sounds of drum and chant. Spencer took the lead, choosing to follow the line of the woods that bordered the lawn. That way they could reach the fire unseen and evaluate the situation. But as he rounded the corner of the house he thrust out his hand to stop the others. Not ten yards away Michael stood, his back to Spencer, facing another tall man unlike Michael in feature but so identical in form and stance that he could only be the elusive brother.

In the glow of the still-hidden fire Spencer could read that man's face. If Michael's face were as hardened with anger and determination, as Spencer imagined it must be, an epic battle was about to begin. Though neither brother appeared to move, Spencer's Noantri senses detected an effect unfamiliar to him: both seemed to pulse with the rhythm of the chant and the drum.

At Michael's side a smaller man was standing. Spencer recognized him as Lou, Michael's friend. *Oh, young man,* he thought, *move on if you can.* Michael must have been thinking the same, because at that moment, not taking his gaze from his brother, he spoke. "Lou. Go."

Lou looked at Michael and shook himself as if waking from a dream. He darted forward, toward the side of the house where the fire burned, but Edward Bonnard leapt to block his path. He seized Lou's arm and with astonishing speed slammed his fist into the smaller man's face. Lou stumbled, tried to recover, threw two punches that were ineffective. Edward pounded him again and again. Lou sank to his knees. Michael launched himself forward, knocking his brother down.

Michael landed a punch as his brother lay on the frozen ground, but Michael was already injured and Edward was wild with a jubilant anger. He swept a backhand across Michael's jaw. Michael was knocked off-balance and Edward threw him down. In each of the rapid-fire blows Edward rained onto his brother Spencer could see the decades of fury, abandonment, and wounded love.

Michael's right hand shot out and gathered Edward's collar. He jerked to one side and with Edward off-balance, Michael rolled the other way. Edward fell but scrambled back and tackled Michael as he started to stand. Michael fell heavily onto his injured shoulder. Edward punched and pounded and now Michael had no counterattack; even his efforts to defend himself were weak.

Spencer, cursing as he had the night before, threw himself onto Edward's back. Wrapping an arm around Edward's neck, he choked and wrenched until he'd pulled Edward off of Michael.

"This time leave him to me!" Spencer shouted, and it appeared Michael had the sense to do so, because Michael lay panting and then clambered to his feet. For a moment he met Spencer's gaze with such a depth of sorrow in his eyes that Spencer was momentarily stunned. Then Michael turned and ran toward the fire.

As Edward struggled in Spencer's grip, Spencer made out Carbonariis and Thomas Kelly taking off after Michael. Livia appeared beside Spencer and wrapped her arms around Edward to help subdue him.

But to no avail. With a massive roar half of rage, half of joy, Edward twisted and thrashed and exploded to his feet with staggering power. Both Noantri were thrown to the ground. Thudding painfully onto his back, Spencer lifted his head, saw Edward throw a scornful glance at Livia, and then turn his glowing eyes to Spencer with a wild and hungry snarl.

67

No. *No!*

Edward fought the burning ice inside him. He would choose. He'd always chosen. He would Shift tonight only if necessary. For their work. For this dream he'd carried all his life, this dream he shared with Abornazine. They were so close now, and he was in control. In control.

The chant, the drum—no, he wouldn't hear them.

His blood pulsed with them.

No.

His anger, his fathomless rage, always the trigger he used—no.

He tried to step away. He had to get back to the fire. Abornazine would need him.

But the scent of the man on the ground, the man whose blood he'd tasted yesterday, nearly drove him mad.

No!

The man had landed on his back, dazed. He stared up at Edward, and in the man's eyes, something changed. With a small smile, he started to stand. The smile became a grin as he waved the woman back.

Using all his strength, Edward took two steps, three steps, back, toward Abornazine, toward the fire. The man kept walking slowly toward him, as though he understood. As though he knew. Edward couldn't take his eyes off of him as he shrugged out of his coat. The shirt under it was soaked with sweat, and as he stepped closer the wind brought his scent to Edward so powerfully that Edward felt the freezing fire sear his blood.

No. No.

No!

But he had lost. His limbs sizzled, his breath came fast and shallow. Colors faded, sounds sharpened. His craving to devour overwhelmed and conquered. His dream, his friend, everything deserted him. Nothing remained but the desperate need to finish this kill.

He gathered himself. He Shifted. And he sprang.

The man crashed to the ground and Edward slammed a massive paw onto his chest to hold him, but he didn't struggle, just grinned into Edward's eyes. Standing over him, jaws spread, Edward searched his face for fear, searched his scent for terror, found none. Edward saluted his courage and bent toward his throat.

And heard two loud explosive roars, and felt a searing pain.

68

Charlotte stood dumbfounded, rooted. Her ears rang with the sound of gunshots. What had she seen? What had happened? In front of her, Framingham bent over the fallen form with his hands still ready on his weapon. "What the hell?" he kept saying. "What the hell? It's a wolf. It's a goddamn wolf. What the hell? This freak kept a goddamn wolf?"

"Shut up!" she shouted, and that stopped him. He'd arrived just after she had, and he hadn't seen, then. Had she, really? Two men, one of them Michael Bonnard, fighting on the ground near the inert form of a smaller man. Bonnard leaping up, running toward the fire while Spencer George and Livia Pietro tried to hold the other fighter. Two more—those priests, Kelly and Carbonariis—taking off after Bonnard. Charlotte should have followed but the other fighter bellowed and jumped up and it was Tahkwehso. Charlotte's heart stopped, and when it started again she couldn't move. Her blood seemed to pulse with the drum as Spencer George rose and walked slowly toward Tahkwehso and oh my God, oh my God. It couldn't be. Couldn't be. But the voice of Uncle James and the voice of her grandmother and other voices, forgotten or never heard before, whispered and spoke and echoed within her and they all said the same: *It is. What you saw, you saw. Some of the stories are legends, or lessons. But others are memories.* As the voices spoke her spine and fingertips began to tingle and colors grew more vivid. Charlotte felt what she'd so often felt before, and she knew it was true. She had seen a shapeshifter. She'd seen Tahkwehso, seen Edward Bonnard, turn into a wolf.

The wolf, now, lay nearly motionless at her feet. Framingham's bullets had knocked him off of his prey and he'd crashed to the hard earth. His flank rose and fell and she could see weak puffs of breath. Blood steamed as it flowed from under him. Charlotte knelt and reached to stroke the soft silver of his head. He shuddered, and then the breath stopped, and he died.

69

Had he heard gunshots? Thomas didn't know. His heart lurched. Livia! But no, she'd be all right, and so would Spencer. But here, at the fire, what was happening here? Michael Bonnard, about to step over the outer ring of logs, had been seized by Carbonariis. The two men argued, in Mohawk, and not long: Michael threw off the priest's arm and crossed the outer ring. His strength seemed to be failing, though. Pushing forward as if through a headwind, he walked toward the man with the drum, the man who wore the wolf mask. The man danced away and chanted louder, faster. Michael's steps hesitated. The drum's volume grew, too, its tempo increasing. Michael stopped. In the flickering glow of the flames he sank to his knees and began to shiver. His shudders grew but there was a woman a few feet away, also kneeling, wrapped only in a blanket, who didn't move at all. Thomas peered at her: Katherine Cochran! Could it be?

And what should he do? What was right? Stop the Ceremony, that's what Michael had been attempting. Then Thomas would. He jumped over the outer logs and as he did Katherine Cochran let loose a long and echoing scream. The man with the mask and drum increased volume and speed again. Thomas ran toward him but

Carbonariis leapt the outer ring and reached him first. The Augustinian yanked and pulled and tore the mask from the man's head, lifting it high above his own. The chanting and the drumming stopped abruptly. In the sudden silence Michael Bonnard slumped forward and lay unmoving on the ground. Thomas ran to him. He had a hand on Michael's shoulder when a sound from behind made him whip his head around.

70

Katherine felt the moment the rhythm of her heartbeat merged with the cadence of the drum. She didn't understand the words of the chant and she wasn't sure the singer did, either, wasn't sure they even carried meaning in any way she knew. The tones of the song, rising and falling, louder and softer, the changing thumping pulse—these were what rang deep within her, resonating, igniting.

And extinguishing. The Katherine Cochran she had been for four decades began to dissipate, edges blurring, carried away on the music and the wind. She was frightened, afraid of loss; but deep within her a place was being revealed that she had never known, an endless crystalline expanse, as the clouds of who she was shredded and blew apart. Pure, clean, so cold it burned. The chanting continued, the drum picked up speed. The flames blazed higher. When she'd come from the house with the blanket tight around her, she'd shivered in the wind. Now she was still, and the wind meant something else. It pulled her, coaxed her, commanded her presence. The burning ice inside her spread. It filled her chest, seared along her limbs.

Dimly she became aware of dark figures beyond the outer barrier. She heard voices, commonplace human voices, arguing over something that could not matter. A figure leapt into the circle and the singer moved away. The drum faltered, then took up stronger. It gladdened Katherine's heart to hear the sound of the drum, but she didn't need it any longer. The first figure stopped, but another came. Katherine opened her arms and heard her own voice, but it was not hers. A man approached the singer, and they struggled. The drum stopped, but no matter. She threw off her blanket and remained crouched at the fire, knowing her skin was no longer bare before the wind. Then the wind, with a howl, reached down for her, and she spread her mighty wings and answered.

71

Livia climbed to her feet. The woman detective, Charlotte
Hamilton, was kneeling by the wolf-body of Edward Bonnard,
stroking his unmoving head. Her partner, Framingham, who'd
shot him, stood gaping at the inert form. What Livia had heard him
say reassured her he hadn't seen the Shift. Nor, most likely, had the
two uniformed officers who'd run up behind him. Had Hamilton?
Livia thought she had. What would come of that, they'd find out
later.

Spencer leapt up and took off for the fire. As Livia ran after him
she heard the drumming stop. Framingham shouted. His running
footsteps, and those of the other officers, pounded the earth behind
her, but he didn't shoot. Livia was grateful: she wouldn't have
wanted to have to explain away Noantri healing to police officers,
one of whom had just seen a man turn into a wolf.

Spencer reached the fire before she did. He leapt over the outer
ring of logs and knelt beside Michael, who lay unmoving. Livia felt a
stab of fear before her ears picked up Michael's breathing, faint but
regular. Spencer slipped his arm around Michael's shoulders and
helped him to sit, then pulled him close. He whispered to Michael
words Livia could not make out, nor, she knew, was she intended to.

Framingham and the two officers ran up, guns drawn. Hamilton followed, not far behind, looking dazed. The four of them surrounded the group at the fire. Livia took inventory. Sitting with his back to the waning flames, a silver-and-turquoise-draped man, his hair in long gray braids. She hadn't met Peter van Vliet when they'd gone up to his estate but who else could this be? He appeared exhausted and was leaning on a large drum. Just stumbling into the circle, bleeding from his nose, his right eye swollen, was the Asian-featured man whom Michael had tried to protect from Edward. Outside the outer ring Bradford Lane and the indomitable Hilda sat on chairs. Lane was leaning forward, his face shining with excitement. Hilda spoke to him rapidly but calmly, as though engaged in a simultaneous translation. Beyond Michael and Spencer a blanket lay discarded on the ground.

Thomas was nowhere to be seen. Nor was Carbonariis. And if there had ever been an Ohtahyohnee mask here, it was gone, too.

72

Thomas ran down the hill toward the river. He fought his way through the trees and brush. What he'd seen by the fire was seared into his mind.

The sound he'd heard, an odd, inhuman cry, had come from Katherine Cochran. She'd shuddered and seemed for a moment to vanish. Solid once more, she'd thrown off the blanket—but the form under it was no longer a woman. As Thomas stood openmouthed, a giant eagle spread its wings and rose into the inky sky.

He couldn't take his eyes off the huge bird. It turned, swooped, circled. It fought the wind, then rode it, cutting back and forth above. Its screech sliced the night. Higher and higher it swept, until it was small, carried on the wind. Thomas's heart leapt as the bird spiraled up.

But as he watched he saw it falter. It turned, wheeled, seemed unable to find its way. Its massive wings beat in the emptiness; then they stopped. For a moment the eagle hung motionless against the stars. Then it tumbled out of the sky.

Thomas ran now, judging distance, time, led by hope alone. He reached the railroad tracks and sprinted across them to a stony clearing between the track bed and the water. A pale shape lay on the dark ground. He bent over it. Not an eagle. A woman again. Naked, broken, still. The wind gusted, pushing, tugging, asking and demanding, but Katherine Cochran, in the end, was bound to the earth.

73

Framingham didn't know what the hell was wrong with Charlotte. Was it possible she'd been even more freaked out by the wolf than he had? Jesus, the thing almost made him piss his pants, but it was dead now and they had business to do. They were carrying warrants for two of the seven people in front of them and two more warrants for people who weren't there, meaning somebody'd better start looking for them.

He was used to Charlotte taking charge and he waited another thirty seconds because nobody seemed to be going anyplace, but when Charlotte stayed silent he began to give orders. He told everyone to stay where they were, which might have been redundant, and had Petersen call for an ambulance and more backup.

"More backup?" Petersen repeated, looking around warily, as though for danger he hadn't noticed. "Why?"

"We need the manpower and the transport," Charlotte broke in hoarsely, holstering her weapon and stepping up beside him. "We're taking everyone in. Matt, get Ostrander and Sun down here, too."

"Welcome back," Framingham said.

"Where the hell are the priests?"

"Were they here?"

"If you'd moved faster you'd have seen them. They were both over there and they ran in this direction. Where are they? And where's the woman, and where's the mask?"

"Excuse me, Detectives." A woman walked toward them. Livia Pietro, the Italian art historian they'd met at Sotheby's. Well, if Thomas Kelly, who'd also been at Sotheby's that night, was tangled up with Spencer George, and George with Michael Bonnard—and the two of them certainly looked tangled up right now—he supposed he shouldn't be surprised to find Pietro here, too. "It's cold out here," Pietro said. "Perhaps some of these people should be indoors?"

Charlotte looked at Pietro, then fixed on the two figures on chairs. "Are you Bradford Lane?"

"If it's me you're shouting at, young woman, I certainly am. Who exactly are you?"

"Charlotte Hamilton, detective, NYPD."

Framingham watched the coat-swaddled old man in the thick dark glasses. The heavy woman beside him kept up a constant stream of whispers even as Charlotte spoke. Description, Framingham realized. The old man could hear the dialogue; she was setting the scene.

"I'm investigating two homicides and grand theft," Charlotte said. "I need to question everyone here but I have no warrant for your premises. I do have warrants for some of these people and I can get others."

"Oh, for God's sake! Did you just threaten to arrest me if I don't let you into my house? People have been stampeding through all day. Why don't you just ask?"

The seven people around the fire got to their feet. Lane leaned on the arm of the heavy woman, George and the young Asian-looking man supported Bonnard, and Livia Pietro helped the long-haired man with the drum to stand. At gunpoint that none of them seemed to notice, they were shepherded into the steamy heat of Bradford Lane's conservatory.

74

Where are the priests? And who was the woman and where is she?" Charlotte demanded again. The suspects—every damn one of these people were suspects, in her mind—were seated in the conservatory now, though Bonnard, Spencer George, and the young man had to make do with the steps to the living room. Petersen took up a position at the door to the yard, Klein at the steps. She and Framingham stood in the middle of the floor. They'd searched everyone for weapons and had only found one, a handgun carried by the heavy woman, who claimed to have a permit. Maybe she did; Charlotte's head swirled with a million questions but she was having trouble concentrating. Anger and sorrow pounded her in alternating waves. Framingham eyed her oddly. The vision of the wolf lying on the icy ground kept interfering with the sight of the people and plants and tile floor in front of her.

"Before we get into that, Detective," Bradford Lane spoke up, "I think I have a right to ask who's here. I have no idea what priests you're talking about, but I can tell my house is crawling with people I haven't met. Livia Pietro I do know, and Peter van Vliet, of course. I don't care about the names of any of you police—there are four of you all told, correct?—but that leaves three others, all men, so Hilda tells me. Gentlemen? Who are you?"

The young man, wary but alert, spoke first. "I'm Lou Higbee." He looked Charlotte over and to her added, "Potawatomi." Ah, thought Charlotte. Someone in his background was clearly Asian, but the other kind of Indian made more sense, in this crowd.

"And I'm Spencer George," the Englishman said. He stood from the steps and crossed the room to shake Lane's hand. Petersen moved to stop him but Charlotte waved him back. "And also here is Dr. Michael Bonnard, though I rather fear he's indisposed."

At Bonnard's name, the long-haired man—by process of elimination, Peter van Vliet—lifted his head slowly. He, like Bonnard, had been in some kind of daze, but now he seemed to be coming around.

"That doesn't tell me much," Lane retorted. "Who does that make you?"

Charlotte could feel Framingham watching her, expecting her to shut them all down and go on; but she waited.

"A friend of Michael's," Higbee said.

"Friends of Livia's," Spencer George offered.

"And the brother of Tahkwehso." Van Vliet's voice rattled. "Where is Tahkwehso?"

No one answered. Now Charlotte heard her own voice, with a catch in it she couldn't suppress. "The wolf is dead."

Van Vliet stared at her. He melted slowly back against his chair, as though his strength were draining away.

Now Bonnard straightened, though Charlotte could see that it cost him. "The wolf?" he whispered. "Dead?"

Charlotte nodded.

What reserves Bonnard called upon, Charlotte didn't know, but he pushed to his feet. "I'll go to him."

"I will also." Van Vliet stood.

"No!" Bonnard spun. He looked like ten miles of bad road but van Vliet sank back as Bonnard spoke in a voice filled with quiet menace. "All this is your fault. You're not welcome. Stay here."

"Damn right he'll stay," Framingham said. "You will, too. No one leaves."

"No, it's all right," Charlotte said. "Petersen, go with him. But keep back. Give him room. He wants to say goodbye."

"Charlotte?" Framingham whispered. "He thinks he's that wolf's *brother*. It looks like they all do. And how did you know its name?"

"He can hardly walk," Charlotte said. "He's not going anywhere. Back off, Matt. It's an Indian thing." And it was, though not in the way she was implying. Charlotte was seized with an almost irresistible urge to laugh. The knife-edge of hysterics, she knew, and she forced herself calm; but really, what could be funnier? Poor Framingham lived his life waiting for one of his nutsoid theories to be proved right, and here under his nose this man's brother had turned into a wolf—and he'd missed it.

Spencer George had gotten to his feet when Bonnard did, but he didn't follow him to the door. He touched Bonnard's arm and spoke low. Bonnard met his eyes, and surprised Charlotte with a small, weary smile. He nodded, turned, and pushed out the door. Charlotte watched him disappear around the house, Petersen trailing behind.

She turned back to the others. "Now. What the—" A stirring among them made her whip her head around. By the light of the dying fire she could see a dark shape making its way up the hill from the edge of the woods. "Matt." Framingham dashed out, weapon drawn. The figure stopped and she watched Framingham approach it slowly; but when he neared it he holstered the gun. He threw a supporting arm around the figure, which Charlotte could now see was a man carrying a burden. Framingham helped him to the solarium door and opened it. Father Thomas Kelly entered with the limp, coat-wrapped form of Katherine Cochran in his arms.

75

atherine!" Livia was on her feet and across the room before the detectives could stop her. Katherine was swathed in Thomas's coat; her legs and her head were bare. Deep scratches tracked her face. "Katherine! Thomas, what happened?"

Thomas shook his head. He carried Katherine to the love seat where Livia had been sitting and laid her gently down. Livia knelt by her friend. She stroked Katherine's hair, though she knew before she touched her that all life was gone. Charlotte Hamilton crouched, putting her fingers to Katherine's throat to search for a pulse. She leaned to Katherine's lips to see if she could feel breath, lifted Katherine's lids on blank, staring eyes.

"What the hell happened to her?" the detective demanded of Thomas. "Where are her clothes?"

"She fell," Thomas said.

"And her clothes are in my study," Bradford Lane announced.

Livia, and everyone else, turned to Lane. Hilda had narrated Thomas's entrance in whispers. Now Lane answered Hamilton's question, and repeated, "Her clothes are in the study, Detective. Hilda can show you. She left them there and wrapped herself in a blanket for the ceremony we were doing. The ceremony," he said, "with the drum."

"Drum?"

"I've known Katherine for years. Peter has also, haven't you? Haven't you, Peter?"

"Yes." Van Vliet found his voice, though it was weak. "Years."

"Katherine occasionally brings me pieces she thinks might interest me. Tonight, she brought a drum. Ojibwe, she said, deer hide, with bear tracks and a rising sun. I had to take her word for the bear tracks and the sun but Hilda says they're there. We were trying it out."

"This was the woman?" Hamilton turned to Klein. "The one who brought the bundle?"

"Might have been. Didn't get a good look but—"

"She's the one I saw," Lou Higbee said. "She was carrying something big. Could have been a drum."

"Where's the drum?"

"Peter was using it," Lane answered.

"It's still by the fire," said Framingham. He went to get it.

"You were using it?" Hamilton said. "You were doing some kind of ceremony?"

"Of course, it was bogus. We were making it up as we went along. But it was a nice night for a fire. Katherine was always a little crazy, I have to tell you. This time she really got into it. Came out wrapped in nothing but a blanket. Then Peter's yelping and whooping and suddenly she jumps up and runs downhill. I don't know what happened after that."

"I found her," Thomas Kelly said. "On the rocks by the river."

"You said she fell," Hamilton said.

"She was—moving fast. Then she just dropped. I kept running after her through the woods and finally there she was. She was dead when I got to her."

"What were you doing here?"

"Father Kelly's a new acquaintance," Lane said. "I met him this morning, with Dr. Pietro. Is he one of the priests you meant?"

A blast of cold air entered when Framingham did. He brought the drum to Hamilton. "Could this be it?" he said low, though Livia had no trouble making out his words. "What was in the box? Not a mask, this? What do you think—worth killing for?"

Hamilton shook her head, but in her eyes Livia saw a dark, complex doubt.

"The scratches," Framingham whispered. "The skin under the dead priest's nails." He turned to Lane and in a louder voice asked, "How did her face get scratched?"

"I didn't know it was. I can't see, you know. Maybe when she fell?"

"No, Mr. Lane," Hilda put in. "She had the scratches when she arrived."

"And where's the other priest?" Hamilton said. "Carbonariis, where's he?"

"Father Carbonariis"—Spencer spoke from the steps—"dislikes large gatherings. He came with us under protest and left the moment Detective Framingham discharged his weapon. For which I mustn't fail to thank you, young man. I really believe that wolf would have devoured me entire."

A shadow crossed van Vliet's face at that, but he didn't speak.

"Carbonariis didn't look like he was leaving," Hamilton said. "He looked like he was heading back here, toward the fire."

"Nevertheless," Spencer said. "He's no longer here, is he?"

And neither, Livia thought, was the Ohtahyohnee. Katherine. Her childhood, secretly watching the Seminoles; her lifelong love of Native art; her sense, like Livia's, that the mask at Sotheby's wasn't real. *The ritual objects . . . you vibrate with them, in a way.* Michael had said that. He'd also said, about Shifting, *It's a spectacular feeling—like a cocaine high times ten. Once you've felt it, you want it again.* As Livia looked at the torn, still face of her friend, she also remembered this: *Without teaching and practice, you can't sustain it.*

76

Thomas and Livia sat in Spencer's parlor sharing the soothing silence of friendship. Livia's sadness over Katherine's death was nothing Thomas could dispel; but when he asked if she'd like to be alone, she smiled softly and said, "No, stay with me." The only other thing she'd said, some time later, was, "She must have been so lonely. All her life, so lonely."

Midafternoon sunlight slipped through the windows to brighten the patterned carpet. Last night's wind had swept the sky clear and the morning had dawned fierce and bright. Not that either Thomas or Livia had seen the dawn. They, along with Lou Higbee and Spencer, had passed the night at the Midtown South precinct Detectives Hamilton and Framingham called home. They'd been shuffled in and out of interview rooms and questioned many times; later they found that their stories hadn't quite matched, but according to Lou, who seemed to speak from experience, it was better that way. "Give them the same details, they figure it's b.s. everyone memorized. In real life, most people get most stuff wrong."

Michael had been bundled into an ambulance from where he'd been kneeling by the body of the wolf. Peter van Vliet was taken off with him. The medical examiner sent a van for Katherine Cochran. Thomas led one of the new detectives, an Asian man named Sun (who'd raised his eyebrows at Lou Higbee and gotten a steady stare in return), down the hill to the place where he'd found her.

In the middle of the morning, one by one, they were released. Spencer's jailhouse phone call to a Noantri contact had resulted in a defense attorney from the firm of Quijano and Ennis showing up at Michael's hospital bedside and a whole phalanx of attorneys at the precinct. They hadn't been needed. The detectives didn't seem happy about it but test results showed the skin under Father Maxwell's nails was Katherine Cochran's and her fingerprints were everywhere in the room where Brittany Williams was killed. They speculated she'd returned that evening, possibly ushered in by Brittany herself. They even had motive, or something resembling it, supplied by Bradford Lane, who, as police swarmed around his conservatory and yard, had embroidered bountifully on his account of Katherine as "always a little crazy." Thomas could see that Livia was upset by Lane's characterization but she didn't contradict it.

Thomas heard the front door open, and he stood. From the precinct Spencer had gone directly to NYU hospital to wait while the detectives questioned Michael. Finally Michael had been released by both the law and medical science. Now he stepped into the hallway wearing a crisp new sling. Spencer followed, arms wrapped around bulging plastic bags.

"Greetings," Spencer said, looking almost buoyant. "I hope you're hungry. The café around the corner offers a creditable beef bourguignon." Thomas relieved Spencer of his burdens and Spencer helped Michael out of his coat.

"Michael?" Livia said. "I'm so sorry about your brother."

Michael, thought Thomas, did not look buoyant; but though he seemed beyond exhausted, some of the dark lines on his face had smoothed away.

"I declare a moratorium on conversation," Spencer announced, "until we're seated around the table." He bustled the bags in the direction of the kitchen. Livia went with him. Michael gave Thomas a small smile.

"That's for you and me, right?" Michael said. "They don't really care?"

"They don't need food as we do, no," Thomas said. "Though I've noticed about both of them that they certainly can put it away."

Dishes clattered, silverware clinked, a cork was pulled from a bottle of Pinot Noir. Either Thomas hadn't realized how hungry he was, or the café's beef bourguignon went far beyond creditable; in any case, no words were spoken for the first few minutes after it was ladled out.

Spencer, pouring wine, broke the silence to say to Michael, "If you're concerned about your friend Lou, he'll be along later. I asked him to give us some time alone first. He came under considerable scrutiny, because of his past encounters with the law, but in the end they could find no more reason to hold him than any of us. I must say, under the circumstances he's displaying an impressive degree of equanimity."

Now Michael smiled again. "He's an Indian. Let me ask, though—does he know about you?"

"No. We've told him nothing about the Noantri."

"And you'd appreciate it if I didn't either, and I appreciate that you didn't say that. Don't worry."

"I was in no way worried."

Livia said, "Bradford Lane called. He's had . . . your brother's body wrapped in blankets and he's offering to bury him in the woods on his property."

Michael paused, then shook his head. "I'll take him home. He'd want to be at Akwesasne." After another pause: "That man Lane. Did he see the Shift?"

"See? No," said Livia. "But he knows. He heard it, he felt it. Hilda described it. But not Edward. Katherine Cochran."

"She was the one they were doing the Ceremony for?"

"She became an eagle," Thomas said, marveling at his own matter-of-fact tone. "I saw it, too. But she couldn't—I don't know. Something went wrong."

"My brother's vision was powerful," Michael said quietly. "So strong it created a paradox. It blinded him. He refused the wisdom he was trying to restore."

Spencer reached across the table and touched Michael's hand. "You're feeling a loss only time can soften," he said. "But if you'll allow me, I believe I can relieve your mind of other anxieties. I don't think you need concern yourself about Bradford Lane and his companion. I spoke with Lane. He's absolutely cackling with joy, to have a secret he can take to his grave. Which, as he delightedly points out, will be yawning to receive him soon. It is also his contention that he would instantly be labeled a senile old coot—his words—if he were to advertise what he saw, and further, that of course, he didn't see it. Personally, I believe the part of the whole episode that most astonished him is that Peter van Vliet actually knew what he was doing." Spencer buttered a piece of baguette and went on. "Now Hilda, for her part, is a very devout woman. As far as she's concerned what happened to Katherine Cochran was a miracle from the Lord. Father Kelly has had a long conversation with her and promises others. And she's pleased to see Bradford Lane so happy.

I think she suspects the Lord arranged the whole thing to cheer him up."

Michael nodded. "The police," he asked. "The detectives, and the other two?"

"I was sure Detective Hamilton had seen your brother's Shift," Spencer said, "but apparently she didn't. When I left the precinct house she and her partner were discussing the pros and cons of citing Bradford Lane for harboring wild animals within the city limits. Your only real difficulty, I think, will be with Peter van Vliet."

"No. I saw him before I left the hospital. He's aged twenty years. He didn't know what to say to me. So I talked. In the end I told him to go back home and keep the people calm until I get there. He won't be a problem now." Michael toyed with the stew on his plate, and then looked up. "Where is the mask?"

The others exchanged glances. It was Thomas who spoke. "Father Carbonariis has it. We don't know where he is. But he's passed along a message for you."

"For me?"

"He says he'd rather not see the rest of us again. But if a time comes when you care to speak to him, the Noantri Conclave will put you in touch."

"He'll talk to me?"

"Only to you."

"Good. Good. Then I'll go to him."

"To him?" said Spencer. "But what about your work? Surely now—"

Michael looked at Spencer, and laughed. "My work? I'm through. Rockefeller's probably packing up my lab right now."

"I don't understand."

"Come on, Spencer. I used to be a hotshot minority scientist. Now I'm an Indian with an arrest record."

"The charges were dropped," Thomas said stoutly.

"So? There's no due process in science. Rule number one, don't embarrass your institution." He paused; his voice changed. "Besides, I was wrong. Even if they kept me on, it would be to do the work I've been doing, on smallpox. But I'm done with that. I was looking for the Shifter gene by following the virus. From what Father Carbonariis said, I'll never find it that way."

"Perhaps not," Spencer said. "But you will find it. You now have access to the DNA of the two people at van Vliet's estate whose Shifts were incomplete, and also Katherine Cochran's DNA. That will be of great help, I'm sure."

"Katherine Cochran's? Where the hell would I get that?"

"It could be managed." Spencer's calm confidence almost made Thomas laugh.

"You know, I'll bet if you were involved," Michael said, "it actually could. It doesn't matter, though. This will have to be someone else's work, some other time. It's not mine. The time was wrong."

"Michael. The time is very much right, and the work is yours." Spencer set his glass down. "I believe I mentioned to you that there are scientists among our people. I wouldn't be at all surprised if you were invited to work alongside them. Our laboratories are long-established and well-funded." Michael said nothing. "Come. You and Livia and I will go to Rome and stand before the Conclave. You will tell your story. Rosa Cartelli is already anxious to speak with you, and all those fine ladies and gentlemen will be moved, I'm sure."

Michael looked from Spencer to Livia. He closed his eyes and sat still for a very long time. Thomas wondered if he'd fallen asleep, although he remained upright in his chair. Finally he opened his eyes again and found Spencer. "Thank you," he said. "But I don't know. You're suggesting I disregard the laws, the old ways. Edward did that, and look. To throw in with your people—maybe it's right, but maybe not."

"I think," Spencer said, "in some ways, our people have already 'thrown in' with each other. Have you not wondered, Michael, how it was that in a city of eight million souls you and I found one another? I don't know how many partners you've had, nor am I asking, but over the course of centuries I've had many. Since my Change most have been Noantri. Some, however, have not, and yet I've felt toward them a type of magnetic draw very like that which I've felt toward my Noantri lovers—and toward you. Father Kelly, I apologize if I'm embarrassing you."

"For Pete's sake, Spencer, I'm a priest, not a robot," Thomas snapped; but he could feel the color rising in his cheeks.

"Well said, sir. In that case: Michael, what I mean is this. As many sterling qualities as you possess, and as confident as I am that Aphrodite would have brought us together had we both been Unchanged and—and whatever your word is for those who aren't Shifters—I believe a measure of the attraction we hold for each other is based in our blood."

"I'm not sure I get it."

"Think like a scientist, not like a lover. Your divergence from the majority of humans is genetic. Livia's and mine is also, although in our case the alteration of our DNA occurred in adulthood, not *in utero*. I've told you Noantri have a physical need for proximity. In view of that, an intriguing interpretation could be placed upon my feeling the same attraction, in varying degrees, for my non-Noantri lovers as for those from my people."

"My God. You think it's the same?"

"The cause of the Noantri difference is a microbe. Could not the same microbe, introduced into the human population in a variety of ways, have caused a variety of differences?"

Michael pushed back his chair and walked to the window. The last of the winter afternoon was fading; the street was already in shadow.

"I don't know, Spencer. What you say, it's possible. I think it might be possible. But I can't . . ." Another long pause, his back still to them. "I have to go home. I have to take Edward home. I need to be up there awhile."

"I understand," Spencer said. His voice sounded calm but his eyes were forlorn.

"And after that," Michael continued, "I'll go to van Vliet's estate. I told him. He'll prepare the people. I'm going to ask Lou to go there now, talk to them, wait for me. The ones whose Shifts were partial need to be cared for somehow, and what van Vliet and Edward built has got to be dismantled. The people there have to go home. They know too much, and not enough. The hope they had—it can't be."

"About that, I believe you're correct. But your work can offer a different kind of hope. If you'll accept our help. You've told us your grandmother said your brother's actions would set great changes in motion. The ones he planned were untenable, but perhaps she wasn't wrong."

Michael spoke without turning. "She also said I'd come to a crossroads and have to make a choice."

"This may be that crossroads."

"It may. But knowing that doesn't tell me which direction to choose. Honest to God, I don't know what to do. There's no one who can help me. I have to think. I have to pray. It'll take time."

"Luckily, that's one thing I happen to have."

Now Michael turned from the window, smiling. "I know you do." He came back to his seat and picked up his glass. "I'll leave in the morning."

"I shall miss you. Is there anything I can do to help?"

"Yes." Michael grinned wider. "Be here when I get back."

Charlotte sat in a back booth at the Stonehenge, sipping ginger ale. Frankie'd raised his eyebrows when she ordered it but why the hell should she explain? He'd figure it out soon enough.

She listened to Johnny Cash on the jukebox, singing "I Saw the Light." That's what Charlotte was looking for, here with the music and the photos and the drums on the wall: a little enlightenment. She was wondering what to do now.

As always when that question arose it was answered by the voice of Uncle James: *Come home.* "Home" for Charlotte meant the city where she was born, not the land around Binghamton where so many of her people lived. But this time Uncle James might be right.

She'd seen Tahkwehso, Edward Bonnard, turn into a wolf. She'd thought Framingham had, too, and when it turned out he hadn't she thought at least he'd spot the shreds of clothing hanging on the wolf's body but he hadn't seen those either. When she'd allowed Michael Bonnard to go out and say goodbye she'd ordered Petersen to stay back so Bonnard would have a chance to discard those shreds, which apparently he had.

Her cases were closed. Katherine Cochran, dead in a fall, had likely killed Gerald Maxwell. Yes; but not for a drum. That box at the church had never held a drum. And Cochran hadn't killed Brittany Williams, never mind what the file said. Charlotte was sure, now, that Tahkwehso had done that, leaping from the medical center roof to Sotheby's terrace just the way Framingham's loony theory had it. Poor Framingham. Right for once in his life, and he'd never know.

In the squad room, Charlotte was a golden girl. Captain Friedman loved quickly cleared cases, and he loved even more that this one had actually involved Indians, so putting Charlotte on it was a smart move. And he loved it best that the motives weren't political and the perp was a white woman, at least white enough: a deep background check on Katherine Cochran showed a great-grandmother who was Cree, but nothing in what had happened would cause any stirrings of racial unrest within the five boroughs. One Police Plaza had already called to congratulate the captain.

Charlotte checked her watch. Seven o'clock; the Sotheby's auction would be starting. She wondered how much the mask would bring, and whether, with Katherine Cochran gone, the Met would be bidding. What was the big deal about that mask? Uncle James would know, or some of the elders. Yes, she suddenly thought. She'd take a leave and go up there. How long she'd stay, she wasn't sure, but it might be a long time. She laughed, thinking of Uncle James, waiting patiently all these years. *When you say your name, you'll be reminded.* Keewayhakeequayoo, Returns to Her Homeland. New York City was Charlotte's home, but it wasn't everyone's. She had to think about that now.

She looked around, seeing people she knew and people she didn't, each of them someone with whom she shared blood. The connection she'd felt to Tahkwehso after their night together wasn't about sex, wasn't some crazy variety of love-at-first-sight. It was deeper than those and it wasn't over; in fact, it would never end, now. The tingling in her spine and fingertips, the sharpening of the colors around her, told her that, told her what she couldn't possibly know so soon; but she did know it, and without doubt. And it would affect the rest of her life. Charlotte smiled, thinking of Tahkwehso, and of the woods and fields where she was headed. It was beautiful up there; he'd have liked it, she thought. That was important, now, even though he was gone.

Because she was carrying his child.

ACKNOWLEDGMENTS

We received a lot of inspiration and a lot of help during the writing of this book, and although any errors are solely the fault of the authors, we'd like to thank the following institutions and individuals, some of whom are aware of their part in it, and some of whom probably are not:

The George Gustav Heye Center at the National Museum of the American Indian

The Thunderbird American Indian Dancers

American Indian Community House, NYC

Art Workshop International

Nancy Rosoff and Susan Zeller of the Brooklyn Museum

Tom Govero

Bill Guion

Betsy Harding, Tom Savage, and the late Royal Huber

Barb Shoup and Charles Kreloff

Steve Blier, Hillary Brown, Monty Freeman, James Russell

The Consultant in the Snow (you know who you are)

And as always, thanks to Vanessa Kehren and the team at Penguin/Blue Rider, and to our agent, the calm and unflappable Steve Axelrod.

ABOUT THE AUTHORS

Sam Cabot is the pseudonym of Carlos Dews and S. J. Rozan.

Carlos Dews is an associate professor and chair of the Department of English Language and Literature at John Cabot University, where he directs the Institute for Creative Writing and Literary Translation. He lives in Rome, Italy.

S. J. Rozan is the author of many critically acclaimed novels and short stories that have won crime fiction's greatest honors, including the Edgar, Shamus, Anthony, Macavity, and Nero awards. Born and raised in the Bronx, Rozan now lives in Lower Manhattan.